Side Chick
NATION

Also by Aya de León

The Accidental Mistress

The Boss

Uptown Thief

Side Chick
NATION

AYA
DE LEÓN

KENSINGTON PUBLISHING CORP.
www.kensingtonbooks.com

DAFINA BOOKS are published by

Kensington Publishing Corp.
119 West 40th Street
New York, NY 10018

All Kensington titles, imprints, and distributed lines are available at special quantity discounts for bulk purchases for sales promotion, premiums, fund-raising, and educational or institutional use.

Special book excerpts or customized printings can also be created to fit specific needs. For details, write or phone the office of the Kensington Sales Manager: Kensington Publishing Corp., 119 West 40th Street, New York, NY 10018. Attn. Sales Department. Phone: 1-800-221-2647.

Dafina and the Dafina logo Reg. U.S. Pat. & TM Off.

ISBN-13: 978-1-4967-1579-1
ISBN-10: 1-4967-1579-9
First Kensington Trade Paperback Printing: July 2019

ISBN-13: 978-1-4967-1581-4 (ebook)
ISBN-10: 1-4967-1581-0 (ebook)
First Kensington Electronic Edition: July 2019

10 9 8 7 6 5 4 3 2 1

Printed in the United States of America

Acknowledgments

This book has been a profoundly collective effort. As always, I want to thank my literary team: my agent Jenni Ferrari-Adler, my editor Esi Sogah, as well as Dawn Michelle Hardy, Michelle Addo, Vida Engstrand, and all the folks at Kensington Books. I also could NEVER have written this book without the brilliant consejos of my Boricua peer counselors and leaders: María Judith Colon, Leykamarie Alma, Yara Alma-Bonilla, James "Yimi" Searle, and Nanci Luna Jiménez. My extended Boricua fam: Alicia Bauman-Morales, Yulahlia Hernández, Aurora Levins-Morales, Sandra García Rivera, the Bay Area Boricuas. Also, my immediate fam, Stuart, Dee, Coco, Anna, Larry, Paci, Deva, Neens, and Papi. As well as my women writer/activist crew: Shailja, Pam, and Nanci. My MGMG crew of moms: Nadine, Gail, Debbie, Monisha, and HyoJung. My research/sensitivity reader/consultant/editor/translation dream team: Susan DeFreitas, César del Peral, Daisy Hernández, Marianne Collazo, Elissa Miller, Rachel Aimee, Melissa Reyes, Carolina De Robertis, John Mundell, and Vylma V. I don't know if I could have written this book without the profoundly orienting experience of going to an incredible conference at the University of Chicago: "Puerto Rico, Hurricane María and the Crisis of Colonialism." Thanks to the organizers: the UIC Social Justice Initiative, the Union of Puerto Rican Students, The Puerto Rican Cultural Center, and the Puerto Rican Agenda. Big thanks also to the Boricuas who came to the Bay Area to talk about their feminist work in PR: Zulma Oliveras and Yolanda Arroyo Pizarro. And the many Boricuas out there going hard for la causa who answered my calls for direction, including Eli Jacobs Fantauzzi, Rosa Clemente, and Sofía Quintero. I believe this will be one of the first published novels of Hurricane María in Puerto Rico, but I want to thank Naomi Klein for what I think is the first journalistic book on Hurricane María, which was a critical text for me in the writing of this book. I like to think of *Side Chick Nation* as *The Battle for Paradise* for the set who picks up sexy urban beach reads. But I hope these two books, as well as Edgardo Miranda-Rodriguez's volume *Ricanstruction* are simply the first wave of many, many books about the current struggle for justice in post-María Puerto Rico. And of course, thanks to my Boricua Ancestors, and all the Puerto Ricans holding strong on the island, as well as those of us reaching back from the Diaspora.

Pa'lante.

Juntos.

"Eso es como cuando usted tiene un novio o una novia que tiene una esposa o un esposo. Y usted se queja de que el 25 día de navidad está con la esposa o el esposo y no está con usted. . . .No podemos pretender que nos traten como iguales si nosotros permitimos que nos traten como menos. Y lo que que ha pasado yo creo con María es que la gente ha entendido que no puede seguir consintiendo a una relación de subordinación que permite que nos traten como menos."

"It's like when you have a boyfriend or girlfriend who has a wife or a husband. And you complain that on Christmas day, they're with their spouse and not with you. . . .We can't try to make them treat us equally while also allowing them to treat us like we're less than. And what has happened, I think, with [Hurricane] María is that the people [of Puerto Rico] now understand that we can't keep consenting to a relationship [with the US] of subordination that allows them to treat us like we're less than."

San Juan Mayor Carmen Yulín Cruz
Chicago, Illinois
April 21, 2018

Prologue

Water flooded the storage space as Dulce slept. It seeped through the metal slats in the pull-down door. It pooled on the concrete floor. It rose around the mattress where Dulce was sleeping. Although she was not exactly sleeping, more like in a stupor or a spell from the cocktail of rum and marijuana. It dulled her hearing, so she didn't startle with the shrieking winds and battering rain, and thudding of broken branches against the building. It dulled the panic she would have felt—alone in a storage space where she was living illegally. In a hurricane. And nobody knew she was there.

Water seeped up, turning the mattress into a giant sponge. Soon her back was wet. The crisscross of her racerback tank top, the cotton shorts. The moisture soaked into the fabric, even above the surface of the water she lay in. Inch by inch, the line crept up her feet, her beautifully painted blue toenails, the sides of her arms and legs and torso. It saturated her hair, destroying the remains of the blowout she'd been trying to conserve. She had sweated out the roots, but the tips of her hair had stayed somewhat straight, even in the humidity. She'd kept it up in a ponytail over the last few days, so the ends didn't erupt into tight curls from the sweat on her back and shoulders.

But now, the water rose just above the mattress, soaking her hair, and it bloomed into springing curls all around her head.

Still she slept.

It wasn't until the water seeped into her ears that her body moved at all, beyond the rise and fall of her chest. Her shoulder flinched with the moisture tickling her ear canal, but it didn't wake her. First one side, then the other, as her head was slightly tilted on the mattress. No pillow. But then both ears filled and the tickle was gone. Her body stilled again in sleep. The now full canals dulled the howls of the storm.

The flooding outside was anything but gentle, yet the water could only seep in through the slats in the metal door, and the crack at the bottom above the cement floor. So the water level rose slowly. It crept up gently along her neck, her jawline, her cheekbone. The water sidled up tenderly, like a lover.

Dulce slept, like a maiden awaiting a prince, awaiting a kiss.

Yet she slept on when the water first touched her lips. Only when it began to drip into her mouth did she truly stir. The water, pooling in the back of her throat and making it impossible to breathe properly now. The prince had come. The rescuer on his horse. The discoverer. The pimp.

She flashed back as the water choked her. She recalled his hands around her throat, the bruising press of fingers against skin and muscle and tendon and windpipe. As the floodwater of the hurricane trickled delicately into her throat, her body recalled the searing pain of constricted breath. The scrabbling panic of asphyxiation, her heart was hammering frantically, as if it needed to escape her body to survive. Then the half-blackout, feeling her body slump to the floor, wincing with the sharp press of his boot toe as he delivered a single kick to her hip.

Her hip was soaked now in the floodwater, the left hip.

Her pelvis was tilted slightly, and her left side pointed down toward the sodden mattress. Her right side was slightly raised, the hipbone jutting above the waterline like a disappearing island of brown skin, as water pooled between the tops of her thighs.

Yet she could feel that the real threat was at her throat. Again.

Like that other time, her pimp had sent one of his thugs to kill her. The man had a knife at her throat, as a few dozen women and some of their kids looked on in horror. She had been standing outside the shelter on the icy Manhattan ground in only socks, numb with terror, unable to feel the freezing concrete beneath her feet. Again, the press at her throat. The knife threatening not only skin and muscle and tendon and windpipe, but now her carotid in jeopardy, as well.

More water trickled into her throat, and she coughed weakly, her gag reflex still kicking. And with the gagging, part of her brain began to register the fact that her life was in danger. Some fight or flight response activated her tongue, dragging it into action to spit some of the water out.

Her life was in danger. Her body struggled to wake, but couldn't quite push through her half-sleeping stupor, in which the unbidden memory bloomed in her mind like a nightmare. The time she'd been fool enough to go back to her pimp. And he'd thrown her against a wall. Paint and plaster crashing into her back and shoulder like a drunk driver. When she staggered to her feet, he'd choked her. His thick fingers were more insistent than ever, despite her own hands, gripping his wrists, digging her fingernails into his skin, trying in vain to open the vise of his oppositional thumbs. Yet it was her own grip she could feel loosening as she began to lose consciousness.

That had been Dulce's breaking point. The moment she decided to leave him for good. Or rather, she passed out fear-ing she might die, but deciding to live if she found she had a choice.

That same resolve woke her inside the storage unit.

She sputtered to life, coughing through a burning throat. In total darkness, completely soaked. Her body was sluggish and disoriented with the marijuana and the residuals of rum. She tried to lift her head, but her hair was unexpectedly weighed down with water.

Slowly, through the chemical fog, she rolled to her side. As if in slow motion, she dragged an arm beneath her, propping herself up on one elbow, her mouth fully above the water line.

She coughed hard and gagged, suddenly vomiting. Yet the retching made her a bit more lucid. Even in the total darkness, she was able to orient herself, to make sense of the bizarre combination of mattress and moisture, screaming winds and crashing thuds.

Storage space. Hurricane. Flooding. Fuck.

Chapter 1

Several months earlier . . .

Dulce Garcia crept toward the back door of the nightclub's VIP room on the balls of her stiletto sandals, trying not to wake her boyfriend. He lay, splayed back on the leather couch, in a post-orgasmic half-doze. She spat into an empty beer bottle, and tiptoed to the room's back door. She tried to push it open with her free hand, but it was too heavy. She needed two hands for this.

She stuck the knot of money down into her cleavage, and pushed with both palms flat. The large metal door creaked against rusty hinges. In the humid Miami climate, cheap metal springs like these always rusted. This back door, required by the Florida fire code as a secondary exit, was rarely used. She tried to close it quietly behind her, but the metal was too heavy, and it tipped her forward in the six-inch gold heels.

The slam of metal on metal woke her boyfriend. As she crept away down the dank, concrete hallway, she heard him call to her. His voice was usually loud, but it sounded faint through the thick slab of steel: "Dulce? Where'd you go, *mami*?" She tiptoed down the hallway to the outer door that would lead to the back alley.

But the steel could not contain the roar of rage when he realized his money was missing. She had felt a second bulge in his pants when she unzipped his jeans. As she went down on him, she had slipped the wad of bills out of his front pocket, and palmed it after he finished.

Through the metal, she could hear the slam of the VIP room's other door. He had assumed she'd headed back into the club. She grinned as she pulled the handle for the alley exit, expecting to cut around the corner and hail a cab for a quick getaway. Uber was out of the question. It was his credit card on the account.

But the alley door was locked. She pulled with all her strength, but it wouldn't budge. Either locked or rusted shut. She looked around frantically, afraid she would be trapped. She couldn't retrace her steps through the VIP room—in case he came back looking for her. She ran now, not even trying to be quiet. As she sprinted toward the other end of the hallway, there was a second door that led through a storage room. Either way, she'd need to find her way out through the club. The club where her Dominican drug dealer boyfriend would be assembling his crew of boys to find her, the side chick turned "fucking bitch" who'd stolen his take for the night.

Although Dulce hung with him in the club regularly, she only knew how to get to the different dance floors and VIP rooms. She didn't know behind the scenes. It turned out that the storage room didn't lead back into the club. At least not directly. Dulce hurried past dusty stage props of sparkling palm trees and faded lifesize cardboard cutouts of different celebrities to pose with for selfies. Outside the other end of the room was a different hallway with a trio of doors to locked VIP rooms. At the far end of the hall was a stairwell. She knew that this club was really two buildings cobbled together. If she went up to the sixth floor, there was a walkway that led across to the main building where she had come in.

She needed to hustle, so her boyfriend didn't get his crew to cut her off, trapping her on this end, away from the front entrance.

Dulce ran up the stairs. The first four flights were easy, fueled by adrenaline. But by the last two flights, she began to lag. Dulce's heart beat hard, and the bustier squeezed her ribs like a vise. Between the fourth and fifth floor, she had slowed to a walk, trying to catch her breath.

A stairwell door opened a couple floors below.

"I ain't seen the bitch," a loud man's voice echoed off the concrete. "He just said we need to find her and bring her to him."

Dulce froze.

The voice continued: "Sent me down to look for her on the first floor, the last place he seen her."

Dulce pressed herself against the wall, her heart hammering in her chest as the sound of the man's footsteps receded.

When she heard the downstairs door open and close, she faltered for a second. Then the terror turned to adrenaline, fueling her sprint up the final flight. On the sixth floor, she twisted the knob of one of the VIP room doors hoping for a large party she could blend into. But the room was sparsely populated. A trio of bored looking girls were sitting around drinking champagne, while two guys were doing coke at the high table. They barely looked up at her, as she walked quietly across the room, staying in the shadows. One of the girls on the couch followed Dulce with her eyes.

She walked through and slipped out the door on the far end. In the hall on the other side of the VIP lounge was a coatrack. A blonde bobbed wig hung next to a leather coat and a silver scarf. Dulce grabbed the wig and scarf and ducked into the stairwell to put them on. She pulled her long hair into a loose braid. Fortunately, she'd blown it out for her date tonight, otherwise, she'd never have gotten the wig over the tight curls of her natural hair. As it was, the braid stuck out, too thick to tuck underneath. She wore the silver scarf like a shawl, covering her shoulders and her long braid at the nape of her neck. She crisscrossed the scarf in the front to reveal her cleavage, while concealing the distinctive turquoise-sequined bustier of her dress. It was an ombre fabric, which darkened to navy at the above-the-knee hemline.

Now, she could walk openly through the hallway, peeking out from under the bangs of the bobbed blonde wig. She spotted one of her boyfriend's crew, heading right toward her. Her heart hammered in her throat. Hopefully, he was looking for a brunette in a lighter blue dress, not a blonde in silver and navy.

As he approached, he looked her up and down mechanically.

The door to the VIP room behind her opened, and the movement caught his eye. In the split second he was looking beyond her, she picked up her phone and used it to shield her face. She had gotten the oversized version of the smartphone, and it covered her well.

When he looked back at her, he saw nothing but blonde hair and the Dominican flag phone case, as unremarkable as her caramel skin.

As he walked past, she could smell the mint on his breath as he chewed gum with his mouth open. And under the mint smell was a slight hint of weed.

Behind her now, he was asking the folks in VIP if they'd seen a girl come through.

"Yeah," a woman's voice said.

Dulce didn't dare turn around, but used her phone like a mirror to look over her shoulder.

"I think she went that way," the woman said, pointing in the other direction.

"Where's my scarf?" her friend asked, as Dulce crept around the corner to the walkway between the buildings.

The moment she was on the walkway, she yanked off her

stiletto sandals and took off running, the silver scarf flying half-loose behind her like a superhero cape.

She opened the stairwell in the other building, and began to run down. But on the landing two floors below was a couple going at it.

The woman had her dress hiked up and his pants were below his hips as he pounded between her thighs.

They were blocking the stairwell, and she wouldn't be able to get past. She stepped into the fifth floor hallway to take the elevator. There was another VIP room on that floor. Dulce grabbed a cheap faux leather jacket hanging on the rack outside the VIP room. As the elevator dinged, she shrugged off the scarf and put on the jacket, tucking her braid beneath the collar. Then she quickly slid her feet back into her stiletto sandals. The elevator doors opened, and she pressed in with a group of women wearing ten different clashing perfumes.

The knot of cash was starting to itch her cleavage. Dulce had plenty of time to hunch under the coat and adjust it, as the elevator stopped at every floor.

A pair of drunk guys got on one floor down and proceeded to hit on all the women in the elevator. On the second floor, the guys blocked the women from exiting and kept pressing the door open button, demanding to get their phone numbers.

"We've got a fucking hostage situation," one of the girls said.

"*Pendejos,*" another woman mumbled under her breath.

Dulce pulled a lipstick out of her pocket.

"I'll give you my number," she said. "I think you're hot," she said to one guy. "And I have a girlfriend who would love you," she said to the other. "But you better fucking call me." She recalled the phone number for the pizza place down the street from her apartment, and wrote it across his forearm.

"Don't give me no fake number," he said. "I'm a call you right now."

He dialed the number.

Dulce's felt the panic rise in her chest, but she stayed cool, and turned to the timer app on her phone. She hit one of the sounds, and her phone made the sound of a strumming guitar.

"So suspicious," she said. "Who broke your heart?"

She laughed and grabbed his phone, hitting the end call button. Only the girl next to her heard the faint woman's voice: "Hello, Mariana's Pizza."

"And now I got your number too," Dulce said. "So pick up when I call."

"What's your name?" he asked.

"Mariana," Dulce said, and followed the crowd off the elevator.

The doors opened out onto the dance floor, where the DJ was spinning Latin techno.

Up ahead, she saw two members of her boyfriend's crew, looking around. She pulled out her phone and peered down at it, letting the straight blonde bob fall over her face.

Glancing up from time to time, she turned toward the far wall, away from the two thugs. She weaved between standing tables with people yelling in each other's ears to be heard.

Up ahead, she saw another one of her boyfriend's crew, scanning the room. There was yet another one of his boys near the front door.

She felt a tug on her jacket. "Hey Mariana, wanna dance?" it was the guy from the elevator.

"I was just leaving," she said. "Walk me out?"

"Maybe we could go home together," he suggested.

"Not tonight, baby," she said. But she leaned into him as they walked past her boyfriend's crewmember. She flipped the blonde hair in front of her face and pressed her hip against him as she passed. " 'Scuse me," she said.

The drunk guy from the elevator's hand was slipping down her hip towards her ass.

"Don't get too friendly," she said shaking his hand off.

"I like the way it feels when you move," he said, his breath hot in her ear.

"Really?" she said. "Maybe I can't wait. Maybe you should meet me in the unisex bathroom."

"For real?" he asked.

"Only if you want a little taste," she said.

"Hell yeah," he said. "Let's go now."

She looked down, coyly. "I don't want anyone to see us going in together," she said. "Wait for me. I'll be there in five minutes. I'll knock twice."

"Okay," he said. "Oh fucking kay. I like a woman who knows what she wants."

And then, to seal the deal, she ran her hands from his mid-thigh up to his navel. "Oh, I know what I want. Get in that bathroom."

"*Sí, señora.*" He turned on his heel and headed toward the restrooms.

That gave her ten minutes to get out of there. Fifteen at most, before she had another outraged man looking for her, and he would be searching for a blonde.

She turned the corner past the coat check and saw her boyfriend pacing by the door.

Her heart started to hammer in her chest. She turned and leaned over the coat check half door. A bored, butch woman was leaning against the wall, looking at her phone.

"Which is the ladies' night?" Dulce asked. "Too many dudes in here."

The woman smiled. "I could make it ladies' night for you right now, *mami.*"

Dulce grinned.

"But ladies' night is Wednesday," the woman said.

"I'll be back," Dulce said. "These guys are too aggressive. That guy at the door was hassling me earlier," she said. "I wanna leave, but I don't want him trying to grab my ass."

"Well he's got good taste, but bad manners," the woman said. "He's a sort of big fish in this small pond. He's used to women saying yes to him."

"Tell me about it," Dulce said.

"I got an idea," the woman said. She pulled a heather gray hoodie from the coat check.

"I thought you all didn't allow athletic gear," Dulce said.

"This is mine," the woman said. She put it on Dulce and pulled the hood over her hair and low on her face. Then she put a possessive arm around her and walked her out of the club, right past her boyfriend.

Dulce could smell his cologne, and the scent of sex still on him. She felt a confusing rush of both nostalgia and fear. When things had been good between them, he was intoxicating. He was sexy, had money, and liked to lavish it on her, at least at first. But lately he'd stopped calling every day. He mostly came over for sex and didn't take her out as much. He got texts while they were together, from some new girl whose name she didn't recognize. And he always took time to text the girl back. Dulce didn't want to hang on til he got tired of her. But she had nothing of her own. He'd paid all her bills but never gave her any cash. She'd felt the knot of money and seen her chance to get out with something.

Dulce swallowed hard as she walked past with the coat check woman. He sized them up at a glance and kept looking around.

"So, can I get your number?" the woman asked when they'd gotten out of his range.

Dulce didn't like to lie to women. "No, but thanks for being so chivalrous."

"Okay," the woman said. "Come by one of these Wednesdays."

"I just might," Dulce said, and turned toward the street.

She had money now, so a cab would be no problem. There was usually a line of them out front at this hour.

"How come it's no taxis out here?" she asked the guy at the door.

"Ball game just let out," he said.

"Shit," she said.

"It's about fifteen minutes for Uber right now," he said.

Dulce looked around. The club was in a warehouse district. Nothing around and not safe to walk. Especially when there were no cabs to catch. She had a friend who worked nearby. Maybe she could come get her.

As she called her friend, she kept her eyes on the club.

The number at her friend's job was ringing.

Her boyfriend appeared in the doorway with a few of his crew.

Finally, someone picked up after eight rings. She waited while they located her friend.

One of her boyfriend's crew had something in his hand. An iPad?

Wait! He paid for her phone. Did that mean he could locate her with the phone itself? She hung up quickly and powered the phone off. She dumped it in a trash can on the sidewalk.

Would they be able to find the last place she was?

She hurried up to a pair of girls piling into a Lyft.

"I'm sorry to bother you. My boyfriend is getting really abusive. If he finds me, I swear he'll try to kill me."

"We got you, *mami*," the shorter girl said. "Come on in here with us."

"Oh my god, thank you so much," Dulce said. "I got cash to pay you back for the ride."

The three of them squeezed into the back of the car.

"Sorry," the driver said. "You all requested carpool. Only two passengers."

"What?" the shorter girl asked.

"Do you have another passenger yet?"

He shook his head.

"Well then take me," Dulce said. "I have cash."

"It doesn't work that way," the driver said.

"Oh my god," the taller girl said. "I'll request a ride."

She put the request into the app, and they waited.

From outside the car, they heard a girl yelling. "Get your fucking hands off me!"

Dulce turned to see her boyfriend holding the arm of a girl who looked a lot like her. His boys were standing behind him.

"Sorry," he said. "I thought you were someone else."

"That's assault, bitch," the woman said. "You're lucky I'm not pressing any charges."

"Who you calling a bitch?" her boyfriend asked, reaching under his coat.

"*Enfócate*," one of his boys said. "She was just out here."

Dulce found her voice. "That's him," she hissed to the girls. "That's my boyfriend."

"*Coño*," one of the girls said. "I'll get out and get another car."

"*Mil gracias, mami*," Dulce said, handing her a twenty off the knot in her pocket.

As the girl gathered her purse, Dulce saw her boyfriend walk by the car on the sidewalk. He had one hand on the gun in his waistband, the other hand on the phone at his ear.

As the girl got out on the street side, Dulce could hear her boyfriend through the slightly open window. "You see her anywhere?" he asked into the phone. "My wife's gonna fucking kill me."

"Oh shit," the girl still in the car said. "He has a gun?"

The moment the door closed, the driver took off.

"Is my friend gonna be okay?" the girl asked.

"Definitely," Dulce said, her hand on the knot in her pocket. "He's only dangerous to me."

Chapter 2

The girl was going to the Miami airport. She and her friend worked graveyard shift, and liked to go to the club for a couple hours beforehand.

"Where you headed?" the girl asked in Spanish. Her friend had texted that she was safely on the road, as well.

"To the Dominican Republic," Dulce said. "Thanks for being my ride to the airport."

"You live there or here?" the girl asked.

"I been here for about six months," Dulce said. "Before that I lived in Cuba with my grandmother."

"You Cuban?" the girl asked.

"My dad's side," she said. "But my mom's Dominican. I grew up with my mom in New York."

"How was Cuba?" the girl asked.

"Cool at first," Dulce said. "I got away from a bunch of drama in New York. But then it was boring as fuck."

"Looks like you found some drama in Miami," the girl said.

"Yeah, well I'm done with drama. My aunt lives in a little-ass hick town in the Dominican Republic. No drama there."

The girl shook her head. "You'll get bored again."

"I only need to remember the view of that gun through

the car window. Maybe I'll marry a nice country boy with a shy smile and a big dick."

The girl laughed. "Good luck with that."

In the security line at the airport, she was standing in front of a forty-something businessman. He caught her eye and smiled. "Any chance you're headed to Puerto Rico?" he asked.

He had on a nice suit and a Rolex. He wasn't particularly handsome, with narrow features and thinning, sandy hair. But he looked like he kept himself in pretty good shape.

"Nope," she said. "I'm flying to Santo Domingo."

"Business or pleasure?" he asked.

"Family," she said. "I'll be living there for a while."

"I'll be there next week," he said. "You should have dinner with me. I know a great French restaurant in the capital."

"My aunt doesn't live anywhere near the capital," Dulce said, and they chatted for a while.

"I could send a car for you," he said.

"A car?" she asked. "It's a two-hour drive."

"A car is the least of the things I would do for you," he said with a leering grin. "I'd like to spoil you rotten."

She smiled. "Maybe," she said. "But just dinner."

"Here's my card," he said. "Call me this week and we can set it up." The name on the card was Phillip Gerard. Apparently, he was in real estate.

"I'll think about it," she said, as the agent called her forward. She rummaged around in her tiny club purse, her fingers brushing across her lipstick, a toothbrush kit she bought in the airport, and what was left of the cash she'd stolen from her ex. Her fingers touched firmer paper, and she handed the passport and boarding pass to the agent. The passport was her only documentation. She had never gotten a Florida ID. And she didn't drive.

TSA flagged her for an extra search. She was traveling one

way, last minute, without luggage. By the time she got out of the checkpoint, the businessman was gone.

She went into the restroom and brushed her teeth. Then, alone in the stall, she counted the money she'd stolen. It was a big knot of cash but the largest bills were twenties. Maybe she should have tried to put him off til later in the night, when his take would have been much bigger. Damn, she'd risked her life for a mere thousand.

She looked again at the businessman's card in her purse. She would probably call him. This was the perfect amount of drama. A real estate guy who had money but wouldn't get attached. And she could meet him far from her auntie's prying eyes.

On the plane, she sat next to a young guy with glasses who was typing fast on a laptop. He had on a hoodie that said NADIE ES ILEGAL/NOBODY IS ILLEGAL. He was handsome beneath the coke bottle lenses, with tawny brown skin, full lips, and a short afro.

She smiled at him, but he didn't even look up. Not when she squeezed by him to sit down, or when she leaned across to turn on the air above him, despite the close-up view of her cleavage.

When they made the announcement to turn off electronic devices, he made a quick phone call. "I'm sending it now," he said, and kept clicking the mousepad on the laptop.

"Sir," the flight attendant said. "You need to stow those electronics for takeoff."

"Gotta go," he said into the phone. "Hope it comes through."

As he put things away, Dulce asked: "You a student?"

He laughed. "Is it the baby face? No, I'm a journalist."

"Journalist?" she asked. "You going on location in the DR?"

"Something like that," he said. "We're doing a series on

the aftermath of dictatorships. People are going to Chile, Uruguay, Brazil, Haiti, etcetera. I got assigned to the DR."

"Political reporter, huh?" she asked.

"Everything is political," he said. "And on that note, I'm doing an informal survey of young Latinxs. Are you registered to vote?"

"I wasn't in the States during the last election. And the presidential election before that, I wasn't old enough to vote."

"You gotta get registered," he said. "Blacks and Latinxs are the future."

They compared stories of where they'd grown up. He was Puerto Rican, and had grown up in Harlem. Not that far from her family's apartment in Washington Heights. He was in the Bronx now.

This guy was really easy to talk to. A little preachy, but he had this dimple that kept leaping out when he made an emphatic point, making him look more adorable than condescending.

"What's your name?" he asked.

"Dulce," she said, and realized the businessman hadn't even asked.

"Zavier," he said. "We should keep in touch. I might need to check up on you in the future. Make sure you're voting the right way."

She laughed. "I'll need to get a new phone in the DR."

He handed her his card, and put his personal cell phone number on the back. She slid it into her purse with the businessman's card. If only she could find a man with the personality of this guy and the money of the businessman, or of her Miami boyfriend.

Ex-boyfriend, she thought. Stealing a thousand dollars and running from him must certainly constitute a breakup, right?

* * *

She fell asleep on the plane ride, and didn't wake up til she felt the flight attendant tapping her shoulder.

"You'll need to bring that seat back up for landing," the woman said.

Dulce realized she had fallen asleep on Zavier's shoulder.

"Sorry," she said. She checked to see if she had been drooling. Her mouth was dry. But had she been snoring?

"So is Dolores your given name?" he asked.

"What?" she asked. How did he know? No one ever called her that.

"It's on your boarding pass," he said.

She looked down to see the boarding pass laying face-up on the tray table. "Everybody calls me Dulce except my family."

"What do they call you?" he asked.

"Family secret," she said.

"It's true I'm a journalist," he said. "But you can tell me off the record."

"Not a chance," she said, smiling.

They were interrupted by an announcement that they needed to get ready for landing. Dulce put the boarding pass in her purse and stowed her tray table.

"You were out cold," he said. "You been sleep deprived or something?"

She thought about the life she'd been living in Miami. "Something like that," she said.

"Working a lot?" he asked.

She thought about how much work it was to keep herself up for the ex-boyfriend. Sort of being on call for him all the time. It wasn't the worst work she'd ever done. Back in New York she'd had a pimp from the time she was fourteen to eighteen. That was the worst. By far. She'd ended up in the hospital and almost dead a couple of times.

"Let's put it this way," she said. "I'm looking forward to a nice quiet time with my family in the Dominican Republic."

"Okay," he said. "But I hope you'll call me if you need some excitement."

She looked at him. With his slender waist and open face. He couldn't compare to any of the drama she'd already lived through at twenty. But there was something about him she liked.

"Maybe," she said, for the second time that night. Of the two men she'd just met, she liked Zavier better. But that Rolex and the promise to spoil her beckoned. She knew who she was more likely to call.

Chapter 3

Dulce had also slept on the plane ride from New York to Cuba a year or so earlier.

Marisol Rivera had regarded Dulce in the seat on her left. Across the aisle to Marisol's right were Tyesha, Kim and Jody. Those three women were Marisol's closest friends and her partners in crime. Tyesha was the assistant director at the clinic she ran. But throughout the flight, Marisol kept her attention riveted on Dulce, who was like a twenty-year-younger version of herself. That was probably why Marisol worried incessantly about the girl and had never been able to maintain professional boundaries in their relationship. Transporting a client from her health clinic across international borders was inappropriate and possibly unethical. Maybe even illegal, but she had never let the law stop her.

Marisol took Dulce in when the girl was running from her pimp. Marisol had shot a thug who was trying to slit Dulce's throat. And now, she'd bought Dulce a ticket to Cuba, when both the pimp and his brother were after her. In the line at JFK airport, Dulce had clung to Marisol's arm, afraid that it was all too good to be real.

The way Marisol saw it, she had been meaning to visit her sister in Cuba, and Dulce had a grandmother in Cuba. And

Cuba was a place where Dulce's pimp and his associates wouldn't be able to find her. A win for everyone, except Team Pimp.

Marisol had met the pimp Jerry Rios a few times, and he scared the shit out of her. She'd take Dulce to Siberia if it would get her away from a guy like him.

The first time she'd seen them together, he had towered over Dulce with his broad shoulders and thick frame, like a tyrannosaurus rex. Jerry had brought Dulce and a few of his other girls to Marisol's annual gala. He stood around with an *I'm watching you, bitch* type stalker presence. He was angry that Marisol had sheltered Dulce after he'd beaten her up. Marisol was certain he had shown up to intimidate her.

He had stuffed himself into a shiny pinstripe suit and put on plenty of blingy jewelry. But when he got to the door of the fundraiser, he found out it was five hundred per person.

"Two thousand dollars?" he asked.

"For four people," the girl said.

"I can do math," Jerry said. "You fucking stuck up bitches think I can't do math?"

Marisol heard his raised voice at the door and began walking toward him, her heart hammering. She had seen Dulce's bruises and broken ribs and knew what he was capable of.

Marisol strutted up to them on stiletto heels, the emerald green dress clinging to her ample curves, except the bottom of the mermaid skirt, which swirled behind her.

"I'm not gonna pay two dollars to come up in this bitch," Jerry said to the flustered girl at the registration table. "Let alone two thousand."

"I'm sorry," the girl said. "It's five hundred per person. And I don't have you on the pre-paid guest list."

"You don't think I got that kind of money?" Jerry dug into his pocket. "I got money. Enough to—"

"Jerry!" Marisol called over to him. "Jerry, I'm so glad you could make it!"

Graciousness was the last thing he would expect. He was here to intimidate her, or to pick a fight, but she wouldn't indulge him. She advanced toward the table and picked up a clipboard. "Rivezzo . . . Riordan . . . Jerry Rios." Marisol pulled a pencil from her upswept hairstyle.

"How you know my name?" he asked. "Why you all up in my fucking business?"

Marisol continued, as if he hadn't even spoken. "You should be right here on the VIP list. Obviously, there's been some mistake." She turned to the staffer. "Honey, please make up VIP nametags for Jerry Rios and his friends."

Dulce had on a bright red wig and a pair of shades, but Marisol had her attention trained on Jerry. He was the rattlesnake you needed to keep your eye on.

Jerry's face held its usual scowl, but he stood, uncertain. Marisol made the tag herself. "Can I pin it on you, *papi*, or would you like to do the honors?"

He snatched it out of her hand and put it in his pocket.

"Jody!" Marisol called over to the tall blonde hostess from her crew. Jody stood nearly as tall as Jerry in her heels and glowered back at him.

Marisol smiled and took several flutes of champagne off Jody's tray.

"Please," Marisol said, giving them to Jerry and his entourage. "Be our guests."

One of Jerry's other girls picked up a pamphlet for the clinic and Jerry snatched it out of her hand.

"If you'll excuse me," Marisol said. "I need to go introduce our guest tonight, Delia Borbón."

As Marisol walked away, she heard Dulce say: "Delia Borbón? I love her!"

"Shut up," Jerry said. "We not staying that long."

"There she is!" one of the other girls squealed. Beside the ballroom's small stage, partially hidden behind a partition, Delia Borbón was waiting to go on.

She must have been at least fifty, but her shape was still an hourglass under the gold sequin dress.

She was there to talk about her memoir, *From Red Light to Red Carpet*, where she talked about her time as a stripper.

"Good evening everyone," Marisol said into the microphone. "*Buenas noches.*"

Marisol saw Jerry and his entourage standing against the back wall. He glowered there, arms crossed over his massive chest.

"Thanks for coming out tonight," she said. "Because, in these tough economic times, you're showing that New York cares for its own. That the gorgeous, the fabulous, and the prosperous give a damn about the marginal, the vulnerable, and the so-called expendable. Everybody deserves health care. Delia Borbón knows how hard it is out there. That's why she's here tonight. Like me, she remembers the tightrope young brown women have to walk. And she remembers all the sisters who don't ever write the book, attend the gala event, or even live to tell the tale."

At the back of the room, Marisol saw Dulce reach her finger and thumb under the sunglasses and wipe her eyes.

"And that's where our clinic comes in," Marisol went on. "Every cent we collect tonight will go into our endowment, ensuring that our services can save lives for generations to come."

The audience erupted in applause.

Jerry barked something at the girls, and they all stopped clapping.

But when Jerry went back to glowering silently, Dulce took off the shades, revealing her black eye, and looked straight at Marisol.

Marisol held Dulce's gaze as she spoke.

"Everyone deserves choices," she said into the microphone. "Even sex workers."

Jerry uncrossed his arms and said something to the three girls.

The two other women hustled to the door. But Dulce trailed behind, eyes locked with Marisol. Jerry gave Dulce a yank and she toppled off her heels, sprawling onto the floor. He swung his leg casually, kicking her.

As Dulce hurried to her feet and put her shades back on, Marisol was still speaking specifically to her.

"A woman who's in a bad situation can always find help at our clinic," Marisol said. "We're not afraid to stand up to anyone who doesn't like it."

Dulce adjusted her skirt, and tottered after Jerry.

Marisol had cried when she delivered Dulce into the hands of her grandmother in Cuba. They all had cried. But for Marisol it was bittersweet: it was like the rescue she'd always dreamed of at that age, for a girl who reminded her so much of herself.

Chapter 4

Marisol was still in Cuba visiting her sister Cristina when they got a letter from their cousins in Puerto Rico.

The sisters lay on Cristina's double bed under the fan in the humid Havana bedroom. They had similar faces, but Marisol was curvy and dark while Cristina was slender and fair. They had the do-they-or-don't-they likeness of sisters with different fathers. Their mother had died of breast cancer when Marisol was in middle school, Cristina in elementary. After that, Marisol had fallen solidly into the mother's role. They'd lost touch with these cousins in Puerto Rico after their mother, and then their grandmother, had died in quick succession.

Marisol crowded in closer to Cristina on the bed to see over her shoulder. "You're back in touch with the cousins?" Marisol asked, as she watched her sister open the battered white envelope.

"I found them on social media," Cristina said. "Mostly we just exchange holiday cards."

Cristina smoothed the rumpled paper. "*Querida* Cristina," the letter began in Spanish. "I am so sorry to trouble you, but as you must know, things are really bad here in Puerto Rico with the debt crisis. So bad that the cemetery where *abuelita* and your mother are buried went bankrupt." According to the letter, they'd originally had an agreement to make additional payments to keep their family members buried there, but now the company wanted to use the land for tourism. Their dear departed would be cremated if they couldn't find a new burial plot. No one in their family living on the island could afford to pay. Could Cristina help?

"They're gonna dig Mami up?" Crisitna said. "And *abuelita*?"

The letter was dated a month earlier. There was a phone number. Cristina called, but it was disconnected.

"How come the letter took so long to get here?" Marisol asked.

Cristina sighed. "After decades of the US blockade against Cuba, they still don't have a normal communications infrastructure." Cristina began to pick at the skin around her fingernails, a habit from when she was a kid. "If we can't get through on the phone," she asked, "what should we do?"

"I think I should go see what's up," Marisol said. The return address was her grandmother's old house in Las Palmas, a small town in Southern Puerto Rico.

"I hope you're not too late," Cristina said.

"I can't fucking believe it," Marisol said. "After all the women in our family have been through, at least they should be able to rest when they're dead."

Not only was there no communication infrastructure between Puerto Rico and Cuba, there was also no travel infrastructure. Marisol had a stopover in Miami. Thus, it took nearly five hours to travel the mere eight hundred miles between the two Caribbean capitals.

She had also been delayed on the way out of Florida. The TSA agent on the tall stool had stopped her.

"The age on your passport isn't right," he said. "You should be in your early forties."

"I am," she said.

"But you don't look a day older than thirty," he said.

She smiled at him. "Are you flirting with me, sir?"

She held the US passport next to her face: Marisol Rivera, 5'6" tall, 150 lbs, eyes brown, hair black. Her hair was dark brown actually—long and wavy. Her eyes slanted above the same high cheekbones and full lips in her passport photo.

He frowned, but he waved her through.

If you counted the wait time at the airport, she could have driven there in the same amount of time, if it weren't for all the water.

When Marisol arrived in Puerto Rico, she wasn't the only one who was pissed about the state of things. She drove through San Juan in a rental car, a green coupe. Marisol had spent most of her adult life in New York, so she didn't drive much. It was her first time driving in Puerto Rico, and she took several wrong turns, then got caught up in a demonstration among public workers. According to their signs, they were demanding a living wage and a reliable pension. They had traffic snarled up throughout the capital.

A few hours later, Marisol had made it out of the city, and was listening to salsa on a highway headed into the mountains. God, could this be the same road she had traveled as a kid? So many corporate chains now: American fast food, drugstores, brand advertisements. From the moment they had landed in San Juan, she couldn't believe how much Puerto Rico had changed. Had it been twenty years since she was last there? It looked somehow like a deflated balloon—the corporate chains had blown it up, stretched it til the skin was taut and shiny, but the debt crisis had sucked out all the air. Now it sagged and flapped in the breeze.

An old salsa song came on the radio, and Marisol suddenly found herself filled with nostalgia. But for what? For a Puerto Rico she barely knew anymore? She had been conceived in San Juan. Then her mother had fled to New York to escape her abusive father. She had lived in the Bronx until her mother moved back to Puerto Rico to get away from Cristina's father. Puerto Rico was home for a few years until her mother and grandmother died in quick succession. Then they'd moved back to the states to live with the uncle. The bad men in their life had come in threes, like in a fairy tale. They got away from the first two, but instead of slaying the dragon on the third try, they got burned.

For most of Marisol's life, it had been primarily those two matrilineal graves that had connected her to the island. Suddenly she recognized the twinge of nostalgia as grief. She had cried at her mother's burial, sobbed in her grandmother's arms. But when her grandmother died of a stroke six months later, she was dry-eyed at the funeral. *I've gotta be strong for my sister—for Cristina.*

Who was this uncle who would take them now? She didn't like him and his shrinking wife who seemed scared and wore too much makeup. The wife left soon after the two girls moved to New York.

Suddenly, Marisol heard a thump as several potatoes fell off a truck in front of her and bounced along the highway toward her car. She slowed down and focused on the familiar road. This was the same highway they took every time they went to visit her grandmother in Las Palmas.

Marisol hadn't been there since the funeral. Watching her mother, and then her grandmother, lowered into the Rivera family plot.

And now that plot had gone bankrupt? She had heard things were bad on the island, but this was surreal.

Back in New York, one of her clients at the clinic had started talking about the debt crisis long before it made the news in the US.

Maybe a year before, Clara had been complaining loudly in the clinic lobby. Clara was a transgender woman, tall, butterscotch-colored, and slender hipped, with bright red lips and a gold weave down to her ass.

"Marisol, you're Puerto Rican, right?" Clara had said, but didn't wait for a response. "You got people still there? My parents don't speak to me, but I'm worried about their transphobic asses anyway. You know these motherfucking *yanquis* been bleeding our island dry and now the bill is coming due. Some shady-ass shit. And it's these hedge fund motherfuckers. I have some of them as clients. Cheap and no fucking manners. Just like the goddamn US colonizers. They got trade laws that keep Puerto Rican companies from being able to make money on the imports to our own island. I'm telling you the worst part is that they got some random fucking amendment that we can't go bankrupt, even though the bottom is about to fall out. I don't know how we gonna get out of this shit, girl."

Clara's prophesy had come to pass. Nobody knew how Puerto Rico could get out from under. There were lots of possible strategies, but they would all require that the US financial institutions loosen their stranglehold. It seemed unlikely that the same banks that didn't mind choking the pension funds of white citizens on the continental US would balk at doing the same to brown people on a Caribbean island. Instead of any changes to stranglehold policies, the US president had appointed a fiscal control board that would enforce austerity measures that put debt repayment before human services. Trying to get blood from sand.

Now, as Marisol drove down the highway in Puerto Rico, she tried to get her bearings. The further she got from the capital, from San Juan, the more things looked the same as they had two decades ago. Rural Puerto Rico had changed much less. Narrow, winding roads with thick green foliage and bamboo blocking out the light. Small cafeterias and bodegas on the sides of the road, with little kids running past holding handfuls of bright candy like trophies. Roadside houses in loud colors, with people chatting on concrete porches in chairs. Dogs lolled in shady spots, and chickens wandered by, unperturbed by the cars.

She remembered the way to her grandmother's old house by heart. The only new landmark was a shiny Walgreens, now closed.

Marisol preferred to take the coastal road to Las Palmas. It was a little longer, but she relished driving down a highway that gave her glimpses of the ocean. When she saw the small cluster of boats in the Las Palmas harbor, she knew to turn off onto the winding road that snaked up the hill to the town.

The road passed through the town center, with its pair of restaurants, local bar, small supermarket, and drugstore. There was a single store for clothing and shoes: men, women, and children's.

It was early afternoon when she pulled up in front of the blue stucco bungalow. The house looked much smaller than she recalled, the plaster cracking now, and the concrete steps uneven.

The house next door looked abandoned. Three bald tires lay half-piled on the driveway, each partially filled with old rainwater. Marisol turned back to her grandmother's house, as a teenage girl stepped out onto the porch, a baby on her hip.

"Nidia?" Marisol asked, recalling the square hips, brown skin, and tightly curled hair of her cousin. But how could her cousin look the same after decades?

The girl shook her head. "Not Nidia," she said in Spanish. "I'm Zara. Nidia's my mom."

"Of course," Marisol said, and introduced herself. "I'm your cousin from New York."

Zara brightened and they kissed on the cheek, then she turned and called her mother.

When Nidia stepped out of the house, she gave a shriek of recognition and pulled Marisol in the house and then into a deep hug.

"You came!" she sobbed. "Did Cristina tell you?"

"I tried to call—"

"The phone got turned off—"

"Am I too late? Have they already cremated them?"

Nidia blinked. "Cremated? Oh the graves. No, not yet. I had forgotten—not forgotten, it's just—they're foreclosing on the house."

"What?" Marisol asked. "I thought *abuelito* had it paid off."

"He did," Nidia said. "But when my husband Quique got sick, we had to get a mortgage to pay the bills. And then my hours got cut back to part-time."

"This is Quique?" Marisol asked. She picked up a photo from the side table. Nidia's wedding photo, looking so much like her daughter, with a tall, handsome groom.

Nidia nodded. "A shame you never got to meet him. He died last year."

"I'm sorry," Marisol said. She didn't know what else to say. She had always felt awkward around this particular cousin. They were so close in age, and should have been closer, but the way things went down in the family, they never really had the chance.

Now their lives were so different. Nidia was a widowed grandmother who lived in a small Puerto Rican town. Marisol was an unmarried, childless New Yorker. When their grandmother had died, Nidia was in her mid teens and already pregnant with Julio. Nidia also had a little sister, who lived in Florida now.

Into the quiet of the moment, the baby started to fuss. "I think he's wet," Zara said, and disappeared with him into the rear of the house.

Nidia wiped her eyes with the back of her hand and offered Marisol some coffee.

Over watery cups of something instant, Nidia explained the whole situation:

The cemetery had gone bankrupt. A real estate company had bought the land, and demanded an annual payment to keep the family plot. The family had scrambled to find extra cash, but things had gotten so bad that they couldn't keep up the payments. The family thought the problem was solved when a tourist company bought up a bunch of nearby land, including the cemetery. The company also bought out a credit union that was going under, which held the mortgages on several local properties, including theirs. The company had bought most of the land to set up some sort of resort. They explained that they wanted to keep the cemetery, because it added "charm," and signed new contracts with locals who had cemetery plots. But six months later, the company decided that the cemetery land would be the perfect place for a second motorcycle course.

The way the contract was worded, the company was under no actual obligation to keep the cemetery. It also said they would compensate the families with a certain dollar amount, but they paid in stock options. And the contract was in English, full of legalese, and the family couldn't really tell what it said; but their neighbor's brother-in-law was a lawyer in Miami. He helped set up the deal and they thought they could trust him, but now he wasn't returning their calls. And the company was insisting on having all the graves moved, and the family would need to pay again for a plot somewhere else, and pay for the expenses to move the graves. Or the company would just cremate all the bodies and they could pick up the remains.

Nidia's eyes filled again. "I know that's not what *abuelita* and your *mami* wanted, but I don't know what else to do. Do you think maybe you can keep the urns? If the foreclosure goes through, we won't even have a place to put them. We'll probably stay with my sister in Orlando. There are already five of them in a two-bedroom apartment. But where else can we go? My older son, Julio, is in New York trying to find work. He went to look for our uncle, but couldn't find him. Julio's been living in a homeless shelter."

Marisol was shocked. "Our uncle? Julio was looking for our uncle in New York? Our uncle died more than twenty years ago. You didn't know?"

Nidia shook her head. "There was some bad blood between him and my *mami* when she was alive. They didn't talk. She said to stay away from him, but now she's dead and we're desperate."

"I'm in New York," Marisol said. "I mean, I'm visiting Cristina in Havana now, but I live in Manhattan. I can set you up there. Just let me know what you need."

"Are you kidding me?" Nidia said. "That would be incredible." She let out a choked sob. Marisol put an arm around her, but her cousin waved her away.

"I'm fine," she said quickly. "Just so grateful to have somewhere to go."

"But would you rather stay in Puerto Rico?"

"Not without a house to live in," Nidia said.

"Can I see this contract you signed?" Marisol asked.

Nidia went to her bedroom, and returned with some papers.

Marisol read through them carefully. Her family had been paid in stock for the tourism company. It was no longer worth what it had been valued at the time of the contract signing. But a little research showed that the value had likely been inflated and had probably never been worth that amount.

Marisol seethed as she uncovered the layers of manipulation and deceit. She got the name of the man behind it all, and looked him up on the internet: Davis Evanston, CEO of the tourist company Puerto Cyclo, that been buying up the land. She looked at his photo beside the image of his resort: a fiftyish white guy with a ruddy tan and a smug smile. He was posed beside a motorcycle.

"Remember when you were a kid, and you didn't ever want to leave the playground?" he asked in his YouTube video. "What if you never had to leave? What if the playground never closed? That's exactly what it's like to live in Puerto Rico. No taxes. No regulations. A tropical paradise that's still on US soil. Build your own castle here and live like a king."

Even the images in the YouTube video were misleading. They showed a young white couple walking on the beach past several cozy cottages. Las Palmas had a rocky coastline, and a harbor, but no sand. The town of Las Palmas was up a steep hill from the harbor. There were no houses for the first quarter-mile, until the ground leveled out a bit.

Evanston's Puerto Cyclo resort was a few towns inland from Las Palmas. The resort had a wave pool, a seven-story hotel, a Tiki bar, and the big attraction was the motorcycle course. Really, it was just a couple of acres of former farmland that he allowed guests to tear up with two-wheel vehicles. He was also reselling smaller parcels of land and marketing them as "tax-free fiefdoms." Apparently, it was successful enough that they wanted to dig up the cemetery to make a second motorcycle course. Marisol seethed as she went back to talk to her cousin.

"Is there anything we can do?" Nidia asked.

"I think you might have some legal options," Marisol said.

She looked into her cousin's face. Nidia's brow was furrowed, and she gripped her coffee mug so tightly that her tan knuckles showed pale.

"And of course . . ." Marisol said, meeting Nidia's eyes, trying to determine how much to say. "You probably have a lot of illegal options." The moment she'd said it, she regretted it. She should have asked a bunch more questions before even bringing up anything like this.

But Nidia leaned forward. "Options like what?" she asked.

"This guy stole from you right?" Marisol tried to find the words. "Could you imagine. . . . I mean . . . Would you have any problem . . . ?"

"Stealing it back from him?" Nidia asked. "Are you kidding me? I've thought about it a thousand times. Waiting outside of his hotel and carjacking him. Following him into San Juan and mugging him. But what would I end up with? Fifty dollars? A couple hundred? I'd probably get caught. Besides I cursed him out at a community meeting. He knows my face."

"You really have thought about it," Marisol said.

"Fuck yeah," Nidia said. "I've also thought about hiring someone, but I don't know anyone who could do it, and I don't have any money to hire anybody anyway."

"I have a . . ." Marisol began. Even if Nidia was on board, she was an amateur. It was always a risk. "I have a . . . friend. Here in Puerto Rico. She . . . she has some skills in this area. She might be able to help you."

Nidia's eyes narrowed. "You have to be careful," she said. "People are desperate these days. She might offer to help but really be trying to cheat you."

Marisol shook her head. "We go way back. I trust her. She's . . . she's back and forth to New York. I'd stake my life on the fact that she wouldn't cheat us."

"What's in it for her?" Nidia asked.

"She's got her own score to settle with this guy," Marisol said. "He scammed her family, too."

Marisol drove down to the end of the street and pulled out her cell phone. She called the office manager's desk at the María de La Vega health clinic. It just rang and rang. So she called the office manager's cell phone.

"How's Cuba?" Serena asked.

"I'm in Puerto Rico, actually," Marisol said.

"How's that going?" Serena asked.

"It's really beautiful here," Marisol said. "I think you and Tyesha might be due for a weekend getaway. I could really use some help soaking up all this beautiful sun."

Serena laughed. "I am definitely willing to help, but Tyesha can't leave the office. There's a grant proposal due and a big strategic planning meeting. You remember how it was when you were executive director."

"I certainly do," Marisol said. "But it's a shame. I was really hoping both of you could come. I've got three beds in this hotel upgrade. I'd hate for any of them to go to waste."

"Yeah," Serena said. "That would be a shame. But you know who might be free? I think Lily has some time off. And I know she'd be down to help you soak up some rays."

"Can you call her?" Marisol asked. "Better yet, meet with her in person and convince her to come."

"Consider it done," Serena said.

"Great," Marisol said. "Text me when you can leave, and I'll book tickets."

"Any chance I can bring my boyfriend?" Serena asked.

"Sorry honey," Marisol said. "This is just for the girls on the team."

Marisol came back to Nidia's house a couple of hours later, with a cell phone. She had also booked a pair of plane tickets for her team, and had made a hotel reservation for herself at Puerto Cyclo.

By then it was evening and the mosquitoes were out. She walked to the abandoned house next door and tipped the rainwater out of the bald tires. She didn't want to breed more mosquitoes to bite her baby cousin. Not that the water in three bald tires would really make that much of a difference in the overall amount of Zika virus on the whole island, but she couldn't just let them sit.

"Were you able to speak with her?" Nidia asked.

"She's got a plan," Marisol said "But she needs our help to make it happen."

"Anything," Nidia said. "Except threatening him with a gun, because I know I would lose my cool and shoot that asshole."

Marisol gave Nidia a new cell phone for the two of them to communicate.

"So what does your friend need me to do?" Nidia asked.

"She'll call me tomorrow with the plan," Marisol said. "And I'll pass it on to you."

"Okay," Nidia sighed, slipping the phone into the pocket of her shorts. "I'll get Zara to make up Julio's room for you." With her chin, she indicated a door to the left of the kitchen. Marisol recalled staying there after her grandmother's funeral. The grief reared up and stung like a scorpion. She shook her head.

"Oh no *mujer*, don't trouble yourself," Marisol said. "Besides, my friend says I need to go check in at this guy's tacky hotel to be her boots on the ground." In that moment, Marisol wanted to tell her cousin, "there is no friend—it's just me." But she still didn't know Nidia that well. They may be first cousins, but there was a treacherous streak in her family. For now she'd stick to the "friend" story.

Marisol took her cousins for dinner at a local cafeteria, and then went to the Puerto Cyclo Hotel. The two locations were a study in contrast. The roadside eatery was all locals and open air. The resort lobby was air conditioned with plastic palm trees. Marisol was the only Puerto Rican at the resort who wasn't a service worker.

The rooms were $250 per night, but she'd gotten a deal on the internet. The queen room had a large flat screen TV and muted, forgettable décor.

Marisol spent the next twenty-four hours scoping out the place and talking to her cousin on the phone. Everywhere in the resort were posters saying, "YOU could live here." In the photographs, middle-aged white people participated in a variety of leisure activities. The few Puerto Rican faces were masseuses, athletic instructors, and wait staff.

Puerto Cyclo was on multiple acres of land, and it had a complimentary activities magazine. Along with surfing in the wave pool and a wine tasting, there was a lecture series.

Two days after she arrived, Davis Evanston was scheduled to give a lunch talk in the hotel's dining room, entitled "Two Wheels Are Better than Four: Motorcycles, The Myth of Danger and the Truth about Personal Freedom."

Marisol scoped out the restaurant and would be ready for him. Her cousin had instructions to keep her phone on.

Chapter 5

Every time Dulce visited her aunt in Santo Domingo, the place seemed smaller. When she was there as a toddler, the three bedroom house seemed huge compared to her tiny two-bedroom apartment in Washington Heights. Not only did her aunt have a whole house, but a yard in front and back, with chickens. And a shed. Like another miniature house next to the regular one.

When she was seven, they came back again for her great uncle's funeral. He had died from cancer. Her aunt's house seemed smaller on that second visit. In particular, the shed was no longer like a second house, and more like a play structure. Her brother, Santiago, was thirteen and always looking for the next edge. He climbed the tree as he had always done, but now the tree had grown, and with great care, he could edge out on a branch to the roof of the shed.

"Dare me to jump?" he asked their sister Yunisa in English.

"You'll break your legs," she replied in Spanish.

"No I won't," he said. And without further preamble, he leaped off, falling and rolling onto his side in the yard.

Dulce gasped, afraid for a moment he was badly injured.

But then he sprang up, grinning and brushing the dirt off his shorts.

"I wanna try," Yunisa said.

"Me too," Dulce said.

"No, you're too little," Yunisa said over her shoulder, climbing into the tree.

Five minutes later, her sister was also laughing and brushing dirt from the hem of her skirt.

"Santiago," Dulce pleaded. "I want to do it too. Let me do it too."

He rolled his eyes. "You're too much of a scaredy cat."

"I won't be scared," she insisted.

"Okay, fine," he said. "First climb up the tree."

Dulce was a good climber. She was strong from playing on the monkey bars at school with her friends. She easily made it to the roof. She was good at jumping off the bars, too, but this was way further down. Like eight feet. And onto dirt, not those thick black rubber mats at their school. The mats had originally looked like puzzle pieces, but now the edges were crumbling and they had potholes worn in them. Still, she knew the thick spots and how to land safely.

"Bend your knees, Luqui," Santiago called her by his nickname for her. "That's all you have to remember."

She looked over the edge of the roof. Her older siblings looked so small. So short. She was scared. She wanted to take it back. Tell them she changed her mind. But her sister's scowling face made up her mind for her. Yunisa didn't think she could do it, so now she had to do it. She needed to show them both she wasn't a baby anymore.

"Come on, Luqui," Santiago encouraged. "Like the story you wrote about the princess who jumps off the cliff to get away from the dragon and learns she can fly. You're just like her. You can do it. Just bend your knees when you land."

Dulce took one last glance at her sister, the dragon in her life, and jumped. She remembered to bend her knees.

Like her siblings, she rolled on the ground after landing,

but the leap had been more exhilarating than she had ever imagined. She could fly. She wanted to do it ten more times.

But her *tía* was coming out of the house half shrieking. Wasn't it bad enough she had lost her husband? Was she supposed to now have to suffer the loss of one of the precious babies of the family?

"I told her it was dangerous," Yunisa said.

"I'm okay, *titi*," Dulce said. "And I won't do it again."

As her aunt brushed dirt off the knees of her shorts, Dulce looked down at the ground to hide her smile.

That summer, they jumped off the shed roof every chance they got.

A couple evenings after arriving in Santo Domingo, Dulce sat watching TV at her aunt's house. Really, it was her great aunt of course, who had also raised her mother. The aunt was in her late sixties, generous and sharp, and living frugally off her husband's pension. But she was also a devout Christian, and lived a pretty quiet life.

Two days in, Dulce had paid cash for a cell phone, and called the businessman with the Rolex. He hadn't called back yet. By the third day, she'd called the journalist, Zavier. He called right back, but there was a thunderstorm, and the cell tower went down. They'd played phone tag for a couple of days.

The big excitement happened on the fourth night, when her aunt turned on the TV to watch a soap opera called *O Passado Sombrio De Uma Mulher*, or in English, *A Woman's Dark Past*. The program was produced for TV in Brazil, but had been dubbed from Portuguese to Spanish.

On the screen, a young, haughty blonde woman looks bored as an earnest young man holds her hand.

"Izabel," he says. "I know I don't have much to offer

now, but this patent I'm working on. It could change everything. After I finish it, I'm hoping . . . I mean, I wouldn't presume to propose now, but I'm hoping to be able to offer you the life you deserve. I'm hoping you'll marry me."

She turns to him with a patronizing smile. "We'll see when the time comes," she says.

Dulce's *tía* sucked her teeth. "*Izabel es tan sinvergüenza.*" Dulce nodded and got up to put more chicken stew with rice and beans on her plate. Every night her *tía* cooked and they watched TV. Dulce hurried back from the kitchen so as not to miss more of this particular show.

The earnest young man, Guilherme is headed out of the house. He runs into a dark-haired Brazilian girl on his way out. She's the protagonist, Xoana.

She greets him warmly, and asks about his scientific work.

He brightens and begins telling her about the latest experiments. As he talks, the camera zooms in on Xoana, music swells. Her rapt expression makes it clear that, unlike the blonde Germanic girl, Xoana is in love with the young scientist.

"Xoana lives with Izabel," Dulce's *tía* explained. "Since she was a teen and Izabel's mother, La Alemana, rescued her from the favelas. In the cities of Brazil, those are slums."

"I know, *tía*," Dulce said. "I used to watch novelas in Cuba. This one from Brazil was the only one I really liked."

On the screen, Izabel is dressing provocatively to go to a party with her parents, both of whom work at the university.

"You never want to go to their parties," Xoana says. "What's so special this time?"

"Some members of the national soccer team are going to be there," Izabel says excitedly. "It's not every day you get to meet a sports star."

An older blonde woman walks into the room, Izabel's mother, La Alemana. "Well, don't you look fancy," she says to her daughter. "Xoana, are you sure you don't want to come? We could get a babysitter for the boys."

Two rambunctious boys run into the room, one a preschooler and one a couple years older.

"No! No! No!" they shout. "We only want to be with Xoana."

"I need to stay home and study," Xoana says. "And these boys need to clean their room."

"You have to catch us first!" the older boy shrieks and they run out of the room, with Xoana laughing and chasing them.

A handsome older man steps into the room. "Well," he says. "Isn't everyone looking lovely tonight. Are we ready to go?"

Dulce's *tía* pointed to the TV with her fork. "That's not Izabel's father. She's from a previous marriage."

"I know, *tía*," Dulce said. "He's the boys' father. And they treat Xoana like their nanny. Supposedly they took her in and everything, but she's certainly earning her keep."

"No, it's not like that," her *tía* said. "Xoana loves the boys. She enjoys taking care of them."

"Maybe," Dulce said. "But also because she feels obligated."

Dulce's phone rang, and it was Zavier.

"I gotta take this," Dulce said, a smile spreading across her face.

"I'll let you know what happens," her *tía* said, as Dulce walked into the bedroom for privacy.

Dulce lay back on the bed, the phone against her ear. She felt like a teenager. But she had never really gotten to do this as a teen. Talk on the phone to a guy she liked.

"So how's it going?" Zavier asked. "Are you in the capital?"

"Far from it," she said. "My *tiabuela* lives just outside Haina, in a tiny town with nothing going on. I'm so bored, I can't stand it. The big excitement is when a dozen roosters all start crowing at the crack of dawn and wake me up every morning. Oh and going to church with a bunch of old people. I prayed for something even vaguely exciting to happen."

He laughed. "Well, I've filed my story, and I have a couple days free. Can I rent a car and come visit you?"

"Oh my god," Dulce said. "My prayers are answered!"

She gave him her address.

The following day, she walked to the center of town to buy something to wear. She had arrived with only her blue ombre bustier dress, a pair of high heel sandals, and a club purse. Her great aunt had loaned her a couple pairs of drawstring shorts, t-shirts, a few shapeless house dresses, as well as an old dress for church. She didn't have anything cute enough for a date.

Dulce wore a pair of shorts and a tank top into town, both of them fraying. Underneath, she had only her strapless bra from the club. On her feet a beat up pair of slip ons.

People from the area greeted her. "You must be Lourdes's daughter from New York." Apparently, they had all known her mother. Lourdes had been chosen to be in a music video in San Juan. Lourdes had left her two kids—Santiago and Yunisa—with the great aunt in the DR. Lourdes overstayed her visa to Puerto Rico for several weeks, after hooking up with a Cuban guy in the band. When Lourdes told him she was pregnant, he encouraged her to have an abortion. When she asked about the future, he said that it had been fun, but he was moving back to New York.

But Lourdes stayed in Puerto Rico throughout her pregnancy, working as a maid. She wanted to give birth there, so the baby could have American citizenship. After Dulce was born, Lourdes told the Cuban she only wanted one thing: could he get her to New York?

Dulce had traveled to JFK as a lap baby for free. Then Lourdes sent for her two older kids from the DR. Got a job under the table and a place in Washington Heights.

But when Lourdes was injured in an industrial accident, she couldn't sue, because she didn't have papers. Dulce's teenage brother Santiago began supporting the family by selling drugs. And then he got arrested and deported when Dulce was fourteen. That's when everything went to shit. Dulce thought Jerry the pimp was her rescuer. But instead things went from shit to hell.

Dulce walked into the main street of the town. There was only one clothing store. "Nineteen ninety-five called and wants its clothes back," Dulce murmured. But she found a couple of cute pieces that she could work with. What was she gonna do for shoes? She couldn't wear those high heels from the club. They were too much. But these other heels were too out of fashion for a date with a guy who lived in New York. she just ended up buying a gold pair of flip flops. Cute. Classic. They'd have to do.

Dulce sat on the steps of her great aunt's house, waiting for Zavier. The whitewashed bungalow needed a coat of paint. A pair of hens made their way through the grass in the driveway, pecking at the ground. Beside them, her great-uncle's old Toyota Corolla sat rusting. He'd been dead nearly fifteen years, and her aunt had neither the money to fix it, nor the heart to get rid of it. Besides, her nephew in New Jersey kept promising to come visit and get it running.

Dulce tried to imagine what Zavier would see when he drove up: her kinky hair pulled back in a wild ponytail puff. The pink tank top, the black miniskirt. The shade of lipstick that was a bit too light for her. Sure, the clothes hugged her figure nicely, showed off her curves. But somehow it looked trashy here. In New York she would have dressed it up with some trendy jewelry and fly shoes. Now, she just looked like a hick with a big ass. Like she should be sweeping the house and have a couple of kids.

She liked to be that carefree city girl, that hot girl with the sparkling makeup and cute shoes. Even when she had a pimp she had looked better than this. She remembered those years. She was the only one of his girls who had US citizenship; the others were undocumented. And he held all of their passports. What was it he'd always said to the other girls? If they went back to their backwards-ass countries they'd learn that their pussy was worth a lot less there. "I'm doing you all a favor!"

Eventually, they'd all gotten away from him, but this was probably why they'd stayed. These small houses out in the middle of nowhere. People in your business. Her great aunt had asked too many questions about Zavier. Who was this guy? Where did she know him from? Where was he taking her?

Dulce wasn't sure and didn't really care. Anywhere would be better than here.

When Dulce was a toddler, she'd stayed in this house, in this same guest room, for nearly eight months.

Her mother had gotten an invitation to shoot another video with that same band. But this time, they were in Spain instead of Puerto Rico. The director wanted to continue with the same theme, and wanted the same video vixen. Lourdes didn't hesitate. She sent the now three kids to her aunt's in the

DR and flew to Spain. The video shooting only took a few days, but she rekindled things with Dulce's father. He was living in Spain now.

So their time in the DR stretched on through the months. It was Dulce, her two siblings, and two cousins. Five children slept in the full-size bed, and her great-aunt laid them along the bed's shorter dimension. For years afterwards, she would sometimes get confused when getting into a bed, whether to lay parallel or perpendicular. In some ways, Dulce loved sleeping five-in-a-bed, and having one cousin her same size. She might be the baby of the family, but she wasn't the only baby. Still, she missed her mom terribly.

Who can say how much a toddler understands? Soon her *tía*'s cooing voice turned from "don't worry, *nena*, your *mami* will be back in a few days," to "as always, your *mami* will come get you kids when she's good and damn ready."

Zavier drove up in a silver two-door hatchback. Not fancy, but new enough looking.

"Hold on," she said. "I'm not quite finished watching this line of ants walking by. It's been the thrill of the week."

Zavier laughed.

"So where are we going?" Dulce asked.

"I thought maybe to the beach," he said. "And to lunch. What do you think?"

"Sounds great," she said.

She'd never been to the beach in Santo Domingo. The time her family had come for her great uncle's funeral, there were too many of them to fit in the family's car, and they had no money for rental cars or even public cars. The airline tickets for the funeral had cleaned them out, and they hadn't even been able to afford to fly from New York. Six of them had piled illegally into a car that a neighbor was driving to Ft. Lauderdale. They'd paid for her gas money, then caught a much cheaper flight from Florida.

"Your great aunt's town looks cool, though," he said.

"Are you kidding me?"

"Seriously," he said. "I'm a journalist, but really I'm a writer. I kind of dream of living somewhere quiet and just writing. As long as I have an internet connection."

"Sounds boring as hell," she said. "And lonely."

"Not if I had somebody special there," he said.

"When I was in school I used to love writing," Dulce said. "And I always wanted to be a journalist. You know, the kind that interviews people. In high school, we had this assignment to interview people on the street, and it was the most fun I ever had in school. I even did extra credit."

"Right?" he said. "There's something so exciting about capturing people's thoughts. Their dreams. Finding out what's pissing them off, and how they would like to fix it."

"Yeah, but who the hell would you be interviewing in a small town," Dulce asked. "After like a week, you'd have talked to everybody. I'd want to interview people on the front lines of important things that were happening. Plus, of course, celebrities. Just before I dropped out of school, my English teacher was encouraging me to start writing for the school newspaper."

"Well, I'm actually supposed to interview Ibeyi in the capital before I leave tomorrow. Wanna join me? You could ask a couple of questions of your own."

"Those two Cuban sisters who sing?" Dulce asked.

Zavier nodded.

"Are you kidding me?" Dulce asked. "I'd love to."

He drove them to a beach in a tourist area, over an hour away. It wasn't until they got to the restaurant and she heard some people speaking English, that she realized she'd been speaking Spanish with Zavier the whole time.

He treated her to lunch. She had Chinese food, something she hadn't had in ages.

As they ate, he asked, "Who's your greatest rapper of all time?"

"English or Spanish?"

"Spanish first,"

"Migranteza," Dulce said.

"Yes!" Zavier said. "That's the shit!"

"They're so ratchet," Dulce said. "But conscious, too. It's like, a little something for everybody."

"And the beats," Zavier said. "That DJ is a fucking genius. She mixes the Caribbean beats with that Afropop and seventies soul and is just killing it."

"Okay we agree in Spanish," Dulce said. "So what about in English?"

"Thug Woofer is the greatest rapper of all time."

"What?" Dulce asked. "Thug Woofer? The king of the $kranky $outh?"

"He's gotten beyond that," Zavier said.

"Based on what?" Dulce asked. "That dancehall song he did with Bumboozala."

"He's changed," Zavier said. "Did you listen to his Melvyn album?"

"I heard one track," Dulce said. "It was like reading someone's diary. I want hip hop I can dance to."

"He seriously took it to the next level, though," Zavier said. "What he was revealing about himself. His past. And then he pulled out of that album deal with Car Willis. And now his new album, Man.Hood. If you take all his stuff and listen to it continuously, it's like, how men of color need to evolve. It's really fucking deep."

"I'm glad he's evolving, but I can't dance to that shit," Dulce said. "That's why I love Nashonna. She's my number one."

"Nashonna?" Zavier asked. " 'What the stripper had to say'?"

"You need to listen to what that stripper has to say," Dulce said.

"But she never talks about anything else," Zavier said. "It's all the same. 'I'm sexy. I'm too busy for love. I rap as good as the boys. I used to strip but now I make money doing hip hop. Girl power!' Every single song."

"Not every song," Dulce protested.

"She never takes on any other topics," Zavier said. "Woof takes on police brutality. He has that new song encouraging everyone to vote, 'Blast the Last Disaster.' Nashonna doesn't have the range."

"People always try to dismiss her," Dulce said. "But when her book comes out, you'll see."

Zavier shook his head. "Lyrically, she's a lightweight," he said.

"We'll have to agree to disagree," Dulce said.

"Send me some lyrics then," Zavier said.

"What do you mean send?"

"Email them," he said.

Dulce shook her head. "I'm not on email much."

"Instagram?" he asked. "Facebook?"

"I never liked Facebook," she said. "And I hardly use my Instagram account. But I'm on twitter."

"Fine," he said. "Tweet me some lyrics."

"What's your handle?"

"@ZaviJourno."

"Cool," she said, pulling out her phone. "I'll tweet you right now."

She grinned as she pulled up the app on her phone and typed from memory. Then she tagged him in the tweets and hit send.

Zavier pulled out his phone. He read:

The word according to @ThatGirlNashonna
"All these boys tryna teach me something
Act like the teacher and we're at school

Always got some kind of lesson they planning
Like just cause I'm hot I gotta be a fool?" (1/2)

"But now you got hit with the unexpected
You just might not pass this class
You better go sharpen your number two pencil
Cause the number one rapper's gonna whup that ass."
(2/2)

Zavier raised his eyebrows. "Okay," he said. "Okay, I see how it is."

"You gonna write back," she asked.

"I'm thinking," he said, looking at his phone.

"You're not thinking," she said. "You're googling."

"I refuse to answer the question on the grounds that it might incriminate me," he said.

She grabbed his phone. "RatchetLyrics.com? And you call yourself a journalist?"

"I'm just using it as a secondary source to verify the quote," he said, reaching for the phone.

"You are such a liar," she said. "Fake news! Fake news!"

He cracked up. "Give me my phone, *chica.*"

She laughed, and when she put the phone in his hand, he wrapped his fingers around hers.

"So, you gonna pull up those Thug Woofer lyrics or what?" she asked.

He smiled and looked in her face. "I was going to, but I suddenly got very distracted."

Dulce looked down and focused on using the chopsticks to get the food to her mouth. "Whatever," she said. "You just got defeated by Nashonna, that's all."

After lunch, they walked through the tourist part of the area. She bought a swimsuit and a couple pairs of cute shoes.

She would have bought a dress, but the tourist sizes were apparently for women who didn't have as much ass as she did.

It had been ages since she'd been to the beach. She'd gone to Coney Island with her family a bunch of times. Her boyfriend had taken her to Miami Beach, but they hadn't gone in the water. She'd just been arm candy in a couple of clubs and part of the entourage as he handled business on the strip.

Zavier had a slender triangle of an upper body. Broad shoulders and a narrow waist. A smooth mosaic of hair across his chest. In the loose trunks, his legs were tawny and lean, the hair on his calves flashing auburn in the sunlight.

He dove into the water and started to swim away from the shore.

She hesitated.

He turned around. "Hey, are you coming or what?"

"I can't swim," she said.

"You've got to be kidding me," he said. "What kind of *Caribeña* can't swim?"

"The kind that gets raised in Washington Heights," she said.

"But didn't you come here a bunch as a kid?" he asked. "Your aunt's house isn't that far from the beach."

"Both the beaches and the rivers near Haina are so polluted," she said. "My *tía* wouldn't let us swim there."

"Come here, then," he said. "I'll teach you."

They waded out to waist deep water. The beach was in a cove, so the waves were gentle.

"Here's what you do," he said. "Lean back and just float. I'll hold you up."

She felt awkward, laying in his arms, but she could feel the tight six pack of his belly against her side.

"That's it," he said. "Just relax."

"How do you know I'm not gonna sink?" she asked.

"I'm looking at you in a swimsuit," he said. "You got plenty to hold you up."

"Fine," she said laughing. "So my ass won't sink. But I'm worried about my head going under."

"Then dunk your whole body," he said, lowering the arm that had been beneath her legs. "Get used to the water."

Her feet slowly drifted down to the ocean floor.

"Come on," he said. "I'll do it with you."

He held her hands, and together, they went under.

She came up laughing. The ocean was warm and she felt safe with him. As the salt water ran down from her hair, she was glad she hadn't wasted money on a blowout.

And then she lay in his arms, relaxing, feeling her body floating.

"Okay," he said. "I'm gonna take my arms away."

For a second, she floated but then she tensed and began to sink.

She sputtered and grabbed him around the neck.

"You had it there for a minute," he said, putting one hand around her back and the other under her knees.

She tried it again, and this time she got it.

Floating felt amazing. Like she could let go of everything she'd ever worried about.

"Float with me," she said.

"That's a tall order," he said. "I'm all skin and bone. Not much to float."

"You got a little ass there," she said.

He laughed. "Whatever I got is muscle," he said. "Muscle sinks, too."

"Fine," she said. "We can take turns. I'll hold you up."

"What self-respecting Caribbean man would let his date hold him up in the water?"

"The kind of Caribbean guy who carries the weight of the world on his shoulders and could use a break," Dulce said. "Besides, fuck these people. You'll never see them again."

He laughed. "All very good points," he said. "If you ever tell anyone about this, I'll deny it."

"Your secret is safe with me," she said.

And he lay back in her arms. After a few minutes, he even fell asleep.

As she looked down at him sleeping, Dulce felt strange. She'd never had a man trust her like this before. Relax with her. She thought about the men she had messed with. Her longest relationships were with a pimp and a drug dealer. She didn't think she'd ever seen either of them relax.

The sun went behind a cloud, and there was less glare off the ocean. She was able to really look at Zavier. His face was beautiful without the glasses. Chiseled. His hair floated around his head in a curly halo. His eyelashes were long, and the muscles in his arms and chest were firm, even as his entire body was relaxed.

He was good-looking, but not in any way that was familiar. With Jerry, she had been fourteen, and there had been the sense of excitement that being with an older man would make her grown, somehow. That some of the power would rub off on her. With her ex from Miami, it was that sense of being chosen. That he could have any girl, but he wanted her. He was the full deployment of the original fantasy she'd had about Jerry. A man who would take care of her. But Jerry was a sham because he wanted her to fuck other guys for money. Ultimately—as Marisol had revealed to her—she was the one taking care of Jerry with her sexual labor. In contrast, her ex in Miami only wanted her for himself. But she had been naïve to think that it could last. A man like that has a parade of side chicks.

Zavier was a whole different type. In the past, he wouldn't have even shown up on her radar. This guy might be some kind of boyfriend material. After he woke up, she'd be sure to ask if he was married.

The sun came out from behind the clouds. Zavier began to squint behind his closed eyes. He opened them, then blinked and stood upright.

"Oh wow," he said. "How long was I out?"

"Just for a minute," Dulce said.

"Sorry," he said.

"Why are you sorry?" she asked. "I fell asleep on you on the airplane,"

"It's rude to fall asleep on a date," he said. "I don't want you to think I'm not excited to be with such a beautiful woman. But there's a way I can just relax with you and be myself."

"I know what you mean," she said. "It's like I've known you for much longer than a couple weeks."

"Really just a couple days if you count the times we've actually been around each other," he said.

From the water, she heard a *paletero* yelling that he had popsicles.

"Let's get some," she said.

"I left everything but my key in the car," he said.

"I got some cash," she said, and pulled a few coins out from under her breasts in the swimsuit. Dulce never let herself go anywhere without a little money.

"A woman of many talents," he said.

"You have no idea."

The two of them sat on the towels they had bought, and ate the *paletas*. He got strawberry and she got mango.

When she had been with her ex, she'd eaten ice cream with him a few times. Each time it was about licking it in a way that would turn him on. But with Zavier, she wasn't putting on a show.

She felt the cool, sweet mango in her mouth, the sun on her face, the sound of the waves, and the presence of the guy next to her. She never wanted the day to end.

* * *

When he dropped her off at her great aunt's house, they both knew she couldn't ask him in. So she expected that he would make a move on her in the car. She didn't have any condoms, so she planned to explain that and give him a blow job.

After he stopped the car, she waited for him to make a move. To kiss her or something. They sat there for an awkward moment.

Then he jumped up. "Shit, where are my manners?"

He stepped out of the driver's side and came around and opened her door. She was stunned, and it took her a moment to rally. Was something wrong? He didn't think she was sexy?

He reached a hand in, and took hers. Then he kissed her gently on her knunkles and led her out of the car.

"I had a really nice time," he said.

She didn't trust her voice, so she just nodded.

Still holding her hand, he walked her up to the bungalow's door. "Can I come back and see you again tomorrow?"

She nodded again.

His grin was huge. "Noon at the latest. I want to spend as much time with you as I can."

He gave her a soft kiss on the cheek, and then he was gone.

She stood there in the moonlight, dazed by the chivalry and disoriented from her body having revved up for sex that didn't happen.

She might have stood there all night if her great aunt hadn't opened the door.

"*Carajo, nena*, are you coming in or what?"

She stepped in and closed the door behind her. Confusion still filled her body, but beneath it all was the excitement for tomorrow.

Chapter 6

Marisol's team, which consisted of Lily and Serena, landed in Puerto Rico by 6 AM the following day. They picked up a blue compact from the car rental, and drove to a small-town bed and breakfast between San Juan and Las Palmas.

Marisol was waiting in their room.

"How was the trip?" she asked, hugging them both. "Any trouble in the airport?"

"No problem," Lily said, opening the checked luggage and pulling out some of the items Marisol had requested: a satellite phone, two burner phones, and a flame lighter with an extra-long reach. Lily had buried the items under a bunch of costumes. Nothing they had was technically illegal, but they didn't want to raise any questions.

Puerto Rico didn't have the same type of customs as sovereign Caribbean nations, but Lily had taken extra care to disguise the biggest item they had brought, a spike strip. Although the strips targeted cars and not people, they were considered weapons. These accordions of jutting nails were used by law enforcement to stop fleeing suspects. Just set one of them in a vehicle's path for an instant tire blowout. They were commercially available for personal security, and you could buy them online. Or, in Lily's case, you could get them on short notice from a thuggish on-and-off hookup you knew in Brooklyn.

Lily had disassembled the spike strip and made it look like part of a carnival costume. She'd sewn the spiked bars onto the back of three pairs of leather boots, then she'd stuck bright blue feathers onto each spike. She even packed a trio of blue leotards, two blue wigs and a headdress to make it look more believable.

Serena had packed the other disassembled pieces of the spike strip, as well as the screwdriver and nails. The two women had flown on separate reservations, checked their suitcases, and made sure to sit far apart on the plane. Fortunately, neither of them had been searched.

"So who's the target?" Serena asked.

Marisol showed them a photo on her phone. "This guy," she said, pointing to the fiftyish grinning white man. "Davis Evanston, the CEO of Puerto Cyclo." She pulled up another photo of a black car. "And this is what he'll be driving."

Marisol spent the next ten minutes showing the the two new arrivals how to set up the satellite phone to follow the GPS tracker she had put on Evanston's car. Then she loaded a geolocator site and put in a set of coordinates.

"This is the location where you should wait for him," she said, pointing her finger to a dropped pin on a winding road in the mountains.

"Why here?" Lily asked.

"Notorious for bad cell service," Marisol said.

"Which is why we needed the satellite phone," Serena said.

"So after we blow out the tires on the car, do we rob the guy?" Lily asked.

"Nope," Marisol said. "You know I don't like to rob, just to burgle."

"What's the difference again?" Serena asked.

"Robbing is more intimate," Lily said. "When you burgle, the mark isn't there."

"So why stop the car?" Serena asked.

"You're my alibi," Marisol said.

"So while he's stranded out on the road, you're gonna burgle him?" Lily asked.

Marisol nodded. "I'm about to burgle the fuck out of this asshole."

On her way back to the Puerto Cyclo resort, Marisol stopped by her grandmother's house in Las Palmas. She put two numbers in the burner phone and gave it to Nidia.

"This first number is my burner phone," Marisol said. "Call me if there are any problems. This second number is the one you call when I send the signal."

Nidia nodded.

"Here's my credit card and ID," Marisol said. "Just sign a scrawl for my name on any receipts."

"Should I have Zara straighten my hair with the curling iron so I can look more like you?" Nidia asked.

Marisol nodded. She and Nidia had faces that looked passably alike. Similar height. Marisol had encouraged Nidia to wear a loose dress to hide the differences in their body shapes. If Nidia straightened her hair it would be difficult for any casual observer to say that she wasn't Marisol. Even if they were shown a photograph later.

"So here's the big challenge," Marisol said. "How's your English?"

"I understand it better than I speak it," Nidia said.

Marisol nodded. "So speak Spanish in the restaurant," she said. "Just like I would. But you have to say one phrase in English like a native."

"What phrase?" Nidia asked.

" 'No worries,' " Marisol said.

"Noh wodies," Nidia said back to her.

"Okay," Marisol said in Spanish, conjure up your inner-*yanqui.* "Nooooeeeee."

Nidia laughed. "Noooohhh."

Marisol laughed, too. "Watch my mouth," she said in Spanish. "Noooooeeeee."

Nidia mimicked Marisol's lips: "nooooeee."

"Perfecto!" Marisol said. "You're halfway there. Now try the second part: Wurrrrrieeezzz."

"Woodieezz," Nidia said.

"Wurrriezz," Marisol said. "Just do the vowel sound. Uuuuurrr."

"Uuuuhhhh . . ." Nidia tried it, and burst into uncontrollable laughter. "This is a totally unnatural way for the human mouth to move. No wonder *yanquis* don't know how to act."

Marisol laughed, too. "You're probably right," she said. "Try again."

Half an hour later, Nidia could say it with a straight face. "No worries."

"Yes!" Marisol said. "You did it. Here's your prize." She handed her the long reach flame lighter.

"And this is to set the fire?" Nidia asked, turning it over in her hand. She took a while to get the hang of pressing in the button with her thumb and pulling the trigger with her finger. After a few tries, a flame shot out of the tip.

"Nicely done," Marisol said. "When we do it for real, don't light too many papers. Maybe just one section of a newspaper. Or better yet, a stack of Puerto Cyclo's fucking tourist brochures."

"That'll be easy," Nidia said. "For a while now I've been taking them from the bar where Zara works."

Marisol grinned. Again, she felt the pull to tell Nidia that there was no friend, that she was the thief. But she hadn't gotten this far by being careless when her emotional guard was down.

She smiled at Nidia. "You're gonna be great at this," she said. "Now I gotta get back to the resort."

By 12:25 that day, Marisol had finally gotten the hang of the rented motorcycle. She'd practiced in sneakers, but now she was riding in her stiletto pumps. She felt like a cliché in the tight spaghetti strap top, the short shorts, and the high heels, but she was determined to get Davis Evanston's attention.

And so it was, that at 12:45, she revved the bike loudly and drove along the road past the picture window of the hotel's restaurant.

The CEO speaking at the podium looked up from his audience. From behind her shades, Marisol saw him watching her. She had choreographed it perfectly: a woman roaring slowly by on a motorcycle, her voluptuous ass barely contained on the bike's seat, and her long dark hair flowing behind her.

Marisol pulled up to the hotel entrance, parked, and walked into the restaurant. Above the podium, there was a huge motorcycle mounted on the wall where the heads of animals might be.

Evanston was taking questions. Marisol carefully ignored the CEO and got a table facing away from him, looking out the window at the unnaturally blue wave pool.

She ordered lunch, and when the pathetic salad arrived fifteen minutes later, Evanston himself was serving her.

"Wow," she said with a bright smile. "You must be short of staff to have the owner waiting tables."

"I was concerned about you," he said, setting down the salad. "You really should wear a helmet."

She shrugged. "I know. I'm bad," she said. "But I came here to feel free. Unencumbered by all the constraints of my regular life in the states. Care to join me for lunch Mr. Evanston?"

He slid into the chair opposite her. "Call me Davis," he said and extended his hand.

"Marisol," she said, and he clasped her fingers in more of a squeeze than a shake.

"You have great taste," he said. "You picked the best of our rental bikes."

She let out a tinkling laugh, the kind she saved for clients and marks. "I like to feel power between my legs."

She took a bite of the salad as the waiter came by and the CEO ordered his lunch.

As soon as the waiter left, a white guy around Evanston's age came by the table.

"Great talk, Davis," he said.

"Thanks," Davis said, then turned to Marisol. "Meet Phillip Gerard. He's my real estate genius. And a bit of a rogue. Phil, isn't there a warrant for your arrest in Costa Rica? Something about a young girl going missing?"

Marisol's stomach clenched, and she had to work to keep her composure. She maintained her smile, despite a wave of nausea, as Gerard kissed her hand.

"Davis is just jealous because I'm richer and more hand-some," Gerard said. "So he's stooping to the level of gossip. Not a good look, Davis."

"Oh come on, Phil," Davis said. "This woman looks old enough to drink in all fifty states. She's obviously not your type."

"You could have fooled me," Gerard said. "You look like an ingenue."

Marisol giggled and it sounded shrill to her own ears.

"If you ever decide to skip the middle man and go straight to the top, give me a call," he said. He was making a move, and still hadn't asked her name.

"I'll take your card," she said.

"Oh no, you won't," Davis said. "Run along, Phillip. I think there's a high school tour coming in soon."

"I'll be at tonight's lecture, as well," Gerard said, winking at her as he walked away.

She turned back to Davis Evanston. "With friends like that," Marisol said, trailing off the cliché.

"So . . ." he fumbled. "You know who I am. You even know who my unscrupulous friends are. Tell me a little about yourself."

Marisol didn't want him to google her online and find that she ran a health clinic for sex workers. Fortunately, there were many women named Marisol Rivera. One was sort of YouTube famous, and she dominated any google searches.

"I live in Florida," she lied. "I had a project that paid off recently, so I guess now I'm an investor." On reflection, she realized that the latter part of what she'd said was true.

A steak arrived for him and he began to slice it, the sharp knife cutting the meat into thin strips.

"I like how you handle that bike," he said.

"I like how you've handled this resort," she said. "Tell me about your operation."

He talked for maybe fifteen minutes. ". . . such an unprecedented investment opportunity . . . really could use more women investors . . ."

None of the content was important. But she listened with her full attention, waiting for the chance to jump in.

". . . the same architect who did our offices . . ."

"I'd love to see your office," she said. "Especially if it has some of the same visual themes." She waved vaguely toward the giant bike on the wall.

"We have this same artist's work throughout the property," he explained.

"Of course," Marisol said. "I was just hoping you could show me your office." She smiled widely. "As a start."

He brightened with her lightly flirtatious tone. "Of course," he said. "Would you like to stop by after lunch?"

"I've got nothing but time," she said.

* * *

At 1:42 Marisol sent a text to Nidia on the burner phone. **heat things up in 10 minutes. call in 15.**

The offices were on the top floor. The elevator that accessed them was down the hall from the restaurant, which closed at midnight. The front desk stayed open 24-hours, and she also noted the housekeeping and grounds office, where they probably had overnight staff.

There was a security desk in the lobby. She managed to look at the guard's camera feed. Front door. Lobby. Parking lot. Restaurant entrance. That was it.

On the penthouse floor, she was pleased to see that the air vents were ground level. Good. It would be much easier to get in. But when they got to his office, she was disappointed that the door opened with a card instead of a key. She could pick a regular lock, but she didn't know how to bypass a card system. She couldn't rig the door to stay open, because he'd be in and out too many times today. She'd have to crawl in through the vent.

The office was bright and chilly, with the stale flavor of overdone air conditioning. On the walls were more of the motorcycle art. This time tires with sparkling rims.

"I just love these," Marisol said, noting which of the pieces might cover a safe.

She looked at his wall clock, also a tire theme, and noted that it was 1:54.

At 1:57, Marisol was not surprised when they were interrupted. His office phone on the fake wooden desk rang. He had been standing uncomfortably close to her, droning on about how the artist really understood the inherent sensuousness of circles, when the call came in.

"Excuse me," he said, and picked up the phone.

Even from across the office, Marisol could hear the raised voice of the woman from the front desk.

"A fire," the woman said. "A guest says there's a fire in one of the cottages. I've called the fire department and I sent housekeeping with an extra extinguisher."

He had barely hung up the phone, when he began to sprint for the door.

"I'll be back," he stammered over his shoulder.

He didn't close the door behind him. Marisol shut it carefully.

She could feel her heart beat faster as she searched behind the wheel art until she found the safe. A MuscleMan. No extra security features to the lock. She felt the urge crack it. But not now. He would be back as soon as he realized the fire was a ruse. Fortunately, it had gotten him out of there. If it hadn't, Plan B was for Nidia to pull the fire alarm. Marisol would have taken advantage of the confusion.

She had scoped the architectural plans online. She knew the air conditioning vent connected to the hallway. She pulled out her screwdriver and replaced the air vent's real screws with fakes. From inside the vent, she'd only need to push and the grate would open for her. Hopefully the safe would do the same.

By the time Davis Evanston came back, she was sitting calmly, flipping through one of the hotel brochures.

"Is everything okay?" she asked.

"Just some papers in a trash can caught on fire," he said. "Some guest overreacted. Sorry to leave you waiting."

"I like a man who protects his investments," she said.

"Let me make it up to you," he said. "Dinner? On me?"

"Sure," she said. "But your dining room leaves something to be desired. How about in San Juan? I'll be there for a meeting this afternoon."

He agreed, and suggested a high-end restaurant. They set dinner for eight.

Marisol went back to her room and called Nidia on the burner phone.

"I was so scared when I set the papers on fire," Nidia said. "And even more scared when I called. I did it like you told me. Hysterical, but not over the top. Did they buy it?"

"You did perfectly," Marisol said. "Are you in San Juan yet?"

"About another half hour," Nidia said.

Marisol gave her the name of the high-end restaurant Davis Evanston had suggested. "Be there at eight."

"What do I order in a place like that?" Nidia asked.

"Whatever you want," Marisol said. "Bring some dinner home for Zara, too."

"It'll be a pleasure," Nidia said.

That evening, Serena and Lily stood out on the dark road between Las Palmas and San Juan, right at the spot where Marisol had dropped the GPS pin. Serena seemed jumpy with the darkness, the mosquitoes, and the chirping of frogs. But Lily seemed more relaxed than when she was in New York.

"This place reminds me of home," Lily said. "Same climate. Same foliage. Same style of houses. Same feeling at night."

"Not me," Serena said. "We were from Athens. It's warm, but not like this. And not always so muggy. My hair is nothing but frizz."

"Would you ever go back?" Lily asked.

Serena shook her head. "Greece is finally getting out of the dark ages in LGBT rights," she said. "But my family's too religious. I wouldn't have anybody there."

Lily nodded. "Plus that new boyfriend isn't trying to leave Manhattan."

Serena smiled. "Except maybe for one of the boroughs."

"I still feel torn," Lily said. "I miss my mother, the feel of home. Brooklyn used to be a little West Indies, but the gentrification now." She sucked her teeth. "We not there like we used to be. This place brings it all back."

The two women watched the little dot on the screen move down the road toward their location. They had an estimated half hour til it reached them, so they headed back to their own vehicle, hidden in some shrubbery nearby.

Cars only went by every few minutes, but the timing would be tight.

They needed to make sure to target the right vehicle, and they didn't want to get hit. It was difficult to hear cars coming in the darkness with the loud sounds of the insects and frogs.

The two of them waited on the rural road for the black car to come. Glancing from time to time at the GPS, the two women huddled by the roadside and plucked a few last feathers from several row of spikes.

Lily had reassembled the spike strip. When it was collapsed, it was a dense rectangle of metal, but when it was expanded, it was a lethal row of Xs that had spikes on parallel diagonals and connected to make a row of diamond shapes.

Finally, Lily pulled off the last of the feathers and collapsed the spike strip.

"He's due in about five minutes," Serena said. "You ready?"

Lily nodded, then opened the car door and walked up to the road.

They heard a vehicle coming from the opposite direction. It wasn't safe to step out while cars were coming from either side, because drivers often ignored the center line on these curving roads.

The GPS estimated that he'd be there in three minutes. A minivan went by in the other direction.

"Now?" Serena asked.

Lily listened. Was that a car? It was hard to peel the sound of the retreating van apart from any new traffic. The insects and frogs buzzed loudly, drowning other sounds. Yes! That was a car.

"I hear something coming," Lily said. "But too close to be him. He's still a full minute away."

"Damn," Serena said. "The cars must be pretty close together."

"We can't run the risk of harming someone who's not involved," Lily said.

"Yeah, but we can't afford to miss him," Serena said. "And you could get hit."

"I'm a fast runner," Lily said. "That'll have to be good enough."

"Okay," Serena said. "I'll go further down the road. I'll shriek like a bird if the cars are close together."

Serena slipped back into the darkness and around the curve of the hill.

Lily crouched by the side of the road, just behind a tree.

The sound of the car grew louder, and she took a deep breath.

From around the bend, Serena called like a bird. So not this car, but the next one.

Blinding headlights flashed toward Lily, and her body tensed for the leap.

A small coupe made its way around the corner. Five people inside. The windows were open and Lily heard laughter.

The moment it passed, she sprang from her spot at the edge of the asphalt. She ran halfway across the road, pulling the spike strip, which opened behind her.

Lily began to dash the rest of the way across the road, and headlights bore down on her. They were coming from the other direction. A taxi careened toward Lily, swinging wide toward the shoulder on its own side and just missing her. Fortunately, it also swerved out of the path of the spike strip.

Lily dove into the greenery on the far side of the road, just as Davis Evanston's car came around the curve.

She heard the explosion sound as the tires blew. The car teetered a bit on the busted tires, and as it did so, Lily darted back into the street and dragged the spike strip back toward their own car. She slid it behind her into the bushes like a huntress, returning with a huge tropical snake.

"Did he see you?" Serena asked.

"No," Lily said. "How about the folks in the taxi? Did they hear the blowout?"

"I doubt it," Serena said. "They didn't slow down or turn around."

"Good," Lily said. "I think we're done here."

"So what do we do now?" Serena asked.

"It's the Caribbean," Lily said. "We go to the bar and celebrate."

"But it's so late," Serena said. "And this is such a small town."

"No matter how small the town," Lily said. "There's always a bar open late."

Davis Evanston cursed when his tire blew out on the way to San Juan. Unfortunately, he got the flat along a portion of the road with notoriously bad cell phone service. He honked, attempting to get the attention of a blue compact, but the driver zoomed by without stopping. He tried flagging down cars, but with the twists in the road, he nearly got himself killed.

It was 8:45 by the time he had walked to a place where he got decent reception. He called for roadside assistance and then called the restaurant in San Juan. The host was able to find a woman dining alone, about the right age. She fit the description and answered to the name Marisol Rivera.

Davis launched into a long explanation about how he wasn't the type of man to leave a lady waiting. She really must forgive him. And Davis cursed this backwards island where consumer goods were of such low quality that even new tires were half bald and the roads were strewn with detritis sharp enough to cause multiple flat tires. When he had finally ranted himself out, the woman on the other side of the phone said, "No worries."

As Davis was waiting for a tow truck on the side of the road, Marisol was waiting for the right moment to creep past the front desk staff.

A large party of Midwestern tourists came in with a mountain of luggage, and she took that opportunity to slip into the hallway. She caught the elevator to the penthouse floor. Once she arrived, she unscrewed the air vent and crawled in, leaving the grate in place behind her with clips.

At first, the only sound was the slide of fabric against metal. But as she wriggled through the tiny space to the office, a sudden burst of laughter came throught the grate. She froze.

"Well don't let my dad hear you talk like that," a young female voice said. "He doesn't trust any man who won't ride a motorcycle."

Marisol felt the swell of panic in her chest. Who was in the office? She had been so careful to make sure Evanston didn't have a partner. She hadn't counted on a daughter. The young woman continued to flirt, but Marisol couldn't hear the response. She must be on the phone.

Then the air came on. Marisol began to panic, as she felt cold pressure against her feet, pushing up toward her ass in the vent. The back half of her body was freezing, but the front half was overly warm. She began to sweat.

At least the noise of the air covered the sound of Marisol's movement. She inched toward the office, until she could see through the slats. A young blonde woman sat with her feet up on the desk.

The girl blathered on. Marisol carefully tried to control her breathing, but the feeling of panic continued to rise.

Finally the girl interjected her own monologue: "Why is it so damn hot in here? Hold on—" She set down the phone and walked over to the vent.

Marisol knew intellectually that the girl's pupils would be adjusted to the office's bright light. Yet she had had the irrational fear that somehow the young blonde would be able to detect the glint of light on Marisol's eyes, her hair, her skin beading with sweat in the dark vent.

A pale hand waved in front of the grate. The hand began to open and close the slats for the air. The bright image of the girl in the office flashed on and off like a peep show.

Marisol's panic spiked. What if the daughter really tried to adjust the grate? With the fake screws Marisol had put in, would it fall off?

The girl left the grate open and walked to the desk: "Let me call you back from my cell. By the time maintenance comes to fix it I'll have melted in this heat. They say Puerto Rico is part of the United States, but I know the third world when I see it. It'll take five minutes to get down to my suite."

After she heard the door click shut, Marisol pressed hard on the grate and it fell onto the rug. She wriggled herself out, and screwed it in behind her with real screws.

Then she went to work on the safe with her stethoscope. Five minutes later, she had cracked it.

Inside, she found nearly $100,000 in cash, several types of bonds and what looked like more of the same stock options Nidia had. She took all of it, and crammed it into her bag.

Just as she was ready to walk out the door, she heard the elevator open out in the hallway. She grabbed the bag, and hid under the desk.

A maintenance man came in, a local. He walked to the grate and put his hand in front of it. Marisol could both feel and hear the cold air pouring in. She felt nearly weak with gratitude that she'd refastened the grate.

On his way out, the maintenance man called down on his

radio. "It's working fine," he said in Spanish. "Fucking Americans. I think they just call to see us jump."

When Marisol heard the *whirr* of the elevator heading back down, she peered carefully into the corridor.

Finding it empty, she refastened the hallway grate, and slid into the stairwell, walking gingerly down to her room. She stashed her take from the safe, then walked down the stairs to the ground floor and slipped out of the hotel.

When Marisol returned from her alleged dinner in San Juan, Davis Evanston was waiting in the lobby, apologetic, with flowers.

"I'm so sorry," he said. "I can't believe I left you waiting."

"Like I said, no worries," Marisol told him. "But I'm tired from the drive. I'll see you next time I'm in town."

He put a hand on her arm. "It's not that late," he said. "It's barely ten. Have a drink with me."

She smiled and removed his hand from her arm. "Some other time."

"It wasn't my fault," he said. His voice was half whining, half belligerent.

"Of course not," she said. "I don't blame you. I'm just tired."

"Come on," he pressed. "Just one drink."

Marisol looked around the quiet lobby. No one was in sight. The thick doors to the bar were closed. The lights were on, but she couldn't see anyone through the window. Was it empty? Was there a bartender? Was the bar even open? Or would Evanston make up the drinks himself?

"Oh . . ." she began coyly. "I don't know . . ."

A grin began to creep up one side of his face.

"You won't regret it," he said.

She smiled and rolled her eyes, a sort of coquettish self-mockery. A giggling sort of *I know I'll regret it in the morning, but . . .*

She would play along to get his defenses down. Head toward the bar and look for a chance to exit. If nothing else, she could reach for the heavy restaurant door and swing it into his face.

But then the elevator dinged, and a trio of middle aged white women tourists stepped out. She recognized them from the lunch talk.

"Oh Mr. Evanston," they cooed.

Marisol shrugged. "I really should get to bed," she said. "I'm gonna take that raincheck."

And then she walked away from him, and slipped into the elevator. One minute he had his hand on her back. The next minute, his hand hovered alone in space.

She smiled and waved at him from the elevator as she stabbed the door close button. He stood helplessly in the knot of tourists, his rage shimmering beneath the surface of his jovial hotel owner's smile.

Up on her floor, she practically ran to her room and locked the door. She put the security latch on, grateful that an owner with a key card couldn't gain access.

Marisol dug in the bottom of her suitcase for the bag of cash and bonds. Not that it would have gone anywhere, but she had to check. She lay down on the bed, curling her body around the bag, as if she needed it for comfort.

I really am too old for this, Marisol thought. Between the safecracking and getting caught in the grate, and then the anxiety of her encounter with Evanston, her adrenaline had spiked several times and was now crashing. One moment she was breathing a sigh of relief, and the next she was out cold asleep with all the lights on.

In the dream, it was Davis Evanston who crept into the hotel room. The security latch did nothing to keep him out.

He reached for the bag of cash and bonds, and the two of them tussled on the bed. Then the dream morphed into a version of a recurring nightmare she'd had for many years. Her uncle's cramped Lower East Side apartment. A teenage Marisol in one twin bed, and her sister in another twin across the room. Marisol not asleep anymore. Never asleep after she heard her uncle come home. The beige wallpaper and suffocating brown marble carpet. Dank. Despite her scrubbing with the ninety-nine cent store's all-purpose cleaner, she could never remove the smell of mildew and bad plumbing.

Eventually at night, her exhaustion would eclipse her will to stay awake. Then the terror at the sound of the front door opening. She felt an overwhelming desperation to run, to hide under the bed, to climb out onto the fire escape before he came into the room. But then he'd find Cristina and she was too little. Her sister couldn't handle it. In the dream, there was always the smell and the feeling of her body crushed under a familiar, hated heaviness. She had never screamed in all the years she'd lived in that apartment, but somehow now, she was able to find her voice.

She screamed herself awake, only to find the heaviness was real. Pressure on her chest. Someone was on top of her. Through her panic, she managed to recognize her surroundings as the bright hotel room. Was it Evanston? How had he gotten in?

She reached to claw at him and felt only the sharp edges of cash and bond bricks through the cloth of a sack.

Marisol gasped and shook the bag of loot off her chest.

She sat up, her heart banging hard against her ribs.

Scrambling for her phone, she called her boyfriend Raul in New York. She shuddered at the memories of the dream as his phone rang and rang. It was four AM, and he was undoubtedly asleep, his ringer probably off. She called Eva, her colleague and sometimes therapist. No luck there, either.

So Marisol sat up, watching television, numb with fear and vigilant. Nobody tried to break in, but Marisol kept all the lights on and didn't even try to sleep.

Later that morning, Marisol checked out. She didn't see Evanston as she wheeled her luggage out of his hotel, full of his cash and bonds.

When she got back to her cousin's house, Zara said that Nidia was at work.

Marisol meant to wait up for her, but she fell asleep on the couch.

She woke up that afternoon to hear Nidia walking in the door.

"*Qué pasó?*" her cousin asked.

Marisol sat up and stretched. "We need to get to a bank," she said.

Nidia grinned, and the two of them headed to the nearest one. They set up an account, got a cell plan for Nidia, and tossed the burner phones.

It would raise red flags if they deposited the money all at once. So Marisol transferred enough money from her personal account to cover the initial payment to get the house out of foreclosure. She would transfer enough each month to cover the mortgage payments. And she'd take the cash to New York to launder it.

Back at the house, Nidia and Zara cried. They'd get to keep their home, the house their grandparents had so painstakingly saved to purchase. And if Marisol helped Julio get a job in New York, they'd be okay.

Later, Nidia walked Marisol to the rented green coupe. "Is there a safe somewhere in San Juan with seventy-five billion in it? Maybe your friend could crack that next? Solve the rest of the problems in Puerto Rico?"

Marisol sighed. "*Ay, nena.* That money isn't in Puerto Rico. It's all in the States. I see it walk by every day in New York."

"On Wall Street?"

"All over Manhattan."

"Goddamn colonization," Nidia said. "That's our money. We fucking worked for that money. For over a hundred years."

"They want us to pay back what they stole from us," Marisol said. "Keep us working to put money in their pocket for another hundred years."

"I just knew we were gonna lose the house," Nidia said, shaking her head. "Tell your friend I don't know how to thank her."

Marisol put her arm around Nidia. "I'll make sure she gets the message."

"My mom always said she regretted not putting her foot down about you girls staying in Puerto Rico," Nidia said.

"What do you mean?" Marisol asked.

"When our uncle came for the funeral and sort of claimed the two of you," Nidia said. "He and his wife apparently couldn't have children. He said they were the obvious ones to take you. My mom objected, but he boasted about what a good life you would have in the US. That maybe if we lived in the capital—in San Juan—he wouldn't insist, because your English was so good. You spoke without an accent. In San Juan you could find opportunities. But my mother would be ruining your prospects if she kept you in a small *jibaro* town like Las Palmas when he could offer you Manhattan."

Marisol was too stunned to speak. She might have stayed in Puerto Rico? With Nidia's mom? Everything might have been different?

"And he was right, no?" Nidia said. "You've made a big success of yourself. You run a clinic. Your sister is a doctor. We read about your clinic's big event. You're hanging out with movie stars like Delia Borbón."

Marisol had faltered then. Unable to find words for the

loss that she hadn't even imagined before. A different path. A different life. Even though her aunt hadn't been able to rescue her, it choked her up to know that she had tried.

Marisol bit back the tears and waved away Nidia's words. "It's really not that glamorous," she said. "You'll have to come visit one of these days and see."

Before Marisol left Puerto Rico, she made one last stop.

In spite of the fact that the cemetery's business had gone bankrupt, the actual graveyard hadn't changed much. The building was still whitewashed wood to match the white marble statue of La Virgen María, arms open in welcome.

As Marisol pulled up to the parking lot, she recalled the funeral, imagined her stoic little eleven-year-old self, staying strong for her sister. Her feet knew the way back to the graveyard.

She followed the narrow stone path, past the banyan, a huge, green-leafed tree with a thick trunk and roots that cascaded down from the branches. Rust peeked through the cracking black paint on the cemetery's wrought iron fence. Marisol opened the gate and let her feet guide her to the northeast edge. She had to pick her way carefully, afraid of stepping on other graves in the overgrowth. The small cemetery was empty of people, except for marble and stone figures of angels and Jesus and Mary, among the crosses and other saints on the headstones and tombs.

Finally, she arrived at her family gravesite. Grass, fallen leaves, moss, and dirt covered many of the headstones; some were so old or dirty, she couldn't read the names, the dates, the *amada esposa*, *querida madre*.

Yet two headstones she knew by heart. "I miss you, Mami," she said to the stone. "I love you. You, too, Abuelita."

She ran her fingers along the indented letters in her mother's name, dislodging some of the dirt. "You know, things got really bad after you guys died." She let out a sudden whoop and chuckle. Always that inappropriate laughter. "It was a lousy thing to do, you know, die? Leave us with your crazy-ass brother." She still couldn't bring herself to say his name. "Well, he has a grave of his own, now," she said.

"Then things got a little better," she said. "A little better for me. A lot better for Cristina."

Marisol had talked to her mother before, believed her mother was watching over her. But now, sitting at the graveside, she wanted to tell it all again. And she found herself whispering this next part, somehow feeling a need to be discreet in the empty graveyard, with faces of Jesus and angels and Marías and Santos watching her: "I started doing sex work, *tú sabes*? I had to do something to support Cristina," she said, as if to justify herself in the eyes of the icons. "You'd be proud of her. She graduated college, and now she's studying to be a doctor in Cuba. I miss her a lot," Marisol said. "I miss all of you."

She picked up a leaf and twirled it in her fingers. "You might be proud of me, too. I started a clinic. Named it after you, Mami. The María de le Vega clinic. We're doing big things in the old neighborhood. Cristina's gonna work for us when she gets back. And remember that hotel in Manhattan, La Fleur? I had a benefit there. I was the one in charge, Mami." Marisol became even more animated when she recalled the presence of the movie star. "Even Delia Borbón came to my fundraiser. She was wearing this wild—"

And then she stopped suddenly. Mami wouldn't even know who Delia Borbón was. Her mother was dead before the Diva became famous. Mami's death had ruined even this. Her mother had missed everything.

Utterly devastated by this seemingly insignificant piece of chronology, Marisol's entire body was suddenly siezed with grief. It pressed the breath out of her, sucked the strength from the muscles in her thighs and core. She collapsed onto the ground and sobbed.

At first only wails, then finally she managed to exhale words. "How could you leave me?" she cried in Spanish, the staccato sobs in counterpoint to the leaden weight of the grief in her limbs. Her breath came in ragged spasms, her face pressed against red dirt, leaves tangling in her hair.

With a surge of rage, she beat on the ground with a fist. "Noooo!" she shrieked into the earth. "Don't leave me with him! How could you?" Somehow in her mind, it was as if her uncle had dragged them away, her and Cristina, as if her mother and grandmother had permitted it by dying. Had cosigned it, sentenced them to a Lower East Side bedroom cell for two girls.

Marisol screamed into dirt, into earth, into the past. Her body thrashed among the fallen leaves. Lizards scurried past her feet, and birds cawed overhead. Finally, her face against the warm red clay dirt, she cried herself to sleep.

The sun was almost setting when she awoke an hour later. Completely disoriented, her neck and shoulder stiff, her body damp on the side that had been on the ground. She sat up, dazed, breathing the moist air; she expected to be in her grandmother's house, under a mosquito net with Cristina, but no. Memory returned. The graveyard. Just a visit. She was grown now.

A mosquito buzzed by her ear. Must have been what woke her. She scratched a spot on her earlobe that itched and burned. She sat up and blinked at the headstones in the fading light.

Suddenly, Marisol laughed bitterly. "It was really shitty of both of you to go and die, you know?" She stood up and pulled a few leaves out of her hair. "But I just might forgive you."

She kissed her finger and placed it on her mother's headstone, then picked her way back out through the bankrupt cemetery.

* * *

After Marisol had returned to New York, she sent an attorney to sue for an injunction against Puerto Cyclo from digging up the graves, and furthermore, challenged the legality of paying with stock options instead of cash, particularly since the contract promised that it would be a cash equivalent, and it hadn't been. The court case was going to take several years, but until it was decided, the graves would be safe.

Chapter 7

Zavier invited Dulce to come with him to the capital. She was excited to go, as she hadn't been there since she was a kid. But on the way, they couldn't agree about temperature controls: she liked A/C and he liked fresh air, so they rode down the highway with the windows open and the air conditioning running full blast. With the blowing air, it was hard to talk, so he played the radio. Mostly merengue, salsa, and the occasional Latin rap.

When they finally parked the car, she asked out of nowhere: "Are you married?"

He busted out laughing. "Excuse me?"

"I had to ask," she said. "I mean it's our second date, and I didn't want to find myself in some kind of don't ask don't tell situation."

"Not married," he said. "Not cohabitating with anyone. No girlfriend. Haven't been on a date in a while. Big crush on Delia Borbón. I do have a picture of her on the inside of my closet door. The one from that action movie she did back in the day where she played the journalist. That's about all I got."

Dulce laughed. Everybody knew that iconic pose.

The two of them stepped out of the car.

"How about you?" he asked. "No boyfriend?"

"I was seeing someone in Miami," she said. "But that's over. It's part of why I left."

She didn't say, *the other part was that he was trying to kill me.*

"Okay," he said. "Looks like we're just two single people out here on a date."

She hooked her hand through his arm. "Two single people."

They went sightseeing around the capital like tourists. They held hands and ate ice cream. A woman came by selling flowers and he gave Dulce a bright bouquet. He was handsome, and so sweet. It was obvious that he really liked her. But it felt like something was missing. Not exactly sex. When he stood pressed close to her in a crowd, she could tell that he was turned on.

"When are you coming back to New York?" he asked. "Today can't be our last time seeing each other."

What could she tell him? New York still wasn't safe? Her pimp was dead, but his brother might still be looking for her?

"I don't really know," she said. "When are you coming back to Santo Domingo?"

"If you're not coming back to New York," he said. "I'll find a reason."

On the one hand, she was excited to see him again. But at some point he'd ask her more about her past, and what would she tell him? In Miami she'd been a mistress? In New York she'd had a pimp?

"So tell me about yourself," she said. "You're what? Twenty-two, but already a serious journalist?"

"I was in college, and I wrote a piece that got in the NYT 'Lives' column. Then they sort of recruited me. You know, 'we got all these old white guys. Let's have this young brown guy.' So they gave me an internship. Unpaid, of course. So I did that, plus school full time, and worked graveyard at a printing company."

"When did you sleep?"

"On the train," he said. "Besides, sleep is overrated."

"No," Dulce said. "Sleep is wonderful. It's good for you, too."

"I'd like to sleep with you," he said.

Dulce raised her eyebrows.

Zavier shook his head. "That came out wrong," he said. "I don't mean sex. I mean sleep. There's something about you that makes me feel . . . I don't know. Peaceful? Connected?"

"You trying to say I'm putting you to sleep?" Dulce asked.

"Not at all," Zavier said. "Being with you makes me feel calm inside. And I guess it shows me that maybe I need more sleep than I thought. Like how I just knocked out in the water. I coulda drowned, but I don't know. I just trusted you. My body was like . . . ahhh . . . I'm safe . . ."

"You make me sound like somebody's grandma," Dulce said. "Putting them down for a nap or something."

"No, Dulce," he said, leaning toward her. "You're not like anybody's grandma. More like somebody to come home to."

He was holding her hand now, leaning toward her. His eyes were locked on hers, like he was trying to see into her.

Dulce felt suddenly sick to her stomach. He didn't know her. Did he think she was some sweet little hick from the boonies in the Dominican Republic? This girlfriend thing couldn't work. Maybe it was safe to go back to New York. But even then, she might run into one of the many men she'd fucked. For money. Or even one of the boys she'd fucked in high school. Just because they asked and she was that desperate for somebody to notice her. She couldn't play house with him in Santo Domingo, when they had no real future. She was stuck here at her aunt's house. Maybe they could have some fun, but this "come home to" shit was not even on the table.

She couldn't let him in, because one day it'd come crashing down. The light he had for her in those eyes would go out. And that would fucking crush her.

She gave him a sudden smile. "I need a drink," she said. She ordered one, downed it, and ordered another.

He suggested that they go to a discoteca and dance. She was just about to say yes when her phone rang. Dulce glanced at it quickly and then paused.

It was the businessman from Miami. She had put his name in her phone. Phillip Gerard.

"Excuse me," she said to Zavier. "I should take this."

She stood on the sidewalk in the front of the restaurant. There was a band playing merengue half a block down. She put her finger in her ear and asked the businessman to speak up.

"I'm here in Santo Domingo," he said. "Did you get my text?"

Dulce looked at her phone. He had texted a picture of his suite. Probably a five-star hotel. Dulce felt a mixture of emotions. She didn't know shit about how to be a girlfriend. But she definitely knew how to come when a powerful man called.

"Sounds good," she said. "But I'm with my cousin."

"I'll come get you," he said. "Tell him I'm your uncle on the Cuban side."

She couldn't have said whether it was the five-star hotel, or the entitled way he directed her, or the fact that he was just a wealthy man. But the next thing she knew, she was telling Zavier that her Cuban uncle had called. And her aunt wasn't doing so well. She needed some urgent medical treatments, and her uncle was going to come pick her up.

Zavier's eyes were concerned. He took her hand. "I'm so sorry," he said.

"She'll be okay," Dulce said. "But I ougtta be there."

"You'll miss the interview with Ibeyi later tonight?" he asked.

"Damn," she said, recalling the Cuban singing duo that would have been her first celebrity interview.

"Family comes first," he said.

"Right," Dulce said. "Family."

And then, without even realizing it was coming, Dulce started to cry.

Zavier came around the table and put an arm around her. Which only made her cry harder.

The more he was kind and concerned, the worse she felt. Like he was showing her every bit of his sweetness she could never have.

And then Dulce was waving goodbye to Zavier, as she walked toward the businessman's Mercedes.

And Zavier just waved back, a frown line of concern between his eyes.

Before they had even taken off in the car, the businessman's hand was on her thigh.

She was wiping her eyes.

"Nice touch with the tears," he said. "Way to sell it."

She resisted the urge to look back at Zavier.

"Let him go," she told herself. "That was never really going to happen."

She took a deep breath and inhaled the new car smell. New luxury car. She looked at the leather and wood upholstery, she touched the luscious fabric of his suit. She felt the purr of the engine beneath and all around her. She had made the right choice. The only real choice for a girl like her.

Chapter 8

Dulce always remembered how she was fourteen and wearing a Minnie Mouse t-shirt when she met Jerry. She and her friend Valeria were smoking some cheap weed in the park when he came up to them. He was a tall hulk of a man. She found his size a little intimidating, but also powerful. Sort of like those superheroes who are so much bigger than the women they rescue. But whereas those men were broad shouldered and narrow-hipped, Jerry was thick all over, and wouldn't be caught dead in a skintight outfit or a cape. He had on a bright, oversized jeans outfit when he approached the two of them. It was just before noon, and she was cutting class.

"How are you fine young ladies doing today?" he asked.

Valeria just shrugged. She was used to getting that kind of attention. She had straight, medium brown hair and light green eyes.

"Fine," Dulce said. She had the kinky hair and the brown skin. The crooked teeth and the dark eyes. She was getting a big ass, but that didn't seem to translate into a boyfriend. Rather men yelling at her in the street and boys who barely had three words for her before they made it clear that they wanted to fuck her.

Maybe Jerry had been looking at Valeria at first, but then he smiled at Dulce. There was an intensity to his focus that she had never felt before.

"Too cool for school, huh?" he asked.

"Too bored," Dulce said.

"Come on Dulce, let's go," Valeria urged.

"Of course your name's Dulce," Jerry said. "You're the sweetest thing in the whole neighborhood."

Dulce smiled and rolled her eyes.

"Can I buy you some lunch?" Jerry asked. "The McDonald's isn't far. And my car is right here."

"What? You gonna offer us candy?" Valeria said. "We're not getting in your car, *viejo.*"

"Fine," he said. "Don't get in my car. Meet me there."

"We're not hungry," Valeria said.

Which was a lie. Dulce was particularly hungry, since they'd missed the school breakfast, and the only reason they were going back to campus was to get the free lunch.

"Meet me there for lunch tomorrow," Jerry said. "At noon. Don't leave me sitting there all lonely, Dulce."

Dulce giggled as Valeria took her hand and led her away.

"You're not thinking of meeting him, are you?" Valeria asked, once they were out of earshot.

"Don't act like you're not sick of cafeteria food, too," Dulce said. "He's offering us a free meal."

Valeria shook her head. "With a guy like that, nothing is free."

Years later, Dulce would look back and realize that the direction of her life had pivoted on the fact that she had English before lunch that year. She loved her English class. Mr. Quiñones was the one teacher who made learning fun. She did her homework and raised her hand in his class. He said she was a really good writer. English had always been her best subject. Especially that year, because they were doing expository essays. She could write down things about her life. Or things that she thought. He would ask questions to help draw out her opinions. And it didn't hurt that Mr. Q was young and handsome.

If Mr. Quiñones's class had been after lunch, then Dulce never would have cut school and gone to meet Jerry. But she had English during third period, and there was nothing to look forward to at school after lunch.

When Dulce arrived at the McDonald's, Jerry had a red rose for her. The bottom was in a small plastic container with a rubber lid that held in the water around the rose's stem.

"I don't really like McDonald's all that much," Dulce lied.

"Where would you like me to take you?" Jerry asked.

Dulce named an Italian chain restaurant in the neighborhood. It was a sort of test. Her sister had said that if a guy took you to a nice restaurant, it meant he was more serious.

"Sure," Jerry said. "You're Dominican, right? I can tell from your accent."

"Yeah," she said. "But my father's Cuban and I was born in Puerto Rico."

"So technically, you're Puerto Rican, just like me," he said. "And a citizen?"

"Yeah," Dulce said. "But none of the rest of my family is."

She told him about her brother getting deported for selling drugs. Her mother being disabled. Her sister with a baby and no job.

If she met him now—at twenty—she would probably notice that he wasn't listening. That his responses were platitudes: "yeah, things are tough all over." Or "right? One fucking thing after another." But at the time, the fact that he was just quiet and let her talk—that the adult man yielded the floor so the young girl could speak actual words—seemed like listening. It was more listening than she'd had from any adult in recent years. Except Mr. Q.

Jerry bought her lunch and even got a pizza to go.

"Take this to your family," he said.

It was the pizza that did it. Jerry wasn't just another one of these boys trying to fuck her. He was a man who was thinking about her whole family. He had heard her. He understood.

The next day at school, Valeria asked, "Did you meet that old guy? Is his name Jerry? I asked around and I heard he might be a pimp."

"He took me to a real restaurant," Dulce said.

"Did you hear what I said?" Valeria demanded. "Pimp?"

"You said he *might* be a pimp," Dulce said.

"Are you saying it's a chance you're willing to take?" Valeria asked.

"You're so lucky," Dulce said. "Your parents are still together. They both work."

"They got no papers," Valeria said. "They don't hardly make shit for money."

"Better than my sister's food stamps," Dulce said. "Now that my brother got deported, we're living off that and a little bit of cash that he left."

Her brother had gotten arrested for selling drugs. ICE sent him back to the Dominican Republic.

"If my sister doesn't find a job this month, we might be on the street," Dulce said.

She had hoped that this crisis would churn her mother into motion. But the depression continued to enshroud her, thick and humid as fog.

"If I have a boyfriend with money," Dulce reasoned. "Then we'll be okay."

"Boyfriend?" Valeria asked, bewildered. "You don't really think that old man is trying to be your boyfriend."

"I think he took me out," Dulce said. "I think he wants to see me again. He talked about being my boyfriend."

Valeria paused and looked at Dulce, as if taking the measure of her for the first time. "All these years we been knowing each other, you been complaining about how your mom and your sister get all caught up in these men and it's like they're brain dead. And I been telling you not to let these stupid boys fuck you, but you're like 'It's nothing. I'm just having fun.' But it don't look like no fun when you're getting called a slut at school, 'cause these boys got no respect."

"No," Dulce said. "But Jerry isn't a stupid boy like them."

"That's right," Valeria said. "And he can see a value in you that you don't even see in yourself. When your so-called boyfriend asks you to fuck some other guy, and there's some kind of money involved, I want you to remember this moment in time. The moment when you became just like your mother and sister and didn't even realize it."

"You don't know," Dulce said.

But Valeria had started to walk away.

"You're just jealous," Dulce said. "Because for once a guy wanted me more than you. A guy with money. A grown man."

Valeria continued to shake her head, but Dulce wasn't sure whether her friend had heard or not.

The first time Dulce and Jerry had sex, he had told her that he loved her. In retrospect, she knew something had always been off about it. If she had just seen the video of his face speaking the declaration, if there had been no sound, she would never have imagined those words. Maybe "Is this seat taken?" or "Please pass the salt." His eyes held no hint of even a smile.

The next day, Dulce sat in geometry class, daydreaming. They were learning that three points can determine a plane, and a plane is infinite.

Pizza. Boyfriend. I love you.

From those three points, Dulce was able to extrapolate an infinite love. An impending rescue.

Her sister Yunisa didn't find a job in time. They illegally subletted the apartment to some artists. Yunisa and Dario moved in with her baby daddy for a while. Their mom went to sleep on a cousin's couch in New Jersey.

The day before they had to be out, Yunisa was packing. "Are you coming with me or Mami?" she asked Dulce.

The baby was screaming, and Yunisa was trying to jiggle him on her hip as she dumped crumbs and wilted leaves out of the bottom of the boxes they'd gotten from behind the bodega.

"I can stay with a friend," Dulce said.

"Valeria?" her sister asked.

Dulce shook her head. "Someone else," she said as she packed her clothes into one of the boxes.

Under any other circumstances, Yunisa would have scrutinized the answer more. Even though the two of them weren't close, it was an older sister's duty to look out for her younger sister.

But the baby was screaming, and the taxi was coming, and the artists were late to pick up the key.

So her sister just nodded and kept packing.

A month later, Yunisa would have a job. Three months later, they would move back into the apartment. But that would come too late.

While Dulce was living with Jerry, while she was totally dependent on him, he asked her to fuck another guy. His brother.

They lived with his brother, and Jerry sold it like he needed her help. He was in between jobs and rent was due and his brother thought Dulce was so beautiful. And his brother was so jealous that Jerry had a girlfriend like her. Would she? Could she do him this favor? Jerry's brother would pay the rent this month and it would be just this once.

In that moment, she thought of Valeria. But she clung to the idea that her friend didn't understand. Dulce had the power. She could help him. He loved her.

And it turned out that Valeria was wrong. Everything didn't change the moment that Jerry asked her to fuck someone else. It didn't even change when Dulce said yes.

It all changed when Dulce came out of his brother's bedroom and Jerry explained that it had all been a test. That she had failed. That this proved she didn't love him. That she was just an ungrateful slut who didn't deserve to be treated well. That he was a grown man and didn't need a little girl to do him any favors. That he was the one doing her a favor. Except he yelled it at her. And slapped her.

So by the time he moved her into his other apartment in the Bronx, where his other girls lived, it didn't matter anymore that he had stopped saying he loved her. And that he didn't often have sex with her, but had a much more steady stream of "friends" having sex with her. It didn't matter because the facts had already been established. He was doing her a favor and he didn't love her anymore because she was a disloyal slut, and it was all her fault.

About a month later, her sister had banged on the door of the apartment in the Bronx.

"Where the fuck have you been?" she asked. "I thought you were with Valeria this whole time. I tried to call but their phone was cut off. I finally had to go by the school. Which you apparently aren't attending."

"Valeria and I haven't been talking lately," Dulce said quietly.

"Well I don't know who the fuck these friends are," Yunisa said. "But pack your shit. We're going back to Washington Heights."

Jerry had walked out into the living room as her sister was speaking.

"Bitch," he bellowed. "I don't know who the fuck you are, but you need to get the hell out of my apartment. Dulce isn't going any fucking where, you got that?" He slung a heavy, possessive arm around Dulce. "Besides, she likes it here. Isn't that right, baby?"

Dulce nodded best she could with the crook of his arm around her neck.

"Don't fuck with what's mine and don't piss me off," Jerry said. "And then we won't have any problems." With every word, he tightened his grip on Dulce's neck.

Stunned, Yunisa backed up to the front door and fled.

A week later, when Dulce went to the corner bodega, her sister pulled her into the narrow aisle between the canned foods and the sodas.

"Come on," Yunisa said. "I can take you home."

Dulce blinked. She couldn't meet Yunisa's eye. She tried to imagine her life back in Washington Heights. How could she return to school? Valeria might have told everyone. She would have no friends. She would be worse than a slut now. A ho. And if that didn't kill her, Jerry promised he would kill her if she ever left.

"Did he threaten you?" Yunisa asked, as if reading her mind. "We'll protect you."

Dulce could't picture it. Her sister, all five-foot-five of her, taking on Jerry, who weighed more than three hundred, easily, and was over six feet? Who did her sister have for backup? Their depressed mother who barely got out of bed? Her baby boy?

"I'm fine," Dulce said, eyes on the stacked up Goya cans of guanabana juice.

"Luqui, please," her sister looked upset, scared. But Dulce just shook her head.

Reluctantly, her sister left.

A week later, two police officers appeared at the door of the apartment. Jerry sent the girls into the back room and invited the officers into the kitchen. Half an hour later, Jerry and the two men were laughing, and Jerry went to get something from the safe. Then, he invited the two officers to meet the girls. Did they want to get to know any of them better?

They picked two of the girls to take into the bedroom. One picked the girl from the Philippines. The other one picked the girl from Haiti.

Jerry was jovial until the cops left, but then he turned to a rage Dulce had never seen. Her sister had called. It was Dulce's fault that he had the cops in his house. It was Dulce that had cost him the hundreds to pay them off. He would take it out of her hide, he said, as in, beat her ass. Four days later, he moved with all the girls to a different apartment.

Chapter 9

Dulce sat in the five star hotel and reminded herself to think of Phillip Gerard by his name and not as "the businessman." She called him Phillip, because he told her to. But he was definitely old enough to be her father. Internally, she thought of him more as Mr. Gerard.

The hotel where he had brought her was even more amazing than in the photo. He took her to the shops and bought her a new outfit, tall black sandals, a floral bikini, a jacket, and a form fitting lime green dress.

The quaint touristy shopping area reminded her a little of her first date with Zavier. She felt a pang in her chest.

"I like the baby blue color on you," Gerard was saying, bringing her back to the present.

Dulce smiled. "Then I'll take the baby blue dress."

She consoled herself with the luxury of shopping. Nice clothes that someone else was paying for.

Gerard made suggestions for the rest of the wardrobe, but not the lingerie.

"Whatever you like," he said.

He had the dresses altered to fit her curves perfectly, and arranged for it all to be sent up to the room. While they waited, he had her soak in the deep Jacuzzi tub. Then he brought up a masseuse for her. She fell asleep on the table.

She woke up when she heard a knock at the door. It was the dress.

"I can't wait to see this on you," he said.

She put it on and modeled it for him.

"Delectable," he said, and put on his suit for dinner.

In the restaurant, he ordered for both of them. Lobster for her and a vegan pasta for him.

Dulce had never had lobster before. The buttery meat melted in her mouth. By the time they got to dessert, she was nearly dizzy from the richness of the food, and the buzz of the sugar and wine.

He took his time with dinner, but she could tell that something changed in the elevator. There was an energy that some men got. A sort of smug confidence that they had paid. Cheap clients in New York apparently got the same kind of excitement as a guy like this who had spent over two thousand dollars, between the food, the wine, the shoes, and the clothes.

From the moment he opened the door, he accelerated.

She was startled when he tore off her clothes. A five-hundred-dollar designer dress, just ripped into two.

It didn't frighten her as much as it distracted her. She found herself wondering: had it ripped at the seam? Could she repair it? But she rallied. She needed to be making all the right sounds of excitement.

"Yes!" she said. "Just take me. Don't make me wait any longer!"

She had put in some lubricant in the restaurant, so she would seem wet for him.

The sex was fast. He only took a moment to survey the lingerie, then ripped that off, too. He didn't use a condom, but she was used to that. She had gotten the birth control shot in Miami, so it wasn't a big deal. He was quick, so she barely had time to fake an orgasm with him.

"That was amazing," she said, with a breathless voice. "You said you were gonna spoil me rotten, but you never said you would spoil me like that in bed."

He grinned. "Get used to it," he said. "I'm gonna be here all week."

The next seven days were more of the same. He bought her clothes, took her out to fancy meals, drove her around in the Mercedes, and they had sex in the hotel room. She learned to pick clothes that zipped and had easy access, so he could continue to play out the rip-off-the-clothes fantasy, but she could still build her wardrobe. He tossed out the first dress, but she retrieved it from the garbage to repair.

There was a small bookstore, and he bought her a copy of Delia Borbón's celebrity biography *From Red Light to Red Carpet*. She asked for the new book by Nashonna the rapper, but they didn't have it.

She had her hair and her nails done. She arranged her hair a little different every day. Changed up her makeup from nude to smoky to bold. Men liked variety, she had learned. In a short-term situation like this, she could change it up and keep his interest.

She got texts from Zavier, asking if she was all right.

She kept her responses vague: **Everything ok. Family drama. You know how it is.**

Mostly, she hung out in the hotel and read or caught up on her soap opera, *A Woman's Dark Past*.

The treacherous blonde daughter, Izabel, has run off with the soccer star. And worst of all, he isn't even from the Brazilian team.

Guilherme is devastated. "If only I had made her see,"

he says to Xoana. "I will be good enough for her one day. But I guess she couldn't wait."

"Don't say that, Guilherme," Xoana says. "You're good enough for any woman. Your experiments are brilliant. She's the one who failed *you*. She failed to believe in you. She took your love for granted."

The two boys run into the room. "Xoana! Xoana! Mama says it's dinner time. You have to join us."

Guilherme stands to go. "I shouldn't be burdening you with my problems," he says. "You have your hands full, with studying and these two."

"It's not a burden, Guilherme," she says. "That's what friends are for. If you want to talk, anytime, just reach out for me."

"You're so kind," he says. "So . . . so kind and generous."

He walks out, blinking, as if seeing her for the first time.

Dulce heard the beep of the keycard in the Santo Domingo hotel. Quickly, she switched off the TV and arranged herself on the bed as if she'd been waiting all day. Then the room door opened, and Phillip walked in. It was showtime.

During the day, Gerard had meetings. She wasn't sure what he did, some kind of real estate development thing. In the evenings, he would sometimes go on and on about work politics: ". . . some whistleblower asshole complaining about. . . ." She put an expression of rapt attention on her face and tuned him out. She'd be thinking about what she might want on the restaurant menu, and how to get him to order it for her. She learned that he liked ingénue: "I've never had caviar before . . ."

She took a selfie in front of the Mercedes, in a designer outfit, with the ocean in the background.

"Got away to the capital for a few days with friends," she posted on Instagram, and hashtagged it #IslandLife.

Zavier didn't have her Instagram, so she wasn't worried that he'd see it. She got another text from him, saying he hoped they'd find a way to connect again soon. Maybe see each other in New York? Maybe when he was back in the Caribbean?

Sounds cool she texted back. As noncommittal as she could be.

At the end of the week, Gerard was leaving for Puerto Rico. "Come with me," he suggested. "I go from there back to the states in a few days, but I'll buy you a round trip ticket."

Dulce shrugged. Why not? She didn't have anything at her aunt's house that she needed.

"Convince me," she said, pulling him by his tie towards the bed. That was the key, she'd learned. Act like she wanted it. Like he was satisfying her.

In reality, Dulce had never had an orgasm. The closest she had come was with the boyfriend in Miami. He went down on her a couple of times. She got excited as he kissed his way from her breasts to between her legs. Was he really going to . . . ? But when he actually got down there, he was so fast and rough. She faked an orgasm just so he would stop.

"You are insatiable," Gerard said, afterwards.

"What does that mean?" she asked.

"Impossible to satisfy," he said.

"Maybe I could be satisfied in Puerto Rico," she said, grinning.

They landed at Luis Muñoz Marin airport in San Juan the next morning.

As they took a taxi from the airport, Dulce found Puerto Rico completely disorienting. It was like a mix of the Dominican Republic and the US. The landscape was Caribbean, but the infrastructure was American. American brands and corporations everywhere. Big highways that got jammed up and looked like New York City.

He rented a Jag this time. By now, she had her own suitcase. Her own designer purse. Her own matching wallet with no credit cards and just the $800 cash leftover from the boyfriend's stash. The only other things in the purse were a cell phone, a passport and an open-ended return ticket to Santo Domingo.

They would be staying at the Vanderbilt Condado Hotel, and the name was somehow familiar for Dulce. When they got there, it was like walking into a jewelry box. The lobby had a glossy marble floor in tones of gold, with glass doors, large mirrors on the walls, and furniture in rich tones of ochre. A curving double staircase of black marble led up to a mezzanine. It was the kind of staircase they had on dating shows. Thirty women would stand posed—one on each step—wearing bikinis or evening gowns, each hoping for the man to choose her.

A woman in a modest uniform ran a dust mop across the floor, and it jogged Dulce's memory. The Vanderbilt Condado. When Dulce's mother had lived in Puerto Rico, she had worked on the cleaning crew. Suddenly, Dulce noticed all the Latinos working there, from the reception area to the bartenders, to the bellhops lugging suitcases in and out.

"I'm so sorry Mr. Gerard," the hotel clerk said. "Your suite isn't quite ready yet. We weren't expecting you for a few hours."

"We caught an earlier flight," Phillip said. "Do you have anything else?"

"Just a regular room," she said. "Our suites are all booked."

"A regular room won't do," he said.

"I'm so sorry," she said. "I'll have housekeeping rush. It should only be another half an hour. Would you like to have a seat in the bar?"

"I have a better idea," he said, and took Dulce's hand.

"What about our luggage?" she asked.

"They'll take it to the room," he said. "Now it's time to do some more spoiling."

Across the street from the hotel was a Cartier jewelers. Dulce's heart began to beat harder. Clothing was one thing, but was he really going to buy her some jewelry?

The display windows were full of diamonds and gold. Rings. Necklaces. Bracelets. Wives got diamond rings. Did side chicks get bracelets? To be honest, she would be happy just to have a purse with the Cartier logo.

When they arrived in the store, a young woman approached them right away. She welcomed them and asked how she could help.

"I was thinking of one of your gold chains," he said. "Something simple."

Was this really happening? A rich man was buying her jewelry. Gold jewelry. From Cartier.

"I'd like the braided chain in all yellow gold," he said. "Eighteen inches."

Somehow that killed it that he knew the size. He had done this before. Had bought this particular bauble for another woman. Probably another side chick. No real thought went into it. Just part of his game.

But when the salesclerk brought out the necklace, Dulce looked at the double chain of flat braided gold strands. The woman lifted Dulce's hair and put the chain on her. He had been right. The length was perfect.

"Will you be needing a bag?" the clerk asked.

"No," Phillip said, and signed the receipt. He turned to Dulce: "I hope the maid is done with the room. Sometimes they're so slow."

Dulce nodded and left the store with the chain around her neck.

* * *

When they returned to the hotel, a tall white man came up to Phillip and greeted him.

"Davis Evanston!" Phillip said. "What are you doing here in the capital? I thought you never left your little tax-free fiefdom."

"I come in to town," Evanston said. "I was here last month for the cryptocurrency summit." Evanston was about Phillip's age, but he had on a Harley Davidson leather motorcycle jacket that was ridiculous for the climate. "In fact," Evanston went on. "I'm here with some of the guys from Puertopia. Come have a drink with us."

Phillip nodded and fished in his wallet for some cash.

"Have them take the bags up," he said to Dulce. "And tip the bellman for me."

He handed her the twenty and the two men walked off, leaving her standing alone in the lobby.

"Wait a minute," Phillip said to Evanston, his voice unnaturally loud as they headed to the bar. "Last time we met, weren't you trying to score with a chick on a motorcycle? How did that go?"

"Well I would have scored," Evanston said. "If I hadn't had a tire blow out . . ." Soon the two men's voices were swallowed by the bustling hotel lobby.

For a moment Dulce felt lost, unsure what to do. She looked around. Beside her was a statue of a sphinx, with the body of a great cat, and the head and torso of a Greek maiden. Dulce felt like that. As if she were put together out of spare parts and not fully human, yet somehow her breasts were always on display.

Everyone else was moving, except Dulce and the pair of sphinx statues.

She felt a tap on her shoulder. "Your room is ready," the woman at reception was handing her a pair of key cards. "Your bags are on their way up now."

Dulce thanked her and hurried to the elevator. She was

hoping to catch the bellman, her fist clutching the crumpled twenty.

When she got to the room, a young man was just walking out of the suite with the gold luggage cart. He had light brown skin and a tight fade haircut.

She thanked him and handed him the twenty.

"Anytime, beautiful," he said in Spanish. "What's your name?"

"Dulce," she said. She walked past him into the room as he held the door for her.

"It's like a nutrition label," he said, grinning at her.

She laughed.

"My name's Christian," he said. "But you can call me the Puerto Rican Sazon Papi. Let us know if you need anything." He grinned at her, and closed the door behind him.

Dulce stepped into the suite. All their luggage was lined up inside the door. A suitcase and a garment bag for Phillip, and the new designer carry-on for Dulce.

The suite was large, with high ceilings, marble floors, and walls of wood and fabric. Afternoon sun streamed in through muslin curtains, illuminating the intricate wood inlay of a long sideboard with hexagonal designs.

For a moment, she felt excited by the luxurious décor. But then, she imagined her mother having to dust the tight crevices of the wood furnishings, having to mop the expanses of marble floor, having to take down the large curtains to wash. All while pregnant.

The story was that her mother worked up until the first contraction, her water breaking on the bus ride home. But mostly, the repetitive physical motion of cleaning would have lulled a baby. As if in recollection of those days, Dulce was suddenly exhausted, and fell asleep on top of the plush comforter, wrinkling her designer clothes, and flattening the curls in the back of her hair.

* * *

When she woke up, she felt dazed and irritated. She went flipping through the TV channels. Mostly American TV. But then she brightened when she realized that Puerto Rico was also showing *A Woman's Dark Past.*

Xoana looks gorgeous in a wedding gown. She stands in a dress shop with her foster mother, La Alemana.

"Do you want to see any more dresses?" the sales clerk asks.

"No," Xoana says. "This is the one."

La Alemana wipes her eyes. "At least I get to see one of my girls get married. Oh, we'll miss you so much, Xoana. The boys will miss you especially."

"I'll come visit," Xoana says. "You'll always be my family."

Later that night, Xoana and Guilherme are at the rehearsal dinner. The wedding is day after tomorrow.

La Alemana's husband is raising a glass. "I suppose for every father giving away a bride, it's bittersweet. In some ways, I feel robbed, because Xoana only came into our lives as a teenager, a few short years ago, and I didn't get to know her from the beginning. At the same time, she has been such a blessing to our family, that I should be grateful for the time we have had. And to Guilherme, I always knew you could do it. We Lutherans talk about 'by faith alone,' and you have worked faithfully, and believed faithfully. What a lovely wedding gift from God, your patent has been finalized, and it looks like we'll not just be losing a daughter, but gaining a very successful son-in-law. To the happy couple!"

As people are toasting, the door opens and Izabel enters. There is a collective gasp.

La Alemana is the first to recover. "Izabel, darling, where have you been? Why didn't you contact us?"

"We can talk about that later," she says. "Right now, it's

Xoana's moment. I heard about it and I had to come. I wouldn't miss my *sister's* wedding for the world."

Dulce slept some more after the soap opera. When she woke, she heard Phillip entering the suite.

"A swim, I think," he was saying.

Dulce nodded and got dressed.

On the beach, the surf was choppier than usual, and she was afraid to go out beyond her knees.

"I can't swim," she said.

"What?" he asked. "I'll teach you."

Dulce felt a twist in her stomach at the memory of her first date with Zavier. The last thing she wanted was to replay the scene with Phillip.

"Oh, I'm a terrible student," she lied. "I can't let you see that side of me."

"Then we'll get you some private lessons tomorrow when I go to work," he said. "I'm determined to swim in the ocean with you before this trip ends."

When they went back into the hotel, he arranged the lessons. At the gift shop, he also bought her a rectangular plastic thing on a cord, the shape and size of a small paperback book.

"What is it?" she asked.

"A water wallet," he said. "To keep your valuables safe while you swim."

It was a cloudy translucent plastic. The sides were soft, but the top was firmly structured with a sealed closure.

"You can keep your hotel key and your phone in there while you go in the ocean," he explained.

"I don't usually take my phone," she said.

"I might need to get hold of you," he said.

Dulce smiled and nodded. A reflex. Of course.

The swim instructor turned out to be an experienced and patient middle-aged European woman. She complimented Dulce on her floating, and taught her a few different strokes.

Dulce had to tuck the water wallet into her swimsuit, or it got in the way.

By the second day, she was a decent swimmer. But as she swam with Gerard, all she could think about was wanting to show her progress to Zavier.

After dinner, they had sex and Phillip fell asleep. Dulce lay awake, feeling the memory of the waves. She was dying to watch her Brazilian novela, but couldn't risk waking Phillip. She had finished *From Red Light to Red Carpet,* and wished she had another book. Eventually, she went into the bathroom and looked at all her social media accounts.

@ZaviJourno had tagged her in a tweet:

@RealThug Woofer on my mind:
"Tryna front with my boys while we drinking top shelf
But I'm thinking bout this girl in spite of myself
Go to the strip club? Whatever. Sure.
But she's the only one I got eyes for.
If lonely was the problem, she'd be the cure." (1/1)

Dulce had told herself that she wouldn't respond. Not to texts. Not anything. But the lyrics got to her. Before she could stop herself, she tweeted back:

@ThatGirlNashonna:
"This girl's running so fast, no time for love.
Running so fast no time for love.
Love tries to slow me for a kiss and a hug.
If love wanna catch me, love better speed up." (1/1)

She stayed up for hours, watching the phone. In case he was still up and would respond. But by four in the morning, she gave up. Why would he be up at this hour? She snorted to herself. Why was *she* still awake? She climbed back into bed and fell asleep.

Chapter 10

Phillip went out early the next morning, something about riding motorcycles. Dulce smiled and pretended to pay attention, but after he left, she crashed out again. When she woke up, she felt around the bed for her phone to see the time. She realized that she had slept for most of the day, and she had a text from Zavier. She vowed not to read it or to check twitter. Instead, she searched for the most recent episode of *A Woman's Dark Past*.

On the night before her wedding, Xoana is alone with Izabel.

"First you took my mother away from me and now my boyfriend?"

"Izabel, you left for a year. You didn't send more than a few postcards. Besides, you never loved Guilherme."

"I was naïve," Izabel says. "I didn't realize how cruel men can be. That soccer player lied to me."

"What about how cruel women can be?" Xoana asks. "How cruel you were. Guilherme was heartbroken."

"Well, you didn't waste any time picking up the pieces."

"It wasn't like that," Xoana says. "Not at first."

"Well you can't seriously mean to marry him in a white dress tomorrow," Izabel says.

"Of course I will," Xoana says. "We haven't even had sex yet."

"But I'm sure you've come close," Izabel says.

"That's not your business," Xoana says.

"I'm not talking about Guilherme," Izabel says. "I'm talking about your past."

"What do you mean?"

"Don't play innocent with me," Izabel says. "I read my mother's notes about you. She rescued you from a brothel. Don't tell me you were a virgin there."

"That was different," Xoana says, tears springing to her eyes. "I didn't choose any of that."

"Ruined is ruined," Izabel says. "And I plan to tell Guilherme. Let him decide if he still wants you."

"And then you think he'll want *you*?" Xoana asked. "The woman who left him, and certainly hasn't returned with her own virtue intact?"

"We'll see what he wants," Izabel says. "I'm tired of you taking what's mine. Leave town and I'll keep my mouth shut."

"I'm not going anywhere," Xoana says. "Except to tell Guilherme the truth."

Izabel grabs her arm. "You really would tell him? You trust that he loves you enough to forgive you?"

"There's nothing to forgive," Xoana says. "I was a child and I was forced. If he doesn't understand the difference, then maybe I don't want to marry *him*."

"If you feel that way, then why haven't you told him?" Izabel counters.

"I don't want to burden him with it," Xoana says. "Because I love him. Because I care about his happiness. Something you wouldn't understand."

"Okay then," Izabel says. "I can see that this is true

love. I'm sorry. I was jealous, but I can't stand in the way of something so strong. I shouldn't have come."

"No, Izabel, you've been like a sister to me. Stay. Come to the wedding. Your parents have missed you terribly. The boys, too."

"Okay," Izabel says. "Let's have a drink to your wedding."

She pours them two glasses of champagne.

Shortly after Xoana drinks, the room begins to spin.

"What did you put in that drink?"

"Only what I had to," Izabel says.

Xoana passes out.

Izabel leaves, but returns later with a strange man. He poses with Xoana in a series of compromising positions. Izabel photographs it all, with Xoana's wedding gown in the background.

"When are you going to leave?" the man asks.

"Why would I leave?" Izabel asks.

"So I can actually have sex with her."

"That's disgusting," Izabel says. "I never agreed to that. Get the hell out."

The next morning, Xoana wakes up on the floor of the dressing room. Beneath her elbow is a manila envelope. She sits up holding her head. Inside are the photographs.

On top is an unsigned note that says: "This would be more difficult to explain. You would do better to just leave town."

Xoana breaks down sobbing.

Later that morning, La Alemana knocks on Xoana's door, but the room is empty.

"Do you know where Xoana is?" she asks her daughter Izabel. "I know you told me she wanted to get ready by herself, but now I can't find her."

"No idea," Izabel says. "It's so strange."

"What are we supposed to do?" La Alemana asks. "Everyone's waiting."

Izabel shakes her head. "I guess we have to go tell them."

As Izabel and her mother walk toward the groom and the assembled guests, Guilherme looks at them with a bright smile of expectation. It gradually dims as he sees their faces.

Inside the dressing room, a pearl pin holds a scrap of paper to the wedding gown: "Guilherme, you are my heart. I'm so sorry but I have to go. I can't explain. Just know that I love you and I always will."

As the camera pulled away from the note, and the credits rolled, Dulce started to cry. It was exactly how she felt about Zavier. It was tearing her apart inside that she couldn't be with him and couldn't be honest with him about it.

Well, at least she could be honest with herself: yes, she wanted to be with him. Some part of her was in love with him. In love? Maybe that was too strong, but when he talked about coming home to her, it opened something in her heart that she hadn't yet been able to close.

When Phillip came to the room, Dulce was still crying.

"What's wrong?" he asked. "No crying. This is supposed to be a fun trip. Only fun."

Dulce shook her head and wiped her eyes. "Oh, I didn't hear you come in," she said. "It's just this sappy soap opera."

She forced a bright smile, putting on her sugar baby face for him.

"That's a good girl," he said.

They had sex, then dinner. It was their last night.

Again, she couldn't sleep well, thinking of Zavier, pressing on her chest against the ache inside.

She knew she should leave it alone, but late that night, she couldn't help but open the message from him.

Scouring through Thug woofer lyrics & thinking of you.

She couldn't bring herself to text. It was too intimate. She tweeted back, tagging @ZaviJourno.

@ThatGirlNashonna:
"This boy is like a song spinning around in my brain
I keep trying to ignore but he keeps staking a claim
And I keep making it plain that I don't have the time
But he keeps jumping the turnstile to this heart of mine."

The next morning, Phillip had to catch a plane back to the states. When he left, he promised to call next time he was in the DR. He traveled frequently back and forth to Miami and New York. She saw him off on his flight to Newark. She was supposed to leave on a flight to Santo Domingo a couple hours later. Instead, she cashed in her ticket. Dulce had no intention of going back to her aunt's house.

She sat down in an empty row of chairs at the airport to figure out a plan. Tickets to New York cost about the same amount as to Santo Domingo. What if she just went for it and surprised Zavier? She could text him: "I'm at JFK! Where are you? Let's meet!"

The more she thought about it, the stupider it sounded. She would look desperate. Delusional. Or like a stalker. How many women dogged out other women on social media for making up stories because a guy sent a couple texts? Because they had some kind of moment with a guy? Zavier hadn't proposed. Showing up like "Baby, I'm here!" and the guy was all "Bitch, who are you?" He'd just said the kind of thing guys say when they're making a move. She would be a fool to put any more on it. And even if he was happy to see her, how long would that last if she told him the truth:

"*Don't worry, bae. My ex-pimp is dead. Now you might just have to protect me from his brother.*" Maybe if Zavier came to visit the Caribbean again . . . Or better yet, decided to settle in the Caribbean . . . Maybe one day they could work something out, where her past wouldn't have to haunt her. But as long as he lived in New York? Nope.

And right now, she didn't have time to be all starry-eyed for some boy who was thousands of miles away. She needed someplace to stay tonight. How much did hotels cost? Hostels? Maybe an AirBnB?

She walked back out of the airport.

"Excuse me," a man approached her. "Do you speak English?"

Dulce smiled. "Sure."

"Maybe you can help me? I can't get Lyft to load on my phone."

"Don't bother," she said. "Lyft doesn't work in Puerto Rico. And Uber doesn't pickup at the airport."

She sized him up. He was tall and lean, with a crisp blazer and jeans. Maybe mid-thirties and balding, but with a handsome face.

"How do I get to my hotel?" he asked. "I don't see any taxis."

"You have to ask one of the guys who dispatches the cabs," she said, walking him down the curb to the taxi stand. "Your first time here in Puerto Rico?"

"Obvious, right?" he said. "I'm from Canada. Going to a sales conference. How about you? Are you from here?"

"No," she said. "I'm from Brazil." The lie came out effortlessly. If he was Canadian and didn't speak Spanish, maybe she could get away with it. She was always pretending to be someone else. The simple Dominican hick. Why not upgrade? Be some businesswoman from Brazil? "My flight back home was canceled," she said, improvising. "I can't get another flight out until day after tomorrow."

"Well, then you have to let me take you to dinner," he said. "As a thanks for the help."

She had to play this right. Reluctant. Unattainable. She gave him a mouth-closed smile. "I'm very flattered, but I really need to get back to my hotel and get some work done. Especially now that I'll be arriving two days later than I'd planned."

"What do you do?" he asked.

"I'm a television writer," she said.

"In Brazil?" he asked.

"Yes," she said. "I write for the show 'A Woman's Dark Past.' Maybe you've heard of it?"

"I'm afraid not," he said. "But if you won't have dinner with me, at least share a cab with me to town."

"I don't know," she said. "Where are you staying?"

He named a hotel in the San Juan neighborhood of Isla Verde.

"I guess so," she said. "I'm staying at the Intercontinental. It isn't far from there."

In Spanish, she gave the driver the name of his hotel and also said there would be a second stop.

The driver put the luggage in the trunk, and they climbed into the back of the cab.

"Okay," she said. "You're in sales right?"

He nodded.

"Well, you have a fifteen minute cab ride to sell me on that dinner."

He grinned. "I accept the challenge."

It wouldn't have mattered much what he said. Dulce was prepared to be won over. He turned out to be of mixed heritage. French Canadian and Indigenous. He didn't like his job. He was bored, selling some sort of tech components. This trip was going to be miserable, but his dinner with her could be the highlight.

She pretended to deliberate. She pretended to be reluctant.

But just before she let the cab take her to the Intercontinental Hotel—where she didn't have a reservation, and which she could never afford—she had a sudden change of heart and said yes.

She kept expecting him to ask where she learned Spanish, to say something about her speaking Portuguese, but he didn't. He really didn't ask that much about her. Or notice that she talked like a New Yorker. Mostly, he talked. She listened. He was charming and funny, sure. But he didn't listen. Zavier listened. He asked her questions.

She blinked and told herself to stop thinking about Zavier. This Canadian was the guy to focus on. The mark. She made sure to drink "too much" at dinner. She flirted. She went to his room, ostensibly to watch her soap opera.

Xoana has moved to the city. It's three years later. Xoana has finished college, and gotten married to a kind doctor. They have a new baby, whom Xoana loves. Yet somehow, her life feels incomplete.

She's wheeling the baby in a stroller when she runs into Guilherme and Izabel in the town square. The chemistry between Xoana and Guilherme is strong and immediate. Neither can speak, but Izabel takes charge.

"I should have known," Izabel says. "You would go back to the city where my mother originally found you."

"I—" Xoana begins. "My own mother was sick—dying in fact. That day I left. I found out. I had to rush. If I ever wanted to see her alive again. I—we only had a moment. Then she passed away."

"I'm so sorry for your loss," Guilherme says.

"I'm sorry, too," Xoana says, then looks up directly at him. "I'm so, so very sorry."

"Well, we can see what you've been up to here," Izabel gestures to the baby. "What can you tell us about the baby's father?"

SIDE CHICK NATION / 117

"My husband?" Xoana asks. "He—he's a doctor. His office is right here. We had lunch together today. I'm just headed home."

"We're married, as well," Izabel says, taking Guilherme's arm.

"We wanted to send an invitation," Guilherme says. "But the family didn't know how to contact you."

"But I sent your mother several letters," Xoana says. "I assumed I never heard back because she was angry with me."

Izabel shrugs. "They must have gotten lost in the mail."

"Of course," Xoana says. "I can see that. So what about the two of you? Are you visiting the city?"

"No, we've moved here permanently," Guilherme says.

"His company has relocated here," Izabel says.

"And what about you?" Xoana asks. "What have you been up to?"

"Well, I was working as a wedding planner, actually," Izabel says. "Our wedding was so beautiful that people began asking me to plan theirs. But I quit because—"

"It's okay," Guilherme says. "We can tell her, she's family. We were hoping for a child. But God will bless us with children when it's time."

"Maybe it's for the best," Izabel says. "I'll be able to re-launch my business here in the city before I'm weighed down with motherhood."

"Of course," Xoana says. "Speaking of motherhood, please send my love to your mother—to your whole family."

"You can count on it," Izabel says, and pulls a somewhat reluctant Guilherme away.

When the Canadian leaned in to kiss her, Dulce was reluctant to turn away from the show. But she had no place else to stay that night. They were having sex by the time the credits came on, and she didn't have to pretend to see her name on the screen.

In the morning, she got up, brushed her teeth, combed her hair, and put on mascara and a light lip gloss.

When he woke up, she pretended to be still asleep. She did a wide-eyed, blinking *where am I?* and feigned embarrassment.

"Oh my god," she said. "I never do anything like—I really need to go."

She rose from the bed, pressing the sheet to her breasts, covering the nipples, but making sure to press the cleavage up and together. She let the sheet fall off one hip.

"No, wait," he said. "Stay. Can't you? Your flight to Brazil isn't til tomorrow."

"I can't—I don't even hardly know you," she tried to look mortified. The ingénue.

"We can get to know each other," he said. "Please. Just stay. Order room service. Go to the spa. You can charge it to the room. Just be here when I get back from this stupid conference."

"I'll think about it," she said.

And so it began. The following day, he begged her to reschedule her flight. "They'll charge me $100," she complained.

"Let me pay it," he said. He dug in his wallet and pulled out a hundred in cash.

She stayed with him all five days of the conference.

In the middle of the week, she got a message on social media that caught her attention. It was from one of the other **girls** Jerry had pimped. "Jimmy got shot. Dead. Figured u wd **wanna** kno."

Dulce stared at the message until the words swam, lost meaning. Not only Jerry, but his brother Jimmy was dead, too? That changed everything. New York City was no longer off limits? She could go home now. But home to what? Her family's two-bedroom apartment in Washington Heights?

She looked around at the four-star hotel room. The fresh white sheets. The flat screen TV. The room service tray. In New York, she'd be Dulce García, Dominican ex-ho. In Puerto Rico, she could be anyone she wanted to be.

After the Canadian left, she walked down the strip to another hotel and sat down in the bar.

Was this going to work more than once? She got hit on by a few guys that didn't appeal to her. Not just because they were older, but their come-on wasn't generous. Maybe she couldn't pull it off. Maybe she should just go back to New York. It was one thing to be a sugar baby with Phillip, a man committed to spoiling her. Or even the Canadian, who was handsome, generous and cheerful. But she didn't know if she could hang out with one of these sullen old men for just room and board.

She waved away a couple of guys, before the bartender brought her a margarita with top shelf tequila. He pointed out the man who had sent it. She smiled and raised the glass to him. He was maybe forty. Handsome. She smiled. When he came over to talk to her, she found him charming. She asked for another drink and reeled him in.

This became her late summer hustle. The businesswoman whose flight was canceled. She pocketed the change fees. She started charging $150. Some airlines did. If guys turned out to be jerks, she "caught" her next flight. If they turned out to be fun, she let them "talk her out of it." She used condoms. They paid for the hotel, all the food, and bought her the occasional gift.

One guy took her on his yacht, which was actually kind of a drag, because he complained to her the whole time about his wife.

But other times, it was room service or fine dining, shopping, and spa treatments.

In her designer carryon, she had four outfits, which she eventually identified as a series of costumes.

A cleavage-bearing silk blouse and pencil skirt: "my flight was canceled."

A spaghetti-strap rayon jumpsuit: "I can't believe I'm still in your hotel room."

A clinging red-orange dress: "pay my plane change fee."

A linen vest-blouse and matching pants: "parting is such sweet sorrow."

All the colors were pale earth tones, except the red dress. The linen outfit only worked on the last day. It wrinkled in the suitcase, but by then she would have had time to order it steamed by the hotel staff.

She kept her hair blown out straight. She wore the Cartier chain. She kept the makeup subtle.

Sometimes, they would tell her how much more "classy" she was than the Puerto Rican women, with their bright colors and loud voices. Dulce would wave away the backhanded compliment with a shrug and a smile, and change the subject. Fuck them if they didn't respect Caribbean women. They were getting hustled by one.

The island had a steady stream of businessmen. Laying in the spa one day, with a woman scrubbing her all over with sugar, she decided she might never leave.

She met Ellis one afternoon when she was between businessmen. She wasn't wearing any of the uniforms, rather her tank top and shorts. She had been swimming, so her hair was kinky, and she had on red lipstick.

She went into a cafeteria to eat some *comida criolla*, and heard him cheering for the Knicks in an accent that broadcast New Jersey, even from across the room. He was African American, well-built, and handsome. She ordered her meal at the counter and sat down on the barstool beside him.

Ellis groaned as the Knicks missed a shot.

"Why isn't their best player in the game?" Dulce asked.

"He took a fall earlier," the young man said. "Where you from?"

"Washington Heights."

"I'm from Newark," he said, and they exchanged names.

After the Knicks' defeat, they continued to chat. Eventually they went out for a drink.

"When you walked in that place, I was like damn, she's fine," he said. "But thank god you spoke English. I got no game in Spanish."

Dulce laughed. It was nice to be with someone brown and handsome, closer to her own age. She thought of Zavier. This guy was more of a hunk, cooler, a total chick-magnet. But still, something about Zavier, with his nerdy glasses and skinny frame—something about the way he looked at her, the intensity of it, dwarfed all the beefcake bodies in the world.

But Ellis had a room at the Intercontinental Hotel. He was some kind of tech whiz. He asked her to stay with him. She said yes. She was herself with Ellis. And perhaps because she wasn't busy playing the role of the Brazilian writer, she couldn't stop thinking about Zavier.

But Ellis was fun. They watched "Love and Hip Hop Miami," ate junk food, and smoked a little weed.

They took excursions into San Juan, not luxury stuff, just checking out the old part of the city, shopping like regular people. She finally found a copy of Nashonna's new book.

When they went out, Ellis picked up the check, because he could charge it to his company. But the company wouldn't reimburse for alcohol. So Dulce paid the bar tab when they went drinking outside the hotel. She didn't really pay attention to how much she was spending. She was so obviously getting the better end of the deal with Ellis paying for the hotel and all the meals.

When Ellis was out at work, he didn't spring for spa treatments, but she did love room service and swimming. Or she lounged around reading and watching *A Woman's Dark Past.*

Xoana is waiting in her husband's OB/GYN office. The baby sits on her lap, playing with her necklace.

Her husband sweeps in. "I'm sorry to keep you waiting darling," he says. "One of my patients had an emergency. I won't be able to make lunch today."

"That's okay," she says. "It's good to get out of the house. These days with just me and the baby can be so long."

"Of course, sweetheart," he says. "I'll see you at home for dinner tonight."

With a quick kiss on her forehead, he sweeps out again.

The baby begins to fuss, and Xoana bounces her. "We missed lunch," she tells the baby. "But now it's somebody's naptime."

As the baby begins to cry in earnest, Xoana puts her in the stroller. "I know you're tired. Let's have a little walk to put you to sleep, no?"

As she steps out of the building, Guilherme approaches her.

"I thought I might see you here," he says.

"I can't really stop to talk," Xoana says. "I've got to get her to sleep."

"I can walk with you," he says. "I'm sure she'll be asleep in no time. You were always so good with Izabel's brothers."

"They must be so big now," Xoana says.

"The older one is turning ten years old."

"What?" Xoana asks loudly.

The baby begins to fuss again.

She reaches into the carriage and soothes her.

"I'm so surprised to find you in the city," Xoana says.

"You used to say that you never liked it here. You wanted to stay behind the scenes. Focus on the science."

"I did," Guilherme says. "I do. But Izabel was restless in such a small town. I want to keep her happy."

"That's so thoughtful of you," Xoana says.

"I have to be honest," Guilherme says. "Part of the reason I moved to the city was that everything back home reminded me of you. I thought if I got away. Maybe then I could just be happy with my life now. Happy with Izabel. But now . . . now I don't think I can." His voice has grown in volume and intensity.

"Shhhhh!" Xoana says. "The baby's almost asleep."

"Don't tell me you didn't feel it," Guilherme says in a choked whisper. "Don't tell me you didn't feel that surge of electricity when we first saw each other. At that moment I knew. I could never be happy with anyone else. Why didn't you tell me that your mother was sick? I would have come with you. We could have postponed the wedding."

"My mother was a prostitute," Xoana says. "I thought she was already dead. I didn't know how to explain it, or if you'd understand."

"I don't know what I did to make you think I would've judged you for your mother's sins," Guilherme says.

"How do you know what my mother's sins were," Xoana says. "Some women don't have a choice about these things. And then, once they've been in that life, every other door closes to them. And some women choose it, and who's to say that's a wrong choice. It's not like most women have so many choices. Women from places like where I came from. Not from fancy places like the town we used to live in. You thought you weren't good enough for Izabel. Where I come from, you would have been like a millionaire."

"There's so much about you I didn't know," Guilherme says. "I was so wound up in myself. I didn't ask the right questions. Now, I wish I had."

"You're right, Guilherme," Xoana says. "There's so much about me you don't know. It wouldn't have worked out, no matter what you asked. Some answers have no questions."

"How can you say it wouldn't have worked out?" Guilherme asks. "After Izabel left me, I found myself falling in love with you. I went to a fortune teller. I've never done anything like that before. She said one sister was my true love, and the other sister was just a bridge to get me to her. After you left, I thought—I assumed you were the bridge. Keeping me connected until Izabel got back. But now—now that I've seen you again, I know that you are the love of my life. Izabel was the bridge. Xoana, you and I are meant to be. Can't you feel it? Nothing can stop us. Nothing can stand in the way of this love we have."

He leans forward and takes her in his arms.

For a moment, Xoana surrenders to it. She melts into his arms, his kiss, his love, the love she barely let herself even think about for so many years.

But then she pulls away.

"It's wrong!" she says. "My husband. My baby. I can't—"

And she hurries off, pushing the stroller between a pair of joggers and leaving him behind.

At that moment in the show, Ellis came into the room and Dulce immediately knew something was wrong. He didn't have his usual grin.

"Baby, I got to cut this trip short," he said. "There's a hurricane warning."

"Okay," she said, and started packing her own suitcase.

"No need for you to leave," he said. "My company has a

deal with the hotel. The room is prepaid til the middle of the month. Feel free to stay the whole time. If you like, I can put your name on the reservation. I'd sit out the storm with you, but I have a big presentation in Houston next week. I can't get stuck here."

Dulce's family had stories of hurricanes. Some were worse than others, but by the end, they had bounced back and were all laughing about it.

After Ellis left, Dulce started getting warnings from the hotel, papers slipped under her door. She had expected to sit out Hurricane Irma on the fourth floor of the hotel. She had imagined herself sitting there, the winds howling and the rain slashing at the windows, but she would be above it all, with good food, good booze, and good weed.

Instead, the written warnings became increasingly dire: "pack all your belongings into your suitcase, and put them in the bathroom. Close the bathroom door."

Then later: "guests will need to be evacuated to the safe room."

She joined a throng of travelers who pressed into elevators and trooped down stairs. They checked her name off a list (thank God Ellis had put her on the reservation) and gave her a special wristband.

She was prepared for the "safe room" to be some kind of dungeon, but it was more like a party. Then they sent her into a ballroom on the second floor, with an open bar and plenty of food. She befriended a pair of young Latinas from Detroit who were in Puerto Rico for a dance competition. One had on bright pink lipstick.

Her friend asked. "Where's that hot as fuck guy we seen you around with?"

"Ellis?" Dulce said. "He had to go back to Houston."

"How you gonna let your man out of your sight?" the dancer with the lipstick asked.

"How'd you let him get out of the bedroom?" the other one asked. "I wouldn't let him wear anything more than a pair of boxers."

"Better yet boxer briefs," the lipstick girl said.

"He's not my man," Dulce said.

"If I'd have known that, I'd have been like 'Hey Ellis, you can take me to Houston!'" lipstick girl said.

"Wait a minute," the other girl put up a hand and scrutinized Dulce. "You got a man of your own, don't you? You were getting a little action on the side?"

"Nothing like that," Dulce said.

"But you have somebody, some kind of way, don't you?" lipstick girl asked.

"Not really," Dulce said, but of course she was thinking of Zavier.

"Did you see that smile?" lipstick girl asked. "You just thought about your real man."

"Your real man must be putting the dick down so hard for you to be like, 'bye Ellis. Have fun in Houston,'" her friend said.

"We haven't even had sex," Dulce said.

"But you were fucking Ellis, right?" lipstick girl asked. "I will personally be heartbroken if all that dick went to waste."

"Yeah, I was," Dulce said with a chuckle.

"And I bet he had you all, *oh yes, papi!*" she gave an orgasmic moan.

Dulce dropped her eyes and smiled. Sex with Ellis had definitely felt good, the same way making out felt good, but nothing even close to bringing her to a climax.

After the first time they had intercourse, he'd asked her point blank: "what about you?"

Dulce had blinked. With the other guys, she'd always faked it as part of the act. But she had been enjoying herself and not bothering to put on a show. He wasn't a client or a sugar daddy. But then, he was looking at her like she was supposed to know. What about her? She had no idea. She opened her mouth, and the "I don't know," was on the tongue that had just been in his mouth, but she couldn't speak.

"You want me to go down on you?" he asked.

Did she? Would she like it? She didn't know that, either. Her Miami boyfriend was a bust, but maybe it was just the way he did it. Suddenly, she felt ashamed. What kind of stupid girl did all this fucking and didn't even know what she liked? Could he see her blush in the dark?

"It just takes me a minute to get comfortable," she had told him, her voice carefully modulated. "I usually come the second time."

So from then on, she faked it.

"Oooh!" lipstick girl said, pulling Dulce from the memory. "They brought out a new plate of desserts."

The three of them joined the rush toward the buffet table, and filled their plates with cookies and small squares of cheesecake and flan.

The hotel had a generator. Even when the power went off in San Juan, the hotel lights stayed on. They continued to prepare food. The three young women were up all night drinking and cracking jokes. In the pre-dawn, Dulce fell asleep for a few hours. By morning, they were all allowed to go back to their rooms.

And that was it. The hotel moved a little slow those first forty-eight hours after the hurricane. A lot of the staff couldn't get in to work. But soon, things were back to normal. Dulce ordered room service. She hung out with her new friends. The dance contest was delayed a couple of days, but they invited Dulce. The girls were good dancers. They came in third.

After her new friends left, things were boring at the hotel.

Finally, her phone came back online. She checked social media, and found @ZaviJourno had tagged her in a series of tweets:

@ThugWoofer
"I been to jail
I shot a gun
Been chased by the cops in a life & death run
But nothing strikes terror in a thug's tatted chest
Than when the time comes for him to express
The love he has for his girl (not to fuck)
But to let her know that she got him fucked
up . . ." (1/3)

"To drop the illusion, let go of control
Admit to himself that he's vulnerable
If he can tolerate the panic
If he can stand the heat
It'll forge him into someone life can never
defeat . . ." (2/3)

"Which is why the best brothers got queens at their
sides
Rocking they own royal queendoms with strength and
pride
So when you meet that queen who's for real for real
You better drop the armor and let her know how you
feel."
#LettingYouKnowHowIFeel (3/3)

Dulce fired back, tagging him in a tweet thread:

@ThatGirlNashonna
"a woman with a goal
whose career is on a roll
can't afford to have a man
so I get it when I can . . ." (1/3)

"but if I keep it real
and reveal the way I really feel
do some serious introspection
see I long for that connection
But let me ask you, sis:
Where's the brother who can handle all this?"
Each Mr. Right that gets anointed
only leaves me disappointed . . ." (2/3)

"So I have the rap spotlight
To keep me warm at night
Curl up with my microphone
And I go to bed alone." (3/3)

Dulce was feeling sorry for herself. Sure, she had a plush hotel room, but not for long. And she was alone. She wished Zavier were there. Or if not him, then Ellis. Even Phillip would have been a welcome distraction. Something to look forward to in the day. Now, her only excitement was the new episodes of *A Woman's Dark Past.*

Izabel follows Xoana, who wheels the baby toward the park, and comes up behind her.

"I've seen the way my husband looks at you," Izabel says. "Whatever is going on between you, I know he won't look at you the same way after he sees those photographs."

Xoana freezes, then keeps walking. "Nothing is going on between us," Xoana says. "I'm married."

"Once a whore always a whore," Izabel says.

"I don't have any designs on your husband," Xoana says. "He married you. Isn't that enough?"

"Not with whores like you around," Izabel says. "Keep away from him."

Night in the city. Izabel climbs in the window of Xoana's house. She slips into the nursery where the baby is sleeping. She approaches the crib, and looks down at the tiny girl. She runs a finger across the child's cheek, and the baby whimpers.

Then Izabel turns to the bottle of water beside the nursing chair. She pours several drops of a clear liquid into the bottom of the empty water glass.

With a last look at the baby, she slips back out the window.

Later, the baby begins to cry. Xoana comes in.

"Hello love," she croons. "Are you awake? Are you hungry?" She sits down in the nursing chair and pours herself a glass of water. She sets the glass down on the table and pulls out a nursing cover.

Her husband walks in with a bottle in his hand.

"I've got it," Xoana says.

"I just got called to the hospital," he says. "One of my patients is going into labor. It might be a while. I just want a moment with the baby before I go."

"So sweet of you," Xoana says.

"Go ahead and finish your nap," he says. "I'll be down in a half hour."

After she walks out, he picks up the baby, and drinks the glass of water.

A little while later, Xoana is woken up by her husband, who comes into their bedroom and gives her the baby.

The husband kisses both of them on the forehead and leaves.

Later that night, the phone wakes Xoana. She leaps up to get it before it can wake the baby, who is in bed beside her.

"Yes?" she whispers into the phone. "Yes doctor . . . is everything okay? I assume my husband is in surgery . . . He what? . . . Yes, I'm sitting down."

Her face crumples, and she begins to sob silently.

A few days later, she's sitting in her living room, when there's a knock at the door. She finds two police officers on her doorstep.

"It's about your husband," they say.

"Please come in," she says. "Can I get you anything?"

The officers exchange a look.

"No thanks," one says.

"We'll get right to the point," the other says. "We're sorry for your loss señora, but we regret to inform you that it looks like your husband was murdered."

"Murdered?" she asks. "But he had a heart attack."

"He did," the first officer says. "But he was a young man, barely forty. The autopsy showed a positive tox screen. Your husband was poisoned."

"Poisoned?" Xoana is shocked.

"Did he eat anything at home that evening?"

"No," she says. "He told me he would grab something at the hospital cafeteria."

"According to the autopsy, he had some pizza, which was eaten by many other patients and staff. There were no other foods in his stomach. No coffee. Only perhaps water. As near as they can pinpoint it, based on the time of death and estimation of how fast the poison would act is that he would have ingested the poison around dinner-time."

"He was here then," she says. "But he didn't eat. I don't know if he drank any water." She blinked. "Poisoned?"

"Did your husband have any enemies?"

"No," she says. "Everyone loved him. Literally every-one. He had so many families who were grateful to him for delivering their babies."

"Any possibility of professional jealousy?"

"No," she says. "Everyone on the staff—"

"Anyone from his past? Anyone who would want to harm him?"

"Not that I know of . . ."

"Señora," the officer says. "We have to ask. There's always the possibility with poison that he wasn't the intended victim. Do you have any enemies? Anyone who would want to harm you?"

It all comes to Xoana in a flash. Izabel demanding that she stay away from Guilherme. The glass of water on the table by the nursing chair. The open window.

But how can she tell them about Izabel without everything about her own past coming out? Don't they always suspect the spouse first? Given her history, the police will suspect she killed her husband for his money. The fallen woman, the reasoning goes, is capable of anything evil.

"No," Xoana says. "I can't think of anyone who would want to harm me."

Both officers rise, and one offers a card. "Thank you for your time," he says. "And again, we're sorry for your loss."

"If there's anything you think of that might help, please don't hesitate to call us."

"Of course," Xoana says, as she walks them to the door.

After she closes and locks it, she walks back into the nursery and picks up the baby.

"With you and God as my witness," Xoana says. "I will find proof that Izabel killed your father, and I will make her pay."

Dulce's cell phone service didn't come back on until a few days after the hurricane. Eventually, she got a text from Zavier:

Headed to Santo Domingo to report on the hurricane.

Are you and your fam okay? Need anything? We may be in your area tomorrow. Are you up for a visit?"

She texted back:

I'm in Puerto Rico. Not sure when I'll be back in DR. Fam is okay. Wish you and me were on the same island. Next time?

Why did she keep torturing herself by drawing this out? It wasn't going to work with Zavier. She needed to stop answering his texts. She deleted his number from her phone. Then later that night, she searched through her deleted photos for the picture she'd taken of his card. She found it and emailed it to herself so she couldn't lose it, even if she lost the phone. She re-entered his contact info. She shook her head even as she was doing it. This was nuts.

But she managed not to text him again. No flirty Nashonna tweets, either. A few days later, he texted that he was going back to New York.

One afternoon, a little over a week later, Dulce was napping on the hotel's king sized bed, and the phone rang. When she answered, it was the front desk.

"We have you scheduled to check out today," they said. "Would you like to stay an additional night?"

"Yes," Dulce said.

"Wonderful," the hotel staff said. "Just come down to the desk with a new credit card."

"I'll be down shortly," Dulce said.

She packed up all her stuff, plus everything in the mini bar, all the soaps and freebies. She dressed in her "my flight was canceled" outfit, and walked out of the hotel without a word.

Dulce went down the street to another hotel and sat at the bar. It was practically empty. No one came to buy her a drink.

"What can I get for you?" the bartender asked.

Dulce ordered a cola. She was surprised when it was four dollars. She waited for an hour, but didn't find any prospects. A few couples sat at tables. The barstools were empty except for hers.

She tried a second bar, this time just asking for a glass of water. "I'm waiting on a friend."

But no new friends showed up.

After the third bar was a bust, Dulce realized she would need someplace to stay. She went to the bathroom and counted her cash. Over eleven hundred dollars. Her "airline change fees" plus a little of the money she'd brought from Miami. Damn, was that all she had left? She could have had so much more. But when men were always treating her, she didn't bother to keep track of where her own money went.

Lodging was the first priority. She couldn't go online for a cheap AirBnB, because they didn't take cash, and she only had enough on her credit card for Uber rides. She looked through a guidebook and found a coupon for a great hotel deal. She took an Uber to the address, only to find out that hotel still didn't have power. She found another hotel in the guidebook, and this time she called first.

The small room with the double bed and no air conditioning was a step down, but she'd find a new sugar daddy tomorrow.

Chapter 11

Saturday, September 16—**Four days before landfall**

A couple days later, she hadn't met anyone new. Hurricane Irma had put a damper on the tourist trade, and there was a temporary lack of businessmen from the States.

She stayed in her hotel on a night-to-night basis. Checking out at noon and checking back in late in the evening, after she hadn't found anyone to stay with.

That Saturday, while she was in the bar of a more upscale hotel, she caught a news report. There was another storm brewing over the Atlantic Ocean. "Potential Tropical Cyclone 15." This meant that possibly another hurricane was on its way.

Two hurricanes in a row? It seemed unreal.

Yet everywhere she went, newscasters were talking about "Tropical Storm 15," and later, "Tropical Storm María." By the end of the evening, forecasters were definitely predicting a hurricane.

So that was that. Dulce shrugged. She'd had a good run in Puerto Rico. But now it was time to get the fuck out. Maybe back to New York. Or back to the DR. Miami was still too dangerous.

* * *

Sunday, September 17— Three days before landfall

The next morning, she asked for a late checkout. She wanted to enjoy every moment she'd paid for at that damn hotel. It was early afternoon when she wheeled her designer bag out in front of the hotel and caught an Uber to the airport.

On her lap in the back of the car, she counted her cash. Money went quickly in Puerto Rico. At least it went quickly when she was paying her own way. Three days in a hotel. Paying for her own food. Paying for taxis and Ubers to get around. She was down to $700.

The airport was madness. Lines everywhere. People were agitated, but underneath it all was panic.

Long before Dulce had made it to a counter, she heard that almost all the flights were full. The rare available seat was selling for thousands. She checked several travel sites on her phone. Nothing cheaper than $1,500 to Miami. $2,000 to New York.

And there were people lining up to get them. All her cash wasn't going to be enough.

First she called Gerard.

He picked up his cell on the third ring.

"Hey beautiful lady," he said. "I hope you're calling to say you're in Miami, and you're waiting in a hotel wearing only a sheet."

"I wish I had such good news," she said. "Actually, it's kind of the opposite. I stayed in Puerto Rico for a while, and now I'm stuck. I'm sure you've heard about the hurricane. Is there any way you could help me get a ticket to Miami? They're the cheapest ones."

"Sorry, honey," he said. "I'm here with my wife, and she would notice if a couple thousand went suddenly missing." He had a little edge in his voice.

"Of course," she said. She didn't want to piss him off. She might need him in the future. "Sorry to overstep."

With a sigh, she called her sister in New York. Her sister never had much in the way of money, but she had a decent job now. Maybe she could do something.

"Oh, so now you call wanting me to give you some money?" her sister said. "But I saw your ass on Instagram. That picture you posted. Why don't you get your 'friends' with their Mercedes and designer shit to help you, huh?" Dulce could hear the baby fussing in the background. "When you were living large did you even think about sending us any money? Of course not. I'm up here supporting Mami and everybody. Not to mention that you're the only one from this family that's set foot on the island in over a decade, and I'll bet you didn't even bother to visit your brother Santiago in jail before you left, did you? But now that you need something you call? Not to mention that *titi* said you went off with some guy to *la capital* and never came back. Was that your 'friend' with the Mercedes?"

"It wasn't like that," Dulce said. Suddenly, she wished she had handled that differently. If she hadn't gone with Gerard, maybe she'd be safe in Santo Domingo now. And she should have visited her brother. She would the next time she was back there. Maybe going off with Gerard had been the wrong choice. Maybe if she had turned him down, she would have a boyfriend like Zavier who would have called her from New York to check on her, instead of someone who was married and didn't really give a damn.

"Well however it was, with whoever you left *titi*'s house with, I can't help you," her sister said. Then yelled in the background. "Will you please shut up Dario? I'm on the fucking phone."

Dulce apologized and signed off with her sister. Now who could she call? There were only a few numbers in this new phone. Her ex in Miami, her mom, her sister, Zavier, Gerard, and the men she'd stayed with in Puerto Rican hotels.

But there was one number she knew by heart. Dulce dialed the cell phone of Marisol Rivera. All circuits were busy, so it took twenty minutes just to place the call. Finally, it was ringing.

Disconnected.

Fuck!

Well if Marisol had a new cell, at least she could call her at work. It took another half hour to get the number for the clinic and place that call, but she finally got through.

"María de la Vega clinic, how can I direct your call?"

"I'm looking for the director, Marisol Rivera," Dulce said, and held her breath.

"Sorry," the girl said. "She's no longer working here. Would you like the new director, Tyesha Couvillier?"

Dulce shook her head, but then realized the woman couldn't see her. "Does Marisol have . . . any new contact information?"

"She's on our board of directors," the woman offered. "You can send a general email to the board and it will get to her eventually."

Dulce took down the email, and the letters on her phone screen blurred. She was stuck. With barely enough cash to get through a week and a sinking feeling in her gut. She reached for a tissue. She didn't want the tears to mar the silk of her designer dress.

Hotels were out of the question now. She had to save money. On her way out of the airport, she took the bus. Traffic was jammed and travel was slow. Everyone was talking about the storm. According to the National Weather Service, María was now a dangerous hurricane that was likely to hit Puerto Rico hard.

Two hours later, she arrived at a storage space in Carolina, a little bit inland from San Juan. It was the kind where you got a key and could come and go twenty-four hours.

She spoke English to the clerk. If she spoke Spanish, they'd hear her Dominican accent and she might not be treated as well.

"I'm worried about my condo," she said. "We're near the beach, and I want to store a few things a little more inland, you know?"

"Of course," he said.

She paid cash for a month, which was their minimum. Actually she paid for two months, because the first month was free. She got the smallest space they had, eight by ten feet, and it cost less than one night at any hotel that wasn't a dump.

Outside, someone had discarded a small card table made of flimsy metal. She scooped it up and it was the first thing she put in the space.

Overhead, there was a bare fixture that hung from the ceiling, but it had an electrical outlet in the side above the bulb. She made a note to buy an extension cord. This might work.

On her way out to get food that evening, she saw a woman dragging a mattress out onto the street.

"Do you need help with that?" Dulce asked.

The woman thanked her profusely. "My granddaughter was supposed to come help me, but everything is moving so slow since the hurricane. The first one, Irma."

Dulce grabbed the other end and together, they pulled it out onto the street.

"Such a shame you're getting rid of this," Dulce said. "It's memory foam."

The woman shook her head. "My son in the US got it for me. He works for a mattress company. But the house flooded in the hurricane."

"It got wet?" Dulce asked.

The woman nodded as they set it on the street. "Mildew. I'm getting rid of it now."

"It doesn't seem moldy at all," Dulce said.

"Not now," the woman said. "But in a few months?" She shook her head.

"Can I take it?" Dulce asked.

"You don't want a moldy mattress," the woman said. "Let me connect you with my son. He can get you a deal."

"Just for a couple of weeks or so til I leave Puerto Rico," Dulce said. "It shouldn't be that bad for a short time."

"Okay," the woman said. But she insisted on giving Dulce the name of the mattress company and of her son. Dulce picked up her phone as if she was writing them down. But instead, she was calling an Uber big enough to take the mattress to her storage space.

She went out again, and returned to the storage space after dark on the bus. She carried a large box, containing only a bag of groceries, an extension cord, and some takeout. You were supposed to enter with a car, but she entered the code and walked in, even as the gate slid wide enough to admit a vehicle.

"Excuse me," she heard a male voice behind her. She turned to see a security guard in the bright exterior lighting.

"Let me help you with that," he said. His words were offering assistance, but the sly grin was all come-on.

"No need," Dulce said. "It's light."

"I would be remiss if I didn't help the customers," he said.

Dulce looked and saw an older man lugging a trunk on a hand cart to a small hatchback.

"How sweet of you to offer," Dulce said, then called to the elderly man. "Señor, do you need help?"

"*Sí, por favor,*" he said.

"This security guard can help the customers," Dulce said. She smiled at the guard. "Thanks so much for the offer." And she disappeared around the corner as the guard went grudgingly to help the old man.

Dulce made sure no one was looking as she slipped into the storage space. She plugged in an extension cord and screwed in a much dimmer bulb. She didn't want anyone to be able to see the light from outside.

She set up the latest episode of *A Woman's Dark Past*, on her phone, then watched it on her mattress and ate the takeout. She had a bottle of rum, a few RampUp! energy drinks, some peanut butter cookies, yucca chips, and a gallon of water. Now that she had the mattress, this place was practically a palace.

Chapter 12

Monday, September 18—Two days before landfall

By five AM, it was official. There was a hurricane warning for Puerto Rico. That day, the storm went through some of the quickest rapid intensification ever measured.

In New York, Marisol became frantic. She had to get Nidia, Zara, and the baby out of Puerto Rico.

She called her travel agent.

"What do you mean there aren't any flights?" she demanded. "They can fly any day, any airline, to any city, any time in the next forty-eight hours. And I'm willing to pay any fucking price."

Marisol took a breath. Her travel agent didn't deserve to bear the brunt of her upset. "I'm sorry," she said. "I'm just really worried about my family."

"I understand," the agent said. "But everyone's trying to get out. There literally isn't a single flight. I can put in an alert if anything becomes available."

"Yes, please," Marisol said. "And thank you. I know you're doing your best."

But it wasn't good enough. She had to find a way. In 2005, she'd had clients who just barely managed to get out from New Orleans, but they could drive. No way to drive off an island. Unless you could drive on water . . . She sat up straight with a sudden thought, and dialed another number.

Why hadn't she thought of Lily earlier? She wasn't only good at deploying spike strips on desolate roads in Puerto Rico, but she also had a Trinidadian cousin with a charter boat.

An hour later, Marisol had him on the phone.

"Clive, I'm wondering if there's any way you could pick up my family in Puerto Rico. There's this other hurricane coming and I can't get them on a flight out."

"Hurricane María," he said. "I hear it's gonna be bad. I won't be able to get there beforehand. It's just not safe to go out on the sea right now. But keep me posted. I can come after the storm dies down. Are they near the coast?"

"Yes," Marisol said. "Las Palmas. It's just up from the harbor."

"I'll look it up, and see if they allow international vessels there."

"Whatever you have to do," Marisol said. "I can pay for you to take them to Miami or whatever port is open. Or even all the way to New York."

"Sure thing," Clive said. "Let's be in touch after the hurricane, and we can make a plan. How's their English?"

"Not that great," Marisol said. "But I think it's about to get better."

Tuesday, September 19 — One day before landfall

Dulce stayed glued to the tiny screen of her phone. "It now appears likely that María will be at Category 5 intensity when it moves over the US Virgin Islands and Puerto Rico," said a spokesman with the National Weather Service. "Preparations to protect life and property should be rushed to completion."

All her property fit in a suitcase. The storage space was to protect her life. She'd gotten as much food as she could from the grocery store. A can opener. Bottles of water.

The Puerto Rican government had opened five hundred schools and other buildings as shelters. But that was a hard pass. She had everything she needed to wait out the storm.

Later that afternoon, she watched the reporting of Hurricane María's devastation on the island of Dominica. Only then did her anxiety rise. She stayed in the unit throughout the day, listening in headphones, trying not to gasp audibly. Every noise she heard outside, she held her breath, afraid she'd be discovered. But the footsteps always passed. She kept her phone plugged in, as she stayed glued to predictions for when, where, and how hard the storm would hit Puerto Rico.

Dulce drank the bottles of RampUp! and stayed on her phone through the night.

The rain had begun, and the power was out. Dulce's anxiety became overlaid with boredom. She needed to save her phone battery for after the hurricane.

Sitting still made her feel nuts, so she pulled out the pedicure stuff. The stone to scrub off the rough skin. The lotion to make her feet soft. The foam to keep her toes apart.

She did the exfoliation by feel. She wet the stone a bit with the drinking water, then scrubbed at her feet in the dark.

She only used the flashlight for nail polish. A base coat of blue, topped in a clear coat with glitter. They sparkled in the beam of the flashlight.

She was usually too impatient to do more than one coat of nail polish. Always too impatient to wait for each coat to dry. She would put on the next one too soon and mess her nails up. But now, she had nothing but time.

Chapter 13

Wednesday, September 20—Landfall

By the wee hours of the morning, Dulce's anxiety had risen again. Outside, the wind clawed at the island. She couldn't see through the windowless room, but the sounds had her panicked. With shaking hands, she rolled most of the marijuana Ellis had left her into a joint and smoked it. She tied up the plastic bag with the last few weed crumbs and tucked it under the corner of the mattress. She just wanted to sleep.

The screaming of the winds made that nearly impossible. And from time to time, she would hear thudding and crashing. Branches torn from trees and siding ripped off of houses turned to projectiles that reverberated when they hit against the concrete and metal of her building.

She needed rum.

Dulce drank half the bottle. As she waited for the alcohol to take effect, she kept her eyes on the tiny screen of her phone and watched the progress of the hurricane toward Puerto Rico. The Technicolor swirl of the storm had moved onto the map outline of the island. Yet her eyes kept straying to two nearby islands, Santo Domingo and Cuba, and both appeared to be safely out of the storm's path. If only she were in either place, she'd be safe and dry and in a house, not a fucking storage space waiting out a dangerous storm. Especially Cuba, where they had successfully evacuated a million people and didn't have a single death during Hurricane Katrina.

Why the fuck hadn't she stayed there? She had Cuba on her mind as the combination of alcohol and weed overpowered the anxiety, and she lay back on the mattress, settling into an uneasy chemical doze.

Chapter 14

Over a year earlier, when Dulce had first arrived in Cuba, she was sure Jerry would come after her. She had a vague memory of drunk dialing him to say goodbye before she left New York. Maybe she had mentioned Cuba? Maybe she had said her grandmother's last name? At some level she knew it was far-fetched.

Just because he had stalked her from The Bronx to Manhattan didn't mean he would stalk her all the way to her grandmother's small town outside Havana. But she felt the clench in her chest every time she saw the back of a tall, heavy man. Every time she caught sight of a thickset guy with straight dark hair, buzzed short at the nape of his neck. There was a tourist from Madrid and a businessman from Bogota, and plenty of locals who fit the description.

Her first couple of months in Cuba, her body was on high alert. Every time she and her family went out somewhere, her eyes scanned for him. Mostly she stayed in the house. Her grandmother was recovering from a stroke, and Dulce was there to take care of her while her uncle worked during the day. They had previously had a caretaker, but now that would be Dulce's job. Everybody in Cuba had a job. But even staying in the house all day, Dulce couldn't relax. Men's voices on the street made her jumpy. Her eyes flew to the door each time it opened. She was certain Jerry would come charging in, furious.

As it turned out, Jerry never stormed into the house. Instead, news of his death slipped in quietly by way of the New York paper her uncle read. "Bronx Man Fatally Shot" was the headline of a story without warning or preamble. "Jerry Rios, 46 . . . pronounced dead . . . .44 caliber bullet . . . shot twice."

And it was as if a switch had been flipped. No longer was Dulce oriented toward terrifying visions of Jerry coming after her in the future. It was as if the news had spun her around several times, turning her in an about face toward the past. After receiving the news of his death, she began recalling every dimension of his brutality, all the times he had come after her when he was alive.

The flashbacks started. Each time she closed her eyes at night, she was reliving the worst of it. The rough sex with him, with clients. The times she'd said yes, but hadn't meant it. The times she'd said no and it hadn't mattered.

The memories descended on her at night like an avalanche. She started hanging out with a party set in Havana, staying out til the wee hours, coming home on the camello buses in the morning, exhausted. She started drinking heavily. She woke from a nightmare in the mid-day and drank half a bottle of rum to quell it. Soon, she'd finished all the liquor in the house.

Her grandmother didn't complain or scold her. But a few days later, a cousin named Josefina appeared from Santiago to stay with them. In her white clothes and colorful beads, Dulce knew she was a practitioner of Santería, the syncretized African tradition that was so strong in the Latin Caribbean. Josefina called it Lucumí.

She gave Dulce a ritual bath, herbs and flower petals and Florida water filling their grandmother's claw-foot tub. She cleansed her with a live chicken, the bird squawking and flailing as Josefina held it by its feet, its wings beating against Dulce's naked skin. She said prayers in Yoruba over her. And through it all, Dulce sobbed and sobbed.

When the nightmares woke her, Josefina was there with a cool palm for Dulce's forehead and a soothing song, her contralto voice flowing with melodies in the liturgical language of Ifá, singing stories of the Orisha and calming the twist in Dulce's chest.

"I feel like he's haunting me," Dulce confessed one day. "I know he's dead, but he just won't leave me in peace."

Josefina lit candles that night. Spit rum onto a stick covered with dusty feathers and bright ribbons. She read broken pieces of coconut.

"He's not here," she said. "He's not at peace, but he's not here. New York, I think."

"Then how come he's got such a hold on me since he got killed?"

"He had a hold on you when he was alive," Josefina said. "But sometimes it not til you're finally safe that you can see just how much danger you've been in."

"What can I do?" Dulce asked. "Can you give me another ritual to cleanse him off me?"

"There's nothing more to do," Josefina said. "Now you just need to allow yourself to feel what it was you weren't able to feel before."

She gave Dulce a couple of prayers to say. And at Dulce's insistence, she gave her a spell: write his name on a piece of paper and put it in the freezer.

Dulce continued to have nightmares. She would lay on the couch next to her grandmother and watch telenovelas and cry.

This was when she began to watch *A Woman's Dark Past*.

Teenage Xoana, in a school uniform, walks down the hallway of a boarding school to the main office. A woman in a neat suit sits behind a desk.

"You wanted to see me, headmistress?"

"You have a visitor," she says.

Tío Juan steps forward from the sidelines. He isn't really her uncle, but a trusted friend of the family.

Xoana gasps when she sees him. "Is it my mother?"

"She's alive," Tío Juan says. "But she's in a coma. You must come see her."

"Your teachers have prepared homework for you," the headmistress says, handing her a packet. "You need to keep up with your classes to maintain your scholarship."

"Of course, headmistress," Xoana takes the packet and exits with Tío Juan.

The next day, Xoana is at the hospital with her mother, a beautiful woman in her mid-thirties. Xoana sits on the side of the bed. A monitor beeps in the background as her mother lies still.

"You would be so proud of me," Xoana says. "My grades have been good. I'm learning to play tennis." She laughs and shakes her head. "Tennis. Who am I turning into? I was hoping it would be easier to make friends playing tennis, but most of the girls have been there for years. It's hard to get close to anyone." Xoana begins to cry. "And I just miss you so much. I had this dream that if I just came home, just held your hand, kissed your cheek, **you**'d wake up. Please, Mamá, wake up." She sobs into her **mo**ther's chest. "How am I supposed to go back to school? I just want to stay here with you." She wipes her eyes. "But I know that school is what you wanted for me. What you still want. I'll go, Mamá. I'll stay strong for you. But you have to stay strong for me. Don't give up on this life. Stay strong."

Tío Juan walks into the room. "Xoana," he says. We have to go."

"Adios, Mamá," she says, and leaves with Tío Juan, holding back tears.

Later, at dusk, they are driving in the car. Xoana is wiping her eyes. She takes several deep breaths and looks around.

"This isn't the way to school," Xoana says.

"We just have to make a brief stop," Tío Juan says.

Later, Xoana sits in a dim room with a single window. Outside, it's completely dark.

The door opens, and Xoana stands up.

"Tío Juan," she says. "Where have you been? I thought—you're not Tío Juan."

"No, sweet thing," the strange man says.

"Where's my Tío Juan?" Xoana asks.

"A girl can have more than one uncle," the man says, advancing toward her.

"Get away from me," Xoana says, as the camera zooms in on the stack of homework on the dresser. In the background, Xoana screams, and the camera fades out.

Each day Dulce lay on the couch, crying beside her grandmother and watching soap operas. And slowly, Jerry began to take breaks from haunting Dulce's dreams. Sometimes she'd dream of her *tía*'s house in Santo Domingo. Or that she was back in middle school and hadn't done her homework for English, the one class she loved, the only subject she excelled in. Or she dreamed that she was flying. Dulce loved those dreams. When she woke up, she didn't feel leaden and could tell that her life still held plenty of possibilities.

Yet even after the flashbacks slowed down, the tears continued.

Her grandmother sat on one end of the recliner sofa, and

Dulce lay with her head in her lap. They watched afternoons of television, until Dulce got up and made dinner. Each night, her uncle would come home and eat with them, bringing groceries and stories from his job as a pharmacist in Havana, and newspapers that talked about the rest of the world, one that Dulce hardly bothered to go out and see.

Yet a couple of months later, Dulce began to take short trips to the local market. Soon, in addition to cooking and keeping house and taking care of her grandmother, Dulce was shopping and even taking directions from her grandmother on keeping the garden.

Eventually, even the crying stopped. And then there was nothing to connect her to her old life in New York, not even the grief.

Until six weeks later, when her grandmother had another stroke. She needed more care than Dulce could give her at home, and the family moved her into a nursing facility. The house was lonely all day. Dulce sat and watched *A Woman's Dark Past* by herself, but it wasn't the same.

Teenage Xoana is in a favela, a poor neighborhood in the city. She sits on a ragged couch with three other girls.

They hear an altercation outside, and a pair of women run in. They're dressed like respectable suburban ladies, one blonde, germanic looking, the other dark.

"Quick, girls, come with us," they say. "We can get help for you."

Xoana jumps up, but the three other girls move more slowly.

"Did Juan send you?" one of the girls asks.

"No," the blonde woman says. "We're here to rescue you."

The girls begin to follow them towards the door.

"The police are right outside," the other woman says.

The girls recoil as if they have discovered that the door is on fire.

"No police," Xoana says.

"We're not officials," the blonde woman says. "I'm from the university, and she's a journalist. We don't have any authority."

"The police are men who can't be trusted with young girls," Xoana says. "You wouldn't bring a wolf to rescue chickens, would you?"

The two women look at each other.

"Where else can we take you?" the blonde woman asks.

"Not to any of the authorities," Xoana says. "But somewhere Tío Juan can't find us."

"We'll figure it out," the blonde woman says to the other. "I'll go tell the police the house was empty. You bring the car around to pick up the girls."

In Cuba, Dulce's uncle decided to move his daughter and her two kids into the house. Dulce was welcome to stay, and he could probably get her a job at the pharmacy. Everybody in Cuba worked. Now that she was no longer her grandmother's caretaker, she'd need to find something. Dulce was in the process of cleaning the house for the arrival of her cousins, when Josefina invited her to come live in Santiago. She liked her uncle, and she enjoyed their visits to her grandmother, but she truly loved Josefina. She finished cleaning the house and her uncle took her to catch the bus.

On the long trip across the island, she met a young Cuban-American man who was visiting from Miami. He was every part of the US that she missed. They flirted the whole ride down, and by the end of the trip, he promised to come by and see her.

Josefina welcomed Dulce with open arms. She had two teenage daughters of her own, but there was a small back room where they put a twin mattress. The next night, the four women of the house were sitting on the couch after dinner watching *A Woman's Dark Past.*

Xoana sits with the blonde woman in the woman's study.

"Why did you pick me to bring to your home?" Xoana asks. "Out of the four girls that you rescued. Why me?"

"I couldn't take four girls to come live with me," the woman says. "I had to choose."

"Yes, but why me?"

There's a knock at the door.

The woman looks up sharply.

"Who is it?" she asks.

In the hallway, we see a blonde, teenage Izabel, standing outside the study door.

"Mamá," Izabel says. "What time are we leaving tonight?"

"You know you are not to bother me while I'm working," the woman says sharply. "I told your father I'd be down at dinnertime."

In the hallway, Izabel storms away with a scowl.

"You want to know why I chose you?" the woman says. "You were different." She leans back in her chair. "When I asked who wanted to leave, you were the first to rise. You were the one who spoke up. You're obviously educated. The other girls were more of what I expected. You weren't. We have a network of families that are prepared to take young women in. I hadn't been part of the network, but for you, I made an exception."

"So you want to—what—study me?"

"I will be doing several interviews, yes," the woman says. "But I also want to do more than get data. I want to make a difference."

"How many interviews?"

"Two or three," the woman says. "I'll find out about your life story, and monitor your emotional responses."

"So you'll interview me," Xoana says. "Do I get to learn anything about you?"

"Not much to tell," the woman says. "My parents immigrated from Germany. They were very focused on education. I defied them by marrying at twenty to a young German man and having Izabel before I finished at university, but the marriage didn't work out. We divorced. Izabel stayed with me. Eventually, I finished my doctorate in psychology. Then I remarried a Brazilian man, and we have two boys."

"Okay," Xoana says. "So I'll do two interviews and that's it?"

"Two in the next week," the woman says. "But then I'll do follow up interviews every year for the next three years."

"So that's the price for living here with you and your family?"

"Xoana," the woman says. "Not everything has a price."

"Maybe not in your world," Xoana says. "But in my world it does."

The novela was interrupted by a knock at the door. As a well-known priest, Josefina was used to people coming to see her at all hours.

But when Josefina opened the door, it was the young man Dulce had met on the bus. Josefina regarded him with narrowed eyes and only asked him in reluctantly.

He invited Dulce out and she eagerly accepted.

Josefina followed Dulce into the bathroom. "He's not good for you," she warned as Dulce put on a bright shade of lipstick for her date.

"Don't worry," Dulce said, regarding her face in the mirror. "I'm just going to have a little fun. Didn't you say I should focus more on the joy in life?"

Josefina sucked her teeth. "That boy is definitely not what I had in mind."

But Dulce went. He took her to a local bar and they drank tequila. They had sex in his cousin's car.

For the first time ever, Dulce insisted that he wear a condom. And he did.

She felt so bossy and powerful. She liked him. But she especially liked this new version of herself. This bolder, sassier version of herself. So when he asked her to come to Miami with him, she went. Hugged Josefina goodbye and thanked her for everything. Then let the guy from the bus buy her a ticket to Miami.

Dulce had a friend from New York she could stay with. But when they first arrived in Miami, the Cuban-American guy said she could stay with him for a few nights. So she did. A few days stretched into a few weeks. By then, he had convinced her to stop using condoms and she had gotten on the pill. Within a month, they had broken up, and she was living with her New York friend. She was deciding whether or not to go back to Cuba when she met a Dominican drug dealer and he had wooed her.

"Stay in Miami and be with me," he said over dinner at a steakhouse.

"How would I get a job?" Dulce asked. "I can't stay at my friend's forever."

"*Mami*, you won't need to work," he said, his voice like the purr of a leopard. "I can take care of everything. Would you do me the honor of letting me pay your bills? Money is nothing to me when it comes to an amazing chick like you."

The attention dazzled her. She said she'd be willing to try it. He moved her into a one-bedroom apartment. She never asked him to use a condom. Not even at first.

Chapter 15

Wednesday, September 20—Landfall

Water flooded the storage space as Dulce slept. It seeped through the metal slats in the pull-down door of the storage space. It pooled on the concrete floor. It rose around the mattress where Dulce was sleeping. Although she was not exactly sleeping, more like in a stupor or a spell from the cocktail of rum and marijuana.

Water seeped up, turning the mattress into a giant sponge. The moisture soaked into the fabric of her clothes. Inch by inch, the line crept up her feet, her beautifully painted blue toenails. It saturated her hair, destroying the remains of a blowout, her hair blooming into springing curls all around her head.

Still she slept.

Her shoulder flinched with the moisture tickling her ear canal. Then both ears filled and the tickle was gone. Her body stilled again in sleep. The now full canals dulled the howls of the storm.

The flooding outside was anything but gentle, yet the water could only seep in through the slats in the metal door, and the crack at the bottom above the cement floor. So the water level rose slowly. It crept up gently along her neck, her jawline, her cheekbone. The water sidled up tenderly, like a lover.

She slept on when the water first touched her lips. Only when it began to drip into her mouth did she truly stir. The water, pooling in the back of her throat and making it impossible to breathe properly now. The prince had come. The rescuer on his horse. The discoverer. The pimp.

Her left hip was soaked now in the floodwater. Her right hipbone jutted above the waterline like a disappearing island of brown skin.

Water trickled into her throat, and she coughed weakly, her gag reflex still kicking, part of her brain began to register the fact that her life was in danger. Some fight-or-flight response activated her tongue, dragging it into action to spit some of the water out.

Her life was in danger.

She sputtered to consciousness, coughing through a burning throat. In total darkness. Completely soaked. She fought through the mental haze to orient herself, to make sense of the bizarre combination of mattress and moisture, screaming winds and crashing thuds.

Storage space. Hurricane. Flooding. Fuck.

Chapter 16

Marisol's cousin had done everything right. In preparation for the hurricane, Nidia had boarded up the windows, stored plenty of water, gotten canned foods, bags of dried rice and beans, a camping stove, a wind-up radio, and plenty of propane.

When Hurricane Georges hit in the late nineties, her mother was still alive. As Mami showed her how to cover the windows and secure the supplies, they both recalled Hurricane Hugo, which had come through Puerto Rico a decade before.

Nidia had developed the habit of saving gallon bottles, and when the warning for Hurricane Irma came up, she had dozens of bottles that she filled from the tap and stacked up. She spent the entire week before Irma getting ready. They had done okay in that first storm, so she just needed to supplement a bit of the eaten food, and refill a few of the gallon jugs of water. New batteries for the flashlights. Additional kerosene for the lantern.

And for the baby: wipes (regular and antibacterial), diapers, infant formula—in case anything happened to Zara, and baby foods he could eat. She had even sealed up the passports and beloved family photos in a zip lock bag. She had consolidated several recommended lists. She had checked and rechecked.

So when her cousin Marisol called, sounding slightly panicked, Nidia was confident. They had gotten through Irma well enough. No need to worry. She'd call when it was over.

Later, she would describe the hurricane to Marisol. If you lay on the tarmac under a jumbo jet when it was taking off, that was what it sounded like. Except it went on for hours, and the whole time, you were terrified that the plane would crush you.

The family had gathered in the back bedroom to wait out the storm. Of all the rooms, it had the smallest window and was on the side of the house away from the hill.

During the night, the baby had grown accustomed to the loud jet engine noise, and now he lay on the bed and slept as Nidia and Zara played dominoes by lantern light. They couldn't play a proper game with only two of them, but Marisol had taught them a different version she'd picked up in the US, where you scored by multiples of fives on the ends. You could play with three or with just two people if you made a pile to pick from when you didn't have a play.

Zara had just scored and was gloating loudly when a huge gust of wind blew the bedroom door open.

Zara's cry of victory turned into a shriek, which woke the baby. The two women looked up to see the roof peeling off the back bedroom, as if the house were a can of sardines. Wind began to drive rain into the suddenly defenseless room.

Zara grabbed the baby, and they all rushed out of the bedroom, but the roof of the living room was being torn off, as well.

"The bathroom!" Nidia yelled, and the two of them ran in.

The baby was shrieking, and Zara sat on the toilet lid to nurse him. Nidia felt panicked. What if the roof of this part of the house came off, as well? She cursed herself and her lists. She wasn't prepared enough. She should have gone to the emergency hurricane shelter.

But it was too late for that now. They needed to wait out the storm the best they could.

She could hear the rain pouring in, and water was already seeping under the bathroom door.

"I'm going to get some of the supplies," she told Zara. Nidia opened the bathroom door, and her daughter's cry of alarm was swallowed by the raging noise of the storm. Even three steps into the living room she was soaked. She crouched as she hurried to the back hallway. Grabbing a bottle of water, the lantern, and a plastic bag of canned food, she turned and ran back into the bathroom.

The two women huddled together and prayed.

Dulce sat dazed on the sodden mattress in the dark and tried to pull herself together. She needed to see. Her phone. She needed her phone. It was rigged up above her. Plugged into the socket on the side of the light switch, with an extension cord to the card table. The phone wasn't charging now, but even without a signal, the flashlight would work.

She stood up, on top of the mattress on wobbly legs. The only sign of light was a dull gray line that ran along the seam of the storage space's door. The interior was otherwise pitch black. She carefully waved her hands out in front of her until the side of her hand touched something. The marijuana caused a bit of a delay in relaying the message to her brain, so it took a minute to get hold of the cord that led to the phone.

The water was up to the middle of her calves, even as she stood on the mattress. Carefully, she followed the extension cord to the phone itself, and pressed the button to light up the screen. In the feeble glow, she could see the slick surface of the rising flood around her, water seeping in between the slats of the storage unit door.

The rush of rising water was deafening. She had to get out.

Ignoring the few texts she'd gotten before her signal went out, she turned on the phone's flashlight. Now that she could see properly, she opened up her wheeling suitcase, blessedly dry on the card table. She pulled out the water wallet Phillip had given her, as well as all her money. Then she stuffed the cash, phone, and charger into the wallet, along with her passport and keys. She left the flashlight on, and she could still see its glow from within the translucent plastic.

Dulce couldn't stand to leave all those designer clothes. The suitcase itself might not survive, but there were thousands of dollars of fashion in there. A little water couldn't possibly ruin all of it. She grabbed the suitcase and waded over to the door, the splashing of the water around her barely discernible from the storm's deluge outside, and the slosh from the slats in the wall that were weeping into the storage unit.

The water was above her knees now. She looked up and realized that water was coming in from nearly the top of the door. Through the fog of the weed and alcohol, it took her a moment to grasp the significance of that fact. It meant that outside, the flood would be over her head. She needed to get out now, or she would be trapped, and the water was rising.

She put the glowing water wallet around her neck, and dragged the suitcase across the mattress to the door. With every step, the suitcase became more waterlogged and difficult to pull.

She slid the bolt open and tried to lift the door, but it was stuck. The pressure of the water outside made it nearly impossible to move.

She gripped with both hands, and could barely lift it.

Outside, the winds continued to howl and the whoosh of water around her was a constant crashing.

Rain beat against the top of the door that wasn't already

submerged. Water was up to her ass now. She waded across the space and grabbed the small metal card table. It was almost completely submerged now. If she could wedge it under the door, she could get out.

She set the table beside her and squatted halfway down, then used both arms and the power of her legs to lift the door. It rose high enough, and she managed to kick the table underwater to wedge it.

Now the water was flooding in fast. The current pressed against her body, pushing her away from the door. She grabbed the suitcase to slide it out ahead of her. She had barely gotten it out in front of her when the card table broke.

The huge metal door came down with a crash, barely missing Dulce's head. She recoiled and fell back into the water. As she floundered to her feet, she realized that now only the suitcase was wedged under the door.

Dulce stood up and the flood was up to her chest. Her heart hammered underwater now. She had to get out before the current rushing in drowned her.

She took several breaths and realized she would have to abandon the suitcase. It was the only thing that could prop open the door. But it didn't leave much room to get through. She crossed herself and plunged back under the water, sticking her feet out first. She could feel the current pulling at her legs outside the space. Her ass stuck under the door, despite the current's pressure. She wriggled hard, but there was no leverage, nothing to push back against.

She swam back in and stood up to breathe, but the water was over her head now. She had stand on top of the mattress to get some air. The panic was rising. She had to try again to escape.

This time, she moved down to another section of the door, one nearer the corner of the mattress. On her second try, she dived under, and stuck her feet out through the open slot below the door, using her arms to push off against the mattress edge. Inch by inch, she wriggled out. She felt like her lungs were burning. It was taking too long.

She pushed herself back into the space and went up for air. The water was nearly at the ceiling. She had to jump off the mattress and bob to the surface to gulp the least bit of oxygen. Up and down she bobbed, trying to think. After several jumps, the mattress shifted a bit, and by the glow of the flashlight, she could see her little bag of weed float up through the water. All the jumping must have dislodged it from under the mattress corner.

She snatched it up and bobbed up for more air. Her head could barely fit between the water's surface and the room's ceiling now.

She raised the bag over her head and untied it, dumping out the weed. Then she filled the bag with air. She jumped up for one final bob, and took in a lungful of air, before diving down under the surface.

She pressed her feet out through the open space below the door. Since the water was a bit deeper, the current at the bottom wasn't as strong now. Dulce pushed with her arms against the mattress. She couldn't use the entire heel of both hands, as she was using one of them to hold the bag shut, like pinching a balloon. She wriggled as best she could, and was about halfway through, when she ran out of air. She pulled the plastic bag to her lips and inhaled the oxygen. A few breaths in and out of the plastic. Then she let the bag go and pushed off with both hands against the mattress. It shifted a bit, not quite giving her the resistance she needed.

She heaved again. Her chest was burning. She was running out of air and now it felt like she was stuck halfway. She needed better leverage. So she grabbed for the suitcase. It was completely wedged under the heavy metal door. She pressed against it with all her strength. Suddenly, with a scrape of metal door against her skin, her body pushed free. She was outside the storage space, her body flowing, tumbling with the current. She righted herself beneath the water and used both legs to press off the ground, pushing her way upward, sputtering to the surface of the water.

She heard the howl of the wind and felt the lashing of the rain. She gulped a mix of air and rainwater, coughing as the deluge of the storm continued to pour on her in the open water, the strong current at the surface dragging her along.

But she couldn't stay up. She was still a beginning swimmer, and her body flailed and began to go down. Yet even in her panic, she remembered floating with Zavier. *Lean back. Let your body relax.* Her life probably depended on it, so she forced herself to breathe, to let her muscles go.

She knew how to do this. How many times had she been fucking some guy to get money for Jerry? How many times had some creep been pounding away in her and she just drifted off? Sometimes with booze or weed, but sometimes just her, commanding herself to drift.

Somehow, she managed it. Her body relaxed amid the screaming wind and rain. She floated down the courtyard of the storage space, the water wallet pressing against her ribcage beneath the tank top.

She floated in a surreal landscape. The sun hadn't set, but the rain and storm clouds obliterated most of the natural light. The floodwater created an artificially high ground level, as if the earth had swallowed up the bottom half of the building. Meanwhile everything above the water line was a murky and ghoulish grayscale of what it had looked like the day before.

Suddenly, the current sped up. Dulce blinked the water out of her eyes and tried to orient herself. The storage space was U-shaped. Rainfall was flooding down from the hills, and getting trapped in the elbow curve of the building. She was moving swiftly with the floodwater now, down along the building's side. In the fading light, she could see that she was on a collision course to crash head-first into one of the second floor storage unit doors. Frantically, she kicked and paddled with her arms to turn her body around, so she was floating feet-first.

Ahead of her, water pounded into the second floor storage spaces. She leaned back in the water, stretching her legs toward one of the metal doors.

The current was too fast now. Was she going to break both of her legs on impact? But this was also familiar, like jumping off the roof of her *tía*'s shed. Yet this time, it was the force of water, not gravity, speeding her toward a collision.

She heard her brother Santiago's voice in her mind: "Bend your knees, Luqui!" And as the current pressed her toward impact, she bent her knees as she hit one of the metal doors, absorbing the shock.

Meanwhile, all around her, water kept rushing, crashing, and it was tossing her around. She couldn't stabilize. She paddled frantically to stay afloat. Her arms and legs were starting to get fatigued. She'd drown if she couldn't find somewhere to rest.

The water was even higher now, and the current ducked her under and slammed her, shoulder-first, into something hard. She grabbed for it, and in the dim glow of the phone flashlight, she could see that it was a railing. Yes! The second floor had an exterior walkway, surrounded by a railing of several parallel metal bars. It was about a foot underwater. Dulce knew if she held the railing and made her way, hand over hand in either direction, she could get to the stairwell in one of the corners. The building had three stories. If she was able to make it to the top floor, she might be safe.

The sky had turned to charcoal, a diffuse not-quite-dark that spit an avalanche of water and wind. In the limited glow of her phone light in the water wallet necklace, she couldn't see which corner stairwell of the building might be closer, but the current was pushing her to the left, so she started moving with it.

As she made her way, the water steadily rose up over the railing, and it became difficult to hold the the top bar underwater and keep her head above the surface. As she got closer to the corner, she could see there was a whirlpool from the inflooding water, filled with debris, but also a perpendicular light post that stuck up well above the water level. She ducked her head under, and used the full length of her arms to shimmy over to it.

When Dulce grabbed the light post in the corner, she was nearly sucked into the maelstrom of branches and debris that had lodged there. Her arms were totally fatigued now. She clung to the light post, but beneath the surface, the current was pressing her body against the railing. With the last of her upper-body strength, she heaved herself up over the top of the railing and into the open stairwell.

Her body tumbled in, but something was caught around her neck. One of her hands grabbed the lamp post so it wouldn't choke her. What the fuck was it? Her water wallet? No. Her free hand scrabbled at her throat and she realized that the Cartier chain had hooked on something. A branch? A piece of roofing? Dulce pulled, but the Cartier chain was stronger than she expected.

Her body was on the inside of the railing, but she was tethered at the neck to the debris somehow. Her flailing feet could nearly touch the building. She held the light post with both hands, but as the water kept rising, she was just able to keep her head above the surface. The current was pressing her toward the building. If she didn't get loose, she could strangle or drown. She contracted her core and pulled her legs up under her, in a fetal position, then planted her feet against the railing. She took a last gulp of air as the water level rose nearly above her head, and pushed off against the railing with all her strength. The chain finally broke, but the momentum sent her tumbling toward the building, with the current accelerating her movement, the water harsh, insistent. She had lost control of the movement of her body. She was another piece of debris in the rapids. The combined force sent her spinning into the stairwell, and she banged the back of her head into the edge of one of the steps.

The building was made of mostly cement, and the impact of her head against concrete and metal stairs was unyielding to her skull. She blacked out for a moment, then the storm woke her with a wet slap to the face.

When she stood up, rising from the water, she felt dizzy. Movement was hard because of her fatigued limbs and sodden clothes, and also because of the strong winds that lashed into the stairwell. She clung to the bannister and moved up to the third floor. The stairwells were open, and rain drove in, but there was a covered part at the corner of the hallway.

In that small piece of shelter, the winds and rain were a bit buffeted. She huddled into a corner, and hugged her knees. She shivered with the cold from the wind, despite the humidity and tropical moisture of the rain.

A few moments later, the water was at her feet again. She shook her head and began to drag herself up the stairs. She had to get to higher ground.

On the landing halfway up between the third floor and the roof, she stopped to rest, protected from the wind and rain. She panted as her heart hammered against her rib cage. It was almost totally dark now. A dimension of dark beyond any she had ever seen. Nothing illuminated anywhere. Except her phone in the water wallet around her neck. She had better save that light.

Carefully, she took the phone out of the wallet and turned off the flashlight. Then she sealed it back up. She leaned against the wall and let her breathing return to normal.

But the water level was still rising. She couldn't rest here much longer. She needed to head up that final flight of stairs leading up to the roof. Halfway up the steps, she collapsed. Her body was beyond exhausted. Her brain was concussed from the blunt trauma. And as she slept, her heart doggedly beat, gradually pumping the last of the marijuana and alcohol out of her bloodstream.

When the storm had finally passed, Nidia got up to survey the damage. It was still raining, but the winds had died down. Zara and the baby were asleep in the bathtub. Thankfully, the part of the roof above the bathroom had stayed intact.

But the rest of the house? Rain drove in through a roofless ceiling. The back wall was just . . . gone. It wasn't really gone. Instead, on the ground behind the house lay the mortal remains of the wall, tangled with mud and foliage. But it was against that wall that Nidia had so carefully stacked her supplies. When the storm had blown out the wall, it scattered everything in the backyard like shrapnel. The water bottles had all fallen and the lids burst off. Gallons and gallons of clean water mixing with the swampy aftermath of the storm. The bags of rice and beans lay in mud, rain drumming down on them. The radio was soaked. The cook stove, the propane, the batteries, the extra kerosene were nowhere in sight. Perhaps they were hidden under something? Hard to spot through the rain in the tangle of fallen leaves and debris?

She searched all afternoon. She found the propane. The batteries. The kerosene and a few more cans of food. But the cook stove was lost (or perhaps looted) and the bottles of water had all opened when they hit the ground. Only one was upright and half full with clear water. The rest had a telltale tint of red dirt. She brought the half-full jug inside. They could use it for something other than drinking. She tried the tap and found that the water wasn't even running.

The roads near Nidia's house were all washed out. In her front driveway, a tree had fallen on the car and smashed the roof in. The windshield and all the windows were shattered. Nidia looked in to see the gas pedal and brake were peeking out from several inches of water. Rain was still coming in the holes where glass used to be.

So that was it. There was no real way to get to the shelter.

When Dulce opened her eyes, the disorientation was complete. The interior of her body was dehydrated and hungover, despite the fact that she was still sodden and surrounded by water.

Through blurry vision she could see that it was light out and the rain had stopped. But it was the sound that was the strangest of all. So silent. No traffic. No human activity. Even the animals were still. No coqui. No crickets. No insects buzzing around. Just an unnatural quiet.

What the hell was going on? From where she stood on the staircase, she could only see the other storage building. The floodwaters had gone down to the first floor, but the area was still flooded. Somewhere at the bottom was a water-logged suitcase, full of designer clothes, with mud seeping in through the wide teeth of the zipper and sluicing across linen and raw silk.

How was she going to get out of here? Was everything flooded or just her building? Maybe she would be able to see something from the roof. She climbed the stairs and stood at the landing. She tried the knob, and it was locked. But when she pulled on the door, it came loose, a sodden piece of paper dangling from where it had been propping the lock open.

Also, from above the door, some cigarettes fell. Whoever had hidden them had slid a lighter in between the cellophane wrapping and the half-full pack.

Dulce scooped them up.

Out on the roof, she looked out to find a sight more disorienting than she could have imagined. From her vantage point, it was as if someone had run a giant rake across the land, scraping leaves and branches off all of the trees, and felling many of the trunks onto houses, cars, and roads. It had raked roofs off some of the houses, and tossed cars into roads and ditches. It had scraped up all the green foliage. Then it had mulched much of what it had raked, mixing roofing tiles with tree branches, an uprooted traffic sign with several pieces of broken lawn furniture. And then, without planting a thing, this malevolent gardener had overwatered their giant yard, leaving pools and rivulets of muddy water everywhere. The corpse of a dead dog floated by, a mixed breed. The frame of a retriever, but a mottled gray coat. The curls of its fur were sodden with water.

Her mind couldn't quite take in the devastation. She reached for the cigarettes. The pack was dry enough to light. She took a long drag, felt a head rush, and abruptly passed out.

Chapter 17

At first Dulce thought she was hearing disco music. Was she back in the club in Miami? Her body was drenched. She usually didn't let herself dance that hard. She didn't like to sweat out a good blowout in her hair. Her eyes opened for a moment, and it was too bright for a club. Rainwater trickled from her sodden hair into her eyes and she closed them tight again. Everything around her was wet. It made no sense.

The sound above her was like fluttering percussion with a whizzing whine in the background. It reminded her of that part of techno music where the beat drops out, and they were ramping up the dancers all over the floor. The pitch gets higher and higher in anticipation. Dulce was waiting for the beat to drop. The thudding one-two of disco. The ramp-up music kept getting louder. Like some DJ was preparing them for the biggest dance explosion ever, but the beat never dropped.

Instead, Dulce heard a woman's voice over the music. The voice spoke to her in Spanish. Was she okay? She wanted to respond, but wasn't sure of the answer. Yes? No? Was this woman the DJ?

Then, above the whining beat, she heard a man's voice, arguing with the woman in English.

"Ma'am," the male voice said. "My orders are just to fly you over the city to assess the damage. We're not supposed to intervene."

"I'm sorry," the female DJ responded. "If I see a woman lying on a rooftop who may need medical assistance, I'm not going to just leave her there. I don't care what your orders are."

Dulce opened her eyes for another brief second and the vision was so surreal. A helicopter hovering above her. A woman with glasses and bobbed blonde hair under an army cap was climbing down a rope ladder to her. Dulce felt the woman touching her neck for a pulse. Asking her questions in Spanish. Dulce still couldn't answer. Her eyes fluttered shut.

The blonde woman half-dragged her back down off the roof into the shade of the stairwell. "I'm coming back for you," the woman DJ said. And then Dulce heard the music fade out, as the helicopter flew off and she slipped back into unconsciousness.

Nidia, Zara, and the baby moved out of their half-roofless home and stayed with a neighbor whose house had fared better. The first post-hurricane days were taken up with just the basics. Preparing food, keeping everyone sheltered, managing makeshift bathrooms. They shared news with families who lived in the immediate cluster of houses, but it was hard to get info from anyone much beyond that. Nobody had electricity, water, or phone service. One family had a radio, but by the second day, they decided to take out the batteries for more urgent needs.

It had continued to rain, which made it dangerous to go much farther from home, because there was flash flooding in Las Palmas's hilly terrain.

By the fifth day, the neighbor's house where they were staying was out of drinking water. Everyone was running out.

The rain had let up for a bit and Nidia carefully waded down the tributary where the road had been. The water was up to her waist, but she was determined to get to a neighbor on the other side of the hill. She asked if they could spare any drinking water. They were almost out too, but they offered a can of juice. "For the baby."

The neighbors with the juice also had a working radio that could be powered with a crank. Nidia learned that power was out on the entire island. Most roads were blocked. Curfew from six PM to six AM. Nidia was worried about her aunt who lived in a town right in the path of the hurricane. But there was no way to find news of her. Nothing to do but pray.

While Nidia was there gathering news, another neighbor came by. A young woman with wet, frightened eyes. Her mother was diabetic and the insulin she depended on needed refrigeration. They had gotten a battery-operated refrigerator and enough batteries, but some of the batteries had gotten damaged. The unit was failing.

"Have you tried using the car battery?" Nidia asked.

"We don't have a car," the young woman said.

"You can use ours," Nidia said. "Come on, I'll get it."

"Who's watching your baby?" the other neighbor asked the young woman.

"She was asleep when I left," the young woman said. "The battery alert sounded on the refrigeration unit, and I just ran over here."

"You should go home," the neighbor said to the young woman. "Your little girl is walking now. If she wakes up, you don't want her loose in the house. Your mother can't keep up with her. I'll go with Nidia to get the battery."

The young woman nodded and hugged them, then ran out the door.

Nidia and the neighbor waded through the mud and water back to Nidia's house and retrieved the battery.

"I don't know how long it will last," Nidia said.

"After it runs out, she can use ours," the neighbor said.

"Any word on the radio about how long they think it'll be til the power comes back?" Nidia asked.

"They don't know," the neighbor said. "Weeks. Maybe even months. She's gonna need to get her mother to an emergency shelter where they have a generator."

From where they stood, Nidia could see the land covered in fallen trees and branches, theirs was one of several towns along a washed out road. The shelter was at least five miles away.

As the neighbor waded off to give the battery to the young mother, something caught Nidia's eye beneath the car. She looked closer and was startled to see the face of her grandmother, bobbing like an apparition in the muddy water.

She reached down and saw the black and white portrait was facing out from her double ziplock bag of passports and family photographs. She snatched it from the water that had pooled beneath the car. As she rotated the bag, she could see that the inside was dry. Through the entire storm, it had mercifully stayed closed tight. She held the bag to her chest, and her body hunched into sobbing. She leaned on the broken car, weeping with gratitude that all her preparation had made the difference in this one thing.

Dulce woke up on the floor of a rescue center.

"Where am I?" she asked.

"Albizu Campos elementary school," the woman said. "But you were in a makeshift hospital for a few days. They say the mayor brought you in."

It was daytime, and she had somehow been moved from the storage building to another place and then to here? She had no memory of it. Looking up at the ceiling, she saw fluorescent light fixtures, none of them illuminated, all the brightness came in through skylights. She tried to sit up to see where she was, but the movement caused a stab of pain in the back of her head where she had hit it. She lay back down and closed her eyes against the throbbing. From the sounds around her, she could tell that she was inside a large school auditorium. She turned her head to the side and opened her eyes. Next to her was a woman with a little boy, who was screaming. Dulce would have thought that she couldn't have slept with a kid screaming, or with her head in such pain. But somehow, she drifted back off.

When she woke up again, it was evening. The last rays of sunlight illuminated the room with a dim glow. Dulce tried to sit up, and moaned as the back of her head began to throb again.

A woman came over to her.

"You're awake," the woman said in Spanish.

"I'm so thirsty," Dulce said. "Can I get some water?"

The woman stepped away and came back with a dropper bottle.

"What are you giving me medicine for?" Dulce asked.

"This isn't medicine," the woman said. "This is the water."

The woman explained that they had begun with enough drinking water for fifty people for three days, but they ended up sheltering over a hundred people. By the time Dulce came in, they were down to only a few gallons of fresh water, and had more people coming in. They expected FEMA or the National Guard to be on the way with more water, but so far they hadn't gotten anything. The woman gave Dulce a dropperful of water every couple of hours.

Slowly, Dulce began to feel more grounded, not quite as dazed. She felt an awkward bulge under her arm. The water wallet. She didn't try to lift her head, but she pressed it with her fingers to make sure everything was still there. The top was slightly open. Had she left it like that?

Running her hands over the outside of it, she felt the phone, the charger, the passport. But where was the cash? She opened it all the way and felt inside in the dusky room.

Her fingers touched the crumpled bills in the bottom, the few coins. But where were the five crisp hundreds? Her life savings. She slid her entire hand into the wallet. They were nowhere. She pulled out the wallet and held it in front of her face. No hundred-dollar bills.

Had she spent them somehow? No. Someone must have robbed her. She had been asleep here in the shelter. Did someone say she had also been in a hospital? As Dulce tried to make sense of the muddle in her brain, she fell asleep again.

When she woke back up, the woman with the water was sitting next to her with a dim lantern.

Dulce blinked and looked over at the lady with the little boy. The woman's back was facing her, curled up. Finally, he had fallen asleep.

The woman with the water fed her two dropperfuls. In the darkness, Dulce couldn't quite read her expression. She looked more solemn than before. Dulce whispered to her: "How's the little boy?" she asked. "Better? He's quiet now."

The woman shook her head: "That little boy is with God, now." She crossed herself and was swallowed by the blackness.

Dulce felt nauseous. The mother's curled back was invisible in the darkness now, but the image burned into Dulce's mind. She couldn't stop seeing it, even though she didn't know if her eyes were open or closed. But eventually she fell back asleep. Or unconscious. So her eyes must have been closed.

She woke in the night to a candle blazing in her face. The woman's hand hovered above her nose. It took a moment to realize that she was checking to see if Dulce was still breathing.

"Can I get some more water?" Dulce croaked.

The woman shook her head. "It's all gone."

From behind the woman, Dulce could hear the drone of a priest in Latin. Last rites. He was praying over the mother.

Dulce tried to focus on the light, a white seven-day candle, like her cousin Josefina used to use in Cuba. She could feel her eyes getting moist. "For the little boy?" she asked the woman.

"For both of them," the woman replied, and moved away with the candle.

Chapter 18

When Dulce opened her eyes again, it was morning. She felt leaden and heavy. Someone had told her she had a concussion. *Con-cu-ción.* The word rattled around in between the Spanish and English-speaking parts of her brain, until it was just percussive sound that made no sense.

Con-cú—con-cush—con-con-con-cu-ción.

Through the garble of sound in her mind, Dulce looked up to see that the woman was offering her a cup of water. An actual cup. Plastic, with a small handle. The kind you get in a cafeteria. It was a little less than half full.

The water was tepid, but she could feel it flow like a river over her cracked lips, her parched throat, her dehydrated interior.

"Sip it slowly," the woman cautioned.

Dulce longed to inhale it. She had the thought that she would give all the money she had for a gallon jug of water all to herself. Then she realized someone had taken all the money she had. Or nearly all.

Her heart sank, and she sipped the small cup of water.

That same morning, a young girl banged on the door of the neighbor's house where Nidia and her family were staying. Nidia, Zara, and the baby were sleeping on a double bed mattress on the living room floor. The banging woke the baby and he started to cry.

"FEMA!" the girl yelled through the window. Apparently, the family who lived at the corner had gotten the Federal Emergency Management Agency on the phone, the part of the US government that is supposed to help when there's a disaster.

Zara sat up, blinking at the bright morning. "Somebody's cell phone works?" she asked in a groggy voice.

Nidia could barely hear her over the screaming baby. "Looks like it," she said, stepping into a pair of shorts and putting on a bra.

The girl ran off to share the news with the next house.

Nidia took the baby so Zara could empty her bladder.

She shushed him gently: "yes, *mi amor. La vecinita* woke you up. But it was good news! Good news! We can talk to FEMA. They're going to help us."

Zara came back. "I barely peed at all," she said. "I'm scared my milk is gonna dry up."

Nidia inspected her daughter's arm. Zara had a vein exactly in the center of the crook of her elbow. It was usually raised. But today, it was flat, almost concave.

Nidia nodded. "I'll try to get some water," she said.

She handed Zara the baby, and hugged them both before she headed out.

The neighbor's house wasn't really at a corner anymore. There was no corner. The ground everywhere was muddy and covered with debris. The difference between street, sidewalk, driveway, ground, lawn, and garden had been obliterated. Landmarks like "the blue house" or "the pair of tall palm trees" no longer existed. But Nidia knew that the platform with the tangle of debris and sodden items was formerly their blue house and underneath where the pair of tall palms had fallen, they would eventually find their driveway. She picked her way down the long road to where the corner had been. As she got closer, she heard animated voices.

The neighbor's house had roof damage, but no major holes, and all four walls were still standing. A line of people spilled out the door and onto the porch.

She waded up and hugged several neighbors. "They have cell phone service?"

"Landline," said a young teacher who lived down the street.

Nidia nodded and inquired about how everyone was doing.

"We buried *abuelito* yesterday," the teacher said.

"I'm so sorry," Nidia said.

"He didn't want to evacuate," the teacher said. "We warned him that he might not survive the stress of the hurricane, but he said that if he died he wanted to die at home. So fucking stubborn."

Nidia hugged him again. He blinked back tears. "We didn't even have time for a proper wake. It was so hot and . . ." He collapsed into the hug and cried for a minute, then he straightened up.

"We can have a memorial for him later," Nidia said.

He nodded, wiping his eyes.

While she waited to get her turn on the phone, Nidia got updates from everyone. The car battery was working for the neighbor's insulin refrigerator. Three people had tried to go to the emergency shelter, but couldn't get through. Someone's nephew in the town nearby had gotten electrocuted by one of the downed wires. They weren't sure if he had died or not. Nobody had any water. She asked if anyone had news of the town where her aunt lived, but nobody did.

A couple hours later, the crowd had thinned a bit, and Nidia had finally gotten into the living room.

"But what about the five hundred dollars?" the middle aged man from across the street was asking in English.

Nidia could hear the FEMA operator's voice, sharp and tight. "The Federal Emergency Management Agency is not an ATM."

"Tell her it's the grant for when your food spoils in the refrigerator," another neighbor said. "Because the power went out."

The man on the phone repeated the information. "No," he said. "We haven't gotten any emergency boxes. Nobody from FEMA has been here. We're not in San Juan. Not so much as a single package dropped by a helicopter."

"I heard they're not getting much food in the capital, either," the man's wife said. "But at least they might be getting some water."

"My daughter is breastfeeding," Nidia said. "I'm worried she's getting dehydrated."

The woman nodded. "We have almost none left," she said. "But we might still have a can of chicken broth. I'll get it for you after my husband gets off the phone."

Finally, the FEMA operator had gotten to the correct screen on her computer, and was taking down his information.

Word had traveled that they had FEMA on the line, and a few more neighbors had come. Nidia sat in the living room with the can of chicken broth in her lap for another two hours. She had talked to FEMA, but needed to wait til everyone else spoke to the operator before they could hang up and she could make another call.

One of the elders in the town was worried about her granddaughter. She lived a couple of towns away, and her husband's alcoholism had been escalating. He was a mean drunk, and had begun to get abusive. The grandmother had begged her to come sit out the storm with her in Las Palmas, but the granddaughter said she would stay with her husband. "He promised not to drink," she had said. "He needs me at home."

When the grandmother had sent some neighbors to check on them, they'd found the husband, drunk on the porch. No sign of the wife. He wouldn't let them in the house.

"He's a monster when he drinks," the grandmother said to Nidia. "He could have done anything during the storm. He could have killed her."

"Don't jump to conclusions," Nidia said. "If he got rough with her, she's most likely in the house hiding her bruises. It'll be okay. We need to pray for her."

When the last neighbor had finally finished their FEMA business, Nidia tried her aunt's landline, but couldn't get through. Then she got the neighbor's permission to call New York.

She dialed the 347 number several times before she stopped getting a recording that all the circuits were busy. It rang twice before Marisol answered.

"Nidia?" Marisol asked. "*Amor*, are you okay? Is everyone okay?"

"We're alright," she said. "We don't have water or power, but we're all safe and sound."

"And the house?" Marisol asked.

And that was when Nidia began to sob. For their house, which was now a roofless, half-walled disaster.

"We should have just fucking let the bank take it," Nidia said. "After all the work you did to save it."

"No," Marisol said. She was crying too, now. "What matters is that you're all okay."

Nidia shook her head. "I don't know how long we can hold out," she said. "We need food and water. The hurricane destroyed all our supplies."

"Can you get to the airport?" Marisol asked.

"Which one?" Nidia asked.

"Any of them?" Marisol asked.

"I don't' think so," Nidia said. "I don't think the smaller ones are open. And there's no way we can get to San Juan. We can't even get to the emergency shelter down the road."

"Do you—" Marisol asked. "Do you think you could get to the harbor?"

Nidia considered this. If she stood up on a chair or something, she could look down the hill and see the harbor from her back yard. "I think so," she said. "But there's nothing going in and out on this end of the island. All the supplies come in through San Juan."

"I know someone with a fishing boat," Marisol said. "If I send him, can you get down to the harbor?"

"I think so," Nidia said. "When I get back to the house, I'll see what kind of shape the harbor is in."

Before she left, she gave her aunt's name to someone who was trying to get through to the radio station. The list would end up with the neighbor who had the radio. Names were written carefully on three pages of notebook paper, and today they added two new names to the list: Nidia's aunt and the other neighbor's granddaughter with the abusive, drinking husband.

On her way back to where she was staying, Nidia went by what was left of her own house. She stood on a felled tree in her backyard and peered down to the harbor.

The water was full of debris: tree branches, wrecked pieces of boats, garbage. But the docks had survived. A boat could probably tie up there if it wasn't too big.

It was late afternoon by the time Nidia got back to the house where they were staying. Zara was drinking water from a cup and giving some to the baby.

"Where'd you find water?" Nidia asked.

"It was a blessing from God," Zara said.

"What blessing?" Nidia asked. "And how do you know it's safe to drink?"

"Don't worry," Zara said. "I cut a bottle open and used it to catch rainwater."

"Without washing it out?" Nidia asked.

"What would I wash it out with?" Zara asked.

"It could be contaminated," Nidia said.

"How could it be contaminated?" Zara asked. "It's rainwater."

"The bottle could have—" Nidia stopped mid-sentence and shook her head. "In future, let's use some antibacterial wipes on anything we catch rainwater in, okay?"

Zara shrugged and agreed. "You're not the only one who can have an idea around here, you know," she muttered.

By the middle of the night, they were all on the back porch. Zara was vomiting into the yard, and Nidia was holding the baby, who was vomiting all over her.

The baby's screaming woke their neighbor, and she came outside, a lantern in her hand.

"What happened?" the neighbor asked, groggy but alarmed.

"I think they drank contaminated water," Nidia said.

"We need Mrs. Talamantez," the neighbor said.

Nidia nodded. Mrs. Talamantez was the former nurse who lived around the corner.

"Go ahead," the neighbor said. "I'll take care of them."

"Are you sure?" Nidia asked.

The neighbor nodded, taking the baby from Nidia, and handing her the lantern.

Mrs. Talamantez's house had been just around the corner, but nothing was simple now. The floodwaters were up to her knees in some places. Nidia had to be careful of downed wires not to electrocute herself, like that one neighbor's nephew. She had to make sure not to trip and fall in, filling her own mouth with contaminated water. Not to mention ruining the lantern.

The lantern only gave her light for a few feet out, so she had to estimate where things would be. It took her twenty minutes in the dark to travel the two blocks.

By the time she got to Mrs. Talamantez's house, she was frantic.

Mrs. Talamantez woke up and quickly put on her clothes. She was a thickly-built, gray-haired woman with glasses.

Then Nidia retraced her steps to take the nurse back to the neighbor's house.

Mrs. Talamantez examined both mother and baby.

"Don't drink any more of the water you had," she said. "Nurse the baby. Nothing for him but mother's milk."

"She's nearly dry," Nidia said.

Mrs. Talamantez nodded. "It'll be easier for her to recover than him. A baby that small can get dehydrated so easily."

Nidia nodded.

"Is there anything you can give us for it?"

The nurse shook her head. "It'll have to work its way out. Since the toilets don't flush, make sure they have a place to go. As contained as possible. We don't want everyone in town to get infected."

In the middle of the night, Dulce woke to the sound of arguing voices in the shelter. It was totally surreal to hear them, whispering urgently, utterly disembodied in the total darkness.

"What the fuck are you doing here?" a woman's voice asked.

"I just needed to know that the kids were all right," a man's voice this time.

"We're fine," the woman said. "You need to go, Pedro."

"Just let me see the kids," he said.

"With what light?" she asked. "We're using every bit of power for basic needs."

"Well, I need to see my kids," he insisted.

"They're fine," she insisted.

"Then I need to spend the night," he pressed. "So I can check on them in the morning."

"You can't take my word for it?" she asked. "The kids are okay."

"All three of them?" he asked.

"What? You think I'd lie to you about that?" she asked. "That if something was wrong with one of our kids, I'd just be sitting here talking to you and not doing anything about it?"

"You've lied about other things before," he said, his voice moving from a whisper to a low grumble. "I need to see for myself."

"Can you all quiet down?" another voice asked from across the room.

"Pedro," the original woman's voice said. "You need to leave."

"Not til I see my kids."

"According to the restraining order, you're committing a crime right now," the woman said.

"Then call the police you fucking bitch," Pedro's voice was a tense growl. "Pick up your phone and call the fucking police. Oh that's right. You got no power and no phone service and the cops are busy with this disaster, so I guess I can stay as long as I fucking want."

"Is there a problem here?" A man's voice spoke. Full volume and hard edged.

"Yeah, my wife won't let me see my fucking kids."

"Soon to be ex-wife," the woman said.

"Did I hear there's a restraining order?" the new guy asked.

"None of your fucking business, you nosy *cabron*," Pedro said.

Suddenly, there was a strong flashlight beam shining on them from across the room. The man and the woman froze. Dulce saw that the woman looked about her age, but much more petite. Wide-eyed but weary, her hair was tied up in a ratty ponytail. Pedro was huge compared to her. It reminded Dulce of her size difference with Jerry. All he had to do was stand over her and it terrified her.

"Papi?" a tiny voice asked.

"Your papi is leaving *mi amor*," the voice behind the flashlight said from across the room. A woman's voice.

"Your papi was worried about you," the mother said soothingly. "Because of the storm. He just came to check that we were okay."

"The storm ripped the walls off the house," the child's voice said from just outside the flashlight beam.

"Tell me more, baby," the father's voice said.

"Unfortunately, *your papi* can't hear more right now," the voice behind the flashlight said firmly. The light bobbed as the woman headed toward them. "He has to leave."

"I'll be back in the morning," Pedro said, standing up. The beam rose and stayed on him.

"No, you won't," the wife said.

"This is a public shelter, bitch. I'll be back."

The child had begun to cry in the dark, and Dulce could hear the mother whispering words of comfort.

Meanwhile, the flashlight followed Pedro until he had walked out the door. His face pale and features sharp in the wash of the bluish light. The moment the door closed behind him, the wife began to gather her things.

"Where are you going?" the voice from the flashlight asked. The beam was still shining on the door. "You can't go out. It's curfew."

"We can't stay here," the woman said.

"I'll put security on the door during the night so he doesn't come back."

"That's not good enough. He always finds a way."

"In the morning, we'll transfer you to a safe house. I know some women who can help. Besides, if you leave now, he might be waiting out there for you."

The woman didn't answer. And soon there was only the sound of the child crying and the mother cooing soothing words of comfort.

Dulce thought of Jerry again. How terrified would she be if there was any chance of him rearing up in the aftermath of the storm and coming after her? God forbid.

It was a long time after the child stopped crying and the mother stopped cooing that Dulce finally fell asleep.

In the morning, Dulce woke early. The sun wasn't fully up yet, but there was enough predawn light that they could see their surroundings. The young woman sat up staring at the door, like a sentry. Beside her, three small children slept, twin babies and a girl of maybe three.

"You okay?" Dulce asked in a whisper. "I couldn't help but hear what went on last night."

"These women better be for real," the young mother said. "Better be able to get me someplace safe."

"I'm sure they will."

"I don't know. Going through the shit I been through, I learned not to trust nobody."

"I know how it is," Dulce said. "I was—I had an abusive guy in my life. And I found a group of women to help me."

"It's not that people don't mean well," the woman said. "It's just that they don't realize what kind of shit they're up against. I mean, we'll go wherever they say. I obviously can't stay here. And I can't go back to a house with no walls or no roof. But I'm not getting my hopes up that they can keep us safe for any period of time."

"I understand," Dulce said. "I had to take it step by step."

They fell into silence. The woman continued to stare at the door.

"Fucking hurricane," she finally said. "Like the storm wasn't bad enough. But like any heavy rain, it got all kinds of slimy motherfuckers creeping out from under rocks. Take advantage of the situation to try to take shit that they think should belong to them. I'll bet he's just one of many."

Chapter 19

Zara and the baby both still had horrible diarrhea the next morning when Nidia went back to the neighbor with the landline. She tried for hours to get through to Marisol but couldn't.

By the time Nidia got home, the vomiting had stopped, but they both still had diarrhea. The chicken broth was gone. Her daughter was weak. The baby was listless. The nurse, Mrs. Talamantez, came over later that night.

"She needs to get to a hospital," the nurse said. "They both need intravenous fluids."

"Should we try to get to the shelter?" Nidia asked.

"The shelter flooded, and they had to evacuate," she said. "But even many of the hospitals don't have power." She slumped down in her chair. "The few that are still open, that is. I don't understand. One of the doctors said the US military has a huge medical ship stationed off the coast of Virginia. Why haven't they deployed it? Those things are literally like giant hospitals that float on water."

Nidia shook her head. "It looks like we're on our own."

"Puerto Ricans pay billions in US taxes," Mrs. Talamantez said. "We're citizens. They should be helping us."

"My cousin has a friend with a fishing boat," Nidia said. "She said he could come get us. But I don't know if Zara is strong enough to get down to the harbor."

"I'll help you get her there," the nurse said. "We can get folks to carry her if she can't walk."

"I'll tell my cousin to have him bring water," Nidia said.

"He needs to bring an IV drip for these two," the nurse said. "And if he can, we're desperate for a few other medical items."

Nidia nodded and wrote down the list.

"I'll go now and call," she said.

"It's not safe," Mrs. Talamantez said. "With the heavy rain, there was another flash flood earlier. In fact, I should stay here tonight."

At dawn, the rain had let up a bit, but the road was nearly waist-deep again. Nidia made her way down to the house on the corner with the landline. She tried repeatedly for several hours, and kept hearing that all circuits were busy. Finally, she got through.

"Is everything okay?" Marisol asked.

Nidia explained the situation and gave her the list.

"I'll call Clive as soon as we hang up," Marisol said, after she took down the list. "I can give him money for the supplies. Can I call you back at this number to let you know when he's coming?"

"You can try," Nidia said. "But there's no guarantee. Because of the rain there's a lot of flooding. But I can see the harbor from our house. I'll check as often as I can. At least once a day. Tell him to wait and we'll come down to the boat."

"What else can I do?" Marisol asked.

"Pray for us," Nidia said.

Marisol hung up with Nidia and dialed the number she had for Clive. No answer. She sent him an urgent text to call her. But how was Clive going to find medical supplies in Jamaica?

She needed to ask her sister, who was a doctor. She called Cristina in Havana, but got no answer. She sent Cristina a text and an email.

Cristina called back first.

"He should come here to Cuba," Cristina said. "If he's in Ocho Rios, he's right by Santiago. I have a friend down there who can put together a rescue kit. Cuba's been trying to send relief supplies, but the US won't let them through."

"That fucking Jones Act," Marisol said.

"Don't get me started about the US and their blockades," Cristina said. "Let me call my friend. I'll call you back."

Clive called back first. Marisol explained the situation.

"I'll leave tonight," he said.

"But what about your charter client?" Marisol asked. "I don't want to mess with your money."

"They prepaid," Clive said. "I'll only have to refund one day worth of fees."

"I can cover that," Marisol said. "But won't you lose this customer's future business if you leave early?"

"Bunch of drunk white boys," Clive said. "I'll let them know I've been asked to join the hurricane relief effort. If they don't understand, then they don't deserve to travel in the Caribbean."

Cristina called back a couple hours later. Her friend could come through with the medical supplies. A few of the doctors would even ride along on the boat if they could fit.

Marisol put Cristina in touch with Clive, but she couldn't get through to Nidia's neighbor to leave a message. She called dozens of times, but all the circuits were busy.

Chapter 20

When she awoke that next morning, Dulce was able to sit up. Her body felt stiff, achy. She had a bump on the back of her head.

The woman who had given her water helped her to her feet and pointed her to the bathroom. She probably could have found it from the smell. The water wasn't running. They had set up buckets. She relieved herself, but noticed that her own shorts were damp with urine. There wasn't anywhere to wash them.

Feeling self-conscious, she walked back to where she had been lying. Sure enough, the blanket she'd been sleeping on had the dank smell of urine, as well.

She sat back down on the blanket and felt totally lost. She didn't know anyone. Not to mention that she felt like a little girl who had just wet the bed. Was she supposed to tell someone? She had no idea what to do next.

She lay on the floor in the large school auditorium. The walls still bore back to school announcements and scores from soccer and basketball games.

The cafeteria tables had all been pulled toward the far end of the room, near the kitchen.

On the other end, there was a row of tables with medical personnel and other staff attending to people as they came in.

Dulce lay on her back and looked up through a skylight, watching a sliver of clouds passing overhead.

When she got up to walk around the room a bit, she saw that someone had put out a bin full of paperback books. There were some young adult novels in Spanish, translations of US teen angst stories that focused on white girls in high school.

As a younger teen, she had read those books from her school library before she dropped out. But then, during her years with Jerry, white girl drama about friends and boys seemed so far from her life. She regarded those stories like kiddie books that began with "once upon a time," or something. In the Jerry years, she had preferred to read gritty urban stories for adults: sex, violence, betrayal, chasing money—they felt like real life. But she only read those books on the rare occasions when she was able to get her hands on them. Mostly, the girls watched TV when they weren't working or keeping house.

But now, in the hurricane, she hungered for something light and innocent. She took a trio of teen books back to her pallet on the floor. She had just started the second book, when a nurse came over to check her out. She was a white woman from the US.

"Head injury, huh?" she asked, handing her a tiny bottle of water.

The nurse made Dulce walk a line, then close her eyes and touch her nose with each of her pinkie fingers. She asked her questions in English: her name, where she was from, the date and time. When the nurse asked who was president, Dulce's face puckered into a scowl.

Before she could even say anything, the nurse laughed. "You're gonna be fine," she said. "You might be sleepy for a few days, but the concussion is healing, and there's no neuro-logical damage."

As the nurse went to move on, Dulce grabbed her arm.

"Is there anywhere for me to wash my shorts?" she asked. "I smell like piss from when I was knocked out."

The nurse put a hand on Dulce's arm. "Sweetheart," she said, her voice gentle, "nobody's worried about that right now. We're rationing the water again. What little clean water we have is for drinking. If it's not quite drinkable, it can be used for washing dishes or hands. I don't recommend bathing in any of the flooded areas. That water could be con-taminated, even though it doesn't smell."

"Contaminated with what?"

"Sewage, bacteria, toxins," the nurse said. "Take your pick."

"I seriously need to go around like this?" Dulce asked.

"Tell you what," the nurse said. "If you're feeling better, you can join one of the crews outside clearing the roads. If it rains this afternoon, you'll get the shower you've been want-ing. Now I gotta go. Lot of people need medical attention."

"Of course," Dulce said. She thought of the mother and baby. How could she be worrying about how she smelled? She got up to put on her shoes so she could help clear the road and realized she didn't have any shoes.

What now? Was she just supposed to wait? Everyone here was eager to get back to their homes. If their homes were still standing. To salvage what they could. But what did she have to return to? A pile of ruined designer outfits? A Cartier chain tangled in a mass of branches, clothes, and trash? This had never been home. She needed to get off this island.

A couple hours later, a man called for volunteers to do some road clearing, and Dulce raised her hand. They distrib-uted machetes, axes, and even a saw. There weren't enough to go around, so they would take turns. Armed with their various weapons, the ragtag brigade marched outside.

* * *

There was too much sky.

The tropics were usually landscapes of trees, bushes, and vines, rising thick up out of the land, towering, blocking out the horizon. But not now. Tall palms had been snapped like toothpicks. Leaves scraped away by wind. The sky stretched out, uninterrupted by greenery, as clusters of naked trunks reached up from the land like claws.

That was the strangest part. How much the sight of the land reminded her of New York winter. The hillsides covered with leafless trees had her recalling the trip they'd taken one Christmas to visit the parents of her sister's boyfriend upstate. The hurricane had made its own winter, like after snow melted in the city and the lumps of trash that had been underneath became visible again, perfectly preserved. Suddenly, Puerto Rico became much more like New York in March, with its barren trees, sodden trash, and people huddled indoors. It had everything but the cold.

They gave her a machete to hack up the brush. One of the men showed her how to swing it safely, so that it came down on the fallen tree branches with maximum chop.

"Watch your eyes," he said, and left her to work.

It took a long time to even hack off a single branch. Some of the other people were much quicker.

After about an hour, she'd managed to clear away a few branches, and had a small sense of accomplishment. From time to time, she'd feel a little lightheaded and would stop to rest.

"You need water?" the head of the crew asked.

"*Sí, por favor,*" she said.

He had her tilt her head back and poured some in from a gallon jug, carefully so as not to spill any.

She licked the drops off the side of her mouth and thanked him.

A little later they took a break for lunch.

"Courtesy of FEMA," the crew chief said.

Several members of the crew groaned as the chief handed out small packets of beef jerky and Cheez-Its.

"Shit," one of the young women said. "We're lucky to have food, *tú sabes*?"

Dulce agreed. "You from New York?" she asked the girl as she tore open the beef jerky packet.

"Upstate," she said. "I just moved back last year. I came for college."

"La Yupi?" Dulce asked, using the nickname she'd heard for the University of Puerto Rico.

The girl nodded. "It's been fucked up though, with the debt crisis and everything," she said through a mouthful of Cheez-Its. "Now with all this, I'll probably end up back in the Bronx."

Dulce tried the jerky. It was nearly as hard as the wood they were chopping. "Are you sorry you came?" she asked.

The girl gave a sudden bark of laughter that also seemed to be partly a sob. "I don't fucking know," she said. "I'll tell you one thing. This shit solved my little identity crisis. I certainly feel like a real fucking Puerto Rican right about now."

After lunch, the sky began to darken. Half an hour later, there was a heavy rain. Dulce heeded the nurse's words. She put her head back and drank. She undid her ponytail and let the rain soak her hair, wash the sweat from her forehead. She raised her arms and scrubbed under her armpits with her bare hands. The hair was growing in under her arms, scratchy against her palms.

She pulled out the front waistband of her shorts and let the water fill them, soaking her underwear, washing away the old urine. Then she pulled out the back waistband and did the same.

After a moment, she went back to clearing, even in the rain, using the machete to hack at the branches.

When the crew came back inside, she asked the nurse to give her a band-aid for a cut on her foot.

"You shouldn't be working barefoot," the nurse said, offering her one, along with an antiseptic wipe. "Why didn't you take your shoes?"

Dulce looked down at a pair of gray athletic sandals with a closed toe. She had never owned shoes like these. Her shoes had always been either sneakers, flip flops, or sexy shoes.

"Those aren't mine," Dulce said. "They belonged to the lady in the bed beside me, the one with the baby."

"The one who died?" the nurse asked.

Dulce nodded somberly.

The nurse sighed. "They're yours now."

The shoes proved to be a size too large, but Dulce stuffed a couple of rags into the toes and then they fit okay.

That evening, everyone lined up for dinner, which was a small portion of beans and rice, and a few swallows of water. They sat on the floor and ate. Dulce sat beside some of the people she met while clearing. It turned out that her friend from La Yupi was there with some of her neighbors, including a pair of middle-aged women who lived in the apartments above her.

"I'm not saying there's much good coming out of this hurricane," she said. "But my aunt is eighty. Her husband is eighty-three. She's bedridden, but strong, you know, her mind is sharp. So before the hurricane, her husband used to boast that he never even *set foot in* the kitchen of their house. His wife did all the cooking and cleaning. Then my niece here took over." She put her arm around the thirtyish woman next to her. "His granddaughter. You did it all, right? Cooking. Cleaning. *Todo*." She turned to the niece. "You tell it."

"Well," the niece began, holding back laughter. "During the hurricane the kitchen flooded. And I was dealing with my grandmother, *tú sabes*. And he was saying 'water is flooding in from the kitchen!' You know? Like 'the British are coming!' or some shit. Like he needed to inform us about it. I was like *coño, tío*, get the *escoba* and fucking sweep the water out. I'm taking care of *abuelita* over here."

The aunt interrupted her: "*Y sabes qué?*" she said. "*Ese macho* got the fucking escoba and swept the fucking water out of his kitchen. And so to keep our spirits up since the hurricane, whenever we visit them, we just do this." She held one fist above another as if she were holding a broom and made a sweeping motion. "And all the women can't stop laughing."

Likewise, the women at the table cracked up.

"*Ha roto su record perfecto*," the aunt said.

"After the gas gets back on it's not like he's gonna go in there and cook," the niece said. "But I'll bet now he'll be able to go in and fix himself a goddamn sandwich."

"Some of these men are so damn stubborn, it takes a fucking hurricane to change their ways," the girl from La Yupi said.

Dulce laughed along with all the women, some of them laughing so hard they cried.

Later that night, Dulce regretted not having taken her blanket out into the rain, as well. The room was totally dark, with just a lantern in the corner where the nurse was talking to a man with a small child.

Dulce's body felt tired, but her mind was buzzing. She was hungry after the small dinner, the paltry FEMA rations, and the time she was unconscious and went without eating before that. She had never been so thirsty in her life.

Not only was her body uncomfortable, but she was never, ever still like this. She felt agitated, raw. There was no light to finish the teen book. Usually, she would watch TV or look at something on her phone. Was her phone even still working?

She pulled it out of the translucent case for the first time. The phone was dry, as were the charger and cash. Phillip was an asshole, but at least he bought her quality trinkets. Although the water wallet was all that remained.

When she pressed the power button on the phone, she was afraid that it would be broken, out of charge, or that the screen would be cracked. But instead it sparked to life. Just like any other day. The phone had no idea she had been through a hurricane, knocked out, covered in piss, had slept beside a woman and baby as they died.

Something about the phone turning on caused her chest to surge with emotion. Not hope exactly, but the idea that something that mattered to her had survived. So her eyes were filled with tears, and it took a moment for her to see the screen clearly and notice that she had messages.

You're running low on data. You have 25% remaining with eight days left. Get unlimited data on the best 4G LTE network in the Caribbean. Switch today.

She deleted the message. The other one was from a number she didn't recognize.

It's Zavier. Texting from a friend's phone. Mine is dead. At the Lumineer hotel in San Juan with press corps. Praying you're somewhere safe to sit out the hurricane. Hit me back when you can. Or better yet come over if you can. xo

The Lumineer Hotel.

The tears started up again. Zavier was worried about her. Somebody cared about her. She knew where to find him. He wanted her to come.

She had a goal now, a destination. She needed to find him and with his help, she could get the hell off this island.

Chapter 21

Clive's boat waited in the Las Palmas harbor. He sat out on the vessel's deck, next to a young doctor from Cuba. The two men looked out onto the steep hillside of spindly, naked trees, and above it, the actual town of Las Palmas. The doctor only spoke Spanish. Clive only spoke English. But Clive understood what was happening. The doctor had the IVs ready for Zara and the baby. He had the rest of the medical supplies in a mid-sized wheeling suitcase, but Clive couldn't imagine how they would get it up the muddy, eroding hill on wheels. They'd have to carry it.

There was a vague track that snaked up the hill. Clive only noticed it after staring at it for hours. Along the track, the treeline was lower, because it had no standing trees, only fallen trunks and branches. Maybe it had once been a road.

Nobody came all morning. Would he and the doctor have to go up into the town and find Marisol's cousins? What if they were too sick to come? Or worse, what if he was too late? He wanted to call Marisol to see if she knew anything, but he couldn't get a signal.

How could he and the doctor even find them? Just start walking around asking for Nidia Rivera? He had a street address, but how could anyone give them directions? From what he understood, there were no discernible streets anymore.

Early in the afternoon, there was a rustle of movement at the top of the hill. The doctor saw them first.

"*Mira*!"

Clive sat up and set down his soda.

The two men saw a small knot of figures emerge from behind a tangle of fallen trees, headed down.

Wordlessly, the two men started up the hill. The knot of people turned out to be a middle-aged woman carrying a whimpering baby, and an older woman and younger man carrying a young woman who seemed barely conscious.

Clive and the doctor met them halfway up the hill and helped carry the two of them down.

The doctor conferred with the older woman, who apparently was named Mrs. Talamantez, and the doctor managed to take both of the patients' pulses as they picked their way down the hill.

The middle-aged woman was crying silently, tears streaming down her face as they did their best to hurry toward the boat.

Nidia wiped her tears. She needed to focus. Once onboard, she went below deck with the doctor and Mrs. Talamantez and helped them hook up Zara and the baby to the IVs.

The doctor sent her above deck to drink water, and she watched as her neighbor helped Clive unload two pallets of bottled water from Jamaica.

Then Clive handed the suitcase to the man.

Shortly thereafter, the doctor and Mrs. Talamantez came back above deck and stepped off the boat.

Nidia translated for them. "She says they need to get to a hospital as soon as possible," she told Clive, struggling again to control her tears.

"Are they going to be okay?" Clive asked.

Nidia's jaw was tight. "We don't know yet."

The four of them were in the open sea off the coast of the Dominican Republic when the baby went from a whimper to a proper cry.

Nidia picked him up.

"Yes, *mi amor*!" she cooed, tears streaming, despite her smile. "Tell me all about it."

Nidia held the baby in her lap. She sat on the foot of the cot where Zara lay. The IV had successfully rehydrated her, but she was still unresponsive.

Half an hour later, the baby had stopped crying, and Nidia brought him out onto the deck. The baby blinked, looking out at all the water, and let out a loud laugh when the wind hit his face.

"How's the mother?" Clive asked.

"I'm praying," Nidia said, biting back tears.

Zara was still unresponsive when the Coast Guard stopped them upon arrival in Miami. Nidia was below deck by her bedside. The IV had hydrated Zara's body—the vein in the crook of her elbow was even fully raised above the level of the skin. But she still lay inert, her breathing shallow.

The space was illuminated by a single candle, flickering in a weighted holder.

"Wake up, *mi amor*," Nidia said. "Just like your precious baby did. It's your turn. Open your eyes. You can do it."

The baby lay next to his mother. He had woken up briefly, drank formula, cried for half an hour, and then fallen back to sleep.

As Nidia squeezed her daughter's hand in a whispered prayer, an amplified voice came from the Coast Guard ship.

"Please identify yourself," the voice thundered. "You do not have authorization to dock in the United States."

Zara scrambled up onto the deck. It was night, and she was nearly blinded by the spotlight of the much bigger ship.

Initially, Nidia was relieved, but Clive stood on the deck with his hands in the air.

"I have refugees from Puerto Rico," he shouted into the wind.

"Keep your hands up," the voice boomed.

Eventually, two officers came aboard the boat. By then, Nidia had gone down and brought the baby up onto the deck.

She pulled the passports and the baby's birth certificate out of a zip lock bag.

Clive showed his Trinidadian passport, as well.

"My daughter needs urgent medical attention," Nidia said.

"We have a protocol," the Coast Guard agent said. "Neither this man nor this vessel has permission to enter the United States."

"I don't want to enter the United States," Clive said. "I was just dropping off these three US citizens so none of them died while your own government wasn't doing a damn thing to help."

One of the agents swiveled around to him. His mouth was tight and his eyes were hidden behind reflective shades. "One more word out of you and you'll be detained while your boat is impounded."

Nidia could see Clive swallow hard. He stood silent and rigid as one agent inspected their documents, then she and her family were allowed aboard the Coast Guard vessel. The first Coast Guard agent watched Clive suspiciously, as if he might run for their boat. Meanwhile, the second agent trooped across the deck with Zara in a fireman's carry over his shoulder.

Nidia expected them to turn their boat around and head immediately to the hospital. But instead, they accompanied Clive back out to international waters, and stood anchored for a while as they made sure his boat was headed away from the Florida coast.

As precious minutes passed, Nidia looked at her unconscious daughter, and her now screaming grandson. She cursed the *yanquis* under her breath.

Chapter 22

On the same day Nidia left Puerto Rico, Dulce woke early with a renewed sense of purpose. She was headed to the Lumineer Hotel in Old San Juan. It was only between ten and fifteen miles away. She could walk.

What was the protocol for leaving an emergency shelter? She didn't really know anyone. But she wanted to let them know she was leaving. Most everyone was still sleeping, so she moved around quietly. She folded her pissy blanket. It seemed absurd to fold something so funky, but she couldn't wash it, and it would be rude to just leave it in a rumpled mess.

The only other person who was awake was the man in the kitchen. He was fat and gray-haired, with several tattoos on his arms. He had a slew of cook stoves going, and had a large pot on each one with water to boil for oatmeal.

She asked him for a bottle of water.

"We'll be distributing water with breakfast," he told her.

"I'm not staying for breakfast," she said. "I'm about to leave."

"Where are you going, *mija*?" he asked. "It's not safe out there."

"I need to get to . . . my family," she said.

"Why don't you wait?" he asked. "Talk about it with the site supervisor when she gets up."

"Everything takes too long," she said. "By the time breakfast is over, I'll have lost three hours. I need to go now if I'm gonna make it."

He shook his head, but he handed her a pair of sixteen-ounce bottles of spring water, and a bag of peanuts, along with a bag of crackers.

"Watch out for downed electrical cables," he warned. "Don't touch any wires."

"I'll be careful," Dulce promised.

"And if you reach any intersections that are clear, be sure to look very carefully, because the traffic signals are all out. There have been a lot of accidents."

"I will," she promised. "Thank you for your work."

"But where are you going?" he asked.

"Old San Juan."

He gave her directions to the Román Baldorioty de Castro Expressway. When she got closer, she would need to find out which of the bridges from Condado or Santurce were open into Old San Juan.

"Should I walk along the actual expressway?" Dulce asked.

"If the roads below are blocked, that's probably a good idea," he said. "You should walk on the left side, facing the traffic, so you can see cars coming. From what I hear, they cleared it just enough that vehicles can get through, but driving slow, you know? There's not much traffic because the businesses and schools are all closed."

"Can I get there today?" she asked.

"On foot?" he asked. "Not by daylight. And they don't allow anyone out after curfew. You need to get to another emergency shelter to stop for the night. There's one at another school about halfway along to Old San Juan."

"How do I find it?" Dulce asked.

He gave her directions. Her landmark would be the Suárez Canal near the airport.

She thanked him again and began to walk out. She had only gotten a few steps when he told her to wait.

He disappeared into the kitchen, then came out with a battered umbrella that had once been white.

"To protect you from the sun," he said.

She gave him a hug. "I can't thank you enough."

"Just be careful out there," he said.

The going was slow. She carefully made her way down the street to the expressway. The only clear part was the area she and the crew had cleared the day before.

She was careful to avoid the many hanging wires, as she picked her way around open water, fallen branches and trees, and so much of people's lives, splayed and sodden on the ground. Family portraits, clothes, dishes, furniture, roofing materials. It was as if someone had poked holes in the roof of someone's house and used it like a salt shaker, sprinkling their belongings indiscriminately onto the land, like a macabre seasoning.

It took her a half hour just to go a few blocks. At this rate, she'd never get to Old San Juan. She stood at the bottom of the expressway off-ramp and listened for cars. After a few minutes, she heard a single vehicle go by, the engine grumbling in a low gear. Slowly, she walked up the ramp, although it felt terribly wrong.

"*Cuidado*," her mother had said every time she was near a street or road. Now she was walking on an expressway.

Like the streets, the expressway was covered with branches and fallen trees. On each side of the expressway, a narrow trail snaked through the debris, just wide enough for a single vehicle.

While keeping out of the way of the cars, she had to climb

over the tree trunks, and some of the larger branches. At first, she kicked the smaller branches aside indiscriminately. But later, she began to throw them off onto the shoulder of the road. If she was walking that way anyway, she might as well help clear.

The umbrella was a godsend. Two of the ribs were broken, but it shaded her head, and that was what mattered. The day began to heat up, and by noon it was blazing. She had eaten the crackers for breakfast. Around one PM, she ate the peanuts. She drank the water slowly, and peed a couple of times on the side of the road.

She only saw a few people over the sides of the expressway, and they were all out of earshot. In the distance, she could occasionally see movement, either individuals or small groups. But mostly she saw wreckage everywhere, particularly trees.

By late afternoon, she had finally crossed over the canal near the airport. Through the chain-link fence, she could see much more activity. Only a few planes in sight, but crews with equipment were clearing the runways of branches and debris.

Her shadow was long across the quiet expressway by the time she had passed the gas station and found the right off-ramp. Her feet hurt in the too-big shoes. She was famished with all the exercise and so little food. She drank the last of the water and hoped there would be more at the rescue center.

She tried to follow the directions the man at the shelter had given her, but the streets between the expressway and the school were completely flooded. Dulce had to walk through waist-deep water.

"You okay?" a trio of teens called to her from an inflatable raft.

"I'm trying to get to the shelter," she said.

"We're going that way," one of them said. "We can take

you." They were two boys and a girl. One of the boys' arms was in a makeshift sling.

It took some maneuvering, but eventually, they got Dulce into the raft without tipping it over.

They exchanged news. Apparently, the US president was finally supposed to visit. Or so they had heard from a friend of a friend, who had heard it on the radio. None of them were particularly hopeful that he would do much to help.

By the time she appeared at the door of the high school, it was starting to get dark.

"We just finished dinner," the woman said. "I'll see if I can still get you a plate."

"Finished?" Dulce asked. It was barely evening.

"We have to work with the sunlight," the woman said.

Dulce recalled that the other school had skylights in both the kitchen and the auditorium. This one didn't have much natural light, and it was far dimmer inside.

Instead of rice and beans, they had cooked a huge quantity of pasta with a thin tomato sauce. She ate the small portion and drank another twenty ounces of water. It gave her the illusion that her belly was fuller. Not exactly full, more of a sloshing feeling inside.

She waited in line for the bathroom for nearly an hour. After she used it, her belly felt empty again and she was totally exhausted. Her body craved meat or beans and rice or even nuts—some sort of protein. But the rations of the day had been exhausted.

One of the people staffing the place found a cot for her. By then it was nearly dark, and—despite her still-hungry belly—she crashed hard, her body totally drained from the heat and the hours of walking.

In the middle of the night, Dulce woke to hear an older man yelling.

"Her oxygen machine isn't working!"

"The generator is still running," Dulce heard a woman with an American accent. She must be one of the volunteers from the US.

"But the power isn't working," the man said, his voice increasingly panicked.

"Could it be the machine?" the woman's voice asked.

"It's practically new," he said.

Suddenly, there was a flashlight beam bobbing. "Double check that the machine is on and the power supply is properly connected," the woman said. "I'm going to check the extension cord."

There was a second flicker of light, and Dulce could see a beam shining on a pair of extension cords, taped to the floor with perpendicular strips of tape, like a railroad track.

Other people were stirring awake. A child nearby started to whine.

"Everything's okay," the woman with the flashlight said. "Go back to sleep, everybody. We're just fixing a little problem here."

"It's not a little problem," the frantic man said, his voice loud and strained. "I've checked the machine, and the power supply. Everything's fine on this end. But the power isn't coming in."

"Just hold on, sir, okay?"

"How am I supposed to hold on?" he demanded. "My wife needs oxygen or she could die."

Several people stood up and offered to help.

"Please," the woman said. "Go back to sleep. I just need to . . . excuse me . . ." she pushed past several people offering assistance.

Ahead, dimly illuminated in the periphery of the flashlight beam, a mother and her young son headed to the bathroom. The boy stumbled on his way in.

The woman with the flashlight turned the beam toward them. Dulce could see the torn tape and the kink in the extension cord.

"I found it!" the woman said. "Please, everyone, back to bed."

She came over and knelt down near the bathroom door, shining the beam on the connection between two extension cords. She pressed them more closely together.

There was a sharp cry from the man. "It's working!"

A few people applauded.

Soon, there was a young man kneeling next to the woman with the flashlight. He had a roll of tape and they were more firmly securing the cords.

Chicago.

The following morning, as Dulce was waking up, she kept hearing one word that didn't belong: Chicago.

She sat up on her cot and saw people walking by with bottles of water. One woman had three bottles.

As she wandered over to the kitchen area, she kept hearing the word Chicago. At the food line, she saw a woman handing out bottles freely.

"We got water?" Dulce asked.

"From Chicago," the woman said. "It's a miracle."

As Dulce drank, the woman told her the whole story. For some reason, FEMA and the US government supplies weren't getting delivered. But some Puerto Ricans in Chicago had raised a ton of money and sent a plane load of supplies on a United Airlines flight they'd secured.

Dulce smiled. Today was going to be a good day, she decided. The day would end with her getting safely to the Lumineer Hotel. Because they day had begun with her drinking miracle water from Chicago.

* * *

She waited until after breakfast to head out, as she wanted to be sure she had as much food as possible. Beside her was a woman trying to get her kids to eat more slowly.

"Not so fast," she said. "You'll give yourselves a stomach ache."

At the next table over, the man from the middle of the night was retelling the story of his wife's oxygen crisis. His voice was jovial now, and he made fun of his earlier panic, his tablemates laughing along.

After breakfast, there was no one to bid goodbye before she headed out with a bag of skittles in the tiny pocket of her shorts. She had a thirty-two-ounce bottle of filtered water in one hand and the battered umbrella in the other.

Her feet hurt. She was developing blisters. She regretted having given herself that pedicure. Right about now, she needed all the tough skin she could get.

She sat down on the cement and pulled the rags out from the toes of the shoes and tied them around her feet like makeshift socks. It helped with the blisters, but now the shoes were too big and kept flopping and falling off.

She grabbed a branch and pulled off several leaves, stuffing them in the front of the shoes. They wouldn't last more than a day, but if there was anything in abundance right now, it was fallen branches and foliage.

She tried walking on the expressway, but there was a bit more traffic on this section, and she almost got hit.

She doubled back and walked along the road for a while, but then she got to a place that was flooded and impassable. She had to retrace her steps, but then she got lost.

She would need to ask someone. As she got further into a residential area, there was more noise. The occasional engine that might be a car or more likely a scooter or motorcycle, which could cut through the smaller open spaces on the roads.

She passed a crew that was working on one of the major roads to remove trees and branches. A truck with chains was attempting to pull a huge tree out of the road. Another man had a chainsaw, and was chopping up trunks and large branches, while a crew of others chopped with machetes and cleared the small pieces away.

There were about a dozen of them, and when she walked by with the bottle of water, they all asked for a drink. She poured it carefully into each of their mouths. By the time they had all had a mouthful, the bottle was only a quarter full.

She asked them how she could get to Old San Juan. They said that the road was impassable, and told here where to cross over the expressway to get on the side of the airport. All the supplies were coming in that way, so the clearest roads led in and out of there.

Two hours later, as Dulce passed the airport, she could see a spot where a massive tree had fallen on the chain link fence. It was leaning down at a forty-five-degree angle. Finally, a fallen tree that might actually work in her favor.

Dulce looked around the part of the airport she could see. Nothing going on at this end, but the work crew had definitely said that the relief supplies were coming in through the San Juan airport. If she showed up here, she would eventually be able to find the area where they had the food and water they were distributing.

At the top of the fencing was barbed wire, but the fallen tree was taller than the fence, so she had a safe path to scale the tree and then climb down the branches that led to the ground.

At the top of the tree, she looked around. She had entered on the far end of the airport from the terminals, and there was no one around here, but she saw some activity in the distance. She carefully climbed down from the tree. The ground was covered with debris like the rest of the island, but the wide, treeless tarmac meant that there were far fewer branches, foliage, and fallen trunks than she had seen most places.

But the lack of trees also meant lack of shade. She crossed over to the closed hangar buildings, her arm fatigued from holding up the broken umbrella.

By the time she had crossed to the busier side of the airport, she was especially exhausted, and slightly faint. So when the truck being loaded full of dead bodies first came into view, she thought she was seeing things. Dulce blinked and rubbed her eyes.

She was walking in between two hangar buildings. There was a narrow strip of shade back here, out of view of the road.

Two men were pulling a tarp off the back of a flatbed truck. The men reached in to take out the cargo. At first she thought they were long sacks of food. Maybe rice or beans, but then an arm swung down from one of the sacks.

Her eyes were vaguely focused in the distance. And what had been an ordinary, daily sight—men unloading a truck—became something surreal, macabre. Dulce shrank back toward the hangar, and stared. The men were loading corpses from the flatbed into a much larger truck.

Five. Six. Seven. Eight. Nine. As Dulce walked toward the apparition, she expected it would somehow dissipate, but instead it became clearer.

Yes.

Twelve. Thirteen. Fourteen. Fifteen. They were definitely loading bodies. By this time, she was close enough to see which looked thicker, thinner, male, female.

They were loading into a larger truck that was connected to a rumbling generator. Was the big truck refrigerated?

Eighteen. Nineteen. Twenty. Twenty-one.

She had counted thirty-five before she was stopped by a US soldier, who pushed a hand hard in her chest.

"This is a secured area. No civilians allowed," he barked in English.

"I—" Dulce said. "I heard I could get supplies here." She looked around. "Water or maybe some food."

"You were misinformed," he snapped.

"I'm so sorry," she said. "I'll leave right away."

"How did you even get in?" he asked.

"There's a fallen tree on the fence, maybe a mile back," she said.

He shook his head. "Not for long. And you won't be leaving the same way you came in," he said. "You'll have a military escort out of here."

"I came from a shelter," Dulce said. "I don't exactly know the way back."

He narrowed his eyes. "Look, I'm not fucking stupid. You're obviously a journalist."

Dulce dropped her eyes. "Okay, you caught me," she said, thinking quickly. "I'm staying at the Lumineer Hotel."

For several hours, she sat on a bench outside one of the empty hangars. She couldn't see much of what was happening, but at least it was in the shade.

"Excuse me," she said to the man who had stopped her. "Can I get a bottle of water, please?"

"I told you," he said. "This isn't a distribution center."

"Come on," another military guy said. "The last thing we need is some journalist dying of heat exhaustion on our watch."

"I don't give a fuck," said the man who had stopped her. "You deal with it."

The good cop military guy came over with a bottle of water.

"Am I being detained?" she asked.

"I don't know," he said.

Dulce drank the water as her anxiety rose. She didn't see anyone for another hour or so.

Then one of the trucks moved, and she had a better view of what was going on around her. She saw military trucks, a few large semis with giant shipping containers on them, and lots of military personnel sort of standing around.

Occasionally, she'd hear their laughter or playful shouts. What the hell were they doing so leisurely?

Another truck pulled up and blocked her view, and the driver and passenger got out. She called to them, but they ignored her.

The spot where they had her sitting was between the hangar and several trucks. Had they forgotten about her? Should she could crawl out underneath one of the trucks? She was thinking about it.

Finally, the bad cop came within earshot.

"Excuse me," she said. "Am I being detained?"

"Not that I know of," he said with a sneer. "Should we be detaining you? Are you confessing something?"

"No," Dulce said quickly. "But you said you needed to escort me out of the airport, and I've been waiting for hours."

"Oh I'm sorry," he said, his tone saturated with contempt. "Is your military escort moving slowly? Your transportation is such a high priority in this total disaster."

Dulce felt like someone was blowing up a balloon inside her chest. She wanted to defend herself, to say she had never asked for any fucking escort, but she kept quiet.

"Well?" he asked, baiting her.

Dulce just blinked up at him.

He turned and stalked away. "Fucking entitled Puerto Ricans," he muttered quite audibly.

* * *

Half an hour later, the good cop came by.

"Excuse me," she said. "Do you have any idea when I can leave? I never asked for an escort out. I'm glad to leave anytime."

"You need an escort for safety issues," he said. "And we don't have extra personnel or vehicles to send. But a patrol goes out after curfew. I assume they'll send you along with them."

Dulce nodded. "Thank you so much." The last thing she wanted was to be stuck on a makeshift military base after dark.

Around seven PM, the good cop came back and walked her across the dark tarmac to a waiting jeep. The driver was a pale military guy with a sour expression. Dulce tensed at the sight of him. There was no record of her in their custody. He could take her anywhere. Do anything to her. These US military guys would rape the women in their own units, let alone the random Dominican chicks they caught in the wrong places.

She was about to say something to the good cop, but what? Make him take her name? Demand some kind of reassurance of safe passage? But as she climbed into the back of the jeep, she saw that the driver's partner was a woman. She thanked the good cop and her new escorts and they headed out.

From what she could see in the headlight beams, they drove through a ruined city.

At one point, she realized where she was, riding along Doctor Ashford Avenue. They drove slowly, because the traffic signals were all out, passing the wrecked upscale bars where she had gone, the ravaged Cartier jewelers across from the Condado Vanderbilt Hotel. This road in the heart of the neighborhood had been her playground for so many weeks. Most of it was shut down. So many buildings damaged.

At one intersection, they stopped to let several military trucks pass along the cross street. In the jeep's headlights, Dulce could see one of the dress boutiques she had visited with Phillip. The display window was smashed now, the plywood hanging askew. The empty mannequin inside was naked and fallen, one leg laying beside her on the waterlogged boutique floor.

Two hours later, the jeep pulled up in front of the Lumineer in Old San Juan. She walked carefully across the cobalt blue bricks to the hotel's front door. Inside, the lobby was illuminated with utility lamps clamped precariously on to various fixtures. Reporters were charging their phones and camera equipment in a bay of outlets, and all the cords were connected to a rattling generator.

The lobby was large, but everyone who was talking on a cell was clustered over at one end where, presumably, the signal was better.

Dulce stepped forward to plug in her phone.

"Sorry, this is for press only," the woman said in English. "Do you have credentials?"

"I'm not—" Dulce began.

"Are you an interview subject?" the woman asked. "Are you supposed to be meeting someone?"

"Zavier Mendoza," Dulce said, recalling his last name from his business card. "From *El Planeta*."

"I know him," she said. "*El Planeta*? He's here freelancing with the *New York Times*. But he's out in the field. You can wait here, but the outlets are only for reporters."

Dulce sat down on one of the plush sofas on the no-signal side of the room. She had stayed at the Lumineer with one of her dates. Will? Gil? He was a businessman from the Midwest.

"Yulin-Cruz is about to speak," one reporter yelled, and

everyone seemed to jump up to go out to see the mayor of San Juan.

Several of them left half-eaten plates of food.

Dulce walked over and discreetly consolidated beans, rice, and bread into a single plate. Then she drew herself back into the shadows to eat it. The beans were cold. The rice was hard. The bread was soggy. And it was the best food she'd ever tasted.

The next thing she knew, someone was tapping her shoulder and calling her name. She stirred and felt the velvet sofa under her cheek. She blinked her eyes open to see Zavier looking down at her.

"Dulce," he said, his face blazing with a grin. "I'm so glad you're okay."

Slowly, she sat up and he pulled her into a hug. She let herself sink into his chest. He was slender, but solid, and she could feel the power of his care for her. She felt a lump in her throat, but wouldn't let herself cry.

"I'm fine," she said in Spanish. "I'm just ready to get out of here. To get back to New York as soon as I can."

"It's easier for press to get in and out," he said. "If you want to assist me for a few days, we'll probably be able to get you out."

"Of course," Dulce said. "How can I help?"

"Tomorrow, you can join me in going around doing interviews," Zavier said. "But right now, I need to go file a story."

"Okay," Dulce said. "Uh, should I meet you here in the morning?"

"Yeah," Zavier said. "Where are you staying?"

"Well, uh," Dulce began. "I was staying in a shelter—"

"Oh shit," Zavier said. "I wasn't thinking. Did you—"

"My place got flooded," Dulce said. "I lost all my stuff. I can't go back."

"Of course," Zavier said. "You can stay with us."

"Us?"

"Yeah, we have a suite. Sort of sleeping in shifts, but mostly people are out in the field twenty-four seven. I've been going for three days straight—just napping on the fly—so I'm definitely crashing tonight, but there's plenty of room for you. Come on, you can rest while I file this story."

"I haven't had any access to news beyond the grapevine," she said. "How bad is it?"

"Most of the island still has no power or running water," Zavier said. "The president finally made a visit yesterday. It was a total circus around here."

"Sorry not sorry I missed it," Dulce said.

Zavier's attention was caught by a tall, black man with graying hair who walked in the front door.

"There's our medic," he said. "Do you need to get checked out for anything?"

"I'm fine," Dulce said.

"It's free," Zavier said. "We call him Obamacare because he actually looks like Obama."

Dulce laughed. "There's nothing wrong with me that a night of sleep won't fix."

"What am I thinking?" Zavier said. "You must be exhausted. Before we go up, are you sure you're not hungry? This is it for food. No room service."

"What?" Dulce asked in mock outrage. "No room service? What kind of dump is this?" She spun on her heel as if she were going to storm out.

"Please señora," Zavier said. "I assure you, our five-to-a-room accommodations are very cozy."

Dulce scoffed. "Señor, I'm used to sleeping one hundred to a room. Plus, I hear you don't have any cots or even floor blankets."

"No, señora, but we do have mattresses," he said.

"Probably with the dreaded box springs," she said.

"I'm afraid so," he said.

"I suppose I'll have to accept that the García family has come down in the world," she said.

"Are you Dulce García of the Washington Heights Garcías?" he asked in mock admiration.

"Yes, but don't tell your society columnist," she said. "I'm slumming it."

He laughed and put on a headlamp. "Let me show you to your room, señora."

The two of them took the stairs up to the third floor.

Inside the room, he sat down at the small desk and turned on a camping lantern.

"Make yourself at home. You want to take a shower? It's gotta be short. Five minutes. No hot water."

"That sounds amazing," Dulce said. "Do you, maybe have a pair of sweats I could borrow or something?"

He looked from her body to his. He had broad shoulders, but a slender build overall. His shirts wouldn't fit over her full bust, and his pants certainly wouldn't fit over her hips and ass.

"You know," he said. "I'm gonna raid my boy's clothes. I think they'll fit better."

He gave her a t-shirt that said EL BOOGIE DOWN and a pair of clean boxers that would fit a much larger man.

Dulce thanked him and disappeared into the bathroom.

From the light of the lantern in the main room, she could see the bathroom would only be illuminated by a seven-day candle, sitting on the sink, which she lit.

She closed the door and turned on the shower. The water was lukewarm, and she stepped in fully clothed.

Grabbing the liquid soap, she lathered over her clothes, then peeled them off and rinsed them, one by one, washing her underwear last. Then she washed her hair and leaned back, rinsing her hair and letting the spray run over her face.

By the time she turned off the water, it had been about six minutes. She wrung out her hair and clothes, and hung them on the shower rod, then dried off and put on the clean clothes.

When she came out, Zavier was on the computer at the desk and didn't even look up.

When she lay down on the bed, the press of the soft, dry mattress against her back was so heavenly, that sleep washed over her like a sudden wave.

Chapter 23

When Dulce woke in the middle of the night, she heard snoring. The sound was coming from across the room. In the murmur between the loud inhalations, she also heard softer breathing coming from someplace closer. As she lay there, listening, she identified several different people. The snoring woman in the next bed. A man sleeping on the floor between the beds. Zavier had gotten the clothes from where he slept. It must be the Boogie Down guy.

And then she felt a slight shift in the bed and realized she hadn't been sleeping alone. Zavier lay beside her. A respectful distance on the double bed. His breathing barely a quiet whisper of air. There were four of them in the room?

And then, as if in answer to her question, a woman got up from the other bed—not the snorer—and walked to the bathroom. Five of them. Just like when she was a little kid. Her sister, her brother, her two cousins, and her. Five of them. All in one room a lot of the time. Five different breathing rhythms.

The woman closed the bathroom door and came back to bed.

Did Dulce need to pee? No. She hadn't drunk enough water.

And then, before she knew it, with the comforting sound of four other pairs of lungs breathing, she fell back asleep.

In the morning, Zavier was shaking her awake.

"Hey," he whispered. "Our ride's leaving in fifteen minutes."

Dulce blinked and nodded.

In the bathroom, her clothes were damp but wearable. She changed and peed, only to feel a stab in her bladder. An infection? Maybe just dehydration. She'd have to see if Zavier had any water. She didn't want to have to test the Obamacare.

She ran her tongue across her teeth and her mouth tasted foul. She hadn't brushed in days. She rinsed a washcloth and put toothpaste on the corner, then brushed her teeth the best she could with that.

When she came back out, Zavier was packing his laptop and talking on his cell phone.

She folded the guy's clothes and put them on top of his duffel bag.

There was nothing for her to pack except her water wallet, which had the passport, her phone, which was dead, and the keys to a storage space that was underwater.

In front of the hotel was a gray van with the driver chain smoking. He turned out to be a white American who didn't speak Spanish. Fortunately, all the windows of his van were open, and most of the smoke blew past her. Meanwhile, the cigarette lighter was rigged up with ports for multiple cables, so she would finally be able to charge her phone.

Most of the seats were full with journalists looking at different tech devices.

"What are we waiting for?" Zavier asked.

"Guy from the *Washington Post*," the driver said.

"Welcome to the fucking queue," Zavier muttered.

"The queue?" Dulce asked.

"For transportation," he said. "This is our unofficial carpool, a four-wheel-drive minivan to transport reporters from the major outlets."

"How are they managing to get all these places with the gas rationing?" Dulce asked. "People in the shelter were saying they waited in line like eight hours to get twenty dollars' worth of gas. Not just for cars, but generators, too."

"It's been really bad for locals," Zavier said. "We have our own gas supply, but it's limited. And it's still hard to get through to so many places. Also, there are a lot of us, so each reporter can only get to a few locations during each day before curfew."

He began skimming throught the newsfeed on his own phone.

As they waited, a young guy from the hotel approached them and reached through the van's open window to tap Zavier on the shoulder.

"Hey!" Zavier said jovially. "*Qué tal?*"

"I might have a tip for you," the guy said. "Something in the hills outside San Juan. I heard there's a santera helping people bury the dead, like a Catholic priest."

"When did you hear this?" Zavier said.

"Last night," he said. "My wife heard it from a neighbor. I thought you might want to check it out."

"Definitely," Zavier said. "Thanks for the tip."

Zavier wrote down the woman's information, and the guy headed back to work.

"Another piece of evidence about the death toll," Zavier said. "A santera in the mountains burying the dead, and yet the official death toll was supposed to be only sixteen."

"Sixteen hundred?" Dulce asked, horrified.

"No," Zavier said. "Sixteen people dead. Total. Governor Roselló upped it to thirty-four day before yesterday. The *Miami Herald* broke the story that it's still too low but—"

Dulce's mouth fell open. "How is that possible? I counted thirty-five bodies at the airport."

"You what?" Zavier asked.

"Dead bodies," Dulce said, and explained what she had seen.

"And he was so eager to get you out of there that they detained you for five hours without any food and water. And then drove you all the way to the Lumineer?"

She nodded. "No food. They did give me some water."

"Oh shit," he said. "We need to get right on this. I'll tell my editor I'm changing up my focus."

During the ride, Zavier got on the phone with his editor, the Puerto Rico Department of Public Safety, and several funeral homes. Then he asked her what seemed like a thousand questions, all the time murmuring in a low voice. Presumably because he didn't want the other reporters to know what he was working on. By the end, she had gone from feeling like she had seen something important, to realizing all the things she hadn't paid attention to: were there any markings on the truck? Did she see the names or ranks on on any of the military guys' uniforms? What branch of the military? Zavier was nice about it, but she vowed to be more observant in the future.

An hour later, they were walking around the back of a funeral home. Dulce shaded her eyes from the bright sun at the back parking lot. "It was a truck like that, but bigger," she said to Zavier. That she was certain of.

The two of them were standing at the edge of the lot, surrounded by broken glass and debris. In front of them was a large truck connected to a diesel power generator.

"Like a semi truck you'd see on the highway," she said.

"And there were thirty-five bodies?" he asked.

"At least," she said. "That was as high as I counted before the military guy stopped me."

"May I help you?" a man's voice asked in Spanish.

They turned to see an elder in a formal guayabera and slacks. He introduced himself as the funeral home director.

Zavier introduced them as being with the *New York Times*. Dulce was a little horrified to have her position so artificially inflated. But she kept her expression neutral and attempted to look however a journalist was supposed to look.

"The official count of deaths related to the hurricane is thirty-four," Zavier said. "In your professional opinion, is that a fairly accurate estimate?"

"There's absolutely no way that's right," he said. "Based on the customers we've had so far and what I've seen in hurricanes before, I'd say it's got to be in the hundreds. If not over a thousand."

"What are conditions like here on the ground for you?" Zavier asked.

"The situation is impossible," the funeral director said. "We have only so much space and resources. We try to send bodies to the morgues, but they're overloaded as well."

"Is it true that the military is helping?" Zavier asked.

"They haven't helped us," the director said. "That truck and that generator you saw? We're paying for that. This is a family business. I don't know how long we can hold out, but people are depending on us, so we're doing everything we can. How am I supposed to turn away a family who just lost a loved one? Whose previous funerals we always handled? But we can't afford to keep operating like this. The cost of running a generator twenty-four hours is going to bankrupt us. But what choice do we have?"

Zavier asked several follow-up questions, and then he was getting ready to wrap up.

"One last question," Dulce said. "Of the bodies autopsied

so far, of the women, are there any who have died as a result of violence?"

Zavier's eyebrows rose.

"None of the bodies we've officially autopsied," he said. "There was one . . . she was pretty young . . . we haven't had a chance yet. I don't know. There are a lot of ways to get bruises in a hurricane. But sometimes you . . . you have a feeling. Maybe."

"Thank you," Dulce said.

"We may contact you to follow up if that's okay," Zavier said.

"Absolutely," the funeral director said. "Whatever I can do to get the word out about the situation."

When Zavier called the transport, they said it would be about three hours til they could pick them up. After some complicated negotiation, it was determined that Zavier and Dulce would walk to the morgue, which was about an hour away on foot, and then they could get a ride to another mortuary near the airport.

On the way, Zavier reached in his backpack for rations: water, beef jerky, and some dried fruit. Dulce started to make small talk, but she realized he was focused on the environment around them. She followed suit. He took a few photos of ruined houses, flooded streets, and looted businesses.

When they got to the morgue, the staff said the facility was overwhelmed with corpses. They had doubled up the bodies and were begging the authorities for additional refrigeration.

"They can't count someone as dead until there's an official death certificate," the morgue attendant said. "And then it has to be entered in the system. But the whole government is shut down. We're just trying to survive. Half our workers can't get here, and the coroner is short of staff, too. Everywhere is backed up with the autopsies. Every aspect of the process is moving slowly except the death rate."

The main attendant offered to show Zavier, who switched his phone into camera mode as the two men headed out of the room. Dulce stayed in the main office where another man was working at a laptop.

"Can I tell you something off the record?" the man asked, looking up from the computer.

"Absolutely," Dulce said.

"My neighbor's niece called day before yesterday," he said in a lowered voice. "Her husband had died during the hurricane and they live outside San Juan. We tried to send a morgue truck, but it couldn't get through. I told her to just go ahead and bury him. People can't even refrigerate their food or their medicine, let alone their dead."

"Can I quote you on that as an anonymous source?" Dulce asked.

He thought for a moment. "Yes," he said.

She wrote down the quote and read it back to him for accuracy.

"And would you like to interview my neighbor's niece?" he asked. "Those roads were impassable for our trucks a couple days ago, but you might get through, especially now that they've been clearing the roads a bit more."

"Definitely," Dulce said, and took down her name and address.

When the van picked them up from the morgue, Zavier asked about going to see the young widow outside of town. The driver said it would be another few hours before he would be back this way. But he had to come by the airport to pick up another journalist.

"Perfect," Zavier said. "Drop us at the mortuary in Carolina. We have some business at the airport. You can pick us up there."

They climbed into the van, and there was one other journalist in the passenger seat.

"Mendoza!" the guy called. He was a tall and white. Mid-30s. He was looking back at Zavier, but he didn't even look at Dulce or introduce himself.

"You working on this death count story?" the guy asked. But it wasn't really a question to get information.

"Yep," Zavier said, and looked back down at his phone.

"Lucky you," the guy said. "A morning at the morgue, huh?"

"Mmm," Zavier said noncommittally.

"I don't know how you do it," the guy said. "I can do war zones, but I can't do morgues. It's like they're just too dead."

"Can you show a little respect, man?" Zavier asked. "The whole island is in mourning."

"Oh come on," the guy said. "It's just gallows humor. We're all in the same boat." He called to the driver: "Hey! This is me just up ahead." He turned back to Zavier. "See you back at the Lumineer."

And then he climbed out of the van. All as if Dulce hadn't been sitting right next to Zavier the whole time.

As they drove away, Dulce sucked her teeth. "I feel a little overwhelmed from all that eye contact," she said.

"What?" Zavier asked. "Did he totally ignore you? Act like you were a lamp or a bookshelf or something."

"Basically," Dulce said.

"He's like the Mike Pence of reporters," Zavier said.

"The what?" Dulce asked.

"It's a journalist joke," Zavier said. "This is your only warning. You're about to be one of us, so you need to know our jokes are corny."

"I could have predicted that," Dulce said.

"That guy really is such a dick," Zavier said. "I guess I've gotten numb to it. Welcome to the world of journalism."

* * *

The folks who ran the mortuary in Carolina said all the same things the other sources had said.

As they walked to the airport, Dulce could see that even a day later, more of the expressway had been cleared.

From outside the airport gate, Dulce was able to point out the area where she had been detained by the military.

Zavier had brought binoculars. He looked through them at all the trucks. There was nothing that looked even remotely like the transportation of bodies from the day before. They did, however, have a bunch of boxes of FEMA supplies: water and what looked like food rations. They were sitting on palates, the sun glinting off the plastic they were wrapped in.

As the two of them stood there, Dulce saw the bad cop from the day before. He was in a jeep that was exiting through a military checkpoint they had set up at the entrance to the tarmac.

"That's him," Dulce said. "The guy who detained me. The passenger."

"Wait here!" Zavier said. He lifted the binoculars, tracked the man for a moment, and jogged toward the entrance.

"Sergeant!" Zavier yelled. Through the binoculars, he had identified the man's rank from his uniform.

The guy looked up behind mirrored shades. Beside him, the driver was conferring with the guard at the checkpoint, studying a map.

"Sergeant," Zavier said, slightly out of breath. "I have several eyewitnesses that saw dead bodies being loaded onto trucks here yesterday. What can you tell us about those cadavers? Are they hurricane victims?"

"No fucking comment," the sergeant said.

"And what about the FEMA supplies on the tarmac today?" Zavier asked. "Are those going to be distributed to the US citizens here in need of food and water?"

"Goddamn media libtards," the sergeant said. "What do you think? We're gonna leave them to rot indefinitely? Relief efforts take time. They just arrived and we're preparing the distribution routes now."

"Is it true that civilian Puerto Ricans from Chicago were able to get food and water to some populations faster than the US government?" Zavier asked.

"Here's a quote for you," the sergeant offered. "The men and women of our military are working hard for the relief effort, despite the naysayers and critics like you. The people of Puerto Rico are lucky to have us here."

"Don't you mean the US taxpayers of Puerto Rico?" Zavier said, but by then the jeep had begun to drive away.

He walked back to Dulce. "What did he say?" she asked.

"Nothing useful," he said. "But I'll keep digging to see if I can find a second source for the article."

He scanned the area a few more times through the binoculars, and called the van pool.

"Can I ask you something?" Zavier asked as they waited for transport to visit the young widow.

"Sure," Dulce said.

"What made you ask that question at the funeral home?" he asked. "About women and violence?"

"Something I saw at the shelter," she said. "Assholes taking advantage of the situation with the hurricane."

"Makes sense," he said. "Any particular story we should be pursuing there?"

"No? Yes?" she said. "I don't know. Seems like women get their asses beat and get killed all the time and it's not really a story. So why would it be news if it's just extra in a hurricane, you know?"

"It's fucked up," Zavier said. "Thanks for helping me keep it on my radar."

The van pulled up and they climbed in. An older guy was sitting in the back talking loudly on a cell phone.

"Nick?" he growled into the phone. "I was on fucking hold for ages. They just got me from the airport, and it's like

I'm on some Supershuttle from hell. I wasn't expecting a god-damn limo, but I expected the vehicle to be heading toward my hotel and not making a two-hour excursion in the other fucking direction."

Dulce and Zavier looked at each other.

"Total asshole," Zavier mouthed.

Dulce nodded discreetly.

"Remember, you begged me to come report in this fucking disaster zone. I didn't win three Peabody awards and a god-damn Pulizer to be roughing it like some fucking cub re-porter."

Eventually he talked himself out. Or Nick hung up. Either way, the van went quiet as they headed up to see the young widow. A half hour later, the guy was asleep.

The widow's house was outside San Juan, and it was slow going, even in the sport-utility vehicle. Parts of the road were in foot-deep water. Other parts were covered in branches, and they had to take the van carefully off-road to get around them. At one point, it looked like they were caught in the mud, but the driver engaged the four-wheel drive, and the ve-hicle leaped forward. Further down that same road was a spot where the concrete had been torn to pieces.

It wasn't really possible to find an address the traditional way, but the driver was able to put in the longitude and lati-tude of the address, and the driver's GPS brought Dulce and Zavier to the right location.

There were no street signs. Not even a real street. And the houses were in different states of destruction. None was still fully intact.

The house they were visiting was half-destroyed.

Dulce and Zavier brought a rescue pack from the van and knocked on the door.

A young woman answered. Mrs. Martinez didn't look much older than Dulce. So young to be a widow. She had her hair back in a disheveled braid and her arm was in a makeshift sling.

Beside her was a toddler that had on a diaper so heavily soiled, it was hanging to his knees.

"Let me carry this in for you," Zavier said, and set it on the counter.

"Bless you," Mrs. Martinez said, looking into the box to find canned and packaged food, water bottles and diapers.

She handed one of the bottles to Dulce with her good hand. "Would you mind?"

"Not at all," Dulce said, opening it for her. Mrs. Martinez took a drink, then gave some to her son. He finished the bottle.

The mother picked up one of the diapers, and tried to get it open, but it was difficult to do with her injured arm.

"Here," Dulce said. "Let me help. I was always changing my nephew."

"You're an angel," Mrs. Martinez said as Dulce picked up the toddler and walked him over to a coffee table that was buckling from moisture.

Mrs. Martinez leaned her head against the back of the couch. She didn't cry audibly, but the tears just ran down her face.

Dulce glanced at her and then back to the toddler. "*Sí, papito*," she cooed. "*Tú vas a tener un panuelo limpio*! Yay!" She lifted both his hands and shook them, as if the baby was cheering. "My nephew used to love that. Looks like you do, too."

The toddler giggled.

In the silence that followed, Dulce changed his diaper. She wasn't sure where to put the dirty one, so she just used the tabs to seal it up, and left it on the coffee table.

Abruptly, Mrs. Martinez sat up on the couch. "We were planning to move to the mainland," she said. "We've been trying to sell this house, but no one was buying. So my husband was working overtime to earn enough for us to fly out. We had tickets for next week. Next fucking week."

"How did your husband pass away, Mrs. Martinez?" Zavier asked gently.

Dulce picked up the toddler in his clean diaper and carried him into the kitchen—or what was left of the kitchen.

"He got hit by a car," she said. "Because the traffic signals were out. Two neighbors carried him to the nearest emergency shelter, but by then it was too late. Maybe if it had been a real hospital they could have saved him, but maybe not." She rubbed absently at her injured arm. "And then we had to bury him there. Because there was no way for the funeral home to get to us. Like it wasn't bad enough that I had to watch him die, but I had to literally bury him myself or watch him rot? My husband, buried with no coffin in the dirt outside an elementary school?"

Dulce looked at the woman through the kitchen door. Mrs. Martinez wiped her eyes with the back of her good arm.

"I wanted to leave sooner for Florida, but he said no. Just let him work a few weeks more. He could get a bonus. We would need the money when we got to the States. He worked so fucking hard. All that work and nothing to show for it. Nothing. Not one fucking thing. When I got pregnant, I wasn't sure I wanted to keep the baby. The economy had gone to shit. I was like, it's such bad timing for us to have a baby. But my husband is so Catholic, you know. He was like God has a plan."

She looked around at the house "Is this God's plan?" she asked, her voice rising.

Dulce began to bounce the baby on her hip as she walked toward the sodden back bedrooms of the house. His mother's voice wasn't quite so loud there.

"Is this God's fucking plan?" Mrs. Martinez asked, her voice even more shrill now. "To have our economy fucking crash and then all the water in the world land on our tiny island. Is God pissing on us?" she demanded. "Is He?"

"It's not God," Dulce heard Zavier say gently. "The United States is pissing on Puerto Rico."

"I guess you're right," she said, her voice quieter now. "The United States is playing God with us. And I look at my son, and he's so beautiful, and I'm glad I brought him into this world because he's the only thing of my husband that I have left—" She choked off into a sob. When she spoke again, her voice was a strangled whisper. "But I'm also sorry I brought him into this world. A world where he's gonna grow up without a father. A world where he's not even two years old, and already treated like shit. *Es una mierda*!" she said.

The child had stayed quiet through the first part of her tirade, but now he began to howl.

"It's okay, *papito*," Dulce said. "It's okay." But the child kept crying, his little hands balled into fists, his face turning scarlet. Because even the toddler could tell that it wasn't okay at all.

On the way back down the hill, they were alone in the van with the driver, and all three of them smoked. Dulce and Zavier shared a single cigarette in the back seat.

"When I was a kid, I always envied Puerto Ricans," Dulce said in Spanish. "Technically, I'm Puerto Rican, because I was born here, but my mom and my brother and sister were born in the DR. I always figured if we had all been Puerto Rican, it would have been different. My mom would have had papers and wouldn't have had to work under the table. My brother wouldn't have gotten deported when they caught him selling drugs." She took a long drag on the cigarette and blew it out the window. She handed the cigarette to Zavier.

"But now, I don't fucking know," she said. "That woman was right. It's all *una mierda*."

Zavier gave a bitter laugh. "Everybody's jealous of somebody," he said. "When I was growing up, I used to envy the kids who lived on the island," He flicked the ash from the cigarette out the window. "They just seemed to know who they were. Nobody was calling them a spic and trying to beat them down on the way to school. They never had to fall on their ass in the snow. They lived in houses with yards and chickens running around. We lived in apartments with rusty fire escapes and roaches. But I always thought I'd get back here. Retire or maybe just live in the US long enough to . . . set myself up as a freelancer and then I could work from here or something. But now?" He trailed off and took a drag of the cigarette. "I don't fucking know."

Dulce took an absent drag on the cigarette and it almost burned her finger. She threw it out of the van, and for a split second she panicked. She had forgotten where she was and worried about fire. It was a reflex. She sat forward suddenly, as if to chase the flaming ember out of the window. Only she could prevent forest fires. Then she sat back in a burst of clarity. Those ads didn't apply to the Caribbean most months of the year, let alone during hurricane season, and especially not now.

After they got back into San Juan, Dulce looked out the window as they picked up a few other reporters around the city. The beauty of the orange and pink sky contrasting with the ruined urban landscape sank Dulce into a state of melancholy.

Zavier's phone rang, startling her.

She still hadn't gotten reaccustomed to the sounds of technology. Before the hurricane, she had just grown accustomed to their constant signals. Calls. Texts. Alerts. Her phone. Her friends' phones. Boyfriend's and clients' phones. But for so may days, there had been no pings and jingles. So when they did happen, they were jarring. Like a nearby siren or a fire alarm.

"*Dígame*," Zavier said when he picked up.

She realized she hadn't checked her own phone since the morning.

Dulce dug it out of her pocket, hoping that she had a signal and maybe Phillip had texted. By now he must have seen the news of the hurricane. She imagined a text where he said he was sorry. He had underestimated the danger. To make it up to her, he was sending her a ticket to Miami or New York or maybe an open ticket to anywhere in the world. She could go to Barcelona. Or even Brazil. Make good on her fake identity.

Instead, when she powered up her phone, she started getting several texts from her family:

From her mother:

Luqui, we're praying you're okay.

From her sister Yunisa:

Luqui, I'm so sorry I was such a bitch when you called and wouldn't help you. You better fucking get out of this okay, or I'll never forgive you.

She laughed out loud and tried calling, but didn't have a strong enough signal. Instead, she texted back:

I'm ok. I'll call when I get a chance. have a friend who might be able to get me home with the press corps.

She tried calling the landline and her family's apartment. She dialed and put a finger in her ear to listen for the sound of ringing. But instead she got a message that her call could not be completed. She hung up.

When she looked up, Zavier was grinning.

"I have good news," he said.

"Great," she said. "I really need a happy ending to this day."

"Delia Borbón's coming," he said.

"Delia Borbón?" Dulce asked, unable to imagine the glamorous film star in this dystopic landscape.

"She's giving a press conference tomorrow in San Juan," Zavier said. "And I got passes."

"Passes?" Dulce asked, eyes wide. "As in more than one?"

"*Dos*," he said. "One for me, one for my lovely assistant."

"I hope that would be me," Dulce said.

"No one lovelier," he said.

As they rode back to the hotel, Zavier went online to see what he could find about Delia Borbón's visit. Next to him, Dulce closed her eyes, so she didn't need to see any more of the broken trees, ravaged ground, and half-collapsed houses.

Chapter 24

Dulce was dazzled by standing so close to one of her idols. As Delia Borbón approached the podium, the questions began.

"Ms. Borbón!" rang through the room like the buzzing of a hive of bees.

Borbón took the microphone and raised her hand for silence.

"I've come here to talk about my humanitarian efforts in Puerto Rico, because my island is facing the biggest ecological disaster of our time. And this is not about forces of nature, this is about where colonization intersects with climate change. This disaster is man-made on both counts, in particular, made by the US, the West, and corporate greed."

She looked down at the reporters. "I hope you all quoted me on that. Before I go on, I need to clarify something. I see reporters here from *TMZ* and *The Enquirer* and other tabloid press. I did not come here to Puerto Rico, in the middle of this disaster to answer questions about my sex life, about my marriage, or about my work history. So, if that's what you flew in here to ask about, you can turn around and fly right back out. Because I'm giving every question about those subjects a big fucking 'no comment' right now, so we can focus on something that actually matters."

In the last twelve hours, Dulce had gotten caught up on Borbón's big scandal. In her memoir *From Red Light to Red Carpet*, and in subsequent interviews, she had always maintained that her sex work had been limited to being a stripper. She had insisted, even when asked very direct and explicit questions about it.

But the previous week, on Reddit, a man had posted a first-person account of getting oral sex from Borbón in the nineties. When asked why he came forward with the story after all this time, he said he wanted to take her down a peg after the comments she'd made about the president being a racist.

In the days since the Reddit story had posted, no one had gotten a comment out of Borbón. She hadn't even been willing to communicate with the media until this press conference in Puerto Rico.

"But it doesn't have to be one or the other!" a reporter yelled out.

"Excuse me?" Borbón asked.

The reporter was a young Latino man.

"I also care about Puerto Rico," the young man said. "I'm Dominican. My island could be next. Many of our readers probably do care more about your personal life than your mission here, but we could craft a story that incorporates both and raises awareness about Puerto Rico."

"Okay," Borbón said. "Fine. Somebody wants to craft a narrative about this disaster that weaves in details of my personal life, then fine. After this press conference, about the hurricane, I'll be glad to have a separate conversation with any of the journalists in this room who are interested. But— wait for it—" she said, and cocked her head to the side.

The room full of journalists wasn't even breathing as it waited for the catch, the caveat.

"The journalists all need to be current or former sex workers," Borbón said.

The room gasped audibly.

"Those are my terms," Borbón said flatly.

Dulce still couldn't breathe. Couldn't get air in or out. Borbón meant her? Delia Borbón would only talk to someone like her?

"Just as I thought," Borbón said. "None of you are qualified to talk to me about my sex life, my marriage or my work history. So back to the hurricane."

Dulce struggled to get her lungs to obey her instructions. She couldn't seem to talk, so instead, she stood up suddenly.

Before she could say anything, Zavier had leaped up next to her and was speaking. "Zavier Mendoza, *New York Times*. We have a freelancer colleague back in New York who is a former exotic dancer. Can we contact her to do a phone interview with you?"

Borbón gave him a withering look. "You think I don't know any sex worker journalists?" she asked. "If I wanted to tell my story to one of them in the States I could have."

Zavier sat down, and pulled Dulce down by the hand.

"Don't say anything here," he said. "These reporters will be all over you."

Zavier had figured it out. He knew. Dulce could feel her face burning as the entire room looked at them. The reporters began to hiss with questions to each other.

"Who is that?" she heard someone ask.

"Is she with some indy press?"

She was afraid to look Zavier in his face, to see what he might be thinking. But he was looking straight ahead at Borbón.

"We shouldn't approach her directly," Zavier whispered. "We'll go through her assistant."

"And one more thing," the star was saying. "I don't want any of you coming to me trying to pretend that the compromises you make in your journalism are the same as sex work."

She surveyed them like a school teacher with naughty children.

"Now back to the matter at hand, the devastation of my homeland, an entire nation, and a people that have been colonized by the United States for over a hundred years. Our blood is on the hands of the US and the hands of the president—who threw paper towels at us? Paper goddamn towels? Are you fucking kidding me? And it's not just this president, but every previous president who was willing to let the US keep sucking the blood of Puerto Rico . . ."

Half an hour later, Borbón had answered all the questions that the reporters had about her hurricane relief efforts, plus several veiled questions like: "Will you be returning to your Manhattan townhouse after this?" Which was really code for: "Are you still living with your New York Congressman husband Kevin Wolinsky, or are you living separately?"

"We're done here," Borbón said. "And I don't want you snakes all hanging around to eavesdrop. Clear the room."

Dulce's heart beat hard as she slipped into the line of reporters and camera operators filing out. Zavier was chatting with a young woman in a Team Borbón T-shirt.

The white woman who had been sitting on her other side during the press conference drifted over to Dulce, but she kept her eyes on Zavier.

"Who's your colleague?" she asked Dulce. "The stripper journalist he mentioned, back in New York."

"Nobody you would know," Dulce said.

"So . . ." the woman asked. "Can I get your card?"

Dulce recalled Zavier's caution.

"I'm out of cards," Dulce said.

"No problem," the woman said. She offered her name and the outlet she wrote for, then stuck out her hand to shake.

"Nice to meet you," Dulce said.

"And you are?" the woman asked.

"I was sitting next to you for half an hour," Dulce said. "And you had no interest in meeting me til now? Why? Because I might know a sex worker who might talk to Borbón?"

"Your generation is killing the profession," the woman said. "With your identity politics and your personal lives on social media." She shook her chest facetiously, and spoke in a high, mocking tone: " 'I'm a stripper so that qualifies me as a writer. Here's a bikini photo.' " She dropped the fake voice. "Here's a newsflash for all of you: writing makes you a writer, not showing your tits."

"I guess Delia was right to only speak to another current or former sex worker if regular journalists are shady bitches like you."

The woman's eyes opened wide.

"That's on the record," Dulce said and walked away.

Once they got outside, Zavier murmured in her ear: "We're headed back to the hotel. Don't say anything in the carpool, ok?"

During the drive, Dulce's anxiety was boiling. Was this even gonna happen? And if Borbón really did give her an exclusive, would Dulce be ready to out herself publicly as a former sex worker? She wished Marisol were here. She would know what to do.

"So," Borbón asked. "What kind of sex work?"

The two of them sat on opposite sofas in a luxury hotel. In daylight, the place was still beautiful, despite the lack of running water. By night it would be illuminated by candles.

What kind of sex work? Dulce felt tongue-tied, trying to remember the woke term she'd learned at the Vega health clinic. "Um . . . full service," she finally said. Girls at the clinic said "prostitute" was kind of a slur. "Ho" was like the n-word. Only cool if people in the group said it to each other.

"Where did you work?" Borbón asked. It was more like Dulce was being interviewed. Interrogated, really.

"New York City," Dulce said. "The Bronx, mostly."

"You still in the business or no?" Borbón asked.

Dulce hesitated. "Before the hurricane, I sometimes had . . . like sugar daddies. But not working for cash. In the Bronx I used to have a pimp, but I got help to get out. From Marisol Rivera at the Vega Clinic."

Borbón's face lit up. "You know Marisol?" she asked.

"She picked me up off the street after I got beat up," Dulce said. "When there wasn't room in the shelter, she even took me up to her apartment. I never coulda got out without her."

Borbón sighed. "She's a special lady," she said. "All heart. If you know her, then you're legit."

Dulce nodded. She didn't really have a recorder, but she pulled out her phone.

"I don't want this recorded," Borbón said. "We can go paper and pen. Old school. Let me know if I'm talking too fast."

Dulce nodded and brought out her notebook.

"Actually, this first part is off the record," Borbón said. "These fucking journalists think they're so goddamn liberal, but their contempt for sex workers seeps into their writing like toxic waste. They don't even know."

Dulce nodded.

"Okay, on the record now," Borbón commanded.

Dulce picked up her pen.

"I just want to begin by apologizing to all my sisters who do sex work for denying the truth all those years. I just thought I could sanitize my past, you know?" Dulce scrawled as fast as she could, and Borbón waited for a moment. "Stripping is legal. It's stigmatized but also kind of glamorized these days. Selling sex? Not so much."

Dulce laughed and nodded. Like the rapper Nashonna might not get that same respect if she'd worked full-service.

"I just thought I'd be able to get away with it," Borbón went on. "I guess in the age of the internet, there's always some asshole who can find a platform to take a woman down. I know I could have just kept denying it. But I thought of the women I had danced with. They also knew I did full-service sometimes. We all did. None of their lives had turned out as good as mine. What would it be like for them if I kept lying? I felt like I was turning my back on them. I decided to speak out."

"Takes a lot of guts," Dulce said.

The older woman nodded. "So I, Delia Borbón, do officially acknowledge that yes, I was a stripper, and exotic dancer, whatever, for years. And those clubs were like . . . what is it Tyesha from the clinic called it? Sharecropping. The more you worked, the more you owed to the venue. Some days you could make enough stripping. But other times, you couldn't. I was facing eviction one of those days, and a customer offered me a lot of money for a blow job. So I did it. Mostly I just danced. But there were always customers who wanted more. I knew the managers wanted us to offer more. I gave maybe a dozen hand jobs. Only two or three blow jobs. Just when I was really desperate for cash. I never did, you know, full sex because other girls said it was harder to do that and get back to dancing without a shower. Plus, they said it was hard to get them to use a condom. So there you have it. One of the three guys whose dicks I sucked has a big mouth and no loyalty or discretion."

Dulce was writing as fast as she could, and realized that she would need to ask a question. Something bold. Something a non-sex worker might not think of.

"What are you most proud of from those days?" Dulce asked.

Borbón's grave face split into a smile.

"Same thing as now," she said. "I'm proud of my hustle. I was determined to chart a path out of the hood."

Dulce nodded as she wrote.

"But not to turn my back on where I came from," she said. "I just had bigger dreams than my parents or what the teachers could imagine for me."

Dulce chose her words carefully: "How has this exposure affected your marriage?"

"Kevin knew," Borbón said. "I never lied to him. I think he benefitted from the lie. Marrying an ex-stripper makes you edgy. Marrying an ex . . . I don't even know what to call myself. I never used the word prostitute in my head."

"Marrying someone who sold sex?" Dulce suggested.

"Yeah," Borbón said. "Marrying someone who sold sex isn't edgy, it's distasteful in this society. It's not distasteful to pimp women so hard in strip clubs that they have to sell sex. It's not distasteful that becoming a mother is the biggest risk factor for female poverty. It's not distasteful that there's no economic safety net. It's not distasteful that women are so underpaid and mistreated on jobs, from blue collar to administrative to professional, that selling sex looks like a better option. It's not distasteful that women are so frequently raped and sexually harassed that it seems like a step up to get paid for sex. Everything in society is set up to pressure women into compromising ourselves, one way or another, but then when we compromise, we get blamed and slut shamed. That's what's distasteful."

Dulce scrawled frantically.

"Do you need me to repeat any of that?"

Dulce did. They spent a few minutes getting it down on the page.

Borbón looked down at her long gold nails. "I've met women who are proud to sell sex," Borbón said. "Or feel empowered by it. But that wasn't my story. I wasn't proud, I just needed the money."

"You don't have to answer this," Dulce said. "But you

know your fans are wondering how Congressman Wolinsky is responding to the news."

Borbón shook her head. "It's been harder on Kevin than he expected. It'd been so long, and we thought I had gotten away with the lie. The crime of omission. We're not separated, but yeah, he did leave unexpectedly to go to Washington, to take a little break."

"What's next for the two of you?" Dulce asked.

Borbón laughed. "A friend of mine suggested couples counseling," she said. "I don't know. I guess if things don't smooth out, I'll consider it."

Dulce thought about Zavier. What would it be like, now that he knew she was a former sex worker? "What would you tell men whose partners have been involved in the sex industries?" Dulce asked.

Borbón looked out the window, then turned back.

"It's really just like loving any woman," she said. "Men are taught that a good woman is pure and doesn't take up too much space or talk back. That she can be controlled. That her sexuality is a force for him to own. For him to use and enjoy. And that's bullshit. Every woman out there was sexually alive before you met her, and thank God. Female sexuality isn't a flower that gets irreparably crumpled after a woman has sex. It's a surging force of nature. Before I married Kevin, my sexuality was alive and kicking. And I used it in the service of my own pleasure, but also for my own survival and to get ahead. And other people took advantage of me and exploited me, and sometimes I participated in my own exploitation. And that's part of the story, too. How I learned to have this power and not let anyone exploit it. And that's all part of what makes me a powerful woman. And Kevin is fucking lucky to be married to someone like me. And if he doesn't respect what he has, then to hell with him!"

Borbón laughed, then put her hand on Dulce's shoulder. "Okay, that last part really is off the record."

"Good," Dulce said. "Because I couldn't keep up."

Borbón chewed one of her gold nails. "I feel like that's the end, but I want to give another line. Some sort of ta-da!"

"What would you say to the man who exposed you?" Dulce asked.

Borbón blew her breath out. "Two things," she said. "First of all, it said he was in an unhappy marriage at the time. Motherfucker, I would never have gone to your wife and talked about what a pathetic whiner you were. Coming into the club, spending your money and begging me night after night for a blow job. Only getting one because you happened to hit me up when my rent was overdue. And second of all, to every woman who's ever made a sexual decision she regretted. That decision did not diminish you. It added to your personal experience. You get to upgrade the system based on what you learned. If it harmed you, you get to heal from it. Nothing about your humanity is ever beyond repair."

Borbón nodded, and Dulce finished writing out the phrase: "nothing about . . . your humanity . . . is ever . . . beyond repair."

"What do you think?" Borbón asked. "Did that sound okay?"

"Are you kidding me?" Dulce asked. "That was amazing. That is about to inspire a whole generation of young women."

"You are the best, *mamita*," Borbón said, and flung her arms around Dulce.

Unexpectedly, they both began to cry.

Borbón waved a hand in a circle in front of her face to indicate her ruined makeup. "This is totally off the record," she said.

Dulce laughed through her tears. "For me, too."

"Sooooo," Zavier said when she came back down to the hotel lobby. "You kind of came in to that press conference as my assistant and totally scooped me and every reporter in the Western Hemisphere."

It was raining heavily outside. They stood around in the lobby waiting for it to let up a bit.

"I never been so fucking disoriented in my life," Dulce said. "I lived through a goddamn natural disaster, and then I was talking to my biggest idol like we were just hanging out on the block or something."

"So, at the risk of seeming like I'm trying to jump on your bandwagon," Zavier said. "I would love to give you some advice, and some help."

"Are you fucking kidding me?" she said. "You better help me. I haven't written anything since high school."

He laughed. "That I can help you with. Piece of cake. But the other thing I think you need to know is that you have to be careful that you don't become the story."

"What do you mean?"

"If people can't get a comment from Borbón, then the story is that she gave her exclusive story to you. People are gonna want to know your name, your history, which publication you're writing for."

"And which publication am I writing for?" Dulce said. "I don't even know."

"You can probably take your pick," he said. "If I were you, I'd get on the phone with different outlets and get them to bid for your story. And then negotiate."

"I don't know how to negotiate with outlets," Dulce said.

"I can help with that, too," Zavier said. "Be a sort of agent on your behalf."

Dulce blinked at him.

"What's in it for you?"

"What do you mean?" he asked.

"Do you want a cut?"

"A cut?" he asked. "*De ninguna manera*. I'm just helping you out as a friend. Some of these reporters are sharks.

They'll try to take you out for drinks and steal the story right out from under you. I might help you with editing, but I'm one hundred percent clear that this is your exclusive story."

"Cool," Dulce said. "I trust you. I wouldn't even be in this amazing position without you."

"I can't believe you thought I'd take a cut," Zavier said. "I'm a colleague, not a pimp—" He stopped suddenly. "Shit," he began. "I'm sorry—I didn't mean to—"

Dulce looked him straight in the face.

"I had a pimp," she said. "In New York."

"You don't have to tell me," he said. "You don't owe me an explanation."

"I met him when I was fourteen. He was the worst thing ever to happen to me. He's dead now. That might have been the best thing ever to happen to me."

"Dulce, I really like you," he said. "I was hoping that after this interview we could maybe pick up where we left off. But now it feels weird. Like I'm trying to make a move because I know about your past."

Dulce shrugged. "Everything is weird," she said. "We're in a fucking disaster zone, eating food out of cans. The phone service comes and goes. I'm sleeping in a room with you and three strangers. We have a camping lantern and I piss by candlelight. There is no normal right now."

"My aunt was a stripper," Zavier said. "I wasn't supposed to know, but I heard her and my mom talking one night. I definitely figured out that her husband started as some sort of sugar daddy. I don't know. Sometimes you gotta do what you gotta do."

Dulce blinked at him. Was he trying to play her? With some fake *I understand* hustle? Maybe. But maybe not. She didn't like the not knowing. So she would let him help her negotiate to find a publisher for this story. Help her write it. Get her back to the US. Maybe she'd even fuck him. But trust that he understood this part of her past? *De ninguna manera.*

* * *

The rain had gone from pouring to simply raining hard. They needed to get going or they'd be stranded after curfew. Zavier offered his waterproof bag for her notebook and she gratefully accepted. The two of them headed out, each crouching against the rain, walking fast.

Halfway to the Lumineer Hotel, the light was fading. The rain finally softened to a drizzle, and without the sound of the downpour they could talk again. Both of them were soaked to the skin, but the evening was warm. It would have been a pleasant rainy stroll if they hadn't needed to make curfew.

"So do you want to publish this under your own name?" he asked.

"Do I have a choice?" she asked.

Zavier shrugged. "If it was me, I might come up with a fake name."

Dulce grinned. "I like it."

They brainstormed ideas on the bridge into Old San Juan.

"You could be Lolita Lebron," Zavier suggested.

"I've heard of her," Dulce said. "Was she an actress?"

Zavier shook his head. "A militant," he said. "She shot a congressman for Puerto Rican independence in the fifties."

Dulce's eyes widened. "Oh, we're going the militant route," she said. "I could be one of those four sisters in Santo Domingo I learned about in high school. The Butterflies. First book I ever read by somebody Dominican."

He grinned. "The Mirabal-Reyes sisters."

"Yeah but my dad is Cuban," she said. "So I need some Cuban roots, too."

"Celia Sanchez," Zavier suggested. "She was part of the Cuban revolution."

"That's it, then," Dulce said. "Celia Mirabal-Reyes. Maybe Celia M. Reyes for short."

* * *

By the time they approached the hotel, it had stopped raining and was nearly dark. Dulce wrung out her hair. Her tank top and shorts would dry eventually.

At the Lumineer, the reporters were sitting around eating canned food and drinking from canteens. Zavier immediately went to the part of the lobby with cell reception to call his editor.

The moment he left her side, one of the *TMZ* reporters came up to Dulce and asked her for the time.

"I don't know," she said. "My phone's not working."

"So crazy here, right?" he asked. "We were eating beef jerky all day yesterday. But we got real food today. Wanna come get some dinner? We have actual salad. Meat that isn't dried. I can get you a plate."

"Sure," Dulce said. What was his angle?

"I didn't get your name," the guy said, and introduced himself.

"Celia M. Reyes," Dulce said.

"Who do you write for?" he asked.

"I'm a freelancer," Dulce said.

"Same here," he said.

They had walked behind the hotel, and in the back courtyard there was a white tent with the smell of institutional food wafting out. They got into a long line.

"I just got back from Delia Borbón's hotel," he said. "Was that you coming out with your friend from the *Times*?"

Dulce shook her head. "Not me," she said.

"I mean, I can see it," he said. "She only wanted to talk to someone who had been in the business. And you were the hottest girl in the room. You could have been a . . . what? Stripper? Cam girl?"

Dulce just smiled at him.

"Dominatrix?" he asked with a huge grin. "You're not that tall, but I can see it. Yes, mistress."

They were almost at the front of the line.

Dulce didn't speak, she just shrugged.

"So you're not gonna kiss and tell?" he asked. "Or maybe no kissing?"

Dulce tilted her head and stared at him.

"No offense," he said.

"None taken."

"She's with me," the guy said, showing his credentials to the woman at the small table.

"I'll put it on *TMZ*'s tab," she said.

The reporter turned back to Dulce. "Or maybe you just lied and said you'd been a pro so you could get the story," he said. "See, there are advantages of being female in this business. I could never have pulled that off."

"Oh I don't know," Dulce said. "I'm sure there are some people in the market for . . ." she looked him up and down, ". . . your type." He was short and balding.

A woman was spooning spaghetti and meatballs from several huge pots. She served them two large plates. Mostly noodles.

"I'm surprised you're not in your room typing away, getting ready to file the story," he said. "She did talk to you, didn't she?"

"You got the wrong girl," Dulce said. "I was in my room reading that profile of her in *The Miami Herald*. Did you know that she walked off the set of the movie she was filming to come here? Apparently, her last words to the director were 'work around me.'"

"Quite the diva," the *TMZ* guy said.

"That's what the director said and he threatened to fire her," Dulce explained. "But Delia said he was racist, and that if someone had left a movie set in LA on 9/11, no one would have threatened to fire them. She still has family on the island."

"Come on," he said. "You talked to her, didn't you?"

"It looks like it might rain again," Dulce said. "I think I'm gonna take my food inside."

The *TMZ* guy looked up at the sky. It was maybe half-full of puffy, white clouds. "Rain?" he asked. "Are you kidding me?"

"How much time have you spent in the Caribbean?" she asked. "My people are from here, and we know when there's a credible threat. See you around."

In the lobby, Dulce slipped quietly into the stairwell, and made sure the guy wasn't tailing her to the third floor.

She knocked on the door. Around the corner, she heard the stairwell door open. Had she been followed after all?

Zavier answered, and she pressed past him into the room, shutting the door quickly behind her. For a moment, they were pressed close, then she pulled up the dish of spaghetti, and held it up between them.

"I brought contraband," she said.

"Good to see how the other half is living," he said. "But no need to ante up, you got it fair and square."

"Are you kidding me?" Dulce asked. "You're the only reason I'm here as a member of the press. The only reason I got this story is you." She remembered she needed to drive home her biggest point. "And you're the one who's gonna get me out of here. Spaghetti is the least I can do to pay you back."

"Oh good," he said. "Because it smells delicious. Is that oregano? I think the only spice I've had in days has been salt."

The two of them sat at the desk and devoured the plate in the fading light.

"So how do you want to approach this story?" he asked.

"I've been thinking," she said. "Since you said I had sort of become part of the news, I'd like to tell my story. It really kind of all lines up. How the US is treating Puerto Rico. How Borbón got pressured to give this guy a blow job. How I—ended up in my situation."

"That sounds—" he was shaking his head.

Of course this was stupid. How did she think she should be put on the same level with a movie star and an international natural disaster?

"That's such an amazing idea," he said. "And a great chance to tie in to larger issues of colonization beyond just Puerto Rico. Yes! This is going to be an incredible piece."

"But you need to do more than just help me," she said. "We need to write it together. Have both our names on it."

"Are you sure?" he asked.

"Definitely," she said. "I want to remain anonymous, though. So I can really tell my story without giving a fuck about what anyone thinks."

Zavier smiled at her. "That's always the best way to write."

For the next four hours, he wrote on the laptop, and she wrote on the tablet. Dulce began by transcribing the interview with Delia, and then wrote about her earliest memories of the star. Watching cable with her brother and seeing Delia Borbón in what she now realized was an R rated movie, and probably inappropriate. But who could forget Borbón standing bare-breasted, in a wide stance. One long leg on the floor and the other foot up on the bed. A sheet draped over one hip, covering her pubic area. She had both hands on the gun, and was pointing it at the lover she had realized was also the killer. The lover that only a few moments before was making her moan (yes, Dulce realized, very inappropriate for her to have seen the film at that age). But Borbón was so powerful. As she confronted him with his misdeeds, he grinned slyly.

"But you knew I was a bad boy," he said. "This has nothing to do with us. That bitch deserved it. It was just business."

"How can you say that?" Borbón asked, a tear falling.

"See?" he had said. "You know you love me. You could never shoot me."

"I know I'll miss you," Borbón had said. "Or I'll miss who I thought you were."

"Think about how you were feeling five minutes ago," he cooed. "You know exactly who I am."

She shook her head but didn't take her eyes off him. "Now that I know you could take a life like that, I have no idea who you are."

They both heard a siren in the distance.

"I gotta go," he said.

"No," she said. "You gotta stay and face up to what you did."

"Sorry I won't even have time to kiss you goodbye," he said.

"Don't try to walk out that door or I'll have to shoot," Borbón said.

He laughed and walked casually to the door. When he turned to blow her a kiss, she looked him in the eye and said, "*Adiós*, motherfucker." And shot him in the chest. His eyes were so surprised.

Many times, Dulce had played that scene with her former pimp, Jerry. She imagined him underestimating her. Then saying those same words, "*adiós*, motherfucker," and him looking so surprised when she shot him. When she was really enraged with something he said or did, when he walked away she would mouth the words and pretend to shoot him with two fingers and her thumb as a fake gun.

She had told Eva Feldman about it, her sometime therapist. Eva had scoffed.

"That movie is a fantasy," she had said. "Besides, when those two meet, they're both adults. She's a reporter at the top of her career. When you met Jerry, you were a child. He was twenty-five years your senior and spent years grooming you so he could manipulate and control you. She was in a consensual adult relationship. You were in a situation of abuse, exploitation, and statutory rape."

She began to write about Jerry, about what life was like in her family before Jerry. About Marisol. About the times she'd seen Borbón in the movies. About how scary it was to stand up in front of a room full of reporters and draw attention to herself. She remembered how much she had liked writing. In elementary and middle school. She had never finished her sophomore year of high school, but Mr. Q had encouraged her. Now, years later, she was finally writing something really important. The words spilled out of her before she could remember that nobody cared what girls like her had to say. She was supposed to be pretty or hot or fiery, and just let guys fuck her.

When Dulce had finished her draft, she walked over to Zavier. His face was bathed in the glow of his laptop, and she looked over his shoulder. As she watched, he typed:

The hypocrisy regarding Puerto Rico is evident, in every dead chicken floating in briny, brown water, in every cement foundation littered with the sodden remains of a family home, in every waterlogged car, in every majestic fallen tree, laying on its side with dirt covered roots, like a red-brown fist. Over a century of extraction, austerity, and neglect has left the island stripped of capital, protection, and increasingly, people.

Dulce felt a lump in her throat. She was in way over her head. How could her jumbled, tell-all about her early life compare to this professional, polished writing that he seemed to crank out, effortlessly.

She retreated into the dark of the hotel room.

"Where are you going?" he asked. "I thought we were gonna compare notes."

She shook her head, unable to speak. "I don't really have much to share."

"Are you kidding me?" he asked. "I heard those fingers ticking on the keypad. Let me see."

"It's not finished," Dulce said.

"A work-in-progress," he said. "I can't wait to read it."

Dulce shook her head. "I'm not ready."

Zavier studied her. "Okay," he said. "I promise to stop asking if you'll read me one passage."

"What's a passage?" Dulce asked.

"One short part of it. Like maybe fifty words."

Dulce chewed her lip. "Okay," she said. "But that's it."

Zavier shrugged. "That's fine," he said. "I just want to get a sense of your voice."

Dulce lowered her eyes to the tablet. She scrolled through what she had written. She didn't realize it at the time, but after the Borbón interview, it was over a dozen pages. She wanted to impress him. But even more than that, she knew he would end up reading all of it eventually, and she wanted him to understand how it had all begun.

"Even though me and my girl were smoking weed that day in the park, it wasn't the weed talking. When Jerry drove up in his car, it was the way he looked at me. She was the prettier one but he singled me out like I was special. Now I know it was probably because I looked thirsty. And I was. My brother had just got locked up for selling drugs and my sister had a new baby and was not taking well to being a mother. She would leave Darito to go out with her friends and I was the next girl in line to watch him since mom was depressed as fuck. I would hang out after school as late as I could to keep from coming home, but eventually I would get hungry, and there was usually a can of something I could open for dinner at home.

Jerry was old and kinda fat, but not too ugly. When he made his face soft, you could see the teenager he'd been. He even had a dimple. But it wasn't his looks that got me, either. It was that he chose me. I had never been chosen before. I never even met my dad. My mom acted like her life was over after they broke up. The senior who said he loved me and took my virginity turned out to have a girlfriend and told all his friends I was a slut. But Jerry looked in my eyes. He had a car. Money. He called me princess. He wanted to take care of me. I was fourteen. I thought I was in the end of a Disney movie where I was going to live happily ever after."

Dulce knew this must be a passage, maybe even two, but she couldn't stop reading.

"Before me and Jerry had sex the first time, he took me to a private doctor, who gave me the birth control shot. 'You don't want to get pregnant like your sister, do you?' he asked me. 'You got your whole life ahead of you.'

"None of the other boys I'd been with before had even asked if I was on birth control. Sometimes I was, and sometimes I wasn't. I guess I was lucky. And that's what I really felt with Jerry at first. Lucky. Even before the first time he asked me to go with another guy, he acted like I had something valuable. Like it was an amazing gift I was giving to him. The lie was like a drug. I wanted that fantasy. Even when I realized I was one of a bunch of girls, I could still rely on him to take care of me. And then later, it wasn't about love. It was about fear. And survival. And then it was just the life I was living. The girls were my friends. He was the boss. We did what we had to do to survive. Only when he beat me up too bad and I went to hospital did I end up going to the Vega clinic and everything started to turn around.

"I understand why Delia Borbón agonizes about what parts of her story to tell. You can't win that battle. If you tell it all, you know people will pity you or just laugh behind your back. They won't respect you. It's hard, because you know that you made some of your choices because you didn't respect yourself. But how the fuck were you supposed to respect yourself when nobody showed you respect? Your dad didn't respect your family enough to stay. Your mom didn't respect her kids enough to let that motherfucker go and keep it moving. The young boys you knew didn't respect you enough to want to hear anything out of your mouth except 'yes, whatever you want.' Your teachers mostly didn't want anything more than an echo of what they believed. The US government didn't respect the country your family came from enough to let your mom or your brother get a legal job. And even though you were a US citizen, you were too young to save your family. So how the fuck were you supposed to respect yourself when a pimp came rolling up, calling you princess and telling you he wanted to make your life golden? You chased that dream down into hell, and you were never free until that motherfucker was dead.

"But even after you were free, you were still in the life. You had no high school diploma, no skills other than fucking and sucking dick, walking in heels and tuning out while men talked about stupid shit with a resting face that looked like you were paying attention.

"So you went from a ho to a hustler, a sugar baby, a luxury companion on good days. But your finances always depended on men and sex and charming the fuck out of people. You didn't know how to find that fourteen-year-old girl in the park and go back to what she would have been if she'd shaken her head to the pimp with the sweet lines, and listened instead to that English teacher who liked her writing, who thought she had a gift. Would she be working retail right now? At a bookstore? In college? With some bullshit baby daddy and a couple of kids?

"And then, the exact same thing that was supposed to be your downfall, your fatal flaw, becomes the thing that separates you from the crowd. Your idol demands: 'who here is a current or former sex worker?' And with that question, she has anointed you, pulled you away from the crowd. And your entire life is changed, once again."

Dulce couldn't look up from the tablet. She hadn't been able to stop herself. The words just kept gushing from her mouth. But now, she wanted to rewind the whole thing. She had said too much. It sounded wrong to her. "Anointed you"? Who used "anointed" and "baby daddy" in the same paragraph. She was all over the place. This was a mistake.

But she looked up and Zavier's eyes were wet. He wasn't crying exactly. But she could see the emotion in his face. Was that pity? It was the last thing she wanted from him.

"You're amazing," he said. "You're a natural. I can't fucking believe you never finished tenth grade."

He ran his fingers through his goatee. "I went to journalism school," he said. "I have an MFA. So I've heard a lot of writing. But I've never heard first draft material as raw and strong as yours. And you are so fucking brave." He swallowed. "You're right. This does have the potential to change your whole life."

She sat there, stunned, unable to fully take in his words, when her mind was constructing another story. She expected scorn, or pity, or him trying to take advantage. But instead he thought her work was brave? Raw? Strong? She couldn't process it.

"Okay," she said. "So what happens now?"

He took off his glasses and rubbed his eyes. Wiped his eyes?

"Now," he said, "we edit."

They worked through the night. They had to switch from the laptop to the tablet, with Zavier running down to the lobby to charge it. He had to be slick to avoid the *TMZ* reporter who wanted to know about the girl he sat next to at the press conference. He had to bribe one of the hotel staff to keep an eye on the charging laptop, for fear the *TMZ* guy would steal the device and try to hack his way in. An exclusive on Borbón could mean thousands. Tens of thousands, depending on what she said and if they had an audiotape. Zavier wasn't taking any chances.

The two of them sat close together at the desk. Dulce wasn't used to being around a guy like this, with all the romantic ten-sion and no sex. She felt every brush of their hands, the press of his thigh against hers as they sat together, his breath on her neck as he stood up to stretch. And yet, she couldn't interrupt the work to tumble him into the bed. Really, she imagined pulling him into the shower. Taking him up against the smooth white tile, with the single candle flickering with the movement of their entangled shadows. But that was just a fantasy. The water would be cold, and they weren't alone. Throughout the night, exhausted roommates would come stumbling into the room with barely a hello. They'd take a leak in the bathroom and collapse into their beds. Not one of them seemed bothered by the editing conversation or the light of the screen.

By five in the morning, they had a draft.

"I think it still needs work," Dulce said.

"Of course it does," Zavier said. "But the structure is there. We've managed to braid it together: your history, Borbón's history, and the history of Puerto Rico that culminated in this disaster."

"I think the writing is really uneven," Dulce said. "Your parts are much stronger."

"I disagree," he said. "I think I have more of a homogenized journalism voice, while you have a more authentic voice. We can smooth that out later. Now need sleep."

The two of them crashed in the bed. Dulce was truly exhausted, and sleep overtook her quickly, but even as she sunk beneath its waves, she was acutely aware of Zavier's body, like an infrared outline in her peripheral vision, pulsing with warmth and intensity.

Chapter 25

Much later that morning, Dulce woke up to the hissing of whispered conversation.

"But I never said we were exclusive," Zavier was saying in a hushed voice, and then he listened for a while.

"No," he said. "That was never our relationship. We always said—" He was sitting in a chair by the window, his body hunched away from her, as if he was hiding both the phone and the conversation.

Of course. Of course he was too good to be true. Of course he had a girlfriend.

"Are you fucking kidding me?" he asked. "I don't care what the legal definition is. I care what we agreed to. Two people. You and me."

The "legal definition"? Did that mean he was married? Well that explained all his so-called gentlemanly behavior. Her sister had explained how that went. These dudes let the woman make the first move so later, when it came out that he was married, he could completely avoid taking responsibility.

She slipped out of bed and peed by candlelight.

When she came out, she picked up her few belongings. The water wallet. Her flip flops. She took a granola bar off the bureau.

But what would she do about the most important thing she had left in that hotel room—her story? She couldn't take the devices it was on. She quickly emailed a copy to herself and went to open the door.

"Hey," Zavier said, lowering the phone. "Where you going? I brought breakfast."

"I gotta go," Dulce said.

"What?" Zavier asked, standing up. As he walked after her, he hissed into the phone. "I gotta go. And this is not over."

"Dulce, wait!" He tossed the phone on the bed and hustled after her toward the stairwell.

"Don't bother," she said.

"What is up with you?" he asked.

"What's up with me?" she asked. "What's up with whoever you were talking to on the phone?"

She pushed open the door to the stairwell. He followed her.

"You heard all that?" he asked, right on her heels as she hurried down the stairs. "Well, it's not ideal, but we need to talk about it. I don't think it really changes things."

"Don't think it changes things?" She spun around to face him. "You don't think it changes things if you're married?" she asked. "Or have you forgotten that I specifically asked you about that in Santo Domingo?"

"Married?" he asked.

"Or wifed up some kinda way," she said. "Maybe it's okay with her if you fuck around, but it's not okay with me." She turned and got in his face: "I'll use your words. 'Relationship' that's not 'exclusive.'" She made air quotes. "Isn't that what you said? 'Two people. You and me'?"

For a moment he just looked at her, mouth open, brow furrowed in confusion. Then he began to laugh.

"Oh you think it's funny?" Dulce asked. "Fuck you."

She turned on her heel and began running down the stairs.

"That was my editor," Zavier hollered after her. "His name is Dave."

Dulce stopped. "Your what?"

Zavier caught up with her. "That was my editor Dave back in New York," he said. "He's insisting that their paper has the right to the Borbón interview because I'm traveling on their dime, and you used the pass with our outlet to get into the press conference."

"You told Dave about the article?"

"Hell no," Zavier said. "I filed my story last night and I've been working with you on the low. But reporters gossip and somebody must have said something. Anyway, they'll pay you freelance rates, but it's nothing like if we'd been able to sell to one of the tabloids."

Dulce felt the good news/bad news mix of emotions. He didn't have a wife or girlfriend? But she also couldn't sell her story for top dollar?

"Your editor Dave wants to run our piece?" she asked. "And I'll get my name in the *New York Times*?"

"If you want," he said. "You wanna go with your real name?"

"I don't know yet," she said. "I can't lie, I was looking forward to that money. But what's going on here is bigger than me getting paid. If we tell Borbón's story and weave it together the way we talked about, that'll get people to learn about what's happening here. And that's probably more important than anything."

Zavier smiled slowly. "So you were mad?" he asked. "You were walking out because you thought I was married?"

"Not necessarily married," Dulce muttered, looking away from him.

"Or in a serious relationship," he said.

"Something like that," she said.

"In other words, you like me?" he asked grinning.

"Why you tryna make me say it first?" she asked.

"Make you say it first?" he asked. "*Chica*, I came looking for you in a fucking hurricane. I broke the rules and smuggled you into my press situation, and you're still wondering if I like you? I can't believe how much I'm feeling you. And I'm up here trying not to make a move so I don't seem like a dick, but yes, *nena*, I'm totally fucking liking you."

Dulce leaned in and kissed him, and he kissed back.

The last time she'd made out with anyone was high school. Those boys descended on her, tongue out, their kisses like beach landings of an invading army. But not Zavier. She was intoxicated by his slowness. He kissed her like he was tasting her, like she was a confection, an elixir, a delicacy he'd been waiting all his life to taste. Her body flushed with the pleasure of it, and she found herself the one hungry for more.

"Let's go back to the room," she murmured in his ear.

"I hope everyone's gone for the day," he said.

"I think they were," Dulce breathed against his neck.

The corridor was empty, and the two of them couldn't keep their hands off each other as they stumbled, tangled in each other's arms, to the door.

Dulce reached behind her to open it, but she had the wrong room. She turned to check the number, and saw it was, in fact, the right room. But it was locked.

"You have your key?" she asked.

"No, I don't have my key," he said laughing. "I ran out without even my phone because the woman I'm feeling so much was walking out for no reason."

"Damn," she said, and the two of them leaned against the door and caught their breath.

They knocked on the door, but Zavier's wish had come true, everyone else had cleared out.

Usually, getting a replacement key in a hotel was an easy task. But the key card encrypting system required electricity and the right staff person to do it, so it would take hours to get back into their room. Fortunately, the tablet was down-stairs at the charging station, and they were able to work on the story while they waited.

Before the hotel could make them a new key, one of their roommates returned, the woman photographer. The two of them followed her back into the room with the look of guilty schoolchildren.

The photographer unceremoniously lay down on the other double bed and she was snoring in less than a minute.

Zavier's phone was inside the room with over a dozen text messages from his editor.

"They want to run the piece," Zavier said. "What do you want the byline to be?"

"Byline?" Dulce asked.

"Who should we say wrote it?" he asked.

Dulce looked at him and her face split into a grin. "Celia M. Reyes."

Zavier grinned back. "You wanna send a photo?"

"Sure," she said, and twisted her hair back into a knot. She stuck a pen into it to hold it in place. Then she pulled a sheet off the bed.

"What's that for?" he asked.

"My sister and I used to use sheets to take glamorous self-ies," Dulce said. "Like we had on ball gowns or some shit."

Dulce draped the sheet over one shoulder, then pulled her tank top down over the other arm, so it looked like she had a one-shoulder strap evening dress.

"I'm watching and learning," Zavier said. "Not sure where I'll use this knowledge, but it's lovely to watch."

Dulce laughed and shook her head.

The room was mostly dim, so she posed near the window. As a final touch, she snatched up his sunglasses and put them on.

"You look like a woman of mystery," Zavier said.

"Perfect," Dulce said, and Zavier took the photo.

"Are we really doing this?" she asked.

"By this time tomorrow, everyone is going to be googling Celia M. Reyes, and some middle-aged postal worker in New Jersey is going to get a lot of unexpected emails."

Dulce threw back her head and laughed.

"Shhh," Zavier said, with a glance at the sleeping photographer. "You'll wake the baby."

He leaned in and kissed her. His mouth hungrier this time, but like he wanted more of something he had already savored. He wrapped his arms around her waist and pulled her closer. She let the sheet fall to the floor, and he kissed her bare shoulder.

"I think you dropped something, miss," he said, grinning, pulling her tank top and bra strap back up.

"Is that mine?" she said. "I don't know if I really need that."

She had just reached down to pull up the tank and take it off, when they heard a keycard in the door.

The two of them sprang apart, and Dulce pulled her shirt back down.

The other woman reporter came back in. An androgynous young white woman with a mop of brown hair and muddy jeans.

"Dave's been freaking out," she said, clearly oblivious to what had just been going on in the room. "Did you file that story yet?"

"We cleared it up," Zavier said.

"He says he wants that paperwork ASAP," the reporter said.

"That's right," Zavier said. "They need all your paperwork before they can run it."

Half an hour later, Dulce handed Zavier a piece of paper with all her relevant information.

He looked it over. "Dolores?" he said. "I remember, from the plane. Your real name."

"That's my government name," she said, with a sly smile. "My real name is Dulce."

"That's what your family calls you?" he asked, eyebrows raised.

"What my family calls me is none of the *New York Times*'s business," she said.

"What if I want to make it my business?" he asked.

"I would say that you are way too nosy," she said. "But since you're an investigative journalist, you should investigate."

"Where do you recommend that I begin?" he asked.

Dulce shrugged. "You have the journalism degree," she said. "You figure it out." She glanced down at the laptop. "Now don't we have a deadline?"

He cut his eyes at her before he got back to work, and the two of them spent the rest of the day going over contracts and then doing edits and rewrites back and forth with the editor.

They couldn't get a moment alone. But they did finish the article.

That afternoon, the two of them stood around in the hotel lobby. Zavier had been on the phone, and Dulce was eating some crackers and spam.

Zavier hung up the phone and walked over to her. "We got that santera interview," he said.

On the way out of San Juan, Dulce saw how much progress had been made clearing the roads. The highways and major thoroughfares had been cleared. But the going was still slow, because most of the traffic signs were out. Even on back roads it took forever, because you never knew if there was supposed to be a stop sign that had been blown down. And the further out of the city they got, the more the roads were still blocked with debris.

It was mid-afternoon by the time the driver pulled the van up in front of a small yellow house. The building looked like it was still in pretty good shape, although the roof of the porch had been destroyed. In the yard was a compact gray two-door car, flipped on its back like a turtle.

He asked the van to wait as the two of them got out and walked up to the porch. Zavier knocked. No answer.

"You looking for Doña Inez?" A middle-aged woman was walking down the rutted road holding the hand of a little boy. In a baby stroller, they pushed a pair of gallon jugs of water.

"*Sí señora*," Zavier said.

"She's in line for water," the woman said. "It'll be another two hours at least."

"*Gracias*," he said.

As she walked off, Zavier told the driver to come pick them up in time for curfew.

The van drove away, and the two reporters looked at the now uncovered porch. Zavier took Dulce's hand. "Let's find a spot out of the sun."

They circled around the back of the house only to find a covered porch that was screened in. Miracle of miracles, on it was a sofa that was actually dry.

The two of them sat for a moment and looked out on the ravaged landscape.

"How come you're so far away?" Zavier asked. He scooted closer on the couch.

She leaned her head onto his shoulder.

"How come you managed to smell so good in the middle of a fucking disaster?" he asked.

Dulce laughed. "Doña Inez ain't the only one that's got some magic."

"Oh really?" he asked. "You gonna show me some magic?"

He leaned forward and kissed her. First just gently with his lips, but then, softly, with his tongue, as well.

"I don't know," she said, pulling back. "Aren't we supposed to be journalists hard at work?"

"Didn't you hear what the lady said?" Zavier asked. "Our interview subject won't be here for a couple hours. I think we need to put in some time rejuvenating ourselves." He was kissing her neck now, her collarbone, her sternum.

"Really?" she asked. "What did you have in mind?"

"Well, you just smell so good," he said. "I wonder how you might taste."

Dulce gasped, as he kissed his way down her chest, nuzzling both her breasts, sliding one hand up under her tank top and kissing the other nipple.

She arched back on the couch, as he slid his tongue down the center line of her rib cage, licking her belly button, teasing his way down to the waistband of her shorts.

When he pulled them down, it was more as if to savor the feeling of his fingers on her hips, her ass, her thighs. The shorts weren't an obstacle, they were a tool of pleasure, as he slid the material down slowly against her skin, then snapping the elastic gently against the side of her ass that practically hung off the couch.

She giggled, and he looked up.

"Does that feel good?" he asked. "Can I please, please taste you, Dulce?"

Her face was burning. She could barely inhale enough air to breathe her reply.

"Yes," she hissed.

He slid the shorts down her legs, exposing her skin to the air, but kissing her belly, all the while. She was too far lost in the pleasure of his touch, both gentle and insistent. She didn't care that her pubic hair was wild and overgrown, she just wanted more of him. More of his lips, his fingers, his tongue.

Achingly slowly, he made his way between her lips. He tangled his tongue in the jungle of hair, making a slow, curving path down.

When he finally slid his tongue all the way in between, licking her clitoris, she sat up with a strangled moan that nearly stopped her breath.

Her body was out of control. She felt hot and clenched and overwhelmed with the power of it. Suddenly the heat of passion turned to shame. What if she didn't look right? Smell right? Taste right? The intensity of the feeling was too much. She felt too open.

"Come inside me," she gasped, and reached into his cargo shorts.

He was surprised, but she felt him in her hands, rock hard.

"Please," she begged.

Her face was raw need.

He slid his own shorts down and entered her. Both of them gasping.

She was back on familiar ground. A man above her. Inside her. But somehow it was all different still. She'd never felt this wet, at least not without lube. And as he stroked in and out, it wasn't the same as previous times. He wasn't the only one swollen. She felt the luscious pressure of her sex against his. With no threat of that sharper pleasure, she could melt into the couch with this feeling, swallowing his moans as he exploded inside her.

And when he collapsed onto her chest, spent and panting, she felt a delicious satisfaction unlike any other she'd had before. Not the ecstasy of climax, but the rapture of intimacy, merging, bliss.

A moment later, he roused himself from the stupor.

"I can't believe I—" he said. "What about birth control? I know my boy has a condom back at the hotel. I was planning on—"

"It's okay," she said.

"But people can't get basic medicine here," he said. "It's not like we can just get Plan B."

"I'm on birth control," she said.

"Oh," he said. "Right. Cool."

"The shot," she said.

He nodded, but didn't say anything as he pulled out and slid his shorts back up.

She stood and pulled on her own shorts.

Had this been a mistake? Should she have played dumb and pretended to be unprotected?

But he slid next to her on the couch and grinned at her. "I gotta be honest," he said. "It's a little awkward. I can't pretend that you got that shot for me." He shrugged. "But I believe in women's health care. And I'm honored to be in a position to reap some of its benefits."

"What position is that?" she asked with a wry smile.

"I'm hoping it's the first of many," he said, and raised his eyebrows.

"Oh my god, so corny," she said.

"You did the setup," he said. "I just delivered the punchline."

"Everybody's a comic," she said, and lay her head against his shoulder, eyes closed against the view of the wrecked hillside, sheltered in the bubble of their post-coital bliss.

When Doña Inez walked up to the house, the sun was low in the sky, and the pair of lovers sat on the now shaded front porch.

They introduced themselves and she let them in.

"I'm sorry I don't have anything to offer you," she said in Spanish. "Other than water, and I don't really trust it."

"No, doña," Zavier said. "We actually brought you some water, plus batteries and canned food."

She thanked them and motioned for them to sit on a pair of living room chairs.

Zavier thanked her for her time. "I wanted to speak with

you, because I heard that you had been burying the dead," he said.

"Absolutely," she replied.

"What gave you the idea to begin burying people?"

"Nothing gave me the idea," she said. "I just did what had to be done. If a woman went into labor, I would have attended to that, too. People died in the hurricane and none of the authorities could get here. You can't leave dead people unburied. It's unclean, both in a spiritual sense and in terms of sanitation."

"How many people have you buried?" he asked.

"Eight," she said. "But five of them were in the same family."

"What happened to them?" Dulce asked.

"They lived in the next town down below," Doña Inez said. "The hurricane ripped the roof off their house, but the car park was still intact. They huddled in the car for shelter. But then there was a flash flood. Water came fast because they were at the bottom of the hill. And it's easy to get trapped in a car. The water shorts out all the electrical. You can't get the windows or doors open. The pressure of the water means you can't even break the windows. The next day, neighbors came to check on them and found the whole family. Mother, father, all three kids. Drowned in the car."

Dulce recalled the flood at the storage unit. She had been at the bottom of a hill, too. The water came fast, faster than she would ever have thought.

"At first, they called me just to pray for the family, but then it became clear that no one was coming to handle the burials. I just said fuck it. For years we didn't need the government or the hospital's help to be born or to be buried. Although the government right now seems pretty committed to killing us."

"You mean the US government?" Zavier asked.

"The US President or the governor of Puerto Rico," she

scoffed. "The first one doesn't care about us, and the second one is ready to sell us down the river to impress the first one."

Zavier scribbled furiously in his notebook. "You said you buried eight people?" he said. "Can you tell me about the other three?"

Doña Inez shrugged. "Word got around the barrio," she said. "Other people died and so their families came to me. How is it possible that only thirty-four people died in this hurricane when I buried eight of them myself?"

After Zavier had asked all his follow-up questions, he stood. "Thank you so much for your time," he said. "And really for all that you've done for the community. Can I have your permission to photograph the house, and the car in your yard?"

"Absolutely," she said. "And by the way, that car out there? It's not mine. I don't know where it came from."

As Dulce stood with him, Doña Inez stopped her.

"Hold on, *amor*," she said to Dulce. "Keep me company a moment."

"Of course, doña," Dulce said.

The moment the door closed, the old woman looked directly at Dulce.

"This hurricane is a curse on many of us, but it came as a blessing to you," she said.

Dulce's mouth fell open.

"There are vultures coming," Doña Inez said. "Those who have no respect for life, who plan to pick the flesh of Puerto Rico. Opportunists. Trump. Roselló. And many others. They plan to twist this disaster into a blessing for them. A payday, but that's not you. You were supposed to be here. This was supposed to change you. Help you find your voice. Connect with your ancestors. You're a city girl, but have a country spirit. You don't need to live in the country, but you need to respect your country roots. You're Dominican, right?"

Dulce nodded. "Your *mami* was from the country, no? She didn't respect it. She couldn't prosper in the city because she didn't respect her roots. Honor your *mami*, but don't follow her example. The city holds dangers for you, but only if you try to become something you're not. Your path requires total honesty. And that boy out there? You should let him know how you feel about him. And you should tell him whatever you've been keeping secret from him. Secrets kill love. Trust me."

"I don't—"

"That boy loves you," she said. "You need to trust that and open yourself up to him."

"But I already—"

The old lady shook her head. "Not your body. Your heart. Don't be ashamed of the stories your body carries. First you need to be known if you truly want to be loved. Don't settle for the love where he can't see all of you. Seeds need light to grow."

Zavier emerged from the front yard. Dulce was still trying to catch her breath from what the older woman had told her.

"I got some beautiful photographs," Zavier said. "Thank you so much for your time."

"Of course," Doña Inez said. "We were just talking about plants growing. There are more storms coming, but you can't stop nature from growing back. The flora will grow back. Puerto Rico, too."

"Can I quote you on that?" Zavier asked.

"You both can," Doña Inez said.

On the way back down the mountain, the woman's words receded into the surreal landscape. In the back of the van, Dulce's skin hungered for Zavier. But they were surrounded by other reporters, and they had to play it cool. She settled for holding his hand, fingers entwined.

When they got back, it was past curfew and almost totally

dark. After the driver dropped them at the hotel, Zavier stopped halfway along the path to the front door. He kissed her with such a passion that Dulce could hardly breathe, but beyond that, she didn't want to. Wanted to breathe his skin, his eyes, his mouth, his hands.

Yet the words of the old woman came back to her. Tell him everything? Even how she'd left him in Santo Domingo to fuck a rich older guy? That her sex work days had lasted right up to hurricane Irma?

The old woman seemed so fierce, though. Burying the dead? And the car that flipped before it could crush her house? Dulce opened up her mouth to say that she wanted to tell him something, but one of their female roommates walked up.

"Did you hear that the mayor of San Juan wore a 'NASTY' t-shirt for TV interviews today?" the photographer asked. "Her latest shot in her battle with The Donald."

"She's battling him?" Dulce asked.

"Oh, you missed all this," Zavier said. "Last week, The White House was calling Puerto Rico a 'good news story.'"

"Are you fucking kidding me?" Dulce said.

"Right?" the photographer said. "The mayor fired back and called it a 'people are dying story.' She just wasn't fucking having it, you know? By the way, looks like we're flying out in the morning. They even got you a ticket, Dulce."

Dulce's face split into a grin. Yes! She would go back to New York with Zavier. It was practically a sign. She didn't need to tell him now what Doña Inez said. She would have her whole life to tell him.

She looked over at Zavier expecting him to be happy, too. But his face was a storm in itself.

"What's wrong?" Dulce asked.

"This is bullshit that he wants to send us back to New York," he said, and pulled out his phone as they climbed the stairs to the third floor.

"You might as well put him on speaker," the photographer said, as the three of them entered the room. "We're all listening to your end of the conversation."

Zavier stabbed the speaker button and put the phone on the small desk. The other roommates were there, and the photographer got them up to speed as Zavier dialed the phone.

"This is bullshit, Dave," Zavier said. "How are you going to send us home now?"

"You know the news cycle," Dave said.

"There are so many developing stories here," Zavier said.

"Zavier," Dave's voice sounded muffled through the connection. "When I sent you, I knew it was a risk because you were Puerto Rican, and you're close to this. You said it would be an asset. And it has been. That Borbón story is fantastic. And we can run your Santería story tomorrow if we get it by midnight. But we didn't send you to be a full-time Hurricane María correspondent for the next six months."

"I'm not asking for six months," Zavier said. "What about six more days?"

"No go," Dave said. "During the president's visit, the news was completely saturated. Come back to New York. Keep pitching me stories about the long-term recovery."

"We need to meet with sources in person," Zavier said.

"That's only for right now," Dave said. "But phone and internet service are being restored."

"In the capital, maybe," Zavier argued.

"Let me put it this way, Zavier," Dave said. "You can continue to freelance there, but not on our dime. And we have a flight for the whole team to come back tomorrow. After that, you're on your own. I gotta go. Let me know what you decide."

"Man, fuck that shit," Zavier said after they had signed off.

The photographer shook her head. "Zav," she said, "it's not sustainable. We need a real night of sleep."

"Yeah," the other woman said. "I need a shower that isn't cold. Food that includes vegetables."

"We can come back," the Boogie Down guy said.

"I don't fucking believe you guys," Zavier said. "I need some air."

He stormed out of the room. Dulce stood there for a moment, uncertain what to do, then turned and ran down the stairs after him.

It took her a moment to find where he'd gone, but he was out behind the hotel smoking with another journalist.

"You wanna talk?" she asked.

"I wanna smoke," he said.

She nodded and took a drag off the cigarette.

"So, do you agree with them or what?" Zavier asked.

"I've been a journalist for all of three days," she said. "I don't think I'm qualified yet to have an opinion."

Zavier put the cigarette to his mouth, and his hand shook. "I feel like I'm abandoning my people," he said. "I can't do it."

His voice nearly cracked; he was clearly fighting to keep control.

"People here were fucking drowning while I was in New York eating organic vegetables," he said. "I mean, I was worried, but I didn't—I wasn't really connected. It was like something I could turn on and off. One day I was worried about the hurricane that's gonna hit Puerto Rico, and the next day, I was distracted by some goddamn athletic shoe sale. Am I gonna be part of the fucking problem now? I'm a fucking *yanqui*. I've got the privilege to pay attention or not. I'm like the goddamn enemy."

"You didn't choose to leave Puerto Rico," she said. "That was your parents' choice. And so what if you didn't realize how bad this hurricane was going to be? Nobody fucking knew. You don't get to kick yourself because you couldn't predict the future. This is just–" She searched for the words. What was it Dr. Feldman had called it when she felt bad that she was the only one in her family that was a citizen? When it felt somehow disloyal if her life went well. "That's some kind of survivor's guilt."

"It's like I've become the colonizer," he said. "I had this dream of returning here to write and retire or raise a family. Some fantasy shit and Puerto Rico could be the backdrop. When I think about PR, it's always been about me. What can Puerto Rico do for me? And you wanna know one of the things that ran through my head when I got assigned to come here? 'This could make my career.' *My* career? *My* fucking career? People are dead, Dulce. More people than they can fucking bury. The least I can do is stay here and tell the fucking story."

"No, baby," she said. "It's not like that at all." At this point, she wasn't just saying it for her ticket off the island. She really cared about him, and she could tell that he was hurting. "You *are* going to tell the story. But this is about the long view. You need to recharge yourself. It's like they say on the airplane. Put on your own mask first."

"I see these guys here who wake up every fucking day and are chopping their people out of disaster with machetes," he said, and stomped the cigarette out on one of the cobalt blue bricks in the street. How am I supposed to go back to New York and sit in pitch meetings in midtown offices with white editors?"

"Because your people need you there," she said. "Without you, nobody will be pitching stories about Puerto Rico after next week."

"I hope you're right," he said. "Because when I get on that plane, I feel like I'm turning my back on my people."

His face was crumpling, and as rigidly as he held his body, it wasn't rigidly enough. The moment she put her arms around him, he collapsed. He folded in her arms and sobbed.

Dulce felt utterly beyond her depth. She couldn't believe he trusted her like this. Part of her thought he was weak for crying. But what the fuck? He'd seen his homeland half-destroyed, helped count the dead, and was supposed to stay dry-eyed?

And there was another part of her, a larger part, that was honored by his tears. That part could tell that she was falling in love with him. Had already fallen. So of course he could show this side of himself. Because this trip, the love they had made on Doña Inez's back porch, the story they had written together, had bonded them for life.

Chapter 26

Dulce was on a plane when the Borbón article finally went live. She and Zavier were flying over the Atlantic Ocean, his head on her shoulder. Her body was exhausted, but she couldn't sleep. Some part of her was just completely shocked and dazed.

Yet there was a ramped up feeling of anticipation on the plane for when they began the beverage service. Dulce asked for bottle after bottle of water. More than she could actually drink. She was hoarding it. Why? She was headed to the US where there would be more. But what if the plane was delayed for some reason? She knew it was irrational, but some part of her was determined never again to be without drinking water.

It was all so disorienting. She couldn't quite accept that the danger was past. And part of the disorientation was knowing that things were getting better for her personally, but things weren't getting better for the people of Puerto Rico. "We're dying here," the mayor had said. And—like Zavier—she felt guilty or selfish or ashamed that her own life had somehow been blessed by this tragedy. She had left the mainland on the run from her boyfriend. Now she was returning with a real boyfriend. One who wasn't married to someone else. He knew all about her past. They had written an article together for the *New York Times*. Jerry and Jimmy were dead, and she could come back home. She would move back in with her family, but maybe she could figure out how to turn this one article into more opportunities. Zavier would help her. Maybe . . . at some point . . . she would move in with Zavier. But she was getting ahead of herself.

So she flew from San Juan to Miami with no luggage, but her head rattling with images and sense memories: glassy-eyed corpses, the full press of Zavier's body on her and in her, and the determined jaw of the old woman in the hills.

In the Miami airport, they landed with several zero battery devices and the expectation that their story was already online. But they didn't have time to stop and charge anything. Their connecting plane to New York was taking off soon.

The two of them hustled through the airport. The terminal looked surreal to eyes that hadn't seen fluorescent lights in over a week. Hadn't seen the trappings of consumerism for even longer.

"It's so fucking weird," Dulce said. "All this shit I took for granted. Fresh water. Food you can buy. Electrical outlets that work."

"Yeah, but we don't have time to stop," Zavier said. "Maybe I'll be able to charge my phone on the plane. You ever notice how the flight from JFK to Miami has all the good food and the good outlets. But the flight from Miami to the Caribbean is the janky-ass old plane? First world versus third world?"

Dulce shook her head. "I don't think I've flown enough times."

"I can't wait to look online," Zavier said. "Just see what kind of traffic the story is getting. How many hits. Check my social media accounts."

He grinned and held her hand as they strode across the airport. When the JFK gate was in sight, it was a level below, down an escalator. Dulce looked over the edge of the mezzanine to see that the status was "boarding," but there were a lot of people in line.

The New York passengers were glossy and fashionable. Dulce looked down at her stained tank top.

"You think I have time to buy a new shirt?" she said.

He nodded and they stepped into a brightly lit airport concession and Dulce was suddenly confronted with choosing between ten different types of shirts. Did she want a pink one that said Miami in rhinestones? Gray with a green and orange gator? Finally, she found one that was blue with a simple palm tree outline. It was an XL, but she bought it anyway, digging a few crumpled bills out of the bottom of her water wallet.

"They're out of the *New York Times*," Zavier said and headed back to a newsstand they had passed. "Yell if they're about to close the gates."

Dulce stood in line to buy the shirt, glancing from time to time at their gate. Her mind kept drifting into a surreal mash up of sex and flooding water, crying women and dead bodies.

"Dulce," a voice startled her out of her daze. She looked up expecting to see Zavier, but it was Phillip Gerard.

"Fate brings us together again," he said. "Same airport. Any chance I can tempt you to come to Panama with me. A beautiful country. Truly."

"What?" Dulce asked. "I just came out of a disaster zone."

"Let me take your mind off all that," he said. "I'll be staying on the beach."

"Forget it," Dulce said.

"I think you need to back off, man," Zavier said. He held several national papers in his hand, like a weapon.

Gerard's back was to him. But then the older man turned around. "I didn't realize she already had company," he said.

In that moment, Zavier recognized the man he had seen in Santo Domingo.

"What the fuck?" he asked. "I thought you said this guy was your uncle. From Cuba."

The man laughed. "More like her sugar daddy from Miami."

Dulce's face flamed and she could feel the snacks from the plane lurch in her stomach. She thought she might be sick. Or spontaneously ignite in a blaze of shame.

"Maybe another time, sweetheart," Gerard said, and strode back the way he had come.

"You—" Zavier stammered. "You acted like it was all so long ago. When you were a teenager. But we were *on a date*, and you left for some . . . older guy you were fucking for money?"

"It wasn't like that," Dulce said. But she could see she'd fucked it up. She couldn't explain it to him like this. She couldn't explain how, when you get turned out as a fourteen year old, you just learn to fuck on autopilot. You don't think about it. You don't think about who you want to be with, you just think about survival. Who can keep you off the street. Who can make sure you get food in the fridge. You follow the money. How it was different now. Now that they'd been together in this different way.

But she had chickened out from telling him about it. Even though the *viejita* had told her to. She knew she should, but she gambled on him never knowing, and yet he had learned and now she didn't look like a girl who didn't know better, she just looked like a liar. What did Jerry used to call her. *A lying bitch whore.*

She shrank from the hurt and fury in Zavier's face.

"Just let me explain," she said. "We can talk about it on the flight."

She held her breath, hoping that somehow he would say yes. She stared at him, the papers held against his chest. The face of the US president. His furious expression and the headline about him firing back at the Mayor of San Juan. She saw the word "nasty."

She looked up to Zavier's face and that's what she saw. He looked at her as if she were nasty.

In the brief second that she stared at him, Zavier said nothing. Then his mouth contracted into a tight circle, and he threw the newspapers with all his strength. The enraged face of the president unfurled and sailed over the mezzanine, newsprint pages fluttered down onto the waiting passengers like big, gray birds.

Zavier turned away from her and stalked back toward the newsstand.

Dulce spun away from his retreating back toward the JFK flight.

Twenty minutes later, they still hadn't closed the plane doors. There was some kind of delay. Zavier could still make it.

Her eyes stayed glued to the front of the aisle. With every new passenger who came in, she felt a jolt of hope that it would be Zavier. But she saw a parade of flight attendants and other airline staff. Finally, she had nearly given up hope and the tears began to fall. Through her blurred vision, a man entered in a blue, short-sleeved shirt. Her heart leaped and she blinked the tears away. But it was a dark-haired white man in a button-down. Not Zavier. They were closing the doors now. He wasn't coming. Wouldn't be joining her. They couldn't talk about it. She'd fucked it up for good.

Now, the jumbled memories of the bodies, and the *viejita,* and the sex, were no longer balanced between possibility and rage. They'd lost the feeling of falling in love to pull her back from the precipice of hopelessness. Now it was all despair and horror, regret, and shame.

Chapter 27

She sleepwalked out of JFK and toward the ground transportation. No luggage. Nothing to declare. Nothing to claim.

She stood there for a moment, totally disoriented. It took a moment for Dulce to realize that the women standing next to her in line for a cab were talking about her. Not about her exactly, but about Celia M. Reyes.

"Isn't it every woman's nightmare," one said. "To have the guy you gave that blow job to twenty years ago pop up in the wrong place."

"No wonder she only wanted to talk to another woman who'd been a hooker or a stripper or whatever," the other woman said. "Someone who wouldn't judge."

"Some of these women need to be taken down a peg, though," the first woman said. "Not Delia, but some of these women get married and act like they were never out here in these streets. Calling other girls all kinds of sluts. Wait til you run into that guy whose dick you sucked in the bathroom at the club."

"And a motherfucker shoulda been grateful and kept his mouth shut, but no," the other woman said.

The two of them laughed.

Dulce walked past the two women to where she could get the bus to the subway. From JFK she barely had the money to take the train. Under other circumstances, she'd flirt with the token booth agent to get through or ask a man on the way to Manhattan if she could share a ride with him. But she had on an oversized airport shirt over a dirty tank top and flip flops. Her shorts had been pissed on and washed out with rainwater, then washed again in the dark. She was sweaty and there was a light film of dirt on her legs below the loose shorts. She hadn't showered since sex with Zavier, which was worse, because she could still feel, still smell him on her skin.

Dulce caught the inbound train, and found a copy of the *Times* on one of the seats. And there it was. Her article. Her article with Zavier. It looked good. The edits didn't compromise the message at all, like Zavier had feared. But she couldn't feel elated. Not since copies of the same newspaper had swooped through the air in the Miami airport.

The muffled voice of the subway train operator announced Fulton Street. She was in Manhattan now, but wasn't sure where she was going. She couldn't go home to that apartment she'd grown up in. Not yet.

Today, she needed what no one in her family had given in a decade: comfort. She needed someone to gather her up in their arms and let her sob. Sob for the man she'd lost. And for the thirty-five dead bodies, and the raging mother, and the santera who buried the dead. For the family of five who died in the car. For the wife of Pedro, whose name she had never learned, whom Pedro could successfully stalk in the chaos, and maybe would find again. For the mother and baby who died right beside her in the shelter while she was sleeping, or knocked out, or whatever. And for all the ruined houses, and people who were still dying beneath the two thirds of the planet's surface that had declared war on that island.

She went to the only place she knew for—what had she called it? Had Jerry called it? A place for broke down whores to go. She went to the Vega clinic.

In the lobby, she felt out of place among the hot girls with fly clothes, tight weaves and flawless makeup. She slunk into the lobby, all her own curves hidden under the giant shirt.

On the walls around them were schedules for the clinic's mobile health van, which served Lower Manhattan. These were interspersed with images of attractive, confident young women from the clinic's demographics that encouraged them to:

Use condoms . . . every time.

Watch your drink.

Recognize the signs of an abusive relationship.

The wall above the reception desk had a framed movie poster for *Live Nude Girls Unite!* featuring three comic book hero styled women, half-naked, with a "Strippers Union" picket sign and fists in the air. There were also posters for the clinic's *Sexy Girl's Guide to Staying Safe and Healthy in NYC.* Dulce had kept it under her bed like a secret holy book when she was with Jerry.

For a few years, she had strode through that lobby, and all the regulars knew her name.

"Excuse me?" Dulce asked the receptionist. "Is Eva Feldman here?"

The receptionist said that her former therapist was on vacation. The girl didn't even recognize Dulce today. Not with her oversized top, kinky brown hair, baggy shorts, and unpainted lips. Even the blue and glittery polish on her toenails was chipped and trashed.

"Want to leave a message?" the receptionist asked. "Dr. Feldman will be back next week."

Dulce shook her head and let herself fade into the background of the lobby. And when the receptionist buzzed the girls into the stairwell, Dulce blended into the crowd. As everyone else went into the multipurpose room, Dulce headed up the stairs, past the administrative offices and therapy rooms.

She was nearly at the top floor when she arrived at a door that had no one going in and out. She knew that this led to Marisol Rivera's private apartment, a studio that opened onto the roof. Or at least it had a while back. And Marisol owned it. No one was moving out of Manhattan unless they got pushed out. Dulce gambled that Marisol would still be there.

She knew it wasn't appropriate to drop by the former director's home. In fact, Dulce's former therapist had told Marisol it was even inappropriate to take clients to her apartment when the clinic's shelter was in overflow. But Marisol had taken her in anyway, and bathed her and put her to bed. She knew she could fall apart in those arms.

Dulce pulled her passport out of her water wallet. She used the thick, laminated edge of the booklet to slip the lock on the hallway door, and went up to the studio apartment.

Dulce took a deep breath and knocked.

The woman that came to the door looked a little like Marisol with curlier hair. They had similar features. But whereas Marisol's body was an extreme hourglass, this woman had square hips and broader shoulders.

Dulce didn't even contemplate English. She immediately began to speak Spanish.

"Is Marisol home?" she asked.

"Sorry," the woman said. "I'm her cousin. She's staying at her boyfriend's. You know Raul?"

Dulce had met him in passing when he was a security guard at the clinic. "Sure," she said. "Maybe I'll catch her there."

As Dulce was preparing to leave, a baby began to cry inside the apartment.

"Zara!" the woman yelled into the hallway.

There was no answer.

The woman propped the door open and walked across the hallway.

"Zara!" she yelled up the stairs that led to the roof. "The baby's awake. You need to come down to feed him!"

"*Ya vengo*," came a younger woman's voice from upstairs.

The woman turned back to Dulce. "When I see Marisol, should I give her a message?"

"No message," Dulce said. "Sorry to bother you." Then she turned and headed down toward the lobby.

On her way down the second flight of stairs, she nearly ran into a woman with a familiar face.

"Dulce, is that you?"

Dulce looked up to see a thirtyish African American woman and a younger white woman with a slender frame.

"It's Tyesha," the black woman said. "What? You don't recognize me in this suit?"

The two of them hugged, but Dulce couldn't find her words.

Tyesha turned to the other woman. "Dulce and I traveled to Cuba together," Tyesha explained, then turned back to make the introduction. "Dulce, this is Serena."

Dulce extended her arm on autopilot and shook hands with Serena. She recognized the clinic's office manager, but she'd never met her officially. The trip to Cuba seemed like a lifetime ago. But it was only a year and change since she left New York with Marisol, Tyesha, Kim, and Jody.

"Were you looking for Marisol?" Tyesha asked. "I'm director of the clinic now."

"And I came to tell you your next appointment is here," Serena said.

"Great to see you Dulce," Tyesha said as she crossed to Marisol's old office.

"I heard a lot about that trip to Cuba," Serena said. "But I must have gotten it wrong. I thought you stayed there."

Before Dulce could even think about it, the tears started to fall.

"Oh honey," Serena said. "Are you okay?"

Dulce shook her head. Why hadn't she stayed? In Cuba, she could have had a whole new life with Josefina. She had a family that had loved her and fed her and taken care of her. She had a good life there, but she just got bored. Like she got bored with Zavier and had to go fuck Gerard. Then she was too much of a punk to own up to it.

She managed to fuck up every good thing that came into her life.

Dulce's knees gave out, and she collapsed onto the stairs and wailed. Serena pressed in close beside her and wrapped her arms around Dulce. Serena was much slighter than her, but her arms held Dulce with surprising strength.

When the fiercest part of the storm had passed, Dulce wiped her face and attempted to pull herself together. "I can't believe I'm falling apart in the arms of a virtual stranger."

"Honey, we're not strangers," Serena said. "We're from the same tribe of women. I don't just work at the clinic. I was a client . . . back in the day."

Dulce nodded and more tears came, but quietly. She relaxed back into Serena's arms and just let herself unclench for the first time since she'd run into Gerard in the Miami airport.

When she finally wiped her eyes and stood up, Serena stood, too. Serena patted her shoulder awkwardly in the narrow hallway.

"Marisol isn't up there, but I can give her your number, if you like," Serena said, guiding her down to the reception desk.

"That would be great," Dulce said. "I came straight here from the airport."

"You're kidding me," Serena said. "If you just came from

Cuba, then you probably don't know what's been going on here."

Dulce opened her mouth to explain that she hadn't been in Cuba, but Serena was going on excitedly. "One of our own just blew up in the *New York Times*." She pulled up a paper from the desk. "Have you seen this? 'Celia M. Reyes.' She got the exclusive with Delia Borbón."

"It's me," Dulce said. "I wrote that." And she began to cry again.

Chapter 28

"So let me get this straight," Marisol was saying an hour later. "You literally just got off the plane from PR?"

Dulce had told Marisol the whole story.

"Do you need somewhere to stay?" Marisol asked. "Our shelter is full to the fire code with folks from Puerto Rico, but I'm sure I could figure something out."

"No," Dulce shook her head. "I can stay with my family. I just needed someplace to land before I had to deal with them."

"Do you need any money?" Marisol asked.

Dulce emptied out her water wallet, and in the bottom were several twenties. As she put everything back, a pair of business cards fell out of her passport. Zavier's and Gerard's.

Marisol reached for Gerard's card.

Marisol froze. Then she looked up sharply. "You know this guy?" she asked.

"Yeah," Dulce said. "He was my sugar daddy for a few weeks. But he wouldn't do shit for me when I got stuck. Lemme rip that up."

"But do you know what kind of business he does?" Marisol asked.

Dulce shrugged. "He said something about real estate."

"More like disaster capitalist," Marisol said. "He's one of the rich guys who's trying to buy up Puerto Rico right now."

"What?" Dulce asked.

"He has this bullshit charity," Marisol continued. "He promises to give food and water to struggling people in Puerto Rico, but it's really just for the people whose houses they're buying up for pennies on the dollar. Promising cash to desperate people, and even promising food and water. They're so damn crooked they won't even foot the bill for the crumbs they're offering to folks whose houses they're practically stealing."

"That's so fucked up," Dulce said.

"Yeah," Marisol said. "Those 'please give to Puerto Rico' signs are all over the hood in NYC. And it's the fucking vultures asking for money while they rip us off."

"I could call a journalist from the *New York Times*," Dulce said. "I know he was talking about all the vultures trying to cash in. He'd probably run with the story."

Marisol walked around to the desk. "Use my—Tyesha's phone. Dial nine to get out."

Dulce took a deep breath and called Zavier's cell.

It rang three times before he answered.

Just hearing his voice, she could feel a lump in her throat. "Um . . . it's Dulce."

"I thought not getting on that plane was enough of a statement," he said. "But if I've gotta say it, then here goes: don't call me, Dulce."

"But this isn't—I mean, I have a news tip for you," she said.

"I don't want it," he said. "I don't want anything from you." He hung up.

Marisol raised her eyebrows. "Oh he was *that* journalist." She came around the desk and put her arm around Dulce. "Are you ok?"

Dulce nodded. She was all cried out from before, but she felt a dull burning in her chest now.

"I just wanted to be able to do something for you," Dulce said. "You know, hook you up with a big reporter. You done so much for me."

"You don't owe me for that," Marisol said. "It's what we do."

They talked for a while longer and then Dulce ripped Gerard's card in two and threw it into the recycling.

Marisol walked her to the door and she gave her another hug.

On her way out, Dulce glanced back over her shoulder and thought she saw Marisol retrieve Gerard's card from the blue bin.

Dulce took the subway up to 168th Street.

She stepped above ground into a changing neighborhood. She saw a pair of white hipsters headed past her into the subway. The girl had rainbow dreadlocks and the guy had a folding bike. But on the street, Dulce still recognized the woman at the corner bodega and gave her a wave. In Dulce's disheveled state, the woman didn't seem to recognize her, but smiled and waved anyway.

Dulce walked down three long blocks to her family's apartment. She didn't really think of it as her home anymore. It had been over half a decade.

She picked up her phone and dialed her mom's number. No answer. The voicemail greeting was a robo-voice that told her the number. She hung up, not even sure why she had bothered calling her mother. It was a sort of ritual. Every time she came home, she would check to see how Mami was doing. Had she gotten up? Was she dressed? Had she taken a shower? Had she eaten? Most of the time, she would walk in to find her mom lying in bed, the TV on—playing the news or novelas. Maybe asleep, maybe awake. If there was a plate near the bed, that was a good sign. Usually, she was in the same clothes from the day before.

Except Sunday. Sundays she got up, dressed and went to church like everything was fine.

Dulce called her sister Yunisa.

"*Dónde stas*?" she asked. "Are you back in New York yet?"

"I'm downstairs," Dulce said.

"No shit," Yunisa said. "Dario, go buzz your *titi* in!"

In the background, she could hear her nephew: "buzzer's broken, Mami."

"Then go downstairs and let her in!" Dulce could hear the door slam in the background. "He'll be down in a—"

Her sister was interrupted by a shriek from the baby.

Yunisa put the phone down, but apparently didn't hang up. Dulce got to hear her alternate between cooing and scolding in the couple minutes it took for her nephew to run down three flights of stairs.

As she waited, Dulce turned off the ringer on her phone. Otherwise, she'd just be hoping against hope that Zavier would call.

When Dario opened the door, she was shocked to see how tall he was. He'd had a mouth full of baby teeth when she'd last seen him, but now he had one front tooth missing and two permanent teeth were just growing in on the bottom.

"Darito!" she said, and pulled him into a huge hug.

"*Caballito*!" he demanded one of the piggy back rides she had given him when they used to see each other.

She tried to heave him onto her back. "*Carajo*," she said. "Has your *mami* been feeding you cement?"

He was disappointed when she insisted he walk up the stairs, but put him on her back the moment they got up to their floor.

When Yunisa opened the apartment door, the place looked so small.

She hugged her sister, and fussed over her new niece. The baby was six months old, and it was Dulce's first time seeing her.

Dario was slipping off her back, and he insisted she put down the baby to give him the promised horsey ride.

Dulce handed the baby back to Yunisa, and galloped around the small living room with Darito on her back. She galloped down the short hallway to the bathroom. She galloped into the bedroom that her sister shared with the kids, trampling piles of laundry and stuffed animals. She galloped into her mother's room, only to find her facing a meteorologist who was predicting rain and a cooling trend.

"Mami, I'm back," Dulce said.

"*Gracias a Diós*," her mother said, but didn't look up.

Dulce galloped back out into the hall.

In the living room, her sister had put baby Belcalis in the play pen. Everyone called her Lali. She was chewing on the end of a plastic cooking spoon.

Dulce's sister was standing next to the door. She was shoving some clothes and a pair of high heel ankle boots into an oversized handbag. She had grabbed a fashionable cropped jacket off the hook by the apartment door.

"I'm going out to the store," she said. "Can you watch the kids for a minute?"

Dulce cocked her head to the side. "The store?" she asked, eyeing the bag. "A minute?"

"Please?" her sister asked.

Yunisa was just four years her senior, but she seemed a decade older. She always looked tired and had a frown wrinkle between her eyes. She worked nine to five at a fast food restaurant, and took care of their mother, as well as her kids.

"Go ahead," Dulce said. "No need to hurry back."

"*Gracias, mi amor*," Yunisa said, and gave Dulce a quick hug before she ran out the door.

Dulce fed the kids dinner and put them to bed. The three of them crashed on the fold-out couch in the living room.

Later that night, she went to check on her mom. She was lying in bed watching TV. Dulce recognized the music from *A Woman's Dark Past*. She climbed into bed behind her mother and they watched together.

Xoana has Izabel by the wrist.

"Let go of me, you whore!" Izabel says. "I still have an envelope that shows you screwing another man with your wedding dress in the background."

"Well, I happen to know that you killed my husband," Xoana says.

Izabel hesitates for a brief second. "Why would I care about your husband?" Izabel asks. "I never even met your husband."

"Maybe you never even saw him," Xoana says. "But he wasn't your target. You were trying to kill me."

"You?" Izabel asks haughtily. She walks slowly around Xoana, looking her up and down. "Why would I be the least bit bothered about killing you?"

"At first I couldn't believe it, either," Xoana says. "I had always thought of you as my sister. Not that you ever cared much for me, but I didn't think you hated me enough to kill me."

"For once, you're right," Izabel says with a shrug.

"I hoped it wouldn't be true," Xoana says. "I hoped it right up until I got evidence that you bought the poison. And still—still, my mind was trying to find some kind of alternative explanation. Until I found the cab driver who took you to our house. It was like a needle in a haystack, but I didn't stop until I found him."

"So what?" Izabel says. "Some lowly cab driver will testify that he took me in his taxi? He could be mistaken. He could be lying. He could have been bribed."

"And the pharmacist who sold you the poison?" Xoana asks.

"Easy to discredit," Izabel says.

"And the testimony of Guilherme," Xoana says. "He told you he still had feelings for me. That he wanted to honor your marriage. He begged you to move back to our home town because it was too painful to see me. He'll testify. He doesn't want to be married to a murderess."

"A murderess?" Izabel asks. "What about a whore? Do you think he'll really take your word over mine when he sees those photos? Without him, you have two low-level strangers. Once I reveal those photos, your case falls apart. No way to establish any motive. You'll just look like a crazy person. A widow overcome by grief. Irrational. Trying to make sense of her husband's death. Or worse yet, a whore trying to steal my husband. Trying to attack me, the daughter of two distinguished professors at the university. You'll be the sewer rat we should never have taken in."

"Go ahead," Xoana says. "Call me a rat. A whore. Savor the taste of the word on your tongue. You think you can wound me with that word? I've survived so much worse. So go ahead and hand over the envelope. I'll give it to Guilherme myself. I told him everything. And he still loves me. He'll come to love my daughter. We'll be a family."

"Lying bitch!" Izabel lunges for Xoana and begins to choke her.

With Xoana's last bit of strength, she pulls the fire alarm. Sprinklers come on, but police also appear. Everyone is quickly soaked.

The officers move in, and pull Izabel off of Xoana.

She is still gasping for breath when Guilherme appears. He ignores Izabel and runs to Xoana.

"My darling, are you okay?"

"Guilherme, how could you betray me?" Izabel asks.

"Betray you?" Guilherme asks. "You are the traitor. Time and time again. And this time you nearly killed the woman I love. I'll never let you succeed."

The police take a screaming Izabel away.

Guilherme takes Xoana into his arms. He kisses her neck where Izabel had bruised her. He kisses her cheeks, her hairline, her lips.

Two fire fighters rush in.

"Someone pulled the alarm!" one says.

"Where's the fire?" the other one asks.

"Right here," Xoana says, as she and Guilherme continue to kiss.

The baby began to cry, and Dulce hopped up to see about her. It took a half hour of walking her up and down the short hallway to get her back to sleep.

Yunisa didn't get home til after three AM. When she came in the door, it woke Dulce. For a moment, she thought she was back in Puerto Rico. She felt the back of her nephew in the fold-out next to her, and heard someone tiptoeing past her in the dark. The memories of Zavier and the Lumineer Hotel flooded back.

But she wasn't in in San Juan. She was in Washington Heights. Never again would she find herself lying next to Zavier. This was her life now.

Her mother was like a ghost who barely spoke to her. Her sister was in way over her head and always looking to tap Dulce for help. Zavier was supposed to be her ticket out of all this. But not anymore.

She lay on the fold-out between the two children and cried silently. The tears ran down the sides of her temples and soaked into the faded floral sheets she'd known since she was born.

* * *

Earlier that night, Marisol had been sitting in the executive director's office with Tyesha and Serena. Marisol was scouring the internet for any information about Phillip Gerard's Puerto Rico racket. Serena was trying to find a money trail for the donations and to get information on Gerard's financial portfolio. Tyesha was working on a grant proposal.

At nine-thirty, two women walked in with a large box of takeout. The Asian girl, Kim, had shoulder-length black hair and a new septum piercing. Her girlfriend Jody was a head taller, with spiky blonde hair, and a frame that would have been decidedly masculine if not for her large bra size.

"Serena said you needed some reinforcements?" Kim said.

"We need a white girl," Tyesha said, not looking up from her grant proposal.

Jody rolled her eyes. "Serena's white," she said. "How come I always get the white girl jobs?"

"First of all, I'm Greek," Serena said. "Which is off-white. And second, we need someone who looks like a waspy heiress."

"You all know I'm really descended from Polish farmers, though. Right?" Jody said.

"Yes, but none of us can even pass as a WASP," Kim said.

"Exactly," Marisol said. "We need that same girl from the Ukrainian mob heist."

"Ugh," Jody said. "I hate her."

"But you still have the wig," Kim said. "And the dress."

Jody made a face like she was smelling something foul.

"Don't worry," Marisol said. "No hand jobs this time."

"Well that's a comfort," Jody said.

Marisol handed her a torn business card that had been taped back together.

"This is the mark?" Jody asked.

"He's a disaster capitalist," Marisol said.

"It's worse than that," Serena said. "He's into cryptocurrency."

"Crypto-what?" Jody asked.

"Money from crypts?" Kim asked. "Like grave robbers?"

Serena shook her head. "No, it's encrypted currency. That is, money that's off the grid. Digital transactions outside the banking system so they can't be traced."

"I heard about that," Tyesha said. "It's like the new money laundering."

"Exactly," Serena said. "A lot of people use it to make transactions with drug money or money that's made from human trafficking, particularly sex trafficking. Less of a trail."

"That should fucking be illegal," Kim said.

"Sex trafficking is," Serena said. "Which is why they want untraceable currency to pay for it."

"Those assholes," Jody said.

"This guy isn't just into cryptocurrency," Marisol said. "He's one of a group of vultures using that money to try to buy up Puerto Rico."

"Are you kidding me?" Kim said. "They're still counting all the bodies."

"One white girl reporting for duty," Jody said. "We need to take this fucker down."

"And you got his cell number from Dulce?" Serena asked.

"Yeah," Marisol said. "He was her sugar daddy for a while."

"Not that I'm trying to get out of anything here," Jody said. "But why don't you ask Dulce to make the move if they already have a relationship?"

"I've risked my life for that girl," Marisol said. "But I can't trust Dulce with something like this. She's too easily manipulated by powerful men."

"I'd have to agree," Serena said. "Me and Marisol nearly died because Dulce slipped up and told Jerry that Marisol was taking her to Cuba."

"That was over a year ago," Jody said. "She was barely

out of her teens when she left. But look at that *New York Times* piece. She's obviously grown up a lot."

"I don't know if you'd be so ready to gamble on her if you'd been the one staring down the barrel of that pimp's gun," Serena said.

"I'm usually pushing Marisol to trust people," Tyesha said. "But this time, I agree."

"Besides," Marisol said. "We don't need someone who looks like they want to get some of his money, we need someone who looks like they want to give him some money."

"Okay," Jody said. "What's the plan?"

"I know these guys had a face-to-face in New York this morning," Marisol said. "You'll call his cell and ask for a meeting."

"And who am I this time?" Jody asked.

"You're the lure," Marisol said. "You'll be pretending to be a big donor."

"No," Jody said. "I meant what's my identity."

"Heidi Honeywell," Marisol said. "Of the Connecticut Honeywells."

Ten minutes later, Jody was on the phone. The team sat around as she called the number from the business card on the speakerphone. So they all heard when the mechanical voice informed them they had reached a number that was no longer in service.

"Dammit!" Marisol said, and banged her fist on the table.

Tyesha shrugged, not looking up from her grant proposal. "You just need to call Dulce and ask if he has another number."

"I don't trust her not to say anything," Marisol said.

"What?" Kim said. "Because in the past she told some of your business to a pimp? That was different. He turned her out as a teenager. Nobody will ever have that same power over Dulce again. Give her some credit."

"It's not about credit," Marisol said. "This guy is worse than a pimp. He's so well connected and has so many resources that he could damage us beyond one pimp with a gun. We can't take that risk."

Serena closed her laptop. "Well we can't pull this heist if we don't have his number. We don't know where he's staying. He doesn't have any property in Florida under his own name. I could find his number, but it'll take time."

Marisol shook her head. "We don't have time," she said. "Right after a tragedy the donations are the highest. Check the hotels near the corporation where they had the face-to-face meet."

"I already did," Serena said. "There are over a hundred four- and five-star hotels in a mile radius."

"*Coño!*" Marisol said.

Tyesha looked up from her laptop. "Marisol, you're gonna have to let something go," she said. "If you wanna do this job, you're gonna have to put some of your trust in Dulce."

"Definitely not," Marisol said. "She's too fucking impulsive. And in some ways naïve. Plus, when money goes missing, the whores are the first ones who get blamed. He'd come sniffing around and I don't trust her to hold it together."

"I agree with Kim that you're not giving her enough credit," Jody said.

"The girlfriends always vote as a bloc," Serena said.

"This isn't a vote," Marisol said. "We're not bringing Dulce on board for this job and that's final."

"Without Dulce, there is no job," Tyesha said.

"There's gotta be another way," Marisol insisted.

"We could look for him at a hundred hotels," Serena said.

"Where he might not even be traveling under his own name," Kim added.

"Then that's what we'll need to do," Marisol said. "Serena, draw up the list. We'll divide up and start now."

Tyesha closed her laptop and stood up. "Marisol," she

said, walking over to the couch. "We can do it your way, but there's a huge risk that we won't be able to find him. Or that we'll be too late." She put her arm around Marisol. "You gotta weigh that against trusting Dulce. And I think you need to call her. After everything your people have been through? I'm not sure you're thinking clearly."

"It's an impossible choice," Marisol said. "Risking everything we've built versus everything he's stolen."

"I don't think you'll be able to live with yourself if this asshole escapes from New York City with all this money," Tyesha said. "Money he swindled from Puerto Ricans in New York to displace Puerto Ricans on the island."

Marisol nodded, and her eyes filled, but she didn't cry. She picked up her phone and called Dulce. Not on speaker. It rang and went to voice mail.

The next day, Marisol finally caught up with Dulce on the phone.

"*Hola nena*," Marisol said brightly. "How are you settling in?"

Dulce shrugged. "The usual. My family's exactly the same. But it's good to be home, I guess."

"Feel free to come by the clinic if you need a break," Marisol said. "Tyesha can always put you to work as a volunteer."

"I might just do that," Dulce said.

"Speaking of work," Marisol said, "can I ask you something?"

"Sure."

"You know that guy," Marisol began. "That businessman Gerard who you spent time with in PR?"

"The one who's ripping off the community?" Dulce asked.

"That's the one," Marisol said. "I know some girls in Puerto Rico who are looking for a sugar daddy."

"How can you even consider that?" Dulce asked. "He's totally pimping *la gente*."

"Excuse me?" Marisol said, an edge to her voice. "These girls are just doing what they gotta do to survive. You of all people should understand that."

"I'm sorry," Dulce said. "Yeah, you looking for a reference? He was okay. Nothing kinky. Didn't even like to fuck that much, just for me to act like I was so hot for him all the time. Also, tell them not to wear their best shit, because he likes to rip things off. And then he'd buy me new clothes. But he never gave cash. Just room and board. And he bought fancy things for me. I got a cash hustle going later, but that wouldn't work now. Not since the hurricane."

"Thanks, Dulce," Marisol said. "Do you have a private number for him?"

"*Claro*," Dulce said. "I can text it to you."

"No need," Marisol said. "Can you just read it off to me?"

"Sure," Dulce said. "Hold on." She pulled up her contacts and read off the number.

"*Gracias, amor*," Marisol said.

"*De nada.*"

An hour later, the crew was in Tyesha's office again, gathered around the speakerphone.

Jody was talking into the mic. The saccharine voice didn't go with her spiked buzz cut or her muscle t-shirt.

"Oh, Mr. Gerard, I'm so glad to have caught you before you left New York," Jody was saying. "I was hoping I could meet you in person for a drink. I think my family would be very interested in donating to your cause . . . Tomorrow at the La Fleur Hotel. Of course I know it. Happy hour? . . . Perfect."

"Sometimes the white girls get the dirty jobs," Kim said with a smirk.

"I have some bad news for you," Marisol said. "We need you to do the real dirty work."

"What? Fucking him?" Kim asked.

Marisol nodded.

"If he was Dulce's sugar daddy, then he likes Latinas with big asses," Kim protested. "Sounds like a job for you, Marisol."

"Nope," she said. "Not only have I met him, but he knows someone who can trace me. Besides, he likes young women. Even his wife is in her twenties."

"Tyesha's younger than me," Kim said. "And has much more ass."

"Tyesha has a grant proposal due."

"Serena . . . ?"

"Will be busy working her computer magic," Serena said, referring to herself in the third person. "And has less ass than you, anyway."

"I want combat pay for this," Kim said.

"Done," Marisol said.

Kim screwed up her face. "I enjoyed being a well-paid ho. But I've really enjoyed being a retired ho. I'm only doing this for the cause."

"Nobody knows like me what a drag it is to come out of retirement," Marisol said. "How can I sweeten the deal?"

"Give me and Jody a hotel room for the night?" Kim asked.

"Okay," Marisol said. "But on another floor. He can't see either of you after the hit. And especially not together. No one can."

"So I guess we'll have to sleep over," Kim said. "And order room service til after he leaves."

"Damn," Tyesha said. "How did they end up having hotel sex, and I'm stuck in the office working on a grant proposal?"

"The cost to be the boss," Marisol said.

"Please," Kim said, cutting her eyes at Tyesha. "Weren't you and your man Woof just at some hotel in London? Like you didn't have hotel sex."

"We totally did," Tyesha said with a grin.

"Come on, ladies," Serena said. "Time to focus."

"Yes," Marisol said. "So for the specs on the hotel . . . The La Fleur has wall safes."

"Aren't those safes digital?" Serena asked.

"Nope," Marisol said. "They have a custom line of superlative safes. The combination gets reset with each new guest."

"So the safecracking is old school?" Serena asked.

Marisol nodded. "Fortunately for us."

"But why would he be getting the donations in cash?" Tyesha asked.

"He won't," Marisol said. "But the hotel encourages their patrons to keep valuables—especially laptops—in the safe."

"Do you have any idea how much security there is on that kind of account?" Serena said.

"I do," Marisol said. "Which is why we need Jody to get the donor info, and then Kim to get us access to his hotel room. If we hack into the account from his laptop, it won't raise a red flag."

"That's assuming I can hack my way in," Serena said.

"If we time it right, you'll have hours to work," Marisol said.

"I'd be more confident if we had a couple days," Serena said.

"Well we don't have that kind of time," Marisol said. "So hack fast."

The hotel La Fleur had loomed in Marisol's memory since she was a little girl. She recalled stopping in there one day when her mother was pregnant with Cristina. Marisol rarely got to spend time with her mom, who worked long hours as a custodian. Cristina's soon-to-be father was still living with them. He wouldn't leave until a few months after Cristina was born. Marisol's mom was glowing with pregnancy and the love of what she thought was a good man.

Marisol wasn't nearly as happy. Everything those days was about the baby. And while her mother was completely in love with the boyfriend, Marisol had her reservations. But this day was special. Someone at work had given her mother a gift certificate to an upscale baby store, and they'd come into midtown Manhattan to redeem it. She'd selected a gorgeous changing table and baby bureau set that would be delivered to their apartment. Afterwards, she and Marisol had gotten an ice cream soda float. Marisol was buzzing from the sugar and just getting to spend time with her mother. She didn't even notice until they were nearly at the subway that she had to pee.

"I asked if you had to go at the ice cream place," her mother had said irritably. "You'll have to wait until we get home."

"They gotta have a toilet in there," Marisol had pointed to the La Fleur Hotel. It was such a big building, with people going in and out, certainly there would be a *baño* inside.

"That place is for rich people," her mother had told her in Spanish.

"I can't hold it," Marisol had said.

"*Coño, mija*," her mother had cursed, but then had taken a deep breath.

"Okay," she told Marisol in Spanish. "We're going to stand up very straight. We're going to walk in like we live there. You're not going to look around at everything."

Marisol nodded, her eyes drifting to the door of this building so special you weren't even supposed to look around inside.

Her mother put a hand under her chin and turned her head back so their eyes met.

"Keep looking straight forward and don't turn your head, you got that?" she asked.

Marisol nodded.

Her mother took off the scarf she had over her head and shook out her hair. Then she took off the shabby coat and folded it over her arm. "The bathroom is just for the people who live here, and we don't live here," her mother said.

"Because they only have one bathroom?" Marisol asked, wondering if it was the same as their apartment.

Marisol's mother laughed. "No, *mi amor*. Because . . . because they're rich. Rich people always have more bathrooms than they need, but they don't like to be very close to anyone."

"I have to go really bad," Marisol said, on the verge of tears. She and her mother had split the root beer float, but Marisol had drunk all the soda.

"We're going to pretend we live here. We're going to pretend we know where the bathroom is. Just follow me." She ran her fingers through Marisol's unruly hair. "We can't ask anyone, because we don't want to make them mad, okay?"

"Okay."

Her mother crossed herself. She never went to church, but she genuflected when she was worried. "It'll be okay, *nena*. It's an adventure."

Marisol always thought of this as her first midtown theft. The unauthorized use of a four-star hotel toilet at the age of six.

Later that afternoon, the team fussed around Jody, making her exterior match the saccharine voice. Long blonde hair, full makeup, and a blue dress with just enough cleavage to dazzle a man, but still within the range of Tri-State-Area WASP.

The Jody that walked into the La Fleur was a totally transformed woman. The spiky hair gone. The muscles camouflaged under a lacy sweater. The taut neck muscles hidden under the long straight blonde hair. Her bright lipstick and dark, falsely lashed eyes marking conventional femininity.

Kim sat further down the bar, with extensions woven in at the nape of her neck, taking her hair from shoulder-length to glam. When Kim had been working, she'd just kept it long, so she wasn't used to the glue that held it in place for the rush job Tyesha had done. She scratched at the back of her scalp with the black plastic stirrer from her drink.

Gerard walked in exactly on time. He was clean shaven and wearing an expensive suit.

Jody gave a dainty little wave from the bar, and Kim nearly spit out her drink.

"Mr. Gerard," Jody said, over the sound of Kim coughing to cover her laughter. "So good to meet you."

"Please," he said. "Call me Phillip."

"I am so thankful to your organization for getting involved in such a messy situation," she said. "I really feel for these poor people. When I found out that they're American citizens? That changes everything."

"I believe, as a nation, we should take care of our own," Gerard said. He handed her a brochure with several brown-skinned people wading through chest-deep water in rural Puerto Rico.

"Let me get right to it," she said. "My family would like to give $20,000."

"Wonderful," he said. "So generous. Would you like to write the check now, or shall we send—"

Jody laughed. "A check?" she asked. "What? You think I'm going to write a check? Is this 1996? The Honeywells wire money. I just need your account number. This is tax deductible, of course?"

"Yes," he said. "Of course." He was a bit flustered. "Let me just—I need to find—"

"I see you weren't quite prepared," she said. She stood to

316 / Aya de León

go, and reached into her purse. "Let me give you a card for my family's foundation. There's a January deadline for grant proposals—"

"No, I assure you Ms. Honeywell," he said. "We accept wire transfers. I just need to find my ledger."

He found it in the briefcase and gave her the account number.

Jody smiled as she took the slip of paper. "I'll send the donation today," she said.

"Thank you," he said. "Please convey my thanks to your entire family."

"I certainly will," Jody said.

He watched her walk out. Her hips switching back and forth on tall stilettos.

When he turned back to the bar to order a drink, he saw the Asian woman had moved next to him.

"Excuse me," she said. "There's a creepy guy over there who won't leave me alone. Can I tell him you're my boyfriend?"

Gerard raised his eyebrows. "You really expect anyone to believe a young, beautiful woman like you would be with an old guy like me?"

Kim giggled. "This is New York. Anything's possible. Besides, don't sell yourself short. You're an attractive guy. And this is a very nice suit."

Apparently, Gerard only ripped up the dresses he had paid for. Kim was a hookup, not a sugar baby, so he let her take off her own dress. Kim had the sedative on her areolas. She didn't kiss clients, and he wasn't the type to go down on her. Besides, the drug would knock her out if it was on her own mucous membranes.

Sure enough, when she did the dramatic unhook of her bra, he took a moment to lick each nipple before the penetration.

She had picked the fast-acting stuff. Which was perfect because he didn't last long. Fifteen minutes later, he had climaxed and was knocked out.

Kim sent a text, and two minutes later, there was a discreet tap at the door. Kim opened it, and Marisol and Serena slipped in.

Marisol pulled a stethoscope from her pocket.

"Safe's over here," Kim said, and pulled aside the portrait behind the mini bar.

Marisol was used to working alone. She wasn't accustomed to having an audience, but Kim and Serena sat watching from the couch in the suite's living room.

As Marisol put on the latex gloves, she felt almost shy. No matter how many safes she opened, she always had a twinge of insecurity that this next one would be the one that bested her. Still, she had trained Kim to open a Superlative. She should think of the other two women as backup instead of critics.

She had a ritual, she always did. It seemed silly with people watching, but it was her talisman. She turned her body toward the wall so they couldn't see as she tapped twice on the door of the safe. Then she put her stethoscope to the door and slowly turned the dial. The pads of her fingers pressed against the serrated surface of the metal. She turned it carefully to the right, then left, then right again. She glanced over her shoulder and saw them watching, and it distracted her.

She started over, this time with her eyes closed, and tapped twice again. She listened for the safe's three-click reply. She relied on the ritual of the two-beat/three-beat call and response in clave rhythm to guide her dance with the safe.

This second time, she cracked it, and when she swung the door open, she turned to her team and did a deep curtsey.

The two women clapped.

Marisol stood up and took the laptop out of the safe.

When Serena took the laptop, Marisol handed her a second pair of latex gloves.

"Do I really need to hang around?" Kim asked.

"In case he wakes up," Marisol said.

"As long as I don't have to service him again," Kim said.

"Service him? Give him another dose of whatever it was? Knock him over the head with a brick? I don't care," Marisol said. "Just as long as he's unconscious until after we're done."

"I gave him plenty," Kim said. "He ought to sleep through the night."

As Serena began to work on Gerard's laptop, Marisol unloaded all the small bottles of liquor from the minibar.

"What are you doing?" Kim asked.

"I want him to think you all had a much bigger party," Marisol said. "It'll explain his headache in the morning."

Marisol began to pour one of the bottles down the sink.

"Wait a minute!" Kim said, snatching it from her.

"What?" Marisol asked. "We can't drink it. We need to be sharp."

"How you gonna throw out free booze?" Kim asked. She emptied her water bottle and filled it with liquor.

"Marisol, can you come here?" Serena asked from the living room.

Marisol walked back out of the bathroom. "What's up?"

"He has an extra level of security on this account," Serena said. "What do we know about him?"

"Not much," Marisol said. "Kim, can you look in his wallet to see if we have names of kids or pets?"

"I have reason to believe," Serena said, "that it is a seven or eight-letter word, beginning with S."

Kim flipped through the wallet. "Not much cash . . ." she reported. "Lots of credit cards."

"Symphony?" Marisol asked.

"No luck," Serena said. "I also tried 'serenade.'"

"Sympathy would fit," Kim said. "But I don't think he's the sympathetic type."

"Pictures of the wife?" Marisol asked. "Kids?"

"Nope."

"Sidecar?" Serena asked.

"Sidechick?" Kim asked.

"Now you're just being ridiculous," Marisol said.

"It's been a long day," Kim said. "I'm getting punchy."

"Anything else in his pockets?" Marisol asked.

"Speaking of side chicks," Kim said. "I think you need to call Dulce."

"I don't think that's a good idea—"

"You don't have to tell her what it's for," Serena said. "But we're not gonna get in here if we don't get this password. I can't just keep trying. Two more tries and I'll be locked out."

Reluctantly, Marisol dialed Dulce on her cell phone.

"Marisol," Dulce said. "What's up?"

Marisol felt something she rarely felt: awkward and unsure. "I was calling to check in on you," she said. "Actually, I was hoping to take you to lunch tomorrow. You busy?"

"I am the opposite of busy," Dulce said. "I'd love to."

"Great," Marisol said. "Meet me at the clinic at noon?"

"It's a date," Dulce said.

"Oh, while I have you on the line," Marisol said. "I had a random question."

"Ask me," Dulce said.

"That businessman you . . . dated," Marisol said. "Was his wife's name Siobhan?"

"No," Dulce said. "I think it was Julianne."

"So strange," Marisol said. "Some S-name associated with him. Maybe one of his kids?"

"He doesn't have kids," Dulce said. "Just a dog."

"The dog's name isn't Siobhan," Marisol said with a laugh. "Is it?"

"I doubt it," Dulce said. "He said it was a male dog."

"I must have gotten it wrong," Marisol said. "I met this woman with the last name Gerard, and a long first name with an S. I thought they might be related."

"Nope," Dulce said. "No S-names I heard. Unless you count his boat."

"His boat?" Marisol asked.

"He calls it the Stampede," Dulce said. "Talks about it all the time. His yacht."

"Of course," Marisol said. "I guess this S-name woman is no relation."

"I guess not," Dulce said. "See you tomorrow for lunch."

"Absolutely," Marisol said.

"STAMPEDE" opened the account.

Kim took the elevator two floors up and knocked on the door of another hotel room.

When Jody opened it, she kissed Kim and said, "I ran a bath."

"I knew there was something about you I liked," Kim said, stepping inside and stripping off her work clothes. Jody walked her into the bathroom, where the light was low and warm.

"They have a Jacuzzi?" Kim asked, looking at the deep tub.

"Not in the standard rooms," Jody said. "But I paid Marisol the difference."

"I definitely like you," Kim said. She slid into the water. Jody slid in behind her and kissed her neck.

"Best girlfriend ever," Kim said.

"Wait til I get the jets going," Jody said.

Soon, the water was whirring with movement.

"And I brought a few things," Jody said.

Kim grinned. "Like what?"

"Like sweet almond oil," Jody said, and put some on her fingertips.

"Do I get a massage?" Kim asked.

"Sort of," Jody said. She slid her fingers across Kim's nipples, and her girlfriend moaned and leaned back against her.

With one long arm, Jody kept stroking her fingertips across Kim's nipples, first one side, then the other. With her other hand, she got some special waterproof lubricant and slid a finger down between Kim's labia.

Kim had been languid with the heat of the water, but now she arched with a moan.

"You're not going anywhere," Jody murmured into her ear, and proceeded to stroke mercilessly.

By the time Kim reached a third climax, the water was turning tepid.

They drained the tub. Jody gave Kim a fluffy robe, and Kim stumbled into bed. Jody joined her a moment later.

"What about you?" Kim mumbled.

Jody laughed. "You're in no shape to do anything about me right now."

She was right. After a couple of minutes, Kim was asleep.

Two hours later, Kim woke up. She had knocked out on top of the covers in the robe. She blinked and looked around. Jody was on the bed next to her in a matching robe, reading a paperback book.

"This room is awesome," Kim said.

"Uh-huh," Jody half agreed, not looking up from her book. She was reading *The Shock Doctrine* by Naomi Klein.

"This room . . . the Jacuzzi . . ." Kim said.

"Uh-huh," Jody said, turning a page.

"And these robes," Kim said. "So cozy, but so breezy, too."

"Yuh," Jody said, eyes glued to the page.

Kim moved around to the foot of the bed on Jody's side. Jody had her knees bent, and her book leaning up against them.

"I would like to demonstrate some of the more exciting qualities of these robes," Kim said.

"Mm hmm," Jody said.

Kim climbed up onto the bed and slid her hands up Jody's calves.

Jody patted Kim's hand. "I'm reading, babe," she murmured.

"Don't mind me," Kim said, sliding her hands up Jody's thighs.

"How am I supposed to read when you're trying to distract me?" Jody asked, laughing.

"Don't blame me," Kim said. "It's not my fault if your book isn't as compelling as I am."

"This book is really compelling," Jody said. "Marisol gave it to me."

"Can your book do this?" Kim asked, kissing Jody's inner thighs.

"That's not a fair comparison," Jody said, leaning the book against her chest.

"How about this?" Kim asked, running her tongue softly against the opening of Jody's lips.

"Definitely not," Jody said, putting the book aside.

"Do I have your attention?" Kim asked.

"I think so," Jody said.

Kim gave a fake evil laugh, and Jody laughed too.

Then Kim slid her tongue up and down Jody's clitoris until her girlfriend was bucking and screaming, half out of the robe. Yet somehow, she had kept hold of the book. She still gripped it in her hand, one finger holding her place.

Chapter 29

The next day, Marisol and Dulce met for lunch across the street from the clinic. It had previously been an old school Italian deli, but now it was a "paleo eatery." Fortunately, they had red meats and baked goods made from yucca, plantain and yam flour. The food was gentrified, but edible.

"I never had no paleo food before," Dulce said. "It's kind of like an empanada if you didn't use as much spices."

They sat at the counter. Beside them, a long line of people waiting to order snaked out the door.

"Glad we beat the rush," Marisol said. "So how is it being back?"

Dulce blew out her breath. "My mom and sister are driving me nuts," she said. "I need to move out. But with what money? I think I'm done with sex work, so how will I be able to afford rent anywhere?"

"What about your writing, Dulce?" Marisol asked. "Or should I say 'Celia M. Reyes'?"

Dulce grinned. "I got that first check, and I was like 'oh hell yeah!' Jerry had me convinced I wasn't good for nothing but fucking. And I was like, where is that asshole buried? Because I wanna dance on his grave and wave my fucking check in his dead face like, 'New York Times, bitch!'"

The two of them laughed.

"I would have gone with you," Marisol said.

"I was so sure I was on my way," Dulce said. "But then I think I missed my window in the news cycle. I coulda sold a secondary story to the tabloids right after I got back. But I was messed up over that guy. And now Delia Borbón did that special with Oprah."

"But you didn't just write that piece on Borbón," Marisol said. "I've seen your name on some of those interviews with hurricane survivors."

"But the big papers aren't looking for freelance Hurricane María content now that it's no longer dominating the news," Dulce said. "And I don't have my journalism hookup anymore."

"Same guy?" Marisol asked.

Dulce nodded. "It was like—for a minute—I thought maybe everything could change. But in some ways it was the same old shit. Some guy comes along and I thought his love was gonna magically turn me into a journalist. Like if I could get him to be my man, everything else would just fall into place. But if I learned anything from you, Marisol, it's not to depend on men. And good things come to those who hustle."

"That is pretty much my philosophy," Marisol said with a laugh.

"So I guess I'll hustle my way into getting paid to write," Dulce said. "Can you help me?"

"Definitely," Marisol said. "What have you tried so far?"

Dulce opened her mouth, then closed it. "Nothing really," she said.

"You were about to say something," Marisol said.

Dulce laughed and shook her head. "It's stupid," she said.

"You let me be the judge of that," Marisol said.

Dulce looked down at the table. "Before I cashed my check from the *New York Times,* I made this, like, tiny photocopy of it," she said. "And I laminated that shit. And I pinned it in my bra for good luck. Left side. Near my heart." Her face flamed hot and she kept her eyes on her plate.

"Are you kidding me?" Marisol said. "That's a great start. Before you can get something, you need to be clear that you want it."

"Really?" Dulce asked.

"*Claro que sí,*" Marisol said. "Next step is to pitch to different editors. I can help with that. There's mainstream outlets, but also sex worker sites like 'Tits and Sass,' that can get your work out there. They don't pay much, but they'll protect your privacy."

Dulce looked up from the plate, but she wasn't ready to meet Marisol's eyes yet. "I want to go for all of it."

Someone called Marisol's name. She and Dulce looked up to see Tyesha and Serena in line to order.

"Hey you two," Tyesha said. "What's up?"

"Just two unemployed ladies having a leisurely lunch," Marisol said.

Tyesha sucked her teeth. "Well we're two working girls getting takeout so we can work through lunch."

The line moved forward slowly.

"Just to add to your workload," Marisol said. "Either of you know of any paid writing opportunities? For Dulce?"

Serena shook her head. "Where's *$pread Magazine* when you need it?"

"Today I saw a grant for gentrification oral histories," Tyesha said. "Some hipster foundation wants people to pour their hearts out, so they can pull quotes to tattoo onto their arms and smelt into commemorative paperweights."

"Oh yeah," Serena said. "That project for displaced people in New York."

"What about the people in your shelter?" Dulce asked. "All those women from Puerto Rico."

"But it's for displaced people in New York," Serena said.

"Wait a minute," Marisol said. "Is it people *in* New York or *from* New York?"

"Let me pull up the email," Tyesha said, opening her smartphone.

As they waited, Serena ordered lunch for them at the counter.

"The language is very clear," Tyesha said. "Subjects must be homeless in New York City due to displacement: eviction, building demolition, rent hikes. And being replaced by owners and residents from a wealthier class."

Dulce pulled out her own phone and read from a dictionary app. "Demolition. Noun 1. an act or instance of demolishing. 2. the state of being demolished; destruction. 3. destruction or demolishment by explosives. 4. demolitions, explosives, especially as used in war."

"Well the Hurricane María refugees are definitely in the state of having been demolished and destroyed," Tyesha said.

"And they're also being replaced by owners and residents from a wealthier class," Marisol said. "All those cryptocurrency billionaires buying up the land."

"I think these hipsters might have signed themselves up to finance our oral history project," Tyesha said. "Lemme forward you the email, cause I'm not writing an additional grant application."

"I might be willing to come out of grant proposal retirement for one more big score," Marisol said. She opened the email, and Dulce looked over her shoulder.

"They want professionals," Dulce said. "I didn't even graduate high school."

"Fuck that," Marisol said. "You're self-taught. You've got a feature in the *New York Times*. You already did oral histories for this population for three different outlets. I'm gonna figure out how to spin this."

"Okay," Dulce said. "What's the word count they want for the final piece?"

"This isn't an article," Marisol said. "We're gonna apply to get you a grant from this foundation. They probably envisioned giving money to traditional academics and journalists and artists to interview families getting displaced. And then they're supposed to have a final product: a book, a report, a film, or an art exhibit. But I'm gonna write a grant that pays you and has a stipend for the participants. I'm gonna write the hell out of this grant proposal, and these motherfuckers are gonna give us this money."

Later that night, the team met in Tyesha's office. Serena sat at the end of the couch. Beside her, Kim lay back on Jody's lap. Tyesha sat at the desk, and Marisol paced across the room.

"So?" Marisol asked.

"It's done," Serena said. "Gerard's charity made a donation of nearly a quarter million to a grassroots organization of Puerto Rican women leading recovery efforts on the island."

Marisol nodded, and suddenly choked up. "I really appreciate all of you," she said. "I know this wasn't really your cause."

"What do you mean?" Tyesha asked. "We help each other."

Marisol laughed and wiped her eyes. "You all are Americans."

"Who you calling American?" Serena asked.

"Yeah," Kim said.

"Okay, maybe not you two," Marisol said. "But every US citizen is technically a colonizer of my island. They been pimping us for over a century. Most people in the US don't give a fuck. But you all do. Enough to risk your asses to help us. I just—"

She fanned her face as if the tears were coming from too much heat.

"Well get ready to look at a zero balance in his account," Serena said. She grinned and turned the laptop around.

"Wait," Jody said. "It says $2,000."

"That can't be right," Serena said.

She clicked a few buttons. "Damn," she said. "They just received a new donation."

"No!" Marisol yelled. "We need to get it. Hack in again."

Serena didn't move.

"I'm serious," Marisol said. "Work your magic and hack that motherfucker again. 'Stampede.' Do it."

"Marisol, we can't," Serena said. "It's too dangerous. We don't have his laptop anymore."

"I may not be the executive director of this clinic anymore, but I'm still the boss of this crew," Marisol said. "Get the goddamn money."

"It's not gonna happen, Marisol," Tyesha said quietly.

"This is bullshit!" Marisol screamed. She picked up the magazines on the coffee table and threw them across the room.

"Not one fucking cent," Marisol said. "Do you hear me? I'm not gonna leave him with one goddamn cent! My people are dying. The government is lying about how many people are dead. The land, the water is toxic. People are gonna keep dying for years, for decades. And this dick is pimping us?? From the time I was eleven years old, somebody was always trying to fuck me. Trying to pimp me. Not! One! Fucking! CENT!"

Marisol picked up the potted plant off the shelf and threw it against the wall. The pot shattered and the dirt exploded all over the wall. Leaves and soil rained down on the expensive carpet. The plant fell upside down into a bowl of condoms leaving the roots pale and exposed in the air.

Marisol reached to throw Serena's laptop, but Tyesha restrained her arm.

Serena pried the laptop from Marisol's hand.

For a moment, Marisol was coiled, poised to fight. But then she shuddered in fury. With a raging howl from deep in her gut, Marisol collapsed onto the sofa.

In the end, she didn't surrender to the sobbing. Rather, she lay passive on the couch as it overtook her. A tsunami of emotion, rearing up in undeniable authority, eclipsing the sky. She stood alone, a brown girl on the beach, awestruck and helpless to resist.

Marisol's body shook with spasms. The tears poured out and she sobbed hard in between waves of brutal grief, where her body clenched and unclenched like a fist.

Chapter 30

Dulce didn't wait to find out if they got the grant. She took her smart phone to the clinic, and interviewed Nidia and Zara. Then she went to the shelter and began interviewing everyone who would talk to her.

Her mother was still depressed and her sister was still bitchy, but every morning, she headed to the shelter to talk to the women. After gathering hurricane stories, she found herself asking girls she knew in the clinic if they would tell their sex-work stories. Marisol helped her pitch two series of interviews to different media outlets: one of hurricane refugees and one of sex workers. Both got greenlighted, but not for as much money as she'd hoped.

Three weeks later, Dulce still didn't know if she'd gotten the grant when Marisol called to invite her to participate in a video project to raise money for hurricane relief. Dulce was to go through her interviews and edit them into a ten-minute video.

Dulce threw herself into the project. Not that it paid much, and the night they premiered the video, she still didn't know if they'd gotten the grant.

She'd decided to do the Puerto Rican oral history work under her own name. So Dulce García was officially on the bill at Marisol's next event: a big gala fundraiser for hurricane relief in midtown. It was another five-star hotel, and she recalled that time at the La Fleur with Jerry. Everything was different now. Maybe not with Zavier, but still different. She had made a small chunk of change and was contributing to buying groceries. Her sister was showing her a little more respect. Yunisa had announced that she was getting someone to watch the kids tonight so she could go to the hurricane fundraiser. Dulce wasn't sure if she was coming to support her, or if she was checking to see if Dulce was telling the truth. Maybe she just wanted the free champagne.

A photographer from the *Times* was there. They had also sent a reporter, but it wouldn't be Zavier. Dulce had learned from his reporting that he was back in Puerto Rico.

The photographer asked Dulce to pose with Borbón, and the staff and refugees from the clinic. She squeezed between Nidia and Zara.

In between shots, she turned to them. "Where's the baby?" Dulce asked.

"Back in Marisol's apartment," Nidia said. "Serena's baby-sitting."

"Smile for the camera, ladies," the photographer said.

Wasn't she smiling? She wondered if maybe it was more of a grimace. Dulce was so nervous, she couldn't quite feel her face. At least she didn't have to go on stage and say anything. But Marisol had insisted that she would need to stand and be acknowledged.

After the photo shoot, Dulce leaned against the wall, unsure what to do. She suddenly felt lost in the vastness of possibilities in this new life. Not that she'd *ever* want to go back to Jerry, but there was something so contained about that lack of freedom. She didn't need to decide what to wear. Where to stand. He always told her. She was rarely expected to speak. She longed for freedom the whole time. But now she longed to know what she was supposed to do with herself at this very grown up party. She had said hello to Delia Borbón, and the star had embraced her warmly. But she didn't know the woman well enough to pal around with her for the rest of the party. Why did she rely on her sister to be her date?

Wealthy people were filling up the tables, along with activist types. Everything about her felt wrong. Her clothes. Her hair. She should have spent the money to get the blowout. But they still didn't know if they were gonna get that grant.

Dulce pulled out her phone and saw a text from Yunisa that she'd be late.

Dulce wondered what she was doing here. She didn't belong. She was practically having a panic attack when Kim and Jody walked by.

"Oh thank god," she said, rushing up to them.

Kim laughed. "It's so easy to get lost at one of Marisol's big gala events."

Dulce nodded.

"Stick with us, kid," Jody said. "We'll protect you from all the drama."

Jody grabbed a trio of champagne flutes and they toasted.

"To justice," Kim said.

They clinked glasses, and over the girlfriends' shoulders Dulce saw the *Times* photographer snap a shot of them.

Kim and Jody had a table with another girl from the clinic named Lily. She was apparently a stripper organizer, but also a slam poet.

Kim and Jody set their purses down, then went to get drinks.

"So it's possible to balance sex work and writing?" Dulce asked.

"Girl, definitely—" Lily stopped abruptly.

Dulce followed her eyes and saw a tall man walking in. From the looks of him, he could have been either black or Latino.

"That's Terence Moreau," Lily said. "He wrote *Filtration System.*"

Dulce didn't recognize the man or the book title. He looked like he was in his mid-thirties, with a bald head, jeans, and a black leather jacket.

Lily waved, and he headed over to their table.

"Lily Johnson," he said, grinning. "The sexiest woman who ever wrote a poem."

He turned to Dulce. "Unless of course you are also a poet, *mon cher.* Then it would be hard to decide."

"This is Dulce," Lily said. "And she's a journalist."

"Then I supposed your title is safe, Lily," Terence said. "Where can I get a drink?"

"Have a seat," she said. "What are you drinking?"

"Bourbon and water," he said.

Lily rose, but Dulce put a hand on her arm. "I'll get it," she said. "I was gonna grab something from the open bar anyway."

She hadn't been planning on getting up, but she didn't really want to make small talk with a flirty guy right now. Not when the drinks were already free.

She got him the bourbon, plus another rum and coke for Lily, and a glass of wine for herself.

When she returned to the table, Lily was asking, "Does that mean you'll be teaching at Columbia next year, or you'll be back at SUNY?"

Dulce didn't wait to hear the answer.

She was lingering by the kitchen door, hoping they would bring out another tray of snacks, when she heard the audience erupt in wild cheering.

Marisol was emceeing the event. "Yes," she said. "You heard me right. Terence Moreau is up next."

More cheering.

"Terence moved to New York as a homeless young refugee from Hurricane Katrina. He wrote rant after rant about the hurricane, and joined one of the New York teams of poets that competed at the National Poetry Slam. He won first place for an individual poet. And later his book *Filtration System* won the National Book Award for poetry. When we reached out to him about performing at this benefit, he didn't ask for any money, he didn't even ask when the event would be. He just said 'yes, I'll be there.' If there's a man who knows what the people of Puerto Rico are going through right now, it's one of the writers that put Hurricane Katrina into words. Please give it up for Terence Moreau."

The audience went wild as he walked to the stage.

After the cheering died down, a young man in the front yelled, "fuck 'em up, Terence!"

Moreau bowed his head and cleared his throat. Then he began by singing:

My, my this American lie
Drove my chevy to the levy
As the water rushed by
And George Bush was drinking whiskey and rye
Singing this will be the day that you die . . .

His voice was gentle, lilting, but then he stopped singing, and his voice turned to a fast, machine-gun delivery:

Modern day middle passage
my people packed in the hold of the slave ship
Superdome
same stench

Line by line, his poem built a searing parallel between Hurricane Katrina and slavery. He framed it as an auction block, where black bodies in crisis were sold to the highest bidder, from the Red Cross' self-serving monopoly on relief funds to the photos of Black Death that made the careers of white journalists to the financial incentives of for-profit prisons.

He wound up the auction with one last sale:

Final contract, rebuilding New Orleans
Big money! Big money!
Good old boy George Bush
Sold to Haliburton
No bid.

He banged suddenly on the microphone like a gavel, and the sharp sound made Dulce jump. Then, before anyone in the audience could catch their breath, he went back to singing.

I met a black girl who sang the blues
And I asked if she had happy news
But she just died and washed away

And I went down to the French Quarter
Where I'd heard the music years before
But the ghost there said the music wouldn't play

And in the streets the children screamed
The lovers cried and the pestilence teemed
But not a word was spoken
The government was broken

And the man who could have done the most
Was grinning in some camera for the Washington Post
As the hurricane
hit
the Gulf Coast
The day the music died . . .

His resounding voice brought it all back for Dulce. By the end of the poem, she had a lump in her throat.

"One more time for Terence Moreau!" Marisol said. "With both these hurricanes, this country's racism and brutality has been exposed for all to see. So they've upped the official death toll for Hurricane María from sixteen to sixty-four, but we know that's still a lie. And now the suicide rate is shooting up in Puerto Rico. People need hope and relief. Which is why we're up here raising money tonight."

Lily walked up to the stage and handed Marisol a piece of paper.

"This just in!" Marisol said. "Not only did Terence Moreau agree to perform free of charge, he also just agreed to donate five thousand dollars!"

As the cheering echoed throughout the room, Kim approached Dulce and handed her a glass of champagne.

"You look like you need another drink," Kim said.

"Definitely," Dulce said, and downed it.

They walked back over to the table, and Dulce hung tight with Kim and Jody for the rest of the evening. The three of them drank lots of champagne. Only much later did Marisol pull Dulce backstage while they showed the ten-minute video of the interviews Dulce had done.

From the wings, Dulce watched, amazed to see her own work on the big screen. The clip was one of the women from the clinic's shelter. She had closely cropped hair and was somewhere in her twenties:

She held a photo of a middle aged, balding man in a tank top and shorts. "This is my father. He died from an infection that was a direct result of the hurricane, a few weeks after. So when we buried him, I cut out the 'made in USA' label on one of my t-shirts and buried it with him. That's my flesh and blood going into the ground. And I know his death was manufactured right here in the United States."

Dulce had watched the clip countless times as she edited

it. But she was stunned to see the impact it had on the audience. People were wiping their eyes.

Backstage, Marisol whispered to Dulce. "I know I said you didn't have to make a speech or anything," Marisol said. "But it would be great if you just said a few words. Are you up for it?"

The booze had given Dulce some unexpected courage, so she found herself agreeing.

After the clip was done, Marisol went back out onto the stage. "Please keep that applause going for the filmmaker," she said. "Dulce García."

Filmmaker? As Dulce crossed the stage, she felt like a preschooler walking in her mother's high heel shoes.

"I don't know if I'm a filmmaker," she blurted out. "But I'm a girl with a camera phone, and a free app to edit video."

The audience laughed.

Dulce shook her head. "I didn't really prepare anything to say, but . . . I . . . I wanted to collect women's stories because I was in Puerto Rico during María, and . . . my people are from the Caribbean, so hurricanes were always just a part of life. But there's nothing natural about these recent storms. Harvey, Irma, María. This is what happens when the people in charge only care about making money, and don't care about the people or the planet. You can't fuck with the environment like we've done, and have ocean temperatures and levels rising and not have crazy shit happen."

She suddenly recalled herself. "Sorry," she said. "Excuse my language."

But the audience clapped to encourage her.

"Fucked up is fucked up!" a woman called out.

"Tell the truth!" one man yelled from the back.

Dulce looked at Marisol, who nodded.

"The truth is," Dulce said. "I just . . . I used to think that environmentalism was some white people drama until this climate change practically fucking killed me. And listen up, this shit isn't gonna be contained to the brown countries for long. People here in New York, you think your money and power can protect you? You can't buy a new ozone layer or a new worldwide food supply if you fuck up the ones you have. So we need to fight for the people of Puerto Rico and to fight for climate justice like we're fighting for our own lives. Because we are."

The audience exploded into applause. She looked out to see them, and her sister was in the front row. And her sister was . . . crying? What? She hadn't seen Yunisa cry since their brother had been deported.

"I just want to shoutout my family," Dulce said. "I couldn't have done it without them. You know? My sister in particular. Cause she taught me how to use a camera phone. Mostly for selfies."

The audience laughed, and Dulce walked off the stage to loud clapping.

Marisol took the mic smoothly again. "Thank you, Dulce. Next up is a young woman I saw recently at the Nuyorican Poets Café. She's in town from California. Yes, the Puerto Rican diaspora is worldwide and coast-to-coast in the US and beyond. This is her poem about the hurricane. Please give it up for Elena Dayo!"

A middle aged black woman with long dreadlocks stepped up to the stage. "This poem is called 'Puerto Rico & Mr. Jones'" she said. And then she gave a little history:

"The Jones Act of 1920, requires that all goods transported by water between US ports (including Puerto Rico) be carried on US ships, made in the US, owned and operated by US citizens. Puerto Rico's debt to the US is roughly equal to the accumulated revenue potential lost by Puerto Rico under the Jones Act."

Like the slam poet before her, she began singing. A gender-flipped version of the old Billy Paul tune:

Me and Mister Jones
We got a thing going on . . .

Then she began to speak, and went back and forth for the rest of the poem between speaking and singing:

America loves me. Lets me wear his chain around my neck. Heavy, heavy gold rope got me living larger than any of the other Caribbean islands. He tells me:

ain't nobody's ships but mine docking up in that port,
baby

He says I belong to him.

We both know that it's wrong
But it's much too strong
To let it go now

He called a few years ago, mad as hell. I told him:

I know I've racked up a lot of debt lately, but it's not like
I don't wanna work. I mean, if you would just let me—I
know the ports belong to you but could I just—? Okay, okay,
stop yelling. Yes, I know I owe you a lot of money. Yeah,
okay. I'll cut back on expenses. Tighten the belt. Austerity or
whatever. We closed a lot of schools. Cut the civil servants. But still, I got this gold chain around my neck. I belong to him now more than ever.

Because he's got his own obligations
And so, and so do I

A little while back, word got around the neighborhood that Irma was coming to kick my ass, and he didn't show up to defend me. But it was cool, right? I'm tough, you know. Not one of those needy chicks. But when María was headed my way, talking bout she was gonna try to take me out for real? She was packing heat, like that bitch was seriously dangerous, okay. I was like *papi, you got me, right? You coming for me, right?*

And the winds came. And the waves crashed. And the houses got beat down. And the fallen trees blocked the road. And the water got contaminated. And the gas supply dried up. And the food rotted in the heat and the dead refrigerator. And the water flooded up to the roof. We up here vomiting. Medicine spoiled. Gangrene set in. Viejitos' rest homes turning to final resting places.

And you didn't come for me, *papi*. You didn't fucking come for me. But you wasn't gonna let nobody else help.
I
belonged
to you . . .

And then she screamed the next two lines, offtune and furious,

Mee-eeee and Mister
Mister Jones!

Since 1900, didn't I send my children to cut your Hawaiian sugarcane? Since 1917, didn't I send my sons to your wars? Haven't I always let your corporate chains put my mom and pop stores out of business? Didn't I let you play your war games on my Vieques for decades? Didn't I let you dump towers full of coal ash when your continental US was too good to clean up its own mess? Open ash dumps for the hurricane to knock down? Now your arsenic, mercury, chromium seeping into my people. And Mr. Jones ain't got a goddamn thing going on to help.

Now he'll go his way
And I'll go mine

Your forefathers threw a hissy fit. Dumped tea into Massachussets Bay to protest King George. How the hell am I gonna get ten stories of coal ash up to Boston Harbor? How do I send this shame back where it belongs? This third world, side chick, shame back?

No, Mr. Jones. You need to act like you got some respect.

As she repeated the last lines of the poem, she faded out some of the words until she said the final line:

No. Jones. Act.

When she finished, the crowd applauded wildly.

"That's right," Marisol said. "We don't just want hurricane relief, we want justice. Repeal the Jones Act! And cancel the debt!"

The applause thundered.

Someone in the crowd yelled out "*Viva Puerto Rico libre!*" Many voices yelled back: "*Que viva!*"

Dulce felt like she was gonna cry. The side chick metaphor sort of undid her. That was just what it was like. Somebody who held all the cards and came just to take and you had to act like you really liked them.

She needed some air. In the packed room, it took her a while to make her way to the door. She felt like she might burst into tears, or maybe throw up. As she pressed through the crowd, Marisol was back on the mic.

"I want to thank you all for being so financially generous tonight," she said. "But there's more that the people of Puerto Rico need from you. Not only your money, but your time, as well. You know you like to go on vacation. Why not spend part of your vacation helping to rebuild Puerto Rico? We got a list of grassroots organizations where you can volunteer to help do all kinds of things . . ."

Dulce finally made it out of the ballroom door, and took the stairs two at a time down to the street. It was an unseasonably warm evening, with temperatures in the low sixties.

Yet her first inhalation wasn't a deep breath but a gasp. In front of the building stood Zavier. His hair was longer and a little wild. He looked thinner. He had on jeans and a pale blue guayabera shirt. And he was smoking. She turned to go back in, but he had already seen her.

"Great speech," he said. He sounded like maybe he'd had a few drinks, too.

"Thanks," she said. "I thought you were back in Puerto Rico."

"Back and forth," he said. "You been reading my stuff?"

"Yeah," she said. "It's good. Especially that piece you cowrote on the increase in violence against women since the hurricane."

"I kept it on my radar," he said, and took a drag of the cigarette. "I been reading your work on Puerto Rico, too." Smoke trailed out of his mouth as he spoke.

Dulce wasn't sure what to say to that. "Thanks for . . . uh . . . coming out tonight," she said.

"It was really . . ." he began. "It had me getting all emotional."

Dulce nodded and pointed to the cigarette. "May I?"

He handed it to her.

"I didn't realize you were the filmmaker," he said. "If I had known, I might not have come."

Dulce took a drag and let the smoke fill her lungs. She used to smoke when she was with Jerry. She'd given it up in Cuba. The times in Puerto Rico didn't really count. It was a hurricane. She'd been tempted since she got back to New

York, but she didn't want to start again. It cost too much money.

"To be honest, that's probably a big part of why I'm so emotional," he said.

"I'm surprised," she said. "It's been months. Plenty of time to move on."

"I've been mostly working," he said. "No time to feel."

She nodded again and took another drag.

"I also been reading your other columns," he said. "The ones about sex work."

"You mean 'Celia's' columns?" Dulce asked with a wry smile.

"I can't get one of those women's lines out of my head," he said. "One of the girls who'd been pimped. The sixteen-year-old."

"'You learn to come when men call you,'" Dulce knew the line.

"I couldn't help but wonder if maybe—maybe some-thing—maybe you—"

Dulce could feel her heart beating wildly now. This was the chance to say it. Not that it would make a difference now, but she had always felt so bitter that she never even had that opportunity to explain.

"Yeah," Dulce said. "That was part of it. Gerard called and I answered."

"I didn't mean to bring all this up," Zavier said.

"It's okay," Dulce said. She swallowed to keep her voice from shaking. "Good to air it out."

He nodded and took another inhalation of smoke.

"There was something else," Dulce said. If this was her one chance, she might as well fucking say it all. "I never really thought any guy would want a future with me. Guys wanted to fuck me, but really be with me? Nice guys? It just seemed like it wasn't gonna work. So I should sort of just get out be-fore I got too attached."

"But what about in Puerto Rico?" he asked. "After I found out you had been a sex worker? You knew I still wanted to be with you."

Dulce wondered if this was like dreaming about a loved one who had died. To wake up and realize all over again that they were gone. Even hearing him say that he had wanted her, wanted to be with her—it was excruciating to hear him describe it in the past tense.

"I should have told you," she said. Confession. She recalled the priest from Puerto Rico. "The *viejita* with the flipped car in her front yard even said so. When you went out of the room, she told me not to keep any secrets from you, but I was scared."

"Of what?" he asked, bitterly.

"Of everything," she said, her voice raised, higher in pitch than she expected. "Rejection. Humiliation. I feel like a fucking fraud all the time these days."

"Most people of color have impostor syndrome," Zavier said. "It's not that unusual."

"You don't get it," she fought for the words. "From the time I was fourteen to the time I was eighteen, I had a guy tell me how deep up my ass to put my thong. Everything I know about sex is how to please a man. I know how to fuck, suck dick, tickle your balls—"

"Enough with the details," Zavier said it as if the words were painful. "You know, I been asking myself since I read what that girl said, could I forgive you? If you even wanted me to. If you even wanted to get back—"

Dulce shook her head. How did he think he was ready to be her man if he couldn't even listen to a few specifics about what she had done, sometimes was forced to do? "I don't think you need to forgive me. I think I need to forgive you."

"*Perdón?*" he said, eyebrows raised.

"Yeah," Dulce said, she felt unmoored, reckless. It was over and she would get her final say. "For not even letting me explain. You think you're so cool with me having been a sex worker as long as it's something that exists all wrapped up neatly in the past and it never has to touch you. When I went off with Gerard, we had only been on a date and a half, and you already felt like you owned me? Yeah, it's fucked up that I lied. And I should have told you. But it's not like I broke a commitment. There's someplace in your mind you had already started thinking of me as 'your girl.' And part of why I lied is because I thought you needed that fantasy. Be honest now. What would you have said that day if I'd told you I was a former sex worker, and that a sugar daddy was calling me? Would you still have thought of me as girlfriend material?"

"If I'm honest?" he asked. "No, but that's just because it brings up a lot of fucking insecurity in me. I grew up in the hood and broke-ass cats like me never got the girls. They went for the guys with money. How would I know that you wouldn't just come when someone else calls in the future?"

"You don't," she said. "You would need to actually trust me. But first you'd need to take the time to lock it down with me. Even after everything we went through together in Puerto Rico, you never actually asked me to be your girl-friend."

"I never asked?" he said. "I was sure I'd asked."

"Trust me," Dulce said. "I was listening really hard for that question."

"Okay then," he asked. "Will you be my girlfriend?"

It was as if all her blood had turned to ice. "Don't play with me," she said.

"Wait," he said. "First I'm supposed to apologize. Dulce, I'm sorry for not giving you a chance to explain what happened. And will you be my girlfriend?"

"Are you serious?" she asked. She wanted to flee. This had to be a trap. Did he want a revenge fuck? Asking if she wanted to be his girlfriend? One more thing a man dangled in front of her to get her off balance, then knock her down.

"Because I will fucking kill you if you're playing with me right now."

"I'm serious," he said, and gave her that searing look into her eyes. The one that made her the most uncomfortable of all.

Her blood had gone from ice to fire. Her face flushed. "This isn't some kind of payback?" she asked. "Get my hopes up only to . . . to . . . ?" The tears were falling now.

He stepped forward and took her hand. "Please, Dulce," he said. "Will you please be my *novia*?"

"Yes," she said, laughing through her tears. "But on the condition that you stop smoking."

"Whatever you say, baby," he stubbed out the cigarette.

Just as he leaned in to kiss her, someone called Dulce's name. It was Yunisa.

"So . . . I just wanted to say I'm headed home," Yunisa said, looking Zavier up and down.

Dulce introduced them.

"Nice to meet you," Yunisa said. "I hope your intentions are honorable."

"Very much so," he said.

Yunisa sucked her teeth, then turned and waved to them over her shoulder. "See you at home, Luqui," Yunisa said.

Zavier turned to Dulce with an openmouthed grin. "Luqui!" he said. "I told you I'd find out. Your family nickname is Luqui? Can I call you that?"

Dulce cut her eyes at Yunisa's retreating back. "I knew my sister would be my downfall."

Zavier's apartment in Brooklyn had once been a single family home, with hardwood floors and tall windows. It had a high-ceilinged living room, a dining room, and a large kitchen with two refrigerators. The walls were decorated with political posters, including one that had a bright, multicolored butterfly that said "migration is beautiful." On the wall of the kitchen was an elaborate chore wheel and a white board that said "RECYCLED paper products, please" and "when you open a new almond milk, please put a date on it w/ a sharpie."

Zavier stood at the kitchen sink and washed his hands.

"I like to scrub the subway off when I come home," he said. He lathered up his hands with dishwashing liquid. Dulce did the same.

A shyness had descended onto her. She was unsure what to say. They dried off their hands and went upstairs.

The second floor had several bedrooms, and another bathroom. Zavier had two small, connected rooms. One had a cozy sofa and desk and the other had a bed and a bureau.

He and Dulce sat down on the couch.

When they had been standing on the street, and she had agreed to be his girlfriend, she was overwhelmed with passion for him. But now, after running into her sister, and a long train ride, she felt awkward. Especially knowing there were other housemates in the apartment.

"How many people live here," Dulce asked.

"There are five of us," Zavier said. "It's a collective. We have rules and house meetings, and stuff."

"So is there like a policy about overnight guests?" she asked.

"Funny you should ask," he said. "We have a boyfriend/ girlfriend policy. No more than three overnights per week. And no sex in the bathroom."

Dulce grinned. "Anything else?" she asked.

"People are expected to just sort of use common sense," he said.

He pulled out his iPhone and plugged it in to a speaker. "Like if people were going to fool around or something," he said. "Common sense would be to put on some music. You know, out of courtesy."

Dulce nodded. "This isn't awkward at all."

Zavier laughed. "I thought I'd just play something familiar," he said. "To put my guest at ease."

"Guest?"

"Or should I say, new girlfriend?" he asked.

"Much better."

And then he put on her favorite Nashonna song. Her heart leaped.

She leaned back against the couch. "This is my jam."

"I had to download it again on the subway," he said. "I deleted it from my phone when we weren't talking."

It was the song she had quoted in one of her tweets. Dulce closed her eyes. She felt the bass of the music, and the melody and rhythm of Nashonna's yearning voice as she sang and rapped about wanting love.

Mastering lyrics has always been my goal
But love is what I want that I can't control
Love shoots like a bullet that I try to dodge
Sometimes love finds me then I sabotage
Say I won't settle for the okey doke
Be sure to ghost good so I don't get my heart broke

Nashonna's words brought it all back. The swell of emotion that he wanted to be with her. She had sabotaged the love of her family twice, and his love once. But not again. She wanted this. She wanted him. She wanted love. And maybe he would break her heart. But she was willing to take the risk.

He had that look again. That searing look, but it was different this time. She had nothing to hide anymore. Suddenly all her fears and hesitation felt ridiculous.

She wrapped her arms around his neck and kissed him. His mouth met hers with an aching hunger, reflecting the yearning of Nashonna's words.

He kissed her ear, her neck, her shoulders each one of her

ribs. She unhooked her bra, and he kissed her breasts, licked her nipples.

When he stood up to take off his shirt, Dulce followed, pressed her tongue into his mouth as he unbuttoned his guayabera shirt. She slid her hands across the smooth muscles of his back, his chest, his shoulders, his sides, his belly.

He was backing away from her.

"Where are you going?" she murmured as he kissed her earlobe.

"To the bed," he said, one hand sliding down the back of her skirt.

Now, instead of him pulling her, she was pushing him. He nearly stumbled over their shoes as he walked backwards.

With both hands, she unzipped her skirt and stepped out of it, along with her underwear, a boring yellow cotton pair. Again, she hadn't waxed anything, but he didn't seem to care. He slid his hands over her hips, gently squeezed her ass, and cupped her pubic mound with one hand.

She groaned at the contact with her vulva, as he slid his entire hand up and down.

She lay back on the bed, and he leaned down above her. Then he used one finger, and traced it up and down through the hair at the opening.

Gently, with each glide back and forth, he worked that single finger just slightly between her lips.

"You're so wet," he murmured.

Dulce could only moan in response.

"Can I come inside you?"

"Yes," she whispered into his neck.

She lay back on the bed, and he followed. When he entered her, she cried out with the sweetness of it.

"Oh my god," he said. "You feel so good. It's all I can do to go slow."

She moaned with his measured stroke.

"Are you loud?" he asked, conspiratorially.

"Am I what?" Dulce asked, confused, getting pulled out of the moment.

"When you come?" he asked. "Are you loud when you come? Should I turn up the music? Roommate courtesy and all?"

Dulce flushed with sudden shame.

His face shifted from sly to concerned. "Did I say something wrong?" he asked. "Are you okay?" He pulled out, but continued to hold her.

"I don't know," she whispered. "I don't know if I'm loud or not."

His brow was furrowed in a frown, but then it smoothed out and his eyes widened. "You've never—"

She shook her head, tears falling silently down her face.

"Oh, *mi amor*," he said, and wrapped his arms more tightly around her.

She cried into his shoulder.

"I—" she began through the tears.

"You don't have to explain anything if you don't want to," he whispered.

She cried for a moment, then sank into the bed. She lay there, face down, a tumble of hair covering her face.

"Hey baby," he said gently. "Can you look at me?"

Dulce shook her head beneath the curtain of hair.

Zavier gently put one finger under her chin. As he lifted her face, he said, "You have nothing to be embarrassed about."

"Easy for you to say," Dulce mumbled.

"I feel honored," Zavier said. "I have the pleasure of giving pleasure to the woman I love."

Dulce's eyes opened wide. "You love me?"

"Of course," Zavier said. "Why do you think I was outside the hotel tonight smoking ten cigarettes? Because I'm in love with you, and I have been since we found each other in a fucking hurricane."

Dulce bit her lip. "I love you too."

"So you have nothing to be embarrassed about with me," he said. "Do you want to try again?"

"Yes?" she said, but it came out like a question.

"So there's this affirmative consent thing," he said. "You need to really want to do this if we're gonna go forward."

"Yes," she said more firmly. "I want to. I'm just . . . a little nervous."

"Good," he said. "Because I really want to do this, too."

She giggled.

"All you need to do is tell me if you like what I'm doing," he said. "Okay?"

She nodded, but he raised his eyebrows.

"Yes," she said.

"Can I come back inside you?" he asked.

"Yes."

Carefully, he entered her.

"Do you like this?" he asked, stroking slowly inside her.

"Mmmmm, yes."

He eased in and out and she moaned with the pleasure of it, but it didn't ignite the fire she had felt when he went down on her.

He tried harder and faster. He tried slower and more intense. It all felt good, but nothing really seemed to get her going.

"You don't have to—" she began.

But he shushed her with a finger across her lips. Then he licked his thumb and slid his hand down below her navel. Slowly, without interrupting a stroke, he slid his thumb between her lips.

She gasped with the intensity of it.

"Yes?" he said, with a delighted, openmouthed grin on his face.

"Yes," she breathed.

"How about this?" he asked, sliding his thumb sideways across her clitoris.

Dulce let out a sharp moan.

He turned his head from her and used a voice command for the speaker system. "Turn the music up to maximum volume," he said loudly.

So with Nashonna's voice soaring in the background, Dulce had her first orgasm. And the music still wasn't loud enough.

The next morning, Dulce got home a little before noon.

"Where you been?" Yunisa asked.

"Most recently at the bank," Dulce said. "I got a cashier's check for half the rent."

Yunisa took the check. "Oh shit," she said. "You paying half the *renta*?"

"Yeah," Dulce said. "My balance is getting low, but I can help out with groceries, too."

"You need to keep a little something," Yunisa said. "Stay sexy for that man of yours. Is he in college?"

"He's got a Masters degree," Dulce said.

"He's skinny but cute," Yunisa said. "You need to keep him. He make good money?"

"Not really," Dulce said. "He lives in Brooklyn with four roommates."

"Where does he work?"

"He's a freelance journalist, but he has this big project working on a radio documentary about colonization and climate change in Puerto Rico."

"Damn," Yunisa said. "He'll be lucky to break even on some shit like that. Why he waste all that time in college if he wanted to be poor?"

"Because that wouldn't help raise awareness about Puerto Rico," Dulce said.

"I know," Yunisa said. "He's obviously got a good heart. And he's good to you?"

"And he knows what I used to do," Dulce said.

"About Jerry?"

"All of it."

"Damn," Yunisa said. "Yeah. He's for real. Don't fuck this up."

Three days later, Dulce walked over to the Vega clinic to meet with one of the new women who had come to the shelter from PR. She had come from a networking event for young journalists of color. She had a pocket full of cards for editors she could pitch. Her head was buzzing with story ideas.

She had her hair loose. Zavier liked it that way. She didn't do it for him, but it was just the way her hair was. She had always flatironed it for men, assuming they liked that better. But if her man didn't prefer straight hair, then good. It was one less thing to have to do.

As she turned the corner to the Vega clinic, a red Mercedes came around the corner and beeped at her. She ignored it, but the driver called her name and rolled down the window. She peered in and saw Phillip Gerard. Was it the same Mercedes from Santo Domingo? Had he shipped it from the Caribbean? No that was ridiculous. He must have rented it.

"So glad to see everything turned out okay," he said. "You need a ride anywhere?"

"No thanks," she said. "I'm not going far."

"Well, can you talk for a minute?" he asked.

Dulce stopped. The whole thing reminded her of when she was walking down the street as a teenager. Grown men used to yell at her from cars. She would do everything to avoid them. Avoid eye contact. Give evasive responses. But she wasn't a teenager anymore. She wasn't going to come when he called, and she wasn't going to avoid him, either.

"Phillip, I'm not interested anymore in . . . whatever it was we had going," she said. The words "I have a boyfriend," almost tumbled out of her mouth. That was her teenage excuse. Even though it wasn't true then, and it was true now.

"Well, can we catch up?" he asked. "I was worried about you. I felt bad about not helping, you know, once I realized how serious the hurricane was."

"Well you certainly haven't wasted any time figuring how to turn things to your advantage," she said.

"What do you mean?" he asked.

"Your real estate group is buying up plenty of Puerto Rican coastline," she said.

"That's not fair," he said. "I have a plan to turn the land I'm buying into a public land trust."

"I'll believe that when I see it," Dulce said.

"No really," he said. "I have the papers right here."

"Let me read the fine print," she said, and walked over to the car.

He pulled out a leather folder. "Look, it's all in here. Have a seat. I'll walk you through it."

The folder said "San Juan Philanthropic Land Trust." She sat down in the passenger seat, and he put the folder in her lap.

When he opened it, the wind blew through the windows, almost scattering the papers.

"Let me roll these up," he said, and as Dulce flipped through the papers, he raised the windows.

It was the click of the locking door that told her something was wrong. But by then, he had floored the pedal and the car screeched away from the curb.

"What the fuck?" she asked.

"Damn bitch," he said. "You thought you were gonna steal my money. I wasn't generous enough to you."

"I never stole a fucking peso from you when we were in the Caribbean."

He tore up the avenue and cut around a taxi.

"Don't fucking play dumb with me," he said. "You know I don't mean that money. I mean the money in the account."

"Since when did I have access to any of your accounts," she asked. "You never even let me use your credit card. I couldn't even sign for meals in the room."

"Lying whore!" he said. "I saw you in the *New York Times* with those two other cunts. The blonde and the Asian chick. Drinking fucking champagne. Celebrating that you took my goddamn money!"

The light had just changed, but he ran the red, barely missing a furniture delivery truck.

Dulce had no idea what he was talking about. Kim and Jody had taken some of his money? How did he even know them?

He turned onto the East Side Highway. Where the hell was he taking her? This wasn't good. He could go anywhere now that he was on the highway. Could drive for miles and miles. She checked his gas tank. Nearly full. He could drive her to Canada if he wanted.

"I barely know them," she said. "If they stole some shit from you, I didn't know anything about it."

"How did they get my number?" he asked.

"I don't know," Dulce said. "Are you saying that I'm the only person you've given it to?"

Shit. She had given Marisol the number. Could Marisol have robbed him?

"Don't act like I'm stupid," he said. "You had the number. She called it out of the blue. Then I saw you together. So we're going somewhere that I swear I will wring your neck til you tell me where I can find my money."

Dulce could feel her stomach drop down in her body.

"My friends were just down the street when you pulled up," Dulce said. "They waved to me. They probably got your license plate."

"You're bluffing," he said. "Nobody knows you're with me. Just like nobody knows yet that I got robbed. Because you're gonna help me get that fucking money back before anyone notices it is gone."

As he spoke, they pulled alongside another car. Dulce turned and banged on the window, trying to alert the other driver.

The woman was singing along to the radio. She had on shades and was swaying to the music. She didn't seem to notice

But Gerard did. He began to drive fast, reckless, avoiding getting close enough to other cars that they could see her. Then he pulled into the right hand lane, so there was nothing next to her, just railing and buildings, and New York sky.

No fucking way. She wasn't going to let him get her somewhere isolated. She looked around for a weapon, but all she had was the leather folder on her lap, and the papers.

Carefully, she unlaced her boot, and slid her foot out of it.

Then, quick as she could, she gripped the instep, and brought it up—heel first—to break the window.

The safety glass shattered, and she opened the folder. Papers flew all around the car. Several stuck to the inside of the windshield. He couldn't see.

"Fucking crazy bitch!" he said.

The car started to careen across the highway.

With a thud, they collided with another car and the Mercedes bounced off it.

Gerard slowed a bit, and scrabbled at the papers on the windshield, pulling enough down so he could see.

But soon, they heard a siren.

The moment Gerard pulled over, Dulce crashed the rest of the glass out of the window and attempted to climb out. She barely felt the scratches of her arms against the crumbling glass.

"Stay in the car, ma'am," the police officer's voice came through over a loudspeaker. It was a motorcycle cop.

Dulce froze, her torso out of the window, the safety glass pressing up through the thin cotton of her shirt.

The officer came toward the car, gun drawn.

"Don't move," he ordered.

Dulce slowly lifted her hands up.

"Sir, hands on the steering wheel where I can see them!"

The officer took his time approaching the car.

"Now we're gonna do this nice and easy," he said. "Sir, step out of the car. Keep your hands where I can see them."

Carefully, Gerard stepped out of the Mercedes, hands above his head.

"Walk around the car and stand next to her," the cop ordered.

Gerard walked around the front of the car. "Thank god you stopped us, officer," Gerard began. "This young lady asked me for a ride, then she simply went crazy. She broke my window—"

"That's a lie," Dulce said. "He kidnapped me. He threatened to kill me."

"Shut up," the cop said.

"She's absolutely—"

"Both of you," the cop said. "Shut up!"

"Now you," he gestured to Dulce. "Keep your hands over your head and exit the vehicle."

"How?" she asked. "I can't open the door with my hands up. Besides, he locked me in."

The three of them stood there, just looking at each other as the cars whizzed by.

A moment later, a police cruiser pulled up. An older officer stepped out, gun drawn.

The younger cop walked over to Dulce, with the gun in her face: "I'm going to open this door," he said. "And you are going to duck your body back through the opening, very slowly, keeping your arms over your head."

As if she were in slow motion, Dulce complied. Soon, she found herself standing out on the highway, one boot and one bare foot on the concrete, the gun pointed straight at her chest.

"Cuff them both," the older cop said.

"Officer," Gerard said. "My name is Phillip Gerard. This young lady solicited me for prostitution. I told her I wasn't interested, but when she told me her sob story, I offered her a ride. I assure you, I've learned my lesson."

"He's lying," Dulce said, as calmly as she could. "He kidnapped me." She was afraid to say anything about the robbery. Could Marisol really have gotten Kim and Jody to rip him off? She didn't want to snitch on them. But without that piece of information, the whole thing didn't make any sense.

Dulce looked down at her bleeding arms. Her single boot. Her raggedy jeans. The wind was blowing her wild hair into her face. She must look a mess. Of course they were gonna believe him. She looked like a feral animal. He looked like the kind of citizen they were sworn to protect and serve.

Gerard was standing just behind her now. The officer still had the gun aimed directly at Dulce.

"Seriously," Gerard said. "The mayor is only a couple of phone calls away for me. Let's talk this over before you cuff me. Her on the other hand? She needs to be restrained for her own protection."

The officer in charge nodded to the younger cop.

He walked forward and commanded that Dulce kneel down. He leaned over and pulled her hands behind her back.

Dulce's heart sank. When they ran her prints or her ID, they'd find her arrest for prostitution. Fuck.

"Excuse me?" a woman's voice yelled. "Officers?"

A car had pulled over behind the cruiser, and the woman had her head stuck out of the window. Dulce could barely see her face, as she was backlit by all the headlights coming behind them.

The older cop headed toward her.

"This woman was signaling for help," she said and pointed to Dulce.

"Ma'am, stay in your car," the cop said. His voice was loud, but the wind was blowing away from the woman. Without the loudspeaker, it swallowed up the sound.

The woman began to exit the car. Dulce looked from the barrel of the younger cop's gun to the middle-aged blonde walking toward them on the side of the highway.

"She was banging on the window," the woman continued. "Trying to get away from that man." The woman had on a long coat, the wind was flapping the hem and blowing her pale, wispy hair to the side.

"Ma'am, get back in your vehicle," the cop insisted.

"I was listening to music, and by the time I realized what I was seeing, he had taken off," the woman said. "But I called 911. Then I saw that it was his red Mercedes that was pulled over. I had to come tell you what I saw. I got off at the next exit and turned around and got back on the highway. These men can't just abduct young girls like that and expect—"

The older officer lifted his gun. "Ma'am, stay where you are."

The woman broke off mid-sentence. Her eyes opened wide, but she didn't lift her hands.

From behind Dulce, Gerard started back up. "This has all been a terrible misunderstanding," he said. "I'm sure I can clear it up. Just let me make that call."

"Don't move," the younger cop said.

"Why is she the one who's been handcuffed?" the woman asked. "And for god's sake, why is she on her knees? Like I said, she was banging on the window for help. I called it in."

"I'm gonna call for additional backup," the older cop said. "And see if I can verify her 911 call."

"Thank you," the woman said. "As I said before, I recognized the car. I recognized the woman."

"Stop talking," the younger cop said.

"I just need to make one call," Gerard insisted.

"You're not going to let him, are you?" the woman asked.

"Just everybody shut up and stop moving!" the young cop said.

He had the gun trained on Dulce. She wished the woman would shut the fuck up, before this nervous babyfaced white boy shot her by mistake.

Behind her, Gerard had one of his hands down from above his head. It was at the level of his neck, now.

"Officer, I assure you," Gerard pressed. "You have no idea who you're fucking with here."

"Please keep your hands up, sir," the younger cop said, although he still had the gun trained on Dulce.

"Don't fall for that," the woman said from the other side of the cop. "This guy is trying to manipulate you with his big shot bullshit."

The young cop half-turned to the woman. "Shut up, ma'am. Just shut up!"

He was still half turned when the older cop slammed the cruiser door.

Dulce saw it all.

How the younger cop twitched at the sudden bang sound. How he was still twisted toward the woman, not looking at her or Gerard. Not looking but his hand responded. His trigger finger. He shot the gun.

Dulce saw it all, as if in slow motion. And she felt a delay in the searing of the bullet into her body. Kept waiting for the impact as the sound of the shot echoed in the air and the wind blew a faint scent of cordite toward her.

Only in the split second later, when she heard the thud of flesh on pavement, did she put together what she had seen in her peripheral vision. Only then, did she realize that it was

Gerard who had recoiled, then crumpled to the ground. She had been kneeling, so the bullet had cleared her and hit him.

"What the fuck?" the older cop asked.

"My god," the woman said. "Oh my god."

The younger cop's mouth was open, but he couldn't seem to put words together. "I didn't—" he stammered. "I thought—"

The older cop rushed to where Gerard lay.

"Call an ambulance," he ordered the younger cop, who stumbled into motion.

The older cop knelt by the man on the ground. In a flash, he had two fingers on Gerard's neck. Then, Dulce could tell by the abrupt change in the cop's speed of movement that Gerard must not have made it. One moment the cop was rushing, and the next, he moved as if underwater, pressing through resistance, lethargy, or dread.

Chapter 31

Six hours later, Dulce sat in a precinct in Queens, waiting for Zavier to pick her up. She was wrapped in a blanket. She had both shoes on now.

They hadn't arrested her, just checked her for warrants. They didn't check the woman who had pulled over. Just taken her statement and let her go. Dulce was too dazed to even say thank you before the cops took the woman back to her car on the highway.

When Zavier arrived, Dulce felt disoriented, disembodied.

"Baby, are you okay?" he asked.

She could feel herself nod, absently.

"Come on," he said. "I parked around the corner."

When they had climbed into the small hatchback, she could feel her body start to shake.

"What happened?" he asked. "Are you all right?"

Dulce shook her head. She couldn't think straight. Couldn't understand what was going on.

"Dulce, you have to tell me what's going on."

"He tried to kill me," she said. "He thought I stole something of his, and he tried to kill me."

"Who?"

"A guy I used to know," Dulce said.

"Did they catch him?" Zavier asked.

"No," Dulce said. "They killed him."

"The cops killed him?" Zavier asked.

Dulce nodded. She couldn't speak.

"Was he black or Latino?" Zavier asked.

"White," Dulce said. "He was a white businessman."

Zavier's eyebrows rose.

"They shot him in front of you?"

Dulce nodded again. She could feel herself falling apart inside.

He pulled her close.

"I'm so sorry, baby," he said, his mouth close to her ear, his voice soft, tender.

She collapsed into him.

When the blanket fell off her arms, he cried out at the sight of the red scratches on her arms.

"It's looks worse than it is," she said.

But he kissed each one of them.

It was his tenderness that undid her. Not even her mother had ever taken the time to so painstakingly and gently kiss every single place she had been wounded.

When the sobbing began, it was at that place where the river meets the ocean. New fresh water trickling from the land to meet the boundless stretch of sea. The reclaiming of this previously lost love was freshwater, but the grief of the motherless daughter has unfathomable depths. Yet they met here, in briny, brackish water streaking down Dulce's face, and sobs undulating through her body like waves, as she wailed, wounded and unraveling in Zavier's arms.

After she sat up and wiped her eyes, she looked Zavier in the face.

"It was that same businessman," she said.

"What?" Zavier asked, confused.

"The one from Santo Domingo," Dulce said. "And from

the Miami airport. The one who pretended to be my uncle. He drove up next to me and wanted to talk. I said I wasn't trying to do—any of what we did before. He said he just wanted to show me something about a charity he was setting up in Puerto Rico. Then he locked the door and drove off."

Zavier's eyes narrowed.

"Why are you telling me this?"

Dulce cocked her head, exasperated. "Because it's gonna be in the fucking paper tomorrow. And I don't want you thinking that I lied to you."

"I don't give a damn who he was," Zavier said. "As long as you're all right and he can't ever fuck with you again, that's all I care about."

He leaned in and kissed her, and she kissed back. She could feel her whole body respond, and she reached to pull him closer to her. Then the gear shift pressed into her ribs, and he bumped his hip on the steering wheel.

"*Coño,*" he said. "This car is too small."

She looked around as if seeing her surroundings for the first time. "Wait," she said. "I thought you didn't have a car."

"I borrowed my roommate's," he said.

She laughed. "Then let's go to your house," she said. "So we can, you know," she made air quotes. "*Return the car.*"

Now Zavier laughed. "Is that what the kids are calling it these days?"

"Are we going to your house or not?" she asked, grinning.

"My roommates are all home tonight," he said.

"Then get them some fucking earplugs," Dulce said with a laugh.

Zavier started the car, and they sped off.

The next morning, Dulce was at the María de la Vega health clinic when it opened. She caught the stairwell door when a few staff entered, and crept up the stairs. She slipped the lock to go up to Marisol's apartment at the top.

Dulce knew that Nidia, Zara, and the baby had their own place now. It was just after nine AM, and she knocked boldly on the door.

Marisol answered, wearing a faded robe. Her face went from curious to pissed off.

"Hold up," she said. "How did you even get in here?"

"I need to talk to you," Dulce said.

"Maybe Eva was right about boundaries," Marisol said. "You need to call first."

"I can't talk about this on the phone," Dulce said.

Marisol's expression changed from pissed to wary.

"Can I come in?" Dulce asked.

Marisol stepped back to let her enter.

"Phillip Gerard got shot by the cops last night," Dulce said.

"Who?" Marisol asked.

"My ex-sugar daddy," Dulce said. "The guy you kept calling me to ask about. The guy whose number you wanted, but you didn't want me to text it to you. The guy your crew robbed."

"What is this?" Marisol asked. "A shakedown?"

Dulce shook her head. "He saw the photo of me and Kim and Jody in the *Times*, and thought I was in on it. He kidnapped me last night and . . . it was a bunch of crazy drama. Anyways, the cops came and shot him by mistake."

"So why did you come here first thing in the morning to tell me this?" Marisol asked.

"It's gonna be in the papers. I just want you to know that I didn't snitch on you all."

"Seriously Dulce," Marisol said. "I have no idea what you're talking about."

"I didn't tell him you were asking about him," Dulce said. "So whatever you did. If you robbed that motherfucker, he deserved it."

"I never even met the man," Marisol said.

"I know why you don't trust me," Dulce said. "It used to be I didn't know how to say no to men. But it's not like that anymore. I'm not like that. Mostly thanks to you and Dr. Feldman."

Marisol nodded. "Eva's good with the boundaries."

"I just didn't want you to worry," Dulce said. "If you read both our names in the papers later today or something. I didn't say anything to him. And he didn't tell anybody about the robbery. Said he wanted to get the money back before his people found out it was gone."

Marisol nodded. "You okay?" she asked. "I mean, since you got kidnapped and you witnessed a shooting?"

"I was lucky," Dulce said. "That bullet wasn't meant for Gerard."

Marisol turned to the kitchenette. "You want some coffee?"

"Sure," Dulce said. She sat down on one of the tall stools next to the kitchenette island.

Marisol put the water on to boil. "When I got back from Cuba, Jerry was waiting for me," she said. "Pointing a gun at Serena and me."

"Oh shit," Dulce said. "I'm so sorry, Marisol." She shook her head. "He always blamed you. For giving me 'ideas.' Like I couldn't possibly have decided on my own that I didn't want to live with a man who beat my ass, made me fuck men for money, and kept all the cash. You didn't give me the idea to leave him, you just gave me the idea that maybe I could leave without him killing me. Which is why I would never have told him it was you that took me to Cuba. Even though I was really drunk that night I called him, I never—"

"I know you didn't snitch," Marisol reassured her. "He said you told him you were going to Cuba, and he put it together that I was the one who took you."

"I just had to fucking tell him," Dulce said. "He told me over and over that I could never get away from him. I had to throw it in his face that he was wrong." Dulce had even thought about repeating the Delia Borbón line *adiós mother-fucker*, but couldn't quite muster the courage.

Marisol shrugged. "It turned out okay," she said. "I finally got to visit my sister in Cuba. I stayed like two months. I never woulda taken the time to get away from New York if it wasn't for you."

Dulce froze, trying to do the math of the timing in her head. "Two months?" she asked. "You didn't come back for two months?" She recalled reading about Jerry's death in the paper about two months after she had arrived in Cuba. "Then it was you!"

"Me what?" Marisol asked. She poured two cups of Bustelo coffee.

"You killed Jerry," Dulce said. "The paper said he got into an armed altercation with someone but they didn't say who."

"Once again," Marisol said. "I don't know what you're talking about."

Dulce laughed. "*Coño*," she said. "That first night, you told me I'd get away from him eventually, one way or another. I guess you made a way."

"*You* made a way," Marisol said. "You kept trying until you succeeded. Now drink your coffee before it gets cold. I've got a police shooting to read about in the paper."

Dulce met Zavier for lunch that day. It was an upscale version of *comida criolla* with organic vegetables and hormone-free meats.

On the walls were pictures of Caribbean farmers.

"Hey baby," he said. "I got you some *carne guisada*." He gestured to a plate across from him. The meat looked familiar, but she was not used to seeing it paired with brown rice and a salad of baby spinach.

"Thanks, *mi amor*," she said. "What was so urgent?" She dug into the plate. She hadn't had anything to eat since the coffee at Marisol's.

"The drama has begun," he said. "A bunch of Gerard's friends have been putting pressure on the cops to do an investigation. Some of the top brass have been calling for the resignation of the cop who shot him. Maybe even criminal charges."

"Excuse me?" Dulce said, her fork hovering in midair. "When that Dominican kid got shot in the Bronx, the cop didn't even get taken off the street."

"Exactly," Zavier said. "So Black Twitter is blowing up because this guy is getting totally different treatment than black and brown people who get shot by the cops."

"You should have seen him," Dulce fumed. "He was like 'I got the mayor on speed dial.' If it wasn't for that woman who saw us, I know I would be dead now, or at least in jail."

"What woman?" Zavier asked.

"The witness," Dulce said. She explained the situation to Zavier.

"The cops are gonna make it hard to get her info," Zavier said. "I'll see if I can get my hands on the police report. Maybe get a name."

"I've got her number," Dulce said.

"You're kidding," Zavier said.

"I got her card," Dulce said, shrugging.

"That's my girl," Zavier said. "Way to investigate."

"I don't deserve any credit," Dulce said. "When I went to get my metrocard, I found this business card in my pocket. It took me a moment to put it together. She musta came to talk to me while I was just sitting there in shock. The memory is hazy. I think she was like 'I don't trust these cops. If they try to blame anything on you, then call me.'"

Dulce handed the card to Zavier. It identified her as a nurse at a local hospital.

"There's one other thing," Zavier said. "Before I call her, can I interview you about Gerard? I won't use your name. Just for background."

Dulce stopped mid-bite. "Are you sure?" she asked. "I mean . . ." As she spoke, the urge to lie, to sugarcoat the truth was strong. But she remembered what Doña Inez had said. "I mean . . . he was my sugar daddy."

"You don't have to answer anything you don't want to," Zavier said.

"I just mean—are you—are you sure you want to know?" she asked.

"Whatever you had with him is in the past," he said. "And it doesn't hurt that he's dead. I'm just being real with that one."

Dulce gave a dry chuckle and shook her head. "Okay, here goes." And she told him.

Zavier took notes at some times, and at others, he just made eye contact and nodded occasionally. He didn't look at her with that piercing look that seared her. But he listened intently. Dulce told it all. From meeting him at the airport to wearing stains of his blood on a highway.

Zavier blew out his breath when she was done. "Wow baby, I'm so sorry that happened to you."

"I think of myself as lucky," she said.

"Really, I'm just so grateful that you're okay," he said. "I don't know what I would do if anything worse had happened to you."

And that was when he gave her that searing look.

"Don't look at me like that," she said.

"Why not?" he asked. "I can't gaze adoringly at my girl?"

"Not if you're trying to turn in this story and don't want your girl to drag you to your apartment in Brooklyn and have her way with you."

"Okay fine," he agreed. "But maybe later tonight, though, right?"

"Yeah, but what about your house rules," she asked. "That would make three times this week."

"Yeah," he said. "And it's only Tuesday."

* * *

Later that night, the news broke that Phillip Gerard, fifty-one, of Miami, who was shot and killed by a NYPD officer, had allegedly kidnapped a young woman and the police were pursuing him while Gerard was driving recklessly at the time. Also, the reporter, Zavier Mendoza, had received an anonymous tip to check out one of Gerard's charities, CityCaresPuertoRico, and found that not only was it a sort of con job, but a quarter million of the money that was under Gerard's direct control had gone missing. Only three thousand was left.

That same night, in Puerto Rico, Doña Inez stood on the back porch of her house. The moon was nearly full, and she sat beneath it, smoking the only cigar she had that had survived the storm.

The green was coming back. She couldn't see it in the dark, but she could feel it. In the daytime, she found tender vines and shoots, and the smallest of buds on some of the broken trees.

The plants would be the first to return. But the people? That was going to be a much bigger fight. She took another puff on the cigar.

She chanted in Yoruba, and blew smoke on an ebony figure. Candlelight flickered off the surfaces of honey, molasses, rum and water on the altar.

She reached her fingers into a calabash on the floor at her feet. She sifted the rich, red soil through her fingers, soil she'd gathered from the spot where the hurricane made landfall on the island. The soil stuck beneath the rings on her fingers. It stuck under her nails and in the crescent moons of her cuticles. It stuck in the lines of her palms. It stuck in the crevices of her fingerprints.

"Give me strength," she prayed, holding the dirt tight in her fist. "Give us all strength to fight, and bless us to win."

* * *

A few hours before dawn, Dulce woke up feeling restless. At first, she thought to wake Zavier to make love again. He lay on his side, arm splayed above his head. The streetlight filtered in through the window and traced a soft glow along the planes of his cheekbones, his eyelids, his jaw. In sleep, he was even more beautiful. Was it really possible that someone like this was her man? She felt a deep yearning, but it wasn't exactly him she was hungry for. Not right now.

She got out of bed and paced around the room. In the glow of New York's never-dark, she could make out the shape of a low bookshelf beneath the windows. She picked up a glass journalism award. What did it feel like to win something like this? To have so many people reading your words? She didn't know, but she wanted to.

She set down the award and crossed to the desk, opening Zavier's laptop. A bluish glow filled the room. She felt a twinge of guilt. She'd only done this before when she broke into her married boyfriend's phone in Miami. She'd felt justified because she was totally dependent on him. If he was getting a new side chick, she needed a heads up.

But now, she didn't bother to open Zavier's email or messages. She could have. Easily. In fact, he should really have better security. But she went straight to the word files and pulled up their draft of the *New York Times* article. At the end were sections they'd cut, six pages of scraps: sentences, paragraphs, outlines, notes. Maybe a third of it was his work, but mostly it was hers. Tangents that just didn't fit in to the article. More of her own eyewitness accounts from the hurricane. A few whole scenes from her teen years.

She had no idea how they fit together. Or if they ever would. But she felt like she was just beginning to tell both sets of stories.

By the time it had gotten light, she had written several pages on each subject. Rough, stream of consciousness. But words. She used the word count feature to tally how many. Something Zavier had taught her.

She heard a rumble from the bed, as Zavier turned over and blinked at her.

"I have one request if you use my computer," he said. "Please tell me you've decided to surprise me by writing my trend piece on men and eyebrow shaping that's due today."

"Eyebrow shaping?" Dulce asked.

"Lad mags keep the lights on," Zavier said, sitting up and scrolling through his phone.

Dulce shook her head. "I don't think I mention the word eyebrow in the twenty-five hundred words I wrote," she said. "I can do a word search."

"Twenty-five hundred words?" Zavier said, looking up from his phone. "How long have you been up?"

"I don't know," Dulce said, suddenly shy. "A couple of hours."

"Well you've broken the first rule of writing," he said. "You're supposed to get coffee first."

"Is that what they taught you in graduate school?" Dulce asked.

"It was pretty much the only thing I learned," Zavier said. "Twenty-five hundred words? Shit. You need a computer of your own."

"With what money?"

"This is Brooklyn, baby," he said. "Give me a hundred bucks and I'll come back in an hour with a hot latte in one hand and a hot laptop in the other."

"Each costing about fifty dollars," Dulce said.

"But maybe you don't need to buy one yet," Zavier said. "Maybe we could get an outlet to loan you one."

"Why would they loan me a computer?"

"Because I pitched a follow-up investigative story about the hurricane," he said. "And I have some interest from a couple of major outlets. I told them I needed an assistant."

"Are you sure?" Dulce asked. "Of course I want to go with you. But I don't have as much experience as a lot of people you know."

"Now that the hurricane is no longer big news, a lot of my colleagues aren't so interested anymore. They've moved on."

"That's fucked up," Dulce said. "So much of the island is still without power. From everyone I've talked to, it's an ongoing disaster."

"Which is why you're such an asset on the team," he said. "You lived through the hurricane, and bring one helluva perspective. Besides, if it weren't for you, I'd still be so deep in guilt that I couldn't have gotten this assignment."

"You haven't gotten it yet," Dulce said.

"But I will," Zavier said. "All I need is a second laptop and some coffee."

"How about a good morning kiss?" she asked.

She kissed him, and he pulled her down onto the bed.

"What about that coffee?" she asked.

"I seem to be waking up without it," he said with a chuckle.

As the two of them kissed and tangled on the bed, a message notification popped up on the open computer. From one of his editors:

I'm greenlighting your Puerto Rico story. How soon can you leave?

Author's Note

When Hurricane María hit Puerto Rico, I was developing a different storyline for my fourth Justice Hustlers book. However, as a member of the Puerto Rican Diaspora, I couldn't think of anything more important to write about than the hurricane, and my editor and publisher supported me in changing course.

In the process of developing this novel, there are a few small inconsistencies with the larger series. There may also be minor inaccuracies about the hurricane and its aftermath, despite my extensive research and consulting with a Puerto Rican sensitivity reader who lived through the disaster. For anyone looking for the town of Las Palmas in Southern Puerto Rico, it is completely fictional. While all other parts of the Justice Hustlers series have been set in real locations, I felt strongly that each actual small town in Puerto Rico had an intimate story to tell, and I didn't want to misrepresent any of those truths. In contrast, the greater San Juan area has so many neighborhoods, and is the area of the Island that I know best. I felt confident that there was room for the emotional truth of Dulce's fictional stories among the millions of urban stories in a Caribbean capital.

And finally, the process of this book has been unlike any other I've ever written. If I had begun with a blank slate for a novel about Hurricane María, I don't know whom I would have chosen to tell the story, or how I would have structured the book. But I didn't begin with a blank slate. Instead, I was working within the confines of a feminist heist novel with a pre-determined set of characters to choose from, and a strong set of genre conventions that draw from suspense, women's fiction, crime fiction, and romance. Like a haiku or a sonnet, genre and character have functioned as a constraint to shape the story—like a pre-determined syllable count or a rhyme scheme. Still, I have been moved and humbled at how the characters of both Dulce and Marisol have spoken to me about this tragedy. Ultimately, I stand by the whole of this book, and by the larger story I am hoping to tell about colonization, climate change, and the need for women of color to be leaders in transforming both. Surprisingly, I have found that heist fiction has proven a fitting genre for this story: as these characters have had to battle law and custom to find small pockets of justice and reparation. Similarly, the extended family of Puerto Rico will have to keep battling laws, customs, history, and entrenched power structures to get the justice and reparations that the island deserves.

Pa'lante.

Don't miss the rest of the
Justice Hustlers series
THE BOSS
UPTOWN THIEF
And
THE ACCIDENTAL MISTRESS
Available now
from
Aya de León
And
Dafina Books